I0627978

# Midlife Crazy

## an erotic romance

Discrete married gentleman seeks elegant lady for lively conversation. No ethnic preference. Prefer mature lady with wide life experience. No smokers or drugs or pros, please. Write to Sweet Gent care of this paper.

# Cody Grey Adams

This is a work of fiction. This means that while it is not factual, it is true to life. The characters and events portrayed here, along with the geographical setting, are all figments of the author's imagination. Any resemblance to a living person or an historical person is purely coincidental. Nor is the unnamed city, or the university located there, based on any particular city or school in the North Star State.

ISBN 978-1-933482-02-6

© Copyright 2012 Cody Grey Adams. All rights reserved. No copy or duplication of this book in any form may be made without the prior written permission of the publisher.

*Gather ye rosebuds while ye may,*
*Old Time is still a-flying*
*And this same flower that smiles today,*
*Tomorrow will be dying.*
Robert Herrick

# The Bet

*Roger.* The whole affair started as a joke, as a flight of fancy fueled by grandiose imagination. The beer may have had something to do with it, too. There were two empty pitchers on the table and what started as a discussion evolved into an argument. This ended with a bet. I could not believe any mature woman in her right mind would even bother to respond to such nonsense. Anne knew her sisters well and had her doubts. Nor did she hesitate expressing them. "You don't know women," she declared, signaling the bar for another round.

Had it been just the two of us alone, nothing would have come of it. Or, if we'd been in the company of strangers. The whole thing would have been forgotten with the morning-after fog. Unfortunately, we were with the usual crowd. Those we called friends egged us on. I'm told the two of us were famous for our eloquence while under the influence. Our heated debates were far more entertaining, it seems, than local talent at the nightclubs.

"What do you mean?" I challenged. Then one of the other women jumped in, taking her side and the debate was on.

"You must be drunk!" I declared at one point. The number of empty pitchers almost equaled the number of people at the table and she had put away more than anyone else.

"I'll show you drunk!" Anne jumped up, seizing a pitcher from a passing waiter. She downed in a single gulp. For a moment she swayed, then glared at me. "Your turn, sailor! Put your mouth where your money is!"

"It's a bet!" I declared. "I'll bet you a kiss!" I grabbed her under the arms and raised her high enough to kiss her lap. She grabbed my ears and pulled me tight.

This brought down the house. Yet, it also brought the manager, who insisted on calling a taxi. "Compliments of the house, Dr. Jahnsen" he told me, hustling us into the foyer. "Someone will bring your car tomorrow."

So the bet was made. Several days passed before either of

us mentioned it. Our memory was a bit confused and we were grateful for that grace. Nor were we pleased that our friends took such delight in filling in the gory details. Or that the story became a campus legend. With every telling it grew the way legends grow. It was months before either of us could do more than laugh politely when someone brought it up.

"Maybe I'll have one of my students do it as a project," I said one evening as we discussed it.

"No," Anne replied. "I think we just need to forget it. I won't hold you to it. We were drunk and the whole thing is silly."

Our friends were of a different mind. Eventually the pressure became too great. "It's been over six months now, Roger," one of them said over barbecue in our back yard. All of them were there, the same crowd, and the beer was flowing. "It's time to shit or get off the pot. Place the ad or admit you were wrong." The others nodded.

"I don't know," I answered. "I don't think it's a good idea. I'm a happily married man. Maybe we could agree to disagree."

"Come on," one of the other wives said. "It's not like you're going to do anything. Right, Anne?"

Anne looked at me. "Oh, I don't know," she said. "Maybe I'll answer his ad. It might be fun." She had a devilish look in her eye, one I knew well.

The others laughed. "See, Roger?" one of the women said. Her name was Shirley. She taught in the English department. "Anne doesn't mind. I'll even help you write the ad."

"No fair!" one of the husbands said. "Roger's got to write it himself. It's supposed to be from a man, not a committee." The other men nodded but their wives kept quiet.

"I'm not in the market," I protested. "I wouldn't know what to say."

"Pretend you're writing it with Anne in mind," Shirley suggested.

"Hell, no!" Mac declared. He was a professor of philosophy. "He's not out for a wife but a lover. It's a whole different thing."

"Is that so?" His wife raised an eyebrow. The group roared.

"Man up, Roger!" Al interjected. He's the one who pushed the issue first, a real asshole. Nor am I alone in this opinion. "Shit or get off the pot."

"All right, say I do it," I replied. "What do I have to do to win?

I don't want to sleep with a stranger."

"You better not!" Anne declared and the group laughed. Then there was silence.

"Come on, folks!" I challenged, forcing the issue. "You're the ones pushing this deal. What do I have to do to lose? Get one or two responses? More?"

"No," said Shirley. "You've got to meet the woman for dinner. What do you think, Anne?"

"It's got to be more than a fluke," Anne replied. "You've got come up with at least three women who are willing to meet you for dinner. It's got to be clear that they have sex in mind afterwards. You have to convince them you do, too. You have to at least get them into their bedroom."

"How will you know I have?" I asked.

"We'll take your word for it. You can describe their bedroom in detail."

"You have to tell us about any birthmarks and tattoos, too!" It was Mac who said this. He was a little drunk already. His wife gave him such a dirty look he repented. "Never mind."

"It can't be your graduate assistants, either," Al declared. The others laughed. Two of my graduate assistants were lesbians. The other two were straight men. It made for interesting chats.

"All right," I said. "It may take some time and I'm not going to rush it. From what I've read, online dating services have more men than women."

"So use several of the services," Helen, one of the other wives suggested. Her husband, Ed, has Parkinson's and was not there. "Or put an ad in the personals."

I looked at Anne. "Are you all right with this, sweet?" I tried to be clear how reluctant I was to do this.

Had we been alone, Anne would have let me off the hook. Yet, the thing had gone too far. There was no way she could back out without losing face. So she nodded. "Of course! I'm the one who took the bet."

"All right," I told them. "I'll get on the ad this weekend. And I'll tell you when it's going to run. Now let's eat this dead pig before it burns."

Later, after the others had gone, I approached Anne again. "Are you sure about this, babe? I don't want anything to come between us."

"It won't," she said, then sighed. "That cabbage salad upset my stomach. I think I'll go on to bed. We can clean up in the morning."

"Go on to bed," I told her. "I'll load the dishwasher and run a load tonight."

"You're sweet. I'm glad you married me."

"I am, too," I answered. Then I kissed her on the forehead and she wandered off to bed.

♣

A half hour later I joined Anne. She was already snoring, something she vehemently denied. I lay there for almost an hour, my mind running a mile a minute. Finally, I got up and went into the kitchen. I dished up some ice cream and retreated to my recliner. Normally ice cream makes me drowsy but not that night. That night it seemed to wake me up and I sat there thinking about the bet. What if someone answered it?

Then my imagination took over. I found myself thinking about a young woman I saw at the post office that week. She was attractive, dressed in a stylish denim skirt that reached below the knee, revealing trim calves and a well-formed derrière. Her feet were shod in plain leather sandals and she wore a simple peasant blouse tucked into her skirt. Her auburn hair was gathered in a single braid that ran half way down her back. And when she dropped something and bent down to pick up, I saw she was wearing no bra.

Then she looked up, caught me looking at her breasts. Yet, she didn't clutch her blouse or even straighten up right away. She smiled, clearly amused at my embarrassment, and picked up whatever she'd dropped. I was too captivated by her wonderful breasts to notice what it was. I wondered if she was going commando, too.

The young woman finished her business at the counter and she turned and smiled at me. It was only then that I noticed how deeply tanned her arms and face were, and how bright this made her hazel eyes. I smiled back. Then she was gone and the lobby seem even more drab. I wondered who she was. I hoped I'd see her again, though this struck me as odd. I was married to a wonderful, beautiful woman, not in the market for a fling.

Yet, I found myself thinking about this young woman as I reflected on the bet. I couldn't get her smile out of my mind and I could still smell the delicate perfume she wore. It filled my imagination, delicately mixed with her own womanly scent. I wondered what it would be like to kiss her full lips, to run my hands down over her nicely rounded derrière. Then I imagined kissing my way down her cleavage as I unbuttoned her blouse. I felt my lips capture an unfettered nipple....

As imagined what might follow, I found myself getting so aroused I thought my shorts would shred. *Get a grip on yourself, Roger!* I scolded. It was the stern voice of my father growling within my skull, a voice I'd grown to hate as a child. I still did, glad he was many years dead.

Then I realized what the voice had said, literally. I had to smile. *Thanks, Dad, I will,* I answered, reaching down to fondle myself. I thought about waking Anne, then decided it would be futile. She was half my weight and had drunk twice as much beer. She was a surly drunk and I knew she would not thank me for waking her. I decided to wait for a better time. I adjusted myself so my briefs didn't bind.

Even so, the memory was vivid. The images simply would not go away. Nor would my erection and trying to think of other things didn't work. I tried the exercises I use to empty my mind, to no avail. Nor was I in the mood for a cold shower. A lusty Valkyrie was riding my soul. I knew the only way I was going to get any rest was to take matters in hand.

Yet, it wasn't that simple. I was wearing a new kind of brief, one guaranteed not to gape. They came with a button in the middle of the fly and I got tangled trying to free myself. The opening was never designed for a man my size. I'd had trouble enough extracting myself to pee. With a full erection there was no way. I reached down and tore off my underpants, hoping to shred them. Life is too short to deal with cranky briefs. I stripped off my tee, too.

Looking down at last, I saw myself standing tall and proud. Only the very tip showed over the edge of its protective hood. It's blind eye was weeping, ready for action.

"Hello, big guy," I murmured, taking him in my left hand. This is like being fondled by a clumsy stranger. Still, it was something different. That night I was wound so tight it didn't matter. I took a deep, relaxing breath and let it out slowly. Then I lay back and began to play.

The sensation was marvelous. It always is. As it grew more intense I slowed down, tried to prolong the pleasure. This only inflamed me all the more. My hips began to move on their own and I felt myself approach the point of no return. I slowed down again, moving very slowly. I wanted to make it last but the feeling was almost more than I could bear. I could hear myself groaning. I hoped it didn't waken Anne. Then I began to twitch and I was past caring.

When the spasms stopped I lay there half awake for a long time, savoring the aftershocks. Then I cleaned up carefully and lay back on the recliner. My mind drifted as odd thoughts flitted across my awareness. *Why is it called jism?* I wondered. *Or is it gism or gysm?* Come made sense, though I didn't like the three-letter spelling. So did duck butter, which is what an earthy friend called it. When I asked how he came up with that, he grinned. "Well, butter is what you get when you churn." He plunged a fist up and down, then added, "And if you don't duck, you're gonna get it in the eye."

I smiled at the memory. I rose to put on my shorts but they were rags. So I sat down again, my mind returning to the bet. Eventually I decided an apology might be the lesser of evils. With that decision made, I fell into a deep sleep.

※

I was still on the recliner when Anne woke me the next morning. The smart thing would have been to tell her about my decision to apologize when I first awoke. Yet, I had trouble coming out of a strange dream and she was in a foul mood, one that was contagious. "It smells like fucking in here!" Anne declared, pointing to my shredded shorts. "Have you been fucking your fist again?"

"That was the only fucking available!" I shot back. "You had your chance!"

"Well, you could have fucked yourself!" she almost screamed, turning on her heel and stalking out of the room.

I started to make a retort but decided to let her have the last word. "Fuck you very much, sweetie!" I would like to have said. "That's exactly what we need to start the day."

※

The mood lasted until late into the afternoon. I managed to reduce one of my graduate students to tears before I relented.

Feeling guilty, I picked up the pile of papers she was assigned to grade. "I had a tough night and a worse day," I told her. "That's no excuse. I'll do these."

"Really?" asked Brenda, half expecting me to change my mind. She knew how much I hated grading papers. She also knew it was the closest I would come to an apology.

I decided to surprise her. "Yeah, it serves me right for being such an asshole. I was way off base."

"Those are your words, Roger, not mine."

I laughed as I put the papers into my briefcase. "Yeah, but you thought it. It's a good thing thoughts don't count."

"Ain't that the truth!" she said, locking the office door behind them. "Have fun grading!" Seeing the look on my face, I knew she wondered if she'd gone too far. We full professors may like to think we're egalitarian but that's only a veneer. Even the best of us are benevolent tyrants.

♣

I was surprised that Anne wasn't home when I got there. So I settled myself in my study to read the term papers. This did nothing to improve my state of mind. They were dull as dog shit, as uninspired as ever. I asked myself a question I'd asked a hundred times before. *How did these students get through high school? Why weren't they taught to write a decent sentence, much less a whole paragraph?*

Then I remembered this was my penance. I tore into the term papers with savage determination, using a red pencil. When I finished, the papers looked like they were bleeding from a thousand slashes. Only three got through without a scratch.

I was so intent grading I didn't hear Anne come in. This did little to improve her outlook. It had not been a good day for her, either. She had little patience for the stupid man who, in her opinion, started it off with a fight. I tried to hug her, as we normally do coming home. She turned away coldly. "I suppose you haven't cooked supper," she grumped.

"Why don't we do take-out tonight?" I asked. It was not my turn to cook but I was not about to point that out.

"That's right, Roger," she said. "Take the easy way out like you always do."

"Check the fucking calendar," I snarled, stung by her unjust accusation. "It's your turn. I'll be in my office, grading papers."

Anne's strident voice followed me down the hall but I tuned it out. I firmly shut my study door, latching it from the inside. Yet, I could hear her cursing like a sailor, banging pots and pans in the kitchen. I sighed. So much for kissing and making up. Since the papers were graded, I took out a legal pad and began to make notes for a lecture. It was for a faculty convocation a few weeks later. The apology had been forgotten.

# CHAPTER TWO

# Decisions

Anne and I were back on more or less loving terms by the weekend. Still, I found myself full of resentment. I'd heard more than I realized walking down the hall. I remembered specific slashes and reflected on what I'd like to have said in riposte. Not that I'd allow myself that luxury. To respond as I might would have escalated the fight to a nuclear level. I was too proud for that.

So I told myself, but the resentment grew. By the time the weekend came, I was thinking out a strategy for losing the bet. I told myself it would serve Anne right if the whole thing backfired. It was not that I wanted to be a cheat. I simply found it pleasant to imagine getting back at her. Yet, I promised myself I'd never follow through.

This was my frame of mind in on Saturday afternoon and I was alone. So I put a great deal of careful thought into my campaign. I write well and at one point wrote advertising copy for a major agency. It was strictly freelance and gave me material for my doctoral thesis. It was a scathing critique of accepted marketing methods.

Oddly enough, I was recruited by several major agencies after I got my degree. I wondered why. It was clear they didn't know what I'd said about them. This was flattering and the pay was great. Yet, I prefer the more relaxed atmosphere of a university.

So I became a popular teacher in the business school of a small college in northern Minnesota. I knew all the persuasive buttons advertisers used to convince buyers of a need they never knew they had. I often entertained my students with specific examples taken from current advertising. While I try to be fair, Mad Ave is fair game. Then, too, there's a wonderful rapport between a speaker and the audience that can be better than sex.

Or maybe it is sexual. The thing I quickly discovered was that the more cutting and acerbic I became, the more the crowd got off on Dr. Roger. The the more they got off on me, the more I got off on the crowd, too. It's seductive and I hate to admit how much I loved it. At first I saw nothing wrong with it. Then I saw a film taken at a political rally in Berlin in the late 'thirties. My students might not be shouting "Sieg Heil!" but the similarity to what I was doing in the classroom was painfully clear.

Anyway, there I was alone in my study on Saturday afternoon. I was planning how to win the bet. The first thing I did before I began was to go through mental exercises I used while working for the agency. These were my own innovation and I'd never shared my secret. Had I chosen to do so by holding seminars, I could have made a pile. However, I've never been motivated by money. I'm motivated by challenge and I consider money a poor way to keep score. For one thing, money is a distraction. Those who have it have to worry about losing it to the tax people or other thieves. It was also very clear to me that money warped relationships. The best example is people who have won the lottery. They often find themselves resented by those they once thought friends.

Personal victory, on the other hand, can never be taken away. I often lectured about Tommie Smith and John Carlos in this regard. Both were American athletes at the 1968 Olympics. They won the gold and bronze medals for the 200 meter race. Yet, as the medals were being given, the two black runners raised their fists in a Black Power salute while the Star Spangled Banner was playing. It was a moving experience to see this on the grainy video I watched many years later. I wish I'd seen it first hand. It was a defining moment in American history.

The point I make is this. While these two brave men were stripped of their medals for embarrassing the American Olympic Committee, there was no taking back what they'd done. Smith set a new world record with his run and until it was broken, it stood as a challenge to other runners. The fact that he had set it could never be denied and their action bore far greater fruit than they ever imagined.

Having a challenge, I plotted my strategy as carefully as a good general does his battle plan. The die was cast. There was no going back and I looked forward to the challenge.

First, I decided to use an assumed name. This would protect Anne an me from unwanted publicity if word got out. Other than that, I'd stick to the truth. While I wouldn't reveal my name or the fact I was doing this on a bet, I'd be completely open and honest about myself. I'd also refuse to talk about my wife. Nor would I violate my own principles. When it came to the moment of truth, I would simply apologize. "I can't do this," I'd say. Then I'd leave.

Even so, there was an element of doubt. I wondered what I might do if an attractive young woman like the one in the post office answered. I might like to think I'd do the honorable thing and walk away. Yet, I wondered if I would. There was something different about her, something that drew me like a magnet. This worried me. I knew it was more than sex.

Next, I tried to center myself and began writing the ad. "Discreet gentleman seeks discreet lady for casual conversation." I smiled when I wrote this. Few people seem to look up common words. Fewer still get beyond the first two definitions. At one point, the word "conversation" meant sexual intercourse. I doubted that many censors or editors were aware of this or even cared. Then I changed "casual" to "lively" and "elegant" to "discreet". I smiled again. The ad had a faintly Victorian flair I found pleasing.

The next lines were easier. "Prefer a mature point of view. Wide life experience a plus." I had to smile at the word "wide" and decided to replace it with "broad." Both were plays on words and I was having fun.

The next item was ethnic preference. How could I express the idea that I was an equal-opportunity fuckist? I thought about this for a few minutes, then decided on "no ethnic preference." This was not strictly true. Tall oriental women and *chicanas* are the most beautiful in the world to me. The ever popular Nordic blonde is lower on my list. I decided what I had would do for the first try. *Keep it simple, Roger,* I reminded myself. *Keep it sweet and simple.*

The only other thing to add was a means of contact. I decided to pay more and use the blind box option most newspapers offer. It was the most secure way to communicate. It was slow but the paper would notify me if I had messages. As an after thought I added "No smokers or drugs."

Looking at what I had, I was satisfied. It got the idea across in a delicate but clear way. It would not offend the politically correct crowd who are quick to take umbrage. Best of all, it didn't give the moral police much room to attack.

**Discreet gentleman seeks elegant lady for lively conversation. No ethnic preference. Prefer mature lady with broad life experience. No smokers or drugs, please. Write Sweet Gent care of this paper.**

I decided that would do for the moment but I had to make it understood that Sweet Gent was married. I made a note on my calendar to set things up the following week. I could refine it then, if necessary.

Now that the project was going I found myself getting excited. It would be interesting to see who turned up. Maybe I should revise it to read "no pros," too. There was no way I wanted to be involved with a call girl or a prostitute. I smiled at myself for making the distinction.

⚜

The following week I was both surprised and shocked when I went to the paper to place my ad. The surprise was pleasant. It came when I walked in and found the young woman I'd seen at the post office behind the counter. The shock came when I found out how much it cost to run the ad.

Despite the cost, I shelled out for a solid month. With no results in that time frame, I would win the bet. I wondered if the others would help with the costs. They might, though Al would object. He had a reputation for being a cheap bastard. That's part of how I define a social asshole.

The young woman at the ad counter glanced over my copy and smiled. Then she read it aloud.

**Discreet married gentleman seeks elegant lady for lively conversation. No ethnic preference. Prefer mature lady with broad life experience.  No smokers or drugs or pros, please. Write Sweet Gent  care of this paper.**

"That's nice," she said. "You have a way with words. The only thing you might add is something about being open minded."

I thanked her and almost asked if she was interested. Then I decided that might be cheating. The clerk was attractive but far too young, and the idea was for someone to answer a blind ad. For a moment I thought about trying to explain this. I decided it was a bad idea. "Let's go with what we have," I said. "I doubt I'll get anyone who isn't open minded."

"I'll call you a week before it runs out," she said, nodding and making a note in her planner. "You know, in case you want to renew. We can save you the expense of having to set it up again."

This sounded plausible. Yet, I somehow knew the young woman was interested in me as a man, too. I wondered why. "Are you a student at the university?" I asked.

"No such luck," she replied. "One of these years, maybe. How about you?"

"No such luck, either," I told her. After all, it was true. I taught there but I wasn't a registered student. "Are you the one who's going to be handling the replies?"

"I could be," she answered. "Would you like that?"

"That would be nice," I said. I wondered what she would be like in bed. Normally I didn't waste time with casual fantasy. This lady was worth an exception. I wondered if she would be as wonderful as I imagined the previous night. *Probably not, I* thought. *She might even be better!*

"All right." She smiled, as if she'd read my thoughts. "When you call, ask for Lucy."

"Lucy in the sky with diamonds?" I quipped. When I saw her confusion I added, "That's an old Beatles song. It was a little before my time."

"What do I call you?" Lucy asked. "Sweet Gent?" Her smile was gently mocking.

"Call me anything but bad in b...," I started to say but stopped myself. "Roger would be fine." I could see she knew exactly what I had started to say.

"How about Jolly?" she asked. "You know, Jolly instead of Bad." She was clearly having fun at my discomfort.

"Well, I better get going," I said. "I'll buy you a cup of coffee sometime."

"That sounds nice. We can have a lively conversation, too."

*You idiot!* I scolded myself as I drove home. *What were you thinking?* I decided the truth is I hadn't been thinking. At least, not above my collar. I was flattered that a young woman like Lucy found me attractive. I was also curious what it would be like to sleep with someone as young as she. *Forget it, old man!* It was an inner voice I rarely heard. *You wouldn't get much sleep! She'd eat you alive and spit you out.* To which I told Jolly Roger, as I came to think of this unknown side of myself, *Yeah, but what a way to go!*

♣

Even at this point things might have turned out another way. Yet, Anne had accepted an eleventh hour invitation to be a presenter at a professional conference. It was in Phoenix and lasted a week. Over the years she'd built a reputation as an architect and was known as an innovative designer. Her specialty was commercial atria and courtyards, though she also did an occasional private home. She'd won awards for her design of homes centered around lavish inner courts. So she was well known in her field and a colleague called to ask her to speak at a major conference.

"It's sort of last minute, isn't it?" I asked. These things are normally arranged months in advance.

"Yes, but it's a great opportunity," she answered, smiling. "Bob Akers will owe me a big favor. He almost begged me to be there. After this last winter, Phoenix sounds wonderful. I'd actually thought about attending before we planned our trip. There are a couple of speakers I wanted to hear."

"What happened?"

"One of the speakers was in a car wreck. He's still in the hospital and won't be coming."

"Will you have enough time to prepare?" I was worried. Great opportunities can blight a career if the presentation doesn't go well. Anne's field was highly competitive and the bar was high. I knew from experience how critical professional audiences can be.

"I could have done it the moment he called," she told me. "The topic is principles of designing inner space. I'm the one writing the latest book on that. I couldn't ask for a better opportunity to promote it."

"That can turn around and bite you," I pointed out.

"Hey, give me a little credit, Roger. I don't have my head completely up my butt."

"That's not what I meant," I tried to explain, but Anne was in a combative mood and it turned into a spat. We had a good time kissing and making up later. Yet, the rancor was still there, biding its time until the next clash.

Part of the problem was that the conference was scheduled over the week of my spring break. We'd made plans to get away for a few days and spend some quality time with one another.

I'd really been looking forward to this. I was more upset about it than I cared to admit.

When Anne suggested that we change our destination to Phoenix, I didn't like it. "No. That won't work. You need to spend time with your colleagues. I don't want to spend the week hanging around by myself. I'll stay home and catch up on my writing. We can do our trip another time."

When I said this, we both knew it wouldn't happen. It had been hard enough to work out the dates given our tight schedules. We were rarely able to get away even for a long weekend This week together had been scheduled months before. I was furious, though I tried not to show it.

The situation was made worse through another glitch. I normally would have driven Anne to our local airport, less than thirty minutes from home. The problem was that she had trouble finding a seat on the flight to the Twin Cities. The best the local agency could set up was flying stand-by. So Anne booked a direct flight out of Minneapolis. It was easiest for her to drive to the airport and park the car in a long-term lot.

Nor did the fact that the only seat available was first class concern her. "Bob is footing the bill this time," Anne said, laughing. "I made him agree to that before I accepted."

I was not amused. "It's the least he could do. Tell him he owes me a big one, too. I hope you charged the hell out of him."

"That's just it." Anne ignored my irritation. "I made him agree to pay me what he was going to pay the original presenter. He didn't like it, but I pointed out that the fee was already in his budget."

That amused me, despite my ire. "Good for you! I'm proud of you, lover. He's the man and you put it to him!"

"In spades!" she laughed, giving me a kiss that curled my toes. "I'll make it up to you, big guy. I promise."

"Well, you better get started," I murmured, nibbling her earlobe. I might be furious but I wasn't that mad.

This always gets Anne going if she's in the mood at all, and we started tearing at one another's clothes. Twenty seconds later we were in bed, her legs spread wide as I kissed my way up each of her wonderful thighs. Then my lips found their target. She gasped and began to moan. She clutched my head as I tasted her, teasing at first, then getting urgent. Just as she was about to go over the edge I stopped. I slid up her belly, dragging myself gently. Then I kissed her deeply, almost pushing her over the edge again. I held us there for a long, delicious moment.

"Your sentence is forty lashes," I told her softly. She felt me slide in an inch. She raised her legs as high as she could, holding them wide with her hands. Then she rolled her hips down and then up to claim another inch. When she did, I moaned and began to push myself into her slowly. "One!" I whispered urgently. I withdrew gradually until only a bit remained inside. "Two," I murmured as I gently pushed my full length in again, this time a bit faster. I'm a big man and she loved feeling me so deep within her. She rolled her hips to meet me again. This time she gyrated as she did. The sensation was incredible, for both of us.

Suddenly we were both at the brink and there was no holding back. "Forty!" I groaned. I began to impale her furiously with long hard strokes. Then I cried out as I filled her sweetness with my own. She locked her legs around me, riding me like crazy and screeching her pleasure. "Oh God!" she cried out over and over. She was thrusting like mad, drawing me ever deeper. Then we both screamed with delight and collapsed senseless in a tangle of arms and legs.

♣

"Damn!" I murmured. Several minutes had passed. It had taken that long before I could speak. "We seem to get better and better at this, don't we?"

"We do," she nodded sleepily. "I felt like I was about to die and afraid I wouldn't. How can it still be so good?"

"To tell you the truth, I don't give a damn," I chuckled, drowsy. "Are you ready for seconds?"

"You've got to be kidding!" she laughed.

I didn't answer. I felt her raise up to look at me, clearly concerned. My eyes had closed of their own accord. I was too far gone to utter the tender words half formed on my lips. The only answer she got was a soft snore.

# CHAPTER THREE

# Loose Ends

Anne left for Phoenix early one Saturday morning, planning to be back the following Sunday. The airline rules required her to stay over a Friday or Saturday night and she was anxious to have a day to herself to perfect her presentation. Her publisher was delighted with what she was doing. They had sent an overnight packet with three proofs and a cover design for her book. The cover was for her to use during her presentation. The proofs were for her to give to colleagues afterward for reviews. It was up to Anne to choose her peer reviewers.

Anne was quite aware how important this was. She needed to give thought to which of her colleagues she trusted enough to ask. Nor could they simply be friends. They needed to be people whose opinions carried clout.

After Anne left, I felt at loose ends and decided to go for a long run. Normally I would have driven the mile-and-a-half to my usual starting point. Yet, it was a nice day and I wanted to extend my run. So after ten minutes of stretching exercises, I took off at an easy lope that covered the ground more quickly than it looks. Less than twenty minutes later I was at the starting point. There I kicked up the pace to a ten-minute mile. The circuit was three miles around and the extra distance would give me a good workout for the day.

I completed the circuit in very good time. I was almost back to the starting point when I felt a cramp beginning in my right foot. I knew better than to try running the cramp out of middle aged muscles. So I slowed to a walk until I arrived at the gazebo near the parking lot. There were benches all around and I sat on one and took off my shoe. I began massaging my foot.

"Are you all right, Roger?" The voice was familiar and I looked up. I saw a woman of average height in her mid thirties. Her hair was pushed up under a baseball cap that had seen better days. I knew she was someone I'd met. But people look very different in running clothes. She was also wearing shades and I couldn't see her eyes.

"Yes, thank you," I replied. Then I added. "I know you but the little gray cells aren't telling me your name."

The young woman laughed. "Well, Poirot, I'm not dressed for work, am I? I'm Lucy from the newspaper."

"Lucy?" I asked. Then I remembered our conversation. "Yes! From the post office, too. Lucy in the sky with diamonds." I was surprised when she mimicked playing a guitar and sang the refrain of the song in a clear soprano.

"It's a weird song," she said. "I looked it up when you mentioned it the other day. I can't make sense of the lyrics."

I laughed. "I'm not sure John Lennon could. Everyone said it was about LSD but Lennon said it was about a picture his toddler son drew of a classmate. It was a crazy time with crazy music."

"I like the Beatles," Lucy told me. "Some of their songs really make sense."

"Everything makes sense when you're stoned," I laughed.

There was an awkward silence. After a moment, Lucy broke it. "You up for a cup of coffee?" she asked.

"Sure," I told her. "We're a long way from a coffee shop. I don't think I could make it there on foot."

"We can go to my place," she said. "I'm a coffee fanatic. Do you like Kenya or do you prefer something else? I have just about every brew they sell." Seeing the question in my eyes, she added. "It's only a half mile from here. Can you make it that far? I can give you a ride home from there."

I shook my head. "No, I'll be all right in a minute. I'd love a cup—whatever kind you prefer."

"Some of them are pretty strong," she told me. "I have decaf if you like yours neutered." The look on her face told me exactly what she thought about decaf.

I shrugged. "It's not noon. Fix whatever you like best. I'd love a cup." I put on my sock and shoe and stood. "Lead on, Lucille."

"Hey, that's a great song," she said, breaking into a twangy tenor as she sang the refrain of the country ballad about a desolate farmer whose wife had left him with hungry kids and a crop to make.

"You've got a wonderful voice," I said. "You do accents well, too."

"It's my secret vice," she said. "All my friends listen to this crap they're churning out now. I like the oldies."

"Oldies are goodies," I replied. The words were innocent. Yet, there was a lot more behind them than I cared to admit.

"Hopefully," she answered, giving me a wry smile. "By the way, my name is actually Lucilla. I got tired of trying to explain it so I go by Lucy."

"The light bearer," I murmured. "Just like Lucifer."

"That's me. Lucy the printer's devil."

"You're full of surprises," I said. Again there was an edge of frisson to my words. Her smile told me that she not only was aware of it, but liked it, too.

☘

When we arrived at Lucy's place, I felt immediately at ease. The building was an old carriage house. It had one large room and what looked like a deep sleeping loft. A picture window looked out over the valley toward a walking trail that ran along the river. "The view of the trail is better up there," Lucy told me, pointing to the loft. "Go on up if you'd like. I'm going to start the brew and grab a shower. We can have our coffee up there." She filled the coffee machine and headed for the bathroom.

I was suddenly aware of how sweaty I was. "I could use a shower, too, if you've got an extra towel," I called after her.

"Sure thing. I'll leave you plenty of hot water," she answered from the bathroom. The door was open and I could hear her clearly. Then her head appeared in the doorway. "Unless you care to join me. There's plenty of room." Seeing my surprise, she smiled and added, "Or not. It's up to you. I wouldn't want you getting lost in here by yourself."

*Well damn, Roger!* I thought. *It's time to shit or get off the pot!* Then I laughed silently. Al couldn't have put it better.

Despite my reservations, I found myself stripping off my sweat-stained shirt and shorts and slipping out of my shoes. Socks and my jockey-strap joined the pile on the floor and I padded into the bathroom. The shower turned out to be a walk-in with no curtain and I found Lucy there, eyes tightly closed and shampoo in her hair. "Is that you, Jolly?" she asked, not waiting for an answer. "Grab that sisal glove and wash my back, will you? Use the blue bar by the shampoo."

"Sure thing," I said, soaking the sisal before I began soaping it. Then I began to scrub Lucy's back, moving the glove in small circles across her smooth skin, beginning at the shoulders and continuing to her waistline. I was surprised to see what a good figure she had and I felt myself becoming aroused.

"God," she said. "That feels good. I haven't had a decent back scratch in ages. Do the hips and legs, too, if you don't mind."

Without a word, I knelt and soaped the glove again. Starting at her waist, I worked my way across Lucy's wonderful buttocks and then up and down each muscular leg. When I got to the place where they joined, I set aside the glove and used the blue bar to soap the division between her buttocks. Then, when Lucy moved her feet apart, I reached in from the back and soaped her vagina. I was surprised to feel no hair.

Setting the soap aside, I reached up again and carefully rinsed the outside of her soft nether lips. Then, starting where her labia came together in front, I slid my middle finger between them, not surprised to find she was wet and slippery. I gently pushed my finger inside, feeling her birth canal contract over and over, trying to draw me in even more. Then Lucy cried out and began to shudder, leaning forward and bracing herself on the tile wall.

"God, you're good!" she said, straightening up and pulling herself away as she turned toward me. "Now it's my turn." Glancing down, she was startled. "My goodness! Big Roger looks jolly." Bending over she carefully rinsed my rigid staff and took me in her mouth, causing me to cry out. Then she laughed and picked up the soap. "Just a preview of coming attractions," she told me. "Now raise your arms."

Starting at my wrists, Lucy lathered each arm and then my neck and hair. Closing my eyes to keep the soap out, I felt her lather my chest and belly, carefully avoiding my full erection. Then she worked her way up and down each leg, ending at my tight scrotum. There she slipped her hand behind them, soaping my crack before slipping a deft finger an inch into my rectum. "You're awfully tense," she said, continuing to massage my anus. "Can you relax a bit? It will feel wonderful."

I lowered my arms and took a deep breath, then another and another. Each time I found myself a bit more relaxed and began to breathe deeply. I discovered Lucy was right. The way she was massaging me felt wonderful. "OK, here comes the good part," I heard Lucy say. I was lost in sensation and found it hard to track her words. "Try not to flinch. Just stay relaxed."

I was startled when Lucy deftly probed my sphincter, gently pushing her finger ever deeper. At the same time, she took me into her mouth as deeply she could. She began to massage my prostate, matching the steady pace she was sucking. The sensation was like nothing I had ever felt before. It was so intense I thought I was going insane and glad of it. Yet, it was over in less than a minute. I found myself exploding, crying out as I discharged my seed into her greedy mouth again and again until I was drained. Then I felt my legs go slack and braced myself against the wall to keep from falling, sliding down the cool tiles until I was sprawled on the floor.

"Roger!" Lucy called, clearly worried. She slapped my cheek lightly. "Are you all right? Talk to me."

"Can't talk," I said with what she later described as a Harrison Ford grin, silly and lopsided. "Give me a minute."

Lucy stood and turned off the water, leaving the shower and returning a moment later with a towel. She began to wipe my face gently. Feeling me trying to rise, she laid the towel aside and gave me her hands, standing to pull me up.

I shook my head and turned to kiss her where she lived. I slipped my tongue in quickly to touch her clitoris. Feeling her shudder, I laughed. "I guess that's what they call a Brazilian wax." I nodded toward her hairless pudendum. I traced it with my finger. "I really like it naked." I looked down at my hairy package. "Does my hair bother you?"

"Not a bit," Lucy laughed. "I see you're a secret red-head. I've never seen a foreskin before."

"We're a covert club. The Ancient Order of Hooded Wonders." She laughed and I began to get up. "Do you have something to eat?" I asked. "I'm starving."

Lucy laughed. "Sure. I can fix you a sandwich. I'd join you but I've had my protein for the day." Seeing the uncertain look on my face, she added, smiling at my confusion, "Hey, I loved it. It felt like a half cup!" Reaching down she cupped my testicles. "Yep, they feel empty. That's too bad. Maybe we can have a lively conversation."

I nodded. "There are some things we probably need to talk about."

"Are there?" she asked. "I'm on birth control and free of disease. Are you?"

I nodded. "I haven't been exposed."

"Good, I didn't think you had. Neither have I. So we don't need to talk about those things. Other than that, I prefer married men."

"You do?" I asked, incredulous.

"Yes, I don't want to date or even get married. I want a fuck-buddy I can count on. Can I count on you, Roger?"

"Yes," I answered. "You can, Lucy. I don't make promises I can't keep." Even as I said this it struck me as hypocritical. I'd just broken some promises I thought I never would.

"I'm not asking for promises, Roger. Just never hit me or cut me down verbally. Or try to change me, either. I can promise you that in return, too. And always be honest with me, Roger. Lies are the worst kind of violence." She smiled. "I'm glad we talked. Now what do you like to eat, besides pussy?"

♣

Over the Dagwood sandwich Lucy put together, I explained the bet. "We were drunk or it would have never happened," I told her. "I'm hoping I don't get any responses. What we're doing is dishonest."

Lucy shook her head. "Not if you follow through, Roger. If you tell someone you just can't do it and walk away, you'll really be hurting her. I'd call it a violent act. It would be kinder to punch her out."

"Then why were all our women friends pushing me to do it?" I asked.

"I don't know. They don't sound much like friends to me. Maybe they secretly hate each other. Women are like that, you know."

"Yeah, well so are men. Al really surprised me. I had him down as a straight arrow."

"Those are sometimes the worst assholes," Lucy said. "I don't know you very well, Roger, but I don't think you're that kind of guy. I would never have brought you here if I did, believe me. I'd rather enter a convent."

Seeing my surprise, Lucy broke out laughing. "I wish you could have seen your expression just now, but don't worry. No way would I ever become a nun. Celibacy sucks." Then she shook her head. "No, I take it back. That's the wrong word. It stinks. About all I can handle is an occasional retreat and I come home as randy as all get-out!"

"You like archaic words, don't you?"

"Yes. I was born in the fourteenth century. What you've seen is the result of beauty cream and aloe vera."

"Wow. You're pretty lively for someone six hundred years old."

"Ha! You ain't seen nothing yet, Jolly Roger."

"Oh? I thought that was a rather jolly rogering."

"God, help us! A pucking funster!"

"That's no worse than a Spoonerist!" I declared, laughing. "Please don't take offense for me saying so, but you don't seem like someone who's never been to school."

"Well, you've seen my library," she said, pointing to one wall that was filled with bookshelves. There was very little room left on them for more. "Or, maybe you haven't. You seemed a bit preoccupied with something else."

"It was lust at first sight!" I declared.

Lucy smiled, then turned serious. "I guess there's something else I need to say. For this to work we've got to be free to love each other. That doesn't mean you can't love your wife, too, but it does mean that we can buy each other sappy valentines and small presents at Christmas."

"How did you get so wise?" I asked.

"I'd be a real dope if I didn't learn something over six hundred years! The real answer is that it took a lot of pain. Some of it wasn't necessary, maybe, but it all brought me where I am now. I like the woman it made me but I'm damned glad to have it safely behind me. It was pretty bad."

"I admire your courage," I told her.

"And here I thought it was my tits and ass!" Then she reached out and gently touched my face. "Thank you, Roger. You're a sweet man. I think I'm beginning to love you a little already. I hope that doesn't scare you off."

I shrugged. "You've had centuries to get used to the idea, Lucy. It's a new concept for me, being able to love someone else, too." Then I looked at her intently. "How old are you, anyway?"

"Oh, God! He's about to tell me I'm young enough to be his daughter. How old do you think I am, Roger?"

"At first I thought you were in your early to mid twenties. The way you think tells me you must be at least thirty."

"Another victory for beauty cream!" she laughed. "I'm almost forty. I will be in six months. Lively old wench, ain't I?"

"So tell me about your library. It sounds like you don't ever throw books away."

"Only the ones I don't like. When you look you'll see everything from astronomy to zoology, with a lot of fiction in the middle. I'm a sucker for a good book."

"So, you'd like books instead of flowers?"

"That's a hard choice, but yes. I do like flowers, though, and potted plants, even more. But good books are best."

"You're someone who never let schooling get in the way of her education."

"No, like the late Mr. Clements, I went for information, not credentials. No disrespect intended, either. I suspect you have degrees upon degrees."

"Not really. I got my doctorate for a union ticket. It allows me to live a life I like. Except for the frigging committees."

"Yes, well, God so loved the world She didn't send a committee," Lucy said. "I hope that didn't offend you, either. People get strange over religion."

"I noticed you called on God a lot," I smiled and she laughed. "That's an area you don't have to worry about," I added. "I like to meditate and do what I call prayer. But it's a long way from church. About the only thing I like about church is some of the music and the fact it's a quiet place to meditate when it's raining. The mall is too noisy."

"All this spiritual talk is getting me wound up." Lucy said with an unmistakable look. "Did I wear you out completely or are you up to an encore? The pun was intended."

"Oh, I think I can oblige you. How about a slow dance this time?"

"It's up to you, Jolly Roger. What's your favorite way?"

"There are two, actually. No, after that last session I'd have to say three." Lucy gave me a wonderful smile. "One is the cowgirl, but let's save that one for your turn. The other is what a guy I know calls angel food. It's a variation of missionary, but it's great. I don't want to hurt you, so you need to tell me if it does."

"Let's pretend we're two horny teens doing it for the first time," Lucy suggested.

"Do we have to get dressed?"

"No, just pretend I'm a shy girl and that you're undressing me for the first time."

"I used to know how to unsnap a bra with one hand."

"Ooh, that sounds wonderful! I can almost feel it!"

"Then stand up." She did and I shook her hand. "Hi, Lucy, I'm Roger. I'd like to kiss you." Lucy looked at her feet shyly, then nodded. I stepped forward and gave her a peck on the lips. When I did so, I poked Lucy in the belly and she laughed. "Oops!" I said. "Maybe we should have worn clothes."

"Girls can still feel it through clothes," she reminded me.

"There is that. Would you like to dance?" She nodded and I tried to hold her close. My erection kept getting in the way and we ended up giggling. "Maybe we need to cut to the chase," I suggested. "Pretend we're somewhere private. Let's move to the couch."

"The loft is more comfortable," Lucy replied and I followed her upstairs. Watching her lovely rump, it was all I could do not to grab her and have her there on the steps. I was aware she knew it, and knew that I knew that, too.

The queen bed in the loft was set next to the railing and overlooked the living area below. It had an excellent view of the walking trail along the river, although I didn't notice any of this at the moment. I was as intent on Lucy as a cat on a mouse and it was difficult for me to restrain myself when she stretched out on the bed, spread-eagle, and smiled at me. I somehow managed to hold myself in check and was rewarded with a kiss that left me gasping.

"Hi, there, beautiful," I murmured. Nuzzling her neck I heard her breathing change. I kissed her again and she opened her mouth, but I didn't give her my tongue. "We didn't do that back then," I said and she nodded.

Reaching out I touched her cheek lightly and ran my hand down her neck, arriving at her breast. Giggling, she pushed my hand away. Then I kissed her again, putting all my concentration into the kiss. This time she didn't push my hand away when I softly touched her breast. "So nice," I told her, kissing her neck as I pretended to unbutton her blouse. Squeezing her breast gently, I reached around and pretended to uncouple her bra. Then I paced my hand below her breast, as if pushing her halter back. I captured her nipple. Leaning down, I kissed it. I began to tease it with my tongue. I felt it grow hard. I moved my hand to the other breast and did the same.

Lucy was breathing heavily by then. I found a perverse pleasure in making her wait. Pretending to lift her skirt I slipped my hand under the imaginary waist of her panties. I slowly worked my way down, kneading the soft skin of her belly. When my hand grazed the top of her labia, Lucy moaned. When I touched her clitoris, she gasped, opening her legs wide. Gently I began running a finger down the outside of her labia. Then I moved up and slipped the tip of two fingers between them. She was hot and wet when I pushed gently into her. Lucy began to move her pelvis around and around.

"I think you're ready," I suggested. Lucy nodded urgently, opening her legs even wider. "I guess I better take off my clothes then," I said and she looked at me in disbelief. "Goodness!" I added, raising myself up and kneeling between her legs. "I think they're already gone."

Still kneeling, I moved forward. I held myself in one hand as I gently moved it up and down the outside of her labia. I was as wet as Lucy and she rolled her hips to meet me. Even so, I pulled back slightly, allowing her only a bit between her nether lips. Moaning, she began to gyrate frantically, driving me crazy. I began to respond, moving ever deeper each time I pushed inside. "Tell me when to stop," I said and she answered with a thrust that claimed most of my length. With the next stroke I was all the way inside her, lightly tapping the bottom of her birth canal.

By then the feeling was so intense I forgot all restraint. Grabbing her ankles I pushed them up until Lucy's legs were resting across her arms and I began to thrust harder and harder. As I did I could hear my body slapping against her as I plunged in again and again and again. She began to moan, louder and louder. She thrust back against me with equal urgency.

Our lovemaking seemed to go on forever. Its intensity grew so great I wondered how I could stand it. Then I couldn't stand it any longer. I began to shudder as I poured out my seed into her warmth. I could hear someone besides Lucy crying out as if in pain. Then I realized it was me, being turned inside out as I emptied myself into her cauldron. It was then that the light began to fade. I felt myself falling into a warm and welcoming darkness.

❧

I had no idea how long I'd been unconscious, but when I awoke Lucy was looking at me, clearly worried. "Are you all right?" she asked.

"Never better," I replied, leaning up and kissing her. She kissed me back warmly but without passion. "How long was I asleep?" I wanted to know.

"You've been out for half an hour," she told me. "Your pulse was regular but I was about to call an ambulance."

"Why?" I said, puzzled but not really concerned.

"You just fell over," she told me. "We came together and then you fainted and fell over. I thought you might have had a stroke."

"At least forty of them," I chuckled. Then I remembered I had said this to Anne not many days before. I felt a pang of regret. "Forty winks," I added. "I think I died and went to heaven."

Seeing that I was all right, Lucy relaxed. She looked at me oddly and I wondered if she had sensed my regret. Then she sniffed the air and smiled. "You must have. I don't smell any sulphur."

❧

We lay in Lucy's loft a long time, talking softly and gently caressing one another. Our passion had been replaced by a mellow tenderness and affection, not unlike what I often felt for Anne. I wondered how I could have known someone so short a while, and yet, could feel so intimate. I shared the thought with Lucy and she smiled. "I was just wondering the same thing," she said softly, kissing me gently. "Your wife must love you terribly."

I nodded but didn't answer for a few moments. Then I said, "I don't think it's just physical, Lucy. I've never experienced anything like this afternoon. It's like our souls touched, or something, and that's what made the sex so good. I don't understand it very well but I think I'm coming to love you a little, too. Does that scare you, too?"

"So coming has made you love me?" she asked with a grin. Seeing the look in my eyes, she added. "I'm not making light of what you just said, Roger. It bothers me a little how much I like you and how much I'm beginning to love you. It feels way too fast but I don't want to give it up." She sighed. "We need to be very careful with each other and I don't like being careful."

"That's funny," I said seriously. "I seem to be breaking free. I live a cautious life, too cautious. It feels good to throw caution into the wind." Then I kissed her gently and sat up. When I did, my eyes were caught by the view from her window. "Wow! You weren't kidding about the view. You're very lucky to have this place."

"I inherited it," she told me. "Along with the two houses on either side. I couldn't afford it on what the paper pays."

"So this is where you grew up?" I asked.

Lucy shook her head and smiled. "This was my father's get-away place. My sister got the main house in St. Paul. We used to come up here in the summer and I loved it. There weren't any other houses around then and we were allowed to bring a couple of friends." Then she turned serious. "It's none of my business, and I'm not suggesting you leave, but don't you need to get home?"

I shook my head. "I'm on my own this week," I said. "I don't even have pets to feed." I explained the situation.

"Would you do me a favor, then?" Lucy asked, looking down shyly.

"Of course, I will," I said. "If I can."

"Would you sleep over? It's been a long time since I've slept with anyone."

I looked at her curiously. "I would be honored, Lucy, but I don't understand. How can that be? You're a wonderful woman."

She looked at me, a wry smile playing around the corners of her mouth. "Yes, but I haven't met any men I'd like to sleep with. I haven't been celibate but with the usual bozos I meet, sex is more than enough. I'd rather sleep by myself."

"So I'm not a bozo, then?" I asked, smiling.

"No, silly," she answered, snuggling close. "Not at all. You're my Jolly Roger." Then she laughed. "What are you doing?"

I had started humming a familiar tune from Down Under and broke into song, "Rogering Lucillia! Rogering Lucillia! I come a rogering Lucilla todee...."

# CHAPTER FOUR

# Close Encounters

*Anne.* I had never been to Phoenix before. Never in my life had I been so glad to set foot on solid ground. Not that the flight had been that bad. It was one of the smoothest I could remember. I enjoyed leaning back into the luxury of my first class seat. The service had been excellent, too, as had the food. It was hard to tell that the entrée had been warmed along with many others in a convection oven. The only thing that gave any hint it had not been prepared from scratch was the ceramic tray that held it. The taste was excellent and nothing had been over-salted. This is a common complaint I have with processed food. This is especially true with canned goods.

The trouble with the flight had not come until the last fifteen minutes. I was looking out the window at the fast approaching ground when a small plane appeared out of nowhere. It was so close I could see the terrorized face of the pilot. Only quick reflexes by both pilots had kept our flight from becoming another grim statistic. I was so shocked I didn't even cry out and by the time I caught my breath, the incident was over.

The only immediate consequence of the near miss was that the pilot of the airliner had to abort our landing. This made the flight twenty minutes longer as he circled around to make a second approach. By the time we reached the concourse, I was shaking so badly I could barely walk. Yet, when one of the attendants offered to help me, I shook off his hand with an angry shrug. "I can manage it myself!" I snapped, and with the advent of anger, the shakes went away. When I arrived in the terminal I was still trembling, but I was in complete, if fragile, control.

When I left the plane and entered the boarding ramp, I was pleasantly surprised by the sensuous feel of the hot, dry air. I took off my outer jacket. The winter might be over where I lived but it was still too cold for shirt-sleeves after the sun went down. It had also been a cold, wet spring and the heat of the desert felt good. It warmed me to the bone, and I began to feel almost calm.

By the time I reached the baggage area I was looking forward to some time in the sun by the hotel pool. The shock of near death was still very much with me but I locked it away firmly. I would deal with it later.

Since I'd be making a presentation, I was wearing a tropical weight business suit in case the airline sent my large bag to Iceland or Tokyo. I'd packed all the bare necessities for my presentation into a carry-on and a large purse that held my laptop and my new swimming suit. At that moment, I could scarcely wait to show it off by the pool. I'd almost been killed and now I was ready to live.

Luck was with me once again. The big suitcase had made it to Phoenix, too. When I picked it up, I wondered why I'd packed so much for just a week. I was glad it had rollers.

Yet, I didn't have to roll it far. As I looked for Bob Akers in the crowd by the exit, I saw my name on a card held by a gorgeous young man. I walked over to meet him. He was quite attractive, so much so I felt goose bumps rise on the back of my neck. At six feet in my stockings, I'm taller than most men but I had to look up to meet the eyes of this hunk. He stood at least six and a half feet over what looked like ostrich cowboy boots. His long powerful legs were covered with stretch jeans that bulged in all the right places. Above a fancy western belt he wore a western-cut shirt over his broad shoulders. Over that was a plain tan leather vest that matched his complexion. His white Stetson made him seem even taller and his jet black hair was woven into braids that hung down over his shoulders.

What attracted me most was his wide smile. It was one that told me that he knew exactly what was on my mind as I approached him. It also told me how attractive I was in his eyes. I felt myself shiver, growing wet.

This had never happened to me before and I found it peasant but disconcerting. At half past forty there have been any number of men I found attractive. Yet, none of them were as distracting as this stud muffin. I knew it had something to do with the near miss, but I didn't care. Then I had to laugh at myself. Stud muffin is not part of my normal vocabulary. The only other man I think about this way is Roger.

"It looks like you're waiting for me," I said as I drew near. I sized the young man up brashly. This was not like me, either.

Just then I didn't give a damn. I was all too conscious how short life can be and felt like kicking the traces.

"It was well worth the wait, Dr. Smyth. I'm Benjamin White Owl, one of Dr. Akers' grad students. I'm very glad to meet you. I'm one of your admirers."

*More like one of his studs*, I thought. "It's kind of you to meet me, Benjamin," I managed to say, offering my hand. When he took it there was a warm, electric feel that coursed down my arm, almost making me catch my breath. The look in his eyes told me he knew what was happening and the bulge in his jeans said he found me as attractive as I did him. "Let's get out of here," I said quietly.

Benjamin nodded and relieved me of my suitcase and carry-on. They were both quite heavy, packed with books. Yet, he handled them like they were grocery bags. "I was supposed to tell you Dr. Akers apologizes for not being here to meet you himself, Dr. Smythe. There was some last minute thing that he had to take care of personally."

*Bob and his power games*, I thought. *Well, that's his loss.* I knew I would never respond to Bob Akers the way I had with Benjamin White Owl. "Call me Anne, Ben. May I call you that?" He grinned and nodded. "To tell you the truth, I'm much more pleased you met me, instead. Do you know where I'm staying?"

Ben nodded again. "Yes, I think you'll like it. It has a private hot tub and a nice place for you to work."

"I hope it has a queen-sized bed," I said. "I like to sprawl."

"King size, m'am. Not too hard and not too soft. I tested it myself." There was no question he knew where we were headed.

When we arrived at the car, I was even more impressed. "I've never ridden in one of these," I said, running my hand over the smooth fender of a white Escalade. "Do people actually take these off road?"

"Around here they do," he replied, opening my door and helping me into my seat. I had to step high to get in and was glad I'd worn flats on the plane. "Let's leave the doors open a minute to let the heat out," he suggested.

"Or we could shut them tight to keep the heat in," I replied. He laughed.

Ben loaded my bags into the rear and climbed into the driver's seat. Once we were on the road, I was pleased to learn the air conditioner worked quite well. I reached over and laid my hand on Benjamin's thigh. This is something I would never have done before. "Are you married, Ben? Or would you rather I call you Benjamin?"

"Everybody calls me Ben," he said, reaching down and rubbing the back of my hand. I was surprised how good this felt. I gently kneaded the powerful muscles I felt under the denim fabric. "No, I'm not married. Not even engaged." He raised his hand and gently stroked my cheek, moving it down over my breast. I felt myself straining back against the leather seat as I suddenly exploded. I almost came again when he reached down and ran his hand up my thigh. "God, you're hot!" he said.

"You ain't seen nothing Yet, stud muffin," I replied. "How far is it to the hotel?"

Ben laughed. "Quite a way," he told me, rubbing my breast again. "At least half an hour. My place is closer but I don't know if my roommate is there or not."

"I guess we'll have to wait," I told him, reaching up and squeezing the bulge in his jeans. He was hard as a rock. "Unless you want me to interview Mr. Big while you drive." I began to unzip his fly.

"We better wait," he answered. "You're about to make me drive off the road."

"All right, we'll wait," I told him, sitting up straight in my seat. *I can't believe I'm doing this,* I thought. Yet, I knew I was not about to stop. "Tell me something about yourself. It will make the time go by faster. I suppose you have to beat the girls off with a stick."

"Yes, but the girls don't hold a candle to you...Anne." He glanced at me to see if I really meant for him to use my given name. I nodded. We were way beyond formality. "You're hot and they're not!"

"Goodness, a poet, too. Why do I think you're stretching the truth, Ben? You don't have to humor this old lady."

"Believe me, I'm not lying," he replied. "You're beautiful, from the inside out."

"You should know," I quipped. "You just about turned me inside out."

"As a lady I know says, you ain't seen nothing yet."

Since I was already checked in, Ben took me straight to my

room when we arrived. He pulled into a slot at the back of the hotel, handed me a plastic key, and grabbed my bags from the SUV. Then he led me a short way down a hallway and stopped, waiting for me to open the door. I was delighted to discover my "room" was a small suite.

Once we were inside Ben dumped the suitcase on the floor and took me in his arms. His kiss was hard and long, almost bringing me over the top again. Then he picked me up and laid me gently on the bed as he began to undress me. I tried to help him but he gently brushed my hands away. "This is my job," he said softly, bending down to kiss my belly before lowering my skirt. I gasped and moaned. I felt my hips rolling up to receive whatever he had to offer.

Slipping off my bra, Ben took one of my breasts into his mouth. He gently played the pink nipple with his tongue as his fingers teased the other, bringing it to full erection. Then he kissed me on the mouth again. His tongue darted skillfully between my lips and teased mine. I grabbed for his shirt, grateful for the snaps that held it together. As I pulled, the snaps sounded like a large zipper quickly moving down. I found the sound incredibly arousing, too. Everything about the man seemed to turn me on.

"Don't go away," Ben murmured in my ear. Standing beside the bed he pulled off his boots and socks, then uncoupled the large trophy buckle on his belt. As he did, he took his time, his eyes playful as he lowered his jeans. Then he hooked his thumbs under the waistband of his white briefs. He began to pull them down slowly. There was a large spot of moisture at the peak of the tent his erection made. As he lowered his briefs, I could see his thick trunk slowly being revealed. Then, just as he was about to pop out, Ben ducked quickly, shucking his shorts and hiding himself. Looking at me and grinning, he slowly stood up. I found myself shivering again at the sight of him. I could feel myself wet with anticipation.

Unable to wait any longer, I threw myself off the bed. Grabbing Ben with both hands, I plunged him into my mouth. I began to suck furiously as I ran my hands up and down his shaft and I was quickly rewarded. Ben grabbed me by the hair, moaning as he followed the rhythm of my hands and mouth. Then he began to convulse and cry out as he released spurt after spurt of his tangy life seed. When he did, I felt myself coming, too, my hips jerking of their own volition with each spasm.

Feeling Ben sway, I reached up and steadied him, easing him down onto the bed. Turning him on his back, I snuggled close as I studied his wonderful love-maker. It was smaller now, but still firm. I gently pulled the foreskin back to reveal a surprisingly pink tip. I'd never seen such a dark penis, almost as dark as the sparse public hair above it, and I looked at him closely. I laid his shaft straight up on his belly. I could see there was no hair on his scrotum. I traced the two large blood veins on either side of his sperm duct with a finger. They seemed very large. So did the spout, and I wondered how it must look when he delivered a massive load.

I felt myself becoming aroused again. I began to play with Ben's staff, kissing it and teasing the tip with my tongue. He was snoring softly, but his member began to respond. Before long it was standing tall. "God," I whispered. "You could fly a flag from that thing."

I felt Ben chuckle. I looked up to see him watching me, a wide smile on his lips. "Damn, woman, didn't you get enough? You wore me out."

"I haven't had you inside me yet, " I answered. I rose up and straddled him, rubbing his breasts with mine. "You just rest and let me have my fun." Sitting up I took most of him inside me. He was thick, which made it a tight fit, but it was also pleasant and I raised myself completely erect. Ben reached up to fondle my breasts, a gift from my Scandinavian ancestors. I felt his full length stretch my love canal. It hurt, but in such a peasant way. I didn't stop. Slowly I began pulling back until half his length was exposed. Then I rolled my hips forward, bringing him in. I felt him grow even harder, stretching me tighter.

Ben started to reach for me. I held up my hands, stopping him. "My turn, cowboy," I said, feeling my vagina begin to contract, drawing him deeper. "It's called rodeo sex. All you're allowed to do is to try and buck this cowgirl off." I leaned back, forcing him even deeper, delighting in the sweet pain. "God, it feels good," I told him.

Before long I felt myself approaching the edge again. This time I slowed down and held back. This was too good to rush and I wanted to feel him release his seed deep inside me. Then it occurred to me I might get pregnant. It was certainly the right time of the month. Strangely enough, the thought of conception didn't trouble me. It actually turned me on and I began to rock back and forth quickly, pressing Ben into me as deeply as I could. "Come on, big guy, fuck me!" I heard myself saying as I began to gyrate, pushing as if I could pump him dry with my vagina. "Give me your seed."

Suddenly I felt Ben stiffen and begin thrusting, too, matching my rhythm. I felt his large tip ramming the bottom of my vagina, driving me wild, and I picked up the pace. Then Ben stopped moving, arching myself against me. I heard him cry out as he began to release his burden. I felt it spurting inside me, time after time. I heard myself cry out as I let myself go, grinding as tight as I could against him. Then I felt myself flying over the edge. I soared higher and higher as each contraction of my body shattered every restraint. Then I plunged into darkness.

♣

When I awoke, I found Ben looking down at me with an odd expression on his face. He reached out and stroked my cheek tenderly. There was no passion in his eyes as he did this. There was only a sense of wonder. It seemed close to adoration. "Anne," he started to say, but the phone rang.

"I better take this," I said. "It might be Bob Akers." Ben nodded and sat back on the bed, taking one of my feet and kissing it gently as he listened to my end of the conversation. I found this wonderfully erotic.

"Hello," I said. Speak of the devil. "Oh, hi, Bob…. Yes, the hotel is lovely…. No, I'd rather wait to meet tomorrow morning…. Yes, that was my plane in the near miss…. No, really. I'm a little scattered right now. Tomorrow morning would be better…. All right, then, I'll meet you in the dining room at nine…. Yes, Ben was very helpful…. Yes, he's an excellent driver…. No, I really don't know where he might be…. Well, I had the impression he had a date…. Oh, that's your car?… Yes, I'll let him know if I see him…. No, tonight wouldn't be good, either. I really do need some time to settle in…. Yes, I'll see you then."

By the time I hung up Ben was laughingly silently. "Your boss wants his car back, if you didn't get the message," I told him. Then I stretched, feeling like a cat after a long nap. I lay back, spread eagle in the center of the bed. "You know what I'd like? I'd like to feel you on top of me. I want to hold you in my arms."

Smiling, Ben lowered himself over my frame until my eyes were looking directly into his. "This time I want to be looking into your eyes when you come," I told him. Surely he must have felt the thrill that ran down my body. "Now give me a kiss, but keep your eyes open." I began to rub my hands up and down his broad back. The smoothness of his skin was delightful.

Ben did as I asked and I could feel him growing firm against me. His length was stretched out beside my body and he lifted up and rolled his hips back. Holding himself in one hand, he ran it down the opening between my labia. I heard myself moan and spread my legs even wider. I rolled my hips down until I felt the tip of his penis rub across my clitoris. Then it slid down between my wet nether lips until it rested at the entrance of my birth canal. I rolled my derrière again to seize a third of his length. Pushing himself forward to meet me, Ben easily pushed the remainder of his manhood all the way in, to the nub. I felt him touch bottom before slowly withdrawing. I saw his eyes loose focus and flutter shut. I grabbed his buttocks, digging my nails in just enough to sting.

"Hey!" He cried, his eyes wide. Then he smiled, realizing I was only getting his attention. I felt him grow even firmer.

Ben pulled himself out until only his tip remained within me. He began sliding in and out, penetrating only a couple of inches before withdrawing and pushing in again. I tried to force him deeper, rolling up until my heels raked his shoulder blades. Try as I might, I could not gain more. I saw his eyes crinkle with humor. "Say 'please,'" he whispered but I answered by lowering my hands to his buttocks. This time my nails dug in hard.

Ben gasped, instinctively pulling away from the pain and impaling himself deep within me. "Not nice," he whispered, still looking into my eyes. "Two can play that game." Suddenly he began to pump forcefully, as if he was trying to drive his rampant staff completely through me. He pulled back until he almost fell out, then plunged in as hard as he could. All without taking his eyes off mine.

I felt like I was being torn in two, but I never flinched. Slamming back against him with all my strength, I felt his balls bounce against my rosebud. They rebounded again and again and again as wave after wave of incredible pleasure overrode the pain and coursed through my body. This drove me even faster.

Then I saw Ben's eyes lose focus again as a great wad of semen shot through his duct. He cried out as his eyes rolled back into his head. Then he began to shudder and twitch. I picked up my pace even more. I pounded him with my pussy without mercy until my own shuddering deliverance came upon me. Then I collapsed beneath his massive chest as the beautiful darkness took me into its welcoming arms.

# CHAPTER FIVE

# Getting Acquainted

I was disappointed when I awoke. Ben had spent the night, giving me little rest. Now he was gone. Getting out of bed I felt like I'd run a marathon. My legs ached from fatigue and I was pleasantly sore in between. Yet, I was also a bit relieved. I was in Phoenix to make a presentation. As pleasant and intense as Ben White Owl might be, I had to keep my wits about me. Still, I couldn't help wishing he was there for one more round.

"Yeah, right, girl," I laughed at the thought. "Much more of that and you wouldn't be able to walk, much less think." Never before had I so fully understood that old expression, "fucking your brains out."

Then I remembered the phone conversation with Bob Akers. All thoughts of Ben White Owl flew out the window. Panic stricken, I looked at the clock. I was due in the dining room in thirty minutes. There was no time to do much more than shower and put on minimal makeup. Nor did I want to be late. Akers was an impatient man. He might come pounding on my door if I was. The last thing I wanted was to be alone with him in a hotel room. While nothing had ever become public, he had a bad reputation among female colleagues. There was no doubt in my mind that Bob Akers would take advantage of a situation if he could.

That morning I outdid myself. I arrived at the dining room at the stroke of nine. I was fresh and casually professional in a modest blue skirt and a white silk blouse worn below a muted brown paisley vest. Akers had wanted to meet at eight and I was glad I'd insisted on nine. I was also glad there was a breakfast buffet. Ben and I never got around to supper the night before and I was ravenous. As I walked across the dining room I wondered how much nutrition was in three globs of semen. Then I felt myself getting aroused. I shut the thought firmly away. No way did I want Akers to sense my mood and think he was turning me on.

I was surprised to see a stranger sitting at the table with Bob. He was a good-looking man. When he stood to be introduced, I saw he was slender and the same height as I. His voice was an almost musical baritone when he told me he was glad to meet me. The fingers that wrapped themselves around mine were long and graceful, surprisingly strong. His well-formed features were quite distinct, made more striking by his café au lait complexion. And there was humor in his dark, intense eyes. Who he reminded me of was a famous African-American singer of my mother's generation. I felt a delicious frisson between us. It was all I could do to keep my mind on what Bob was saying.

"As you know, Dr. Littlejohn will be making the keynote address tonight, Anne. I'd like you to introduce him. I have a basic biography for you but I'd like you to spend some time with him today to get better acquainted."

*Just how well acquainted do you want us to be, Bob?* I thought. I saw a hint of amusement in Littlejohn's eyes, as if he shared the thought. "Thanks, Bob. I'll read the biography later," I turned to our dusky companion. "Your name is very familiar, Dr. Littlejohn, but at the moment I can't place it. "What's your primary interest?"

"Please, Dr. Smythe, call me Michael," he replied, smiling. "We are to be acquainted, so we can at least use given names." His clear Oxford accent placed him somewhere in the Caribbean, possibly Jamaica. "My training was general architecture but my primary interest these days is dynamic space. Are you familiar with that?"

"Of course, Michael, please call me Anne." Bob Akers opened his mouth to say something but I hurried on. "Forgive me for being so slow this morning. I'm quite familiar with your work. I've applied a number of your principles to my plans in designing atriums."

Littlejohn smiled. "I thought I recognized my, um, influence in your work. Though those were quite unique designs. I'm really delighted at this opportunity, Anne. I've wanted to meet you for some time."

*Name the time and place, sweetie,* I found myself thinking. I forced myself to ignore that randy voice within I call Randy-Anne. "How about this afternoon?" I asked. "I'm meeting with Bob most of the morning but I'm free then."

"Would you mind meeting by the pool, or is that too informal?" Michael asked before Akers could break in. "I've spent the last two months in Scotland and I crave sunlight."

"I'm tied up all afternoon," Bob Akers finally broke in. "I can't make it."

"I'm sure we'll do well on our own, Dr. Akers," Michael Littlejohn assured him. "We can meet with you just before the banquet for last minute instructions, if need be."

*This fellow's a smooth one,* Randy-Anne quipped. *What a polite way of telling Bob Akers he ain't invited. Maybe we should skip the pool and cut to the chase.*

*Maybe you should cool your jets!* I answered the voice. *I'm still sore from last night.*

*When did that ever stop us?* Randy-Anne asked and I had to admit she had a point. Michael Littlejohn was a far cry from the stogy college professor I'd expected.

♣

The rest of the morning with Bob Akers was a drag. I had trouble keeping my eyes open and my mind on the subject. This boiled down to what Bob expected of me during the next three days. Finally he slapped his tablet down on the table and asked pointedly, "Is something wrong, Anne?"

"I beg your pardon, Bob," I said, touching his arm lightly. It was a calculated move but Bob was too obtuse to see that and relaxed a bit. "I'm still unsettled about the flight yesterday. You know, I could see the other pilot's face as clearly as I can see yours now." I shivered at the memory. "I'll be all right when I'm up to bat. The show has to go on, regardless."

Akers nodded. "Yes, it does. I can have someone else introduce Dr. Littlejohn tonight if you want."

"No, the busier I am, the better," I assured him. "Getting acquainted with him and talking shop this afternoon is just what the doctor ordered." *The doctor being Dr. Pepper!* Randy-Anne quipped. *Or is it Dr. Popper? Ten is out, but two and four look promising.*

"Let me summarize what you've told me so far." I rattled off a quick summary. It took less than a tenth the time Akers spent giving it. "Did I miss anything, Bob?" I asked. I knew I had not. My memory for details is quite good, even when I'm stressed.

"Wow!" Akers acknowledged. "I better be careful. You might

be able to do my job as well as I can and you're better looking."
Despite my impatience, I laughed. "No way, Bob, but thanks for the compliment. I have neither the interest nor the talent." *Nor could I stand the bullshit,* I thought and heard Randy-Anne tittering. "One thing you didn't mention. Who will be picking us up this evening? Benjamin?"

As much as I'd like to see Ben again, I hoped it was not. I wanted to be available if the chemistry was right with Michael Littlejohn. *Wonder what he looks like in the buff?* Randy Anne asked. *Cut it out! I demanded, shutting the thought away. You'll queer the whole deal!*

*Queer wasn't what I had in mind,* Randy Anne laughed. Oddly enough, she kept quiet after that. I almost missed what Bob Akers was saying.

"...called away on some kind of family commitment. It happens a lot with the Indians, though Ben has been very good about it. He sounded pretty disappointed. The two of you must have hit it off." Akers was looking at me intently and he seemed a bit jealous.

*He sounded worn out!* Randy Anne tittered and I almost laughed aloud.

"What are you smiling about?" Akers wanted to know.

"Nothing," I assured him. "Ben told me some funny stories about his aunts. It's not funny out of context."

"You know that 'aunt' can mean any woman in the extended family of his mother's age group, don't you?" Akers asked.

"No, I didn't," I answered, interested. "Some of my southern cousins call friends of the family 'aunt' or 'uncle.' But that's not quite the same. I read somewhere that the Navajo have a quite complex clan system to prevent intermarriage."

Bob Akers was clearly not interested. *And therefore he is not interesting,* I thought. "I wouldn't know," he said. "That's outside my field of competence."

*So is wiping your ass, shit-heel!* Randy Anne retorted, and I had to pretend to sneeze to keep from laughing aloud.

Bob Akers finally ran out of ammunition and I was glad when I could return to my room. I was developing a headache and needed something to eat. *Something to drink wouldn't be bad, either,* Randy Anne quipped. *We deserve it for putting up with that asshole.*

Although it was after one, I was in luck. Lunch was still

being served in the dining room and there was a buffet. I was pleasantly surprised to see Michael Littlejohn sitting at a table alone. He waved me over, invited me to sit with him. "I'll have another of those wonderful ice cream desserts while you eat," he told me, patting his flat belly. "I'll have to work out an hour longer, but it's worth it."

I was taking a sip of wine when Michael said, "Funny seeing you come in just now. I was just about to knock you up to...." He broke off when I snorted, choking on my wine and almost spraying the table.

"Oh, I'm very sorry," He said, obviously trying not to smile. "I've spent too much time in England. I forgot that means something different over here."

"What were you going to knock me up about?" I replied, laughing as I refilled my wine glass. Fortunately there was no one else in our area of the dining room.

"Oh, dear, I really put my foot in it, didn't I? " Michael asked. "I was going to see if you wanted to go to the pool later in the day. The sun is beastly now."

"We could always sit in the shade," I reminded him. "Why don't we get changed after lunch? When you're ready you can knock me up and we'll see." I smiled to take any sting out of my words and gave him my room number.

"I'm never going to live that down, am I? Well, I hope you don't use it when you introduce me this evening."

"Now, there's a thought, but, no, I won't. There's a price, however." *Woah, girl! You're getting tipsy,* Lusty Anne warned me. *Don't scare him off!*

"And what might that be?" Michael sounded like he thought I was serious, but there was an edge of doubt in his voice.

"Oh, I'll have to think about it," I replied. "But don't worry. I won't embarrass you. I might Bob, but never you." I looked at my empty plate and the empty wine bottle. "It looks like someone at all my food!" I declared.

Michael smiled. "Are you ready?"

♣

When Michael didn't come to my room right away I wondered if I'd misunderstood. The wine had definitely gone to my head. *Did I come on too strong?* I asked myself. It had taken me less than three minutes to change into my new swimsuit and to tidy up a bit. I was about to dial the desk and ask to be connected to his room when I heard a soft knock at the door. When I opened it, he was wearing a black brief that revealed a generous package behind the stretch fabric. Other than that, he wore only flip-flops and a smile. I found myself getting hot and wet.

"Come in," I said softly and he entered, brushing my breasts as he passed by. "I've decided a price," I added.

"Oh?" he asked, his eyebrows raised in surprise.

"Yes," I said. "We're supposed to get better acquainted and I really like your lips. I'd like to kiss them. Do you mind?"

"Of course not," he replied. "Aren't you married, Anne?"

"Well, never mind then. I'm sorry I asked." I was surprised at the bitterness in my voice. I started to turn away but Michael reached out and stopped me cold, grasping my arms with his surprisingly strong hands. A thrill coursed up my spine and I shivered.

"I am not being discourteous," he said, his forceful dark eyes a foot from mine. "I'm trying to be clear. I find you incredibly attractive and nothing would be better than starting with a kiss. I apologize for being insensitive and offending you."

"Hush," I said, slipping out of his grip and putting my arms around him. His chest was warm and smooth and as I moved my hands over his back I felt him growing firm against my legs.

When I looked up, Michael was watching me closely. He leaned down, covering my lips with his own, startling me with the strength of his passion. After a moment I opened my mouth and felt his tongue dart in, exploring the inside of my lips and teasing my tongue. The intensity was so great I began to shudder, overcome by one spasm after another as I slipped my hands beneath his briefs and began to lower them. When I did so, he responded by releasing the top of my bikini, then sliding his long fingers between the cheeks of my derrière, gripping me fiercely with a low growl. A thrill of fear went through me, feeding my passion. I bent down, slipping his briefs down enough to free his feet. As I did, I bumped his stiff dark staff, long and thin like his fingers. I captured it with my mouth, teasing the tip with my tongue, running it all around and tickling the notch at the top.

Suddenly Michael tensed and moaned loudly. It was almost a roar. A moment later my mouth was filled with his hot, tangy seed as he pumped out spurt after spurt across my merciless tongue. Taking a moment to swallow, I milked him until he was dry. He cried out again at the unbearable pleasure I was giving him. Then I felt his hands on my head, lifting me up until I was on my feet. Kissing me like he had before, his hands cradled my taut buttocks, kneading them like bread.

Breaking the kiss, Michael bent down and lifted me in his arms, gently laying me on the bed. "Now I knock you up," he whispered, taking me by the ankles and pushing them to either side of my neck. Then he lifted his rigid staff and teased me by rubbing it up and down against my nether lips, causing me to squirm. I grew even wetter. Slipping the tip of his dark staff into me, he entered slowly, pushing his whole length inside and grasping my knees with his hands, pressing them against my breasts before withdrawing to begin the next stroke. I could barely move, but I pushed back, matching his deliberate rhythm. I growled back at him. I was surprised how much this turned me on. I growled even deeper.

This seemed to excite Michael, too. Changing position, he leaned forward, placing his hands inside my knees and balancing himself on his own. This pushed my legs up until there was nothing between him and my warm, eager wetness. "Damn, you're hot!" He growled as he began to thrust back and forth with rapid short strokes.

I didn't even try to keep pace with Michael, but lay back and absorbed the intense sensations surging through my body. Sore as I'd been that morning, I was surprised how good it felt having Michael so deep inside me. I came again, growling my pleasure. He was thrusting fast, almost like a rabbit. I was so wet now there was little friction. I began to gyrate my hips. When I did, Michael cried out. He clutched himself tight against me, twitching and groaning. I felt him release spurt after spurt of warm fecund seed. Then he collapsed on top of me and I had to push him to one side to breathe.

Still joined together, I lowered my legs and encircled Michael's slender hips. I locked my ankles and held him in place even after I felt him grow flaccid. "So nice to make your acquaintance," I murmured in his ear. He chuckled. It was clear he was drowsy and wanted to sleep.

Releasing Michael, I slipped out of bed. I was wide awake and decided to take a shower. I would have liked another round.

But I needed to get myself together for the evening. The clock told me it was almost four. This meant we had been at it for almost an hour. Even though I felt energized, I was tired. I was also a little light headed. So it was time for a long shower. Then I could take a leisurely hour getting ready for the formal dinner.

Although I had only a minor role in the evening program, I intended to make the most of it. Now, in my forties, I knew I was still good looking in a black cocktail dress. It wouldn't take much to upstage my mostly male companions at the front table. Michael might be the keynote speaker but the night was mine!

♣

The formal dinner was like such things often are. Those who came sat quietly in polite boredom as they endured the opening rituals. Tuning in with half my mind, I thought about the last twenty-four hours with a sense of wonder. Who would have ever suspected the first twenty-four hours to be such a fuck-a-thon? Nothing like this had ever happened to me before. Not even in my wildest dreams had I ever imagined anything like this.

*What had happened to the cautious women I used to be?* I wondered. Part of it was the wine. I was drinking quite a bit these days. Yet, I thought there had to be more to it than that. I decided it was the near-miss, seeing the terror in the face of the other pilot. I'd read about life changing events but I'd never thought it might happen to me. Now, having come so close to death, I felt incredibly alive. The experience seemed to have unlocked a door deep within my soul. It had freed an incredible woman I had no idea was there.

*Who is this woman?* I asked myself. I liked the lady. I resolved to never, ever lock her away again.

*God, I hope not,* answered Randy Anne. *Your normal life is so boring I want to scream!*

*I'm a married woman,* I told her. *I love Roger. I don't want to leave my soul mate.*

*Who said anything about leaving him?* Randy Anne answered. *Why not have your sausage and eat it, too? There is such a thing as an open marriage.*

I repressed the thought as soon as it arose. I focused on the unfolding non-drama of the dinner. It was good I did because Bob Akers was winding up his remarks. He was about to call on me to introduce the keynote speaker. When he did, I got up from my seat and made my way to the podium. I could feel every eye in the place on me. I took my time getting there, walking with a relaxed sway, creating a ripple of interest. I was surprised at just how much this was turning me on. *Who would have ever thought something so ordinary could be so arousing?* I wondered.

Once I was at the podium, I laid out my prepared notes. I slowly looked around the crowded room. As I did, I could sense a frisson of unease running through the crowd and decided to take a risk. "Thank you, Bob," I said. I smiled as I looked at Akers, who had addressed me as Anne. This might be a violation of unwritten protocol, putting myself on his level. Or, better, putting Bob in his place. There was no doubt in my mind that every women in the crowd knew exactly what I had done and why.

"I don't know who that was that you just introduced but I certainly want to meet her before this conference is done." A polite titter ran around the room and I knew I had their attention. "I know this is where I'm supposed to tell you how honored I am to be asked to introduce our keynote speaker, and I do feel honored. I even have notes made up to bore you with, telling you how honored." I smiled, wrinkling my nose and holding up my sheet of notes between my thumb and finger as if it was something smelly.

A man in the back of the room laughed aloud and many of the women were smiling, but some of the men were growing nervous. "So I decided to do something different. We all know who Michael Littlejohn is and the wonderful things he's written about the dynamic use of architectural space. Many of us have used his concepts and those have improved our work. I know I have and I make no bones about it. Using them has made good work into excellent design, and I am very grateful to him for that."

"What I didn't know before today, and what many of you may not know, is the man behind the name." I looked at Michael Littlejohn and smiled. When I did he looked a bit nervous. "It is here I find myself most honored, in being given the opportunity to become acquainted with this brilliant man." Looking at Littlejohn again, I said, "I hope my saying that doesn't give you a swelled head, Dr. Littlejohn, but it's true. I hope everyone here has the opportunity to become acquainted with you during this conference as I have today." To his credit, Michael smiled at me and nodded back.

Turning back to the audience, I continued. "I hope you get to know his wonderful sense of humor. I know you will appreciate his forceful presentation that drives right to the depths of the matter at hand. He truly is a gifted man and he speaks with a silver tongue, clear and concise. So I am honored to introduce this warm, witty human being who goes to such great lengths to share his seminal thinking. Please help me give a warm welcome to Dr. Michael Littlejohn."

As I passed Michael, he smiled and offered his hand. "My turn," he murmured and I found myself scared. What surprised me was how much this aroused me. *God, I thought, is there anything that doesn't turn me on?*

"Thank you, Dr. Anne Smyth," Littlejohn began. "I assure you the pleasure was mine. I was quite familiar with your work, as well, and I found it most delightful to discover the personal depths behind your professional articles. I am certainly one of your fans. I hope we get another opportunity to explore our mutual interests in depth. Your work is dynamic space in person." There were a number of puzzled looks when he said this and several people in the room made notes. The great man had spoken and therefore it needed to be noted. Never mind that these notes might never be read. Many of these folk were academics and note taking was de rigueur.

Fortunately, Michael went on into his keynote presentation. While I found it both informative and challenging, my mind kept slipping back to images of the afternoon. By the time Michael finished his speech, I was ready to throw off my clothes and ravish the man in front of the whole crowd. *And you call me randy,* my newly found companion observed dryly.

The rest of the evening was tedious. I was like a pot simmering on the stove. It was not until late that evening, as I was getting ready for bed, that I would find release. Hearing a soft knock at my door I looked through the peephole. "Room service," said a familiar voice and I opened the portal to admit Michael Littlejohn.

"You naughty lady," he said, smiling as he took me in his arms and kissed me.

"Ooh! Does that mean you're going to spank me?"

# CHAPTER SIX

## Turning a Table

*Roger.* "Want to see a special place?" Lucy asked. It was early morning and we were out for a run along the river trail. This stretch of the path was rarely used by others. It was a long way from a parking area. Yet, Lucy suggested that we run a good distance apart. "It doesn't hurt to be discreet," she told me. "We can meet at the resting place where we turn around. This way we can each run at our own pace."

This made sense and I agreed. Running is not really a social sport and it would give me time for solitude. Lucy and I had been together the entire weekend and I was craving my own company for a while. Our hours together were filled with pleasant conversation and even better sex. There had not been much time alone for reflection and I needed to think about all that had taken place. Even though the weekend would end tomorrow morning when Lucy went to work, it was nice having this brief respite now. I enjoyed her company, maybe a little too much. I was also feeling a bit worn out. *Told you so,* I reminded myself chuckling, recalling my response to first seeing her.

Lucy took off first and was waiting for me at the resting place. It was about two miles from her place and the woods were thick on the bluff overlooking the trail. Below them was nothing but a rock berm sloping to meet the river, barren except for a few stubborn weeds and wildflowers along the edge of the running trail. On the other side of the river was a steep bluff, densely wooded with no buildings in sight. Except for the walking path, we might have been in a wilderness area.

"This is wonderful, Lucy," I told her when we met at the resting place. "How much more special could it be?"

"You'll see," Lucy told me. "It's not far. You can rest there." She took off running up the trail. After a moment I followed her, frowning. Four miles is about my limit. While I can run farther, and had when I prepared myself for a ten-klik run, after four miles it stops being fun.

There was a rock outcropping near the resting place. The river turned back on its course at that point, making a blind bend in the path. I was no more than thirty yards behind Lucy when I rounded the bend. There the path made a reverse turn in the other direction. This gave me a clear view of the trail for at least three hundred yards, but Lucy was nowhere in sight. Stopping to look around, I could see no break in the undergrowth above me. So I walked further up the path, looking for a place where Lucy might have disappeared.

Hearing her laugh behind me, I turned. Lucy was standing on the path not ten yards away. "You couldn't spot it, could you?" she asked.

"Where were you?" I scarcely believed my eyes.

"Right here," she replied. She turned and walking directly toward a solid line of brush. Then she side-stepped and I lost sight of her.

When I followed, I was surprised. There was a game trail hidden behind the first of two lines of brush. Lucy was waiting there. "Come on," she said, reaching for my hand. She led me up the path to a small clearing just below the rocky outcropping. It was covered with a deep stand of grass watered by a small spring. I thought something had grazed there not long ago. The grass was only ankle high near a narrow watercourse that snaked across the middle of the clearing.

I looked around. I could glimpse the path through the trees in both directions if I stood on my toes. Yet, no one would see me if I didn't. There was also a hush in the clearing, as if the brush and trees caught any sound we might make. "How did you ever find this?" I asked.

"Chasing a butterfly when I was a kid," Lucy told me. She moved toward the spring. "Come over here. There's a nice place where we can sit and talk. Or have a lively conversation." Her smile made it clear what she had in mind. She stripped out of her running clothes and bent over the spring. She dipped handfuls of fresh water to wash her face. When she did, I could see the gates of paradise. As she intended, I lost no time shucking my shorts and top.

Lucy was still bent over when I knelt behind her. I grasped her derrière firmly as I leaned forward until I touched the right spot. Then I reached down, gently opening her with my thumbs as I slowly impaled myself within her. There was little resistance when I did. She had obviously been planning this. She was slippery and incredibly warm. I moaned and began slowly rocking my hips back and forth, striking her rump with my belly. Each time I pulled back as far as I could without falling out. As I did, Lucy slowly moved her pelvis round and round, driving me crazy. It didn't take long before I began picking up speed. I began to plunge in and out in short, swift strokes until I cried out. Just as I did, I felt Lucy constrict. She held me deep inside her as wave after wave of incredible pleasure surged over us like thundering surf.

This time I didn't slide off her like I normally did. After a moment's respite I continued to push in and out slowly. I heard myself groan. The pleasure grew ever more intense now that my first urgency was past. As I did this, Lucy began to respond again. She was even wetter now.

"Oh, fuck that feels good!" I moaned. Then out of nowhere it happened again. I cried out and began to come, slamming myself tight against Lucy. I gripped her hips so hard it left marks as I was caught by the intensity of my explosion. I began to twitch wildly, like I was having a seizure.

Then it was done and I fell back onto the soft grass. I stretched out full length before dozing off. My manhood draped across one leg like an empty sock. Lucy saw this and smiled as a tiny drop of formed at the very tip. Then it dripped and ran down my leg.

Lucy seemed to find this very erotic and reached out. Catching the drop with a finger, she caught it and touched it to her tongue. She told me later it tasted sweet and slightly salty, and a little like herself, too. Then she curled up next to me, cupping me in her hand. She laid her head on my chest, listening to the steady beating of my heart. As I looked at her she began to snore softly, drifting off to sleep. A moment later I followed.

♣

I was cold when I awoke. I was cold and ravenous and stiff in all the wrong places. Glancing down I saw Lucy asleep beside me. I wondered what it would be like waking up with her every morning for the rest of my life. Then I shoved the thought aside. I was frightened even thinking it and told myself I was a happily married man. The hidden side of myself, who I was only coming to know, answered. *Yeah, right, champ! That's why you're here diddling Miss Lucy.*

I thought about this a long while. Then I turned and kissed Lucy lightly on the forehead. I whispered, "I love you, Lucy." When I did I was glad she was asleep, though she snuggled closer and made a soft, deep sound of content. Much later she told me that she had heard me.

♣

"You sure make good coffee," I told Lucy. It was Monday morning. We were sitting at her kitchen table, enjoying a leisurely cup. She would leave for work soon and I'd head to my office at the university.

One thing I'd promised myself weeks before was making sense of my desk. Today was the day. The truth is, I hate this kind of housekeeping. Yet, I was at loose ends and there was nothing else I wanted to do. While there are always projects I have going, nothing captured my interest. I felt scattered and this would be a way of getting through the day productively. My reward would be an afternoon run to the special place Lucy had shown me. And if housekeeping got too tedious, I could always distract myself thinking of the evening I'd spend with her.

"Thank you," Lucy smiled. "The secret is high quality beans and good equipment. You really do get what you pay for with coffee." Then she turned serious. "Roger, there's something else you need to know. When I'm involved with someone, I'm monogamous. I never sleep with anyone else. So you don't have to worry about catching anything from me."

I nodded. "I'm obviously not," I answered. "I'm married and we have a good sex life. We don't use condoms, either."

"Is your wife monogamous?"

I shook my head. "I don't know. I think so, but I couldn't swear to it. Anne doesn't seem like she would ever sleep with anyone else, but who knows? I didn't think I would, either."

Lucy gave me a searching look. "Now here you are with a younger woman. How do you feel about that?"

"This sounds like a long discussion," I pointed out. "I'm all right with things as they are, but we need to talk about it this evening. I mean, what if someone answers my ad? You told me I shouldn't back out the way I'd planned."

"Then you need to use a condom," Lucy said. "That's the

safest way."

"So should you and I start using condoms?" I asked. "Anne hates them."

Lucy sighed. "You're right. We do need to talk about this before your wife gets back. I hate them, too, but they're better than taking a risk." She smiled and reached out to touch my face. It was a wonderfully intimate gesture. "I'm getting very fond of you, Sweet Roger. I don't want this to end. You're very special to me."

I reached up and covered her hand with mine. "I know," I said, sighing. "You're very special to me, too, Miss Lucy. We'll find a way to make it work, for all of us. I promise."

Lucy cleared the table. Then she wiped it clean and gave me a look I was beginning to know very well. Sitting on the edge of the table she said, "I think you need to make me late for work. Lying back on the table she lifted her skirt carefully and asked. "Guess who's going commando?"

I stood up and shed the bathrobe I was wearing. I lifted Lucy's legs gently and spread them. I could see she was already wet and ready to go. So I knelt and began to tease her with my tongue and lips. Smelling her tangy juices drove me wild. When Lucy grabbed my head and pulled me closer, I thrust my tongue into her as deep as I could reach. Slowly drawing it out, I felt her grow tense and I plunged my tongue back in while I massaged her clit with my nose. She cried out and I fastened my lips to her. My tongue was moving like a whirling dervish, going round and around. Then she began to shudder violently.

"I can't take it any more!" Lucy gasped, pushing my head back. I stood and plunged myself into her. Then I began to pound her with my pelvis. I held her legs wide and high by the ankles as she dug her nails into my buttocks, pulling me tight. Within a dozen strokes, Lucy began to moan. When she felt me begin to release my seed, she cried out. Joining her voice with mine, I uttered an animal sound of pure joy.

Without thinking, I fell forward onto Lucy's contracting belly. When I did, we heard a loud crack as the table legs gave way. We landed on the floor with a solid THUMP! I was still inside Lucy when we crashed. She gasped as I was driven into her to the hilt. Then she began to shudder as she came yet again.

This scared me. I withdrew immediately and asked if she was

hurt. To my surprise, she began to laugh. "I thought I hurt you!" I declared, still frightened. This made Lucy laugh even harder. She told me later she wasn't laughing at me. At the moment, all she could do was gasp and giggle. After a few moments, I began to smile, too. Then the absurdity of the situation struck me and I began laughing, too.

It took us a good while to calm down and when Lucy looked at the clock, she groaned. "Oh, shit! I'm going to be almost an hour late."

"Why don't you call in sick?" I suggested.

Lucy shook her head. "I don't like to lie," she told me.

I nodded. "I really don't, either." Then I laughed. "I know! Why don't you call in fucked?"

⁂

I was sitting in my office at the university two days later. I was sorting through my mail when the phone on my desk rang. I wondered who was calling and was surprised to hear Anne's voice. "Oh, hi, sweet," I said. My voice sounded brittle, even to me. "How did your presentation go?"

"It went well," she answered. "You sound funny. What are your doing?"

"Pouting, actually," I replied lightly. "That's what I do when I get tired of sorting mail." There was dead silence from the other end of the line. "Come on, sweetheart, you know I'm teasing."

"Do I? Yes, I guess I do. I thought you were going to write this week. Have you even looked at your novel?"

"Several times. I can't seem to get very far. I write a paragraph or maybe two. That's about all I can do. So I've been writing in my journal, hoping it will get me started."

"Your journal? What are you writing there?" Anne demanded.

"What do you think I'm writing? I'm writing about everything that's going on in my life. That's what I always write about."

"I've never understood that," she said. "You go over the same old things. Isn't it enough living it once?"

"It's a healthy way of dealing with the challenges. I've told you this before. When I'm having a hard time with something, writing helps clarify the issues."

"So you're writing about our fusses?"

"No," I laughed. "I'm writing about my part of it, how petty I get and how stupid that is."

"You got that right," Anne answered. I wondered why she was being such a bitch. I thought she was calling to try to set things right. "I don't want you writing about us," she told me.

"I'm not, Anne," I said, more patiently than I felt. "I'm writing about how silly I get, not about you."

"All right, then. But I don't want to read about one of our fights in one of your books."

I sighed. "Why did you call, Anne? To assure me what an asshole I can be?" I could hear what sounded like someone knocking at the other end of the line.

"No. Look I have to go. Someone's at the door. We'll talk about this later. Bye." Anne hung up without waiting for me to respond.

I sat there for a long while, thinking about the call. Then I took out a spiral notebook I used for making writing notes. I took out two pencils and sharpened them. Then I began to write out the conversation we just had, verbatim. After all, I thought, it's good material. It would be a shame to let it go to waste.

# CHAPTER SEVEN

# Coming Home

*Anne.* My flight home from Phoenix was uneventful. Yet, I couldn't completely relax until I was inside the Twin Cities terminal and headed to pick up my baggage. Then I saw Roger waiting for me by the carousel and I slowed down. I realized he had driven up to meet my plane. I was touched by his thoughtfulness.

Even so, he looked different somehow. He seemed even more confident and more relaxed than usual. Yet, there was something else, too, something that made me uneasy. It took me a moment to figure it out. It was guilt, I decided, not his guilt, but mine. I remembered the sense of dread I felt before boarding the plane in Phoenix. *How will I ever explain what happened to Roger?* I asked myself. *Will he ever forgive me?* There was no question in my mind that I loved him with all my heart. But what of this wonderful woman I discovered? Would he love her as much as the Anne he knew before?

All these thoughts went through my mind in a flash. Then he turned and saw me. His face lit up with his wonderful smile and I found myself crying as I ran to embrace him. *What am I going to do?* I wondered. I clung to this beautiful man who shared so much of my life. *What am I going to do?*

*Well, start by fucking his eyes out,* Randy Anne drawled and I laughed without thinking.

"So what's so funny?" Roger asked, frowning. I was sure he sensed something different about me. I was aware of a quiet reserve I'd never had with him before, not even when we first met. I couldn't seem to break out of it and this was frightening.

"Nothing," I replied, smiling and wondering if the difference was not with him, too. "I was just thinking about what I'm going to do to you when we get home."

"Ah," he said, smiling back, but I was certain there was something different between us. Could he still be mad about the change of plans? *That must be it,* I thought and decided to play my high trump.

"I was almost in a midair collision when we were about to land in Phoenix," I told him and explained what had happened.

When Roger didn't respond immediately, I found myself growing angry with him. This was unfair. Roger is always calm in a crisis, something I have always admired. It was only when danger had passed that he allowed himself the luxury of feelings and I relied on him as a tower of strength. But just then I wanted him to be as devastated as I had been. Even though I knew it wasn't his way.

"Well, I can see you don't care!" I snapped and he looked like I had slapped him. I knew he was deeply hurt. Part of me screamed at myself when I saw him pull back and withdraw. It was Randy Anne. *What are you trying to do, you stupid bitch? Drive him away?*

"I'm sorry you had a bad flight," Roger said. His voice was flat and neutral. "I don't see how I'm to blame."

"I didn't say you were!" I snapped. Somehow I couldn't stop myself. *Easy, sweetie,* Randy Anne cautioned. *You're on thin ice. Be careful.*

*You shut up!* I snarled back, so distracted that I missed what he had said. "What?" I demanded, miserable when I saw his carefully neutral features. Driving him away was the last thing I wanted to do but I couldn't stop.

"I said I'll be happy to take the bus home," Roger answered. *Shit!* he thought. *That's all I need.* Lucy was already on the way. It had been an hour since she'd dropped him off. "I really don't want to fight, Anne."

"You never do, do you?" Hearing my own shrill voice almost broke my heart. *What am I doing?* I asked myself. *You're fucking up a perfectly good marriage,* Randy Anne informed me. *Where's Ben White Owl when you need him?* She added sarcastically. *Or Michael Littlejohn?*

Roger nodded. "You're right," he said. "This was a bad idea. My apologies." Turning on his heel he walked out of the baggage area, dialing his cell phone. His shoulders were set and he walked like a centurion going into battle.

Seeing Roger walk away like that, I panicked. I hastily grabbed my suitcase off the baggage carousel and took off after him. By the time I reached the door, he was out of sight. Running across the driveway to the parking ramp, I was almost struck by a passenger bus. The driver blasted his horn and one of the airport police headed my way.

"Do you need help, m'am?" he asked courteously.

I shook my head. "I'm just in a hurry to get home, officer. It's not been my day."

The policeman nodded. "Yes, m'am, but you need to be careful. You want to be sure you make it home." He held up a hand and blew his whistle, stopping traffic. "Drive carefully," he said, waving me across the driveway.

Roger was nowhere to be seen in the short-term ramp. Even though I searched every level, I never spotted his car. Then I saw someone who looked like him standing by the car rental return. Yet, by the time the elevator had taken me down four levels, and I'd crossed the walkway and run the length of the terminal, there was no one there who looked the least bit like him.

Nor could the rental attendant remember anyone of his description. "I'm sorry, m'am," he said. "I see thousands of people every day and I didn't notice."

Fighting back tears, I walked back to the baggage area and waited for the shuttle to long-term parking. When I got to my car I sat there for a long time thinking about what just happened. I've never felt that miserable. I was grateful that Randy Anne refrained from rubbing my nose in the mess I'd made.

♣

*Roger.* "So it was bad," Lucy said. She and I were sitting down for supper at a popular pancake house she knew. It was not far from the airport but was off the beaten track. When she had driven down with me, I'd insisted on paying her to drive my car home. "I've got to be able to explain it truthfully," I told her. "I'm hiring someone to drive my car home." She rolled her eyes when I came up with that one.

Fortunately, Lucy had decided to hang around a while after she dropped me off. I was glad she had. I really don't like riding the bus at all and I might have had to spend the night in the bus terminal. Transportation to our part of the world is tricky.

I nodded, still hurt by Anne's words. "It was terrible. I think she was spoiling for a fight. I think she feels guilty about ruining our vacation plans. Anne has always been into guilt. She was raised Roman Catholic." I sighed. "I wish now I had stayed and toughed it out but I hate fighting. My parents fought all the time, ever since I can remember. It was awful."

Lucy nodded. "I know all about guilt. I was raised an ultra-conservative Lutheran. It took a long time before I came to understand what a mind warp had been done on me. It took even longer before I could give it up. But I did, by the grace of God, as some of my friends say. Then I began to come alive." She nodded solemnly, then shrugged. "Thank God that's behind me."

"I'm surprised you still have religious friends," I said, glad to change the subject. "I used to have some very devout friends. After a while they all turned judgmental. I don't know why."

"Oh, I didn't say these were religious friends. Many of them don't have much time for religion. They're spiritual people, though. Very much so."

This surprised me. "I don't understand," I told her. "What's the difference?"

Lucy seemed uncomfortable. "I don't want to offend you, Roger. There's a lot about you I don't know."

"You won't," I assured her. "I refuse to be offended, even if you call me a dip-shit."

Lucy smiled. "That's actually a term of endearment." She looked at me intently. "All right, Roger, I'll take a risk with you. In for a penny, in for a pound."

She paused a moment to gather her thoughts. "All the religious people I know seem to be focused on rules They also seem to expect the world to live by their rules. Spiritual people seem to focus on their relationship with whomever or whatever they call God. They seem to do more praying and a lot less talking about what they believe. They seem a lot more tolerant, too. I hope that doesn't offend you."

"Not at all," I answered. "Where in the world did you run into such people?"

Lucy looked very uncomfortable. "They were there all along. It was when I went to recovery that I began to be able to see them."

"Recovery? You mean…."

Lucy nodded, looking at I as if she expected me to bolt out the door. "Yes, lover, I mean I'm a recovering addict. Pills were my passion, pain pills. I have to watch it with other things, too, like alcohol. Aspirin is about the strongest thing I'll take these days."

"So that's why you're so strong on coffee. I hear they drink a lot of that at meetings."

Lucy chuckled. "And most of it is terrible! That's why I started bringing my own. That led to trying out about every kind I came across. Do you have any idea how many varieties of coffee there are?"

"Quite a few, I imagine. Why did you think I might not like it that you were in recovery?"

"Are," Lucy corrected. "It's present tense, Roger. I am in recovery and will be the rest of my life. I go to two or three meetings every week."

"Is that what makes you so passionate?"

Lucy laughed. "Actually, that's one of the reasons I stay clean. Sober sex is incredible. You wouldn't believe the difference." Then she turned serious again. "Please be honest with me, Roger. Does my being an addict bother you? Even a little?"

"How could it? I'm an addict, too."

Lucy was flabbergasted. "You are? You sure don't seem like it."

"I'm addicted to Lucy in the sky." I smiled and took her hand. "I need a fix."

Lucy shook her head sadly. "This isn't a joking matter, Roger. Recovery is a life and death thing for me. I need you to take it very seriously."

"I am very serious," I told her. "You're very good for me, Lucy. You're good to me, too. I really enjoy your company."

Lucy shook her head again. "Roger, we're on a slippery slope here. Right now you're pissed off at Anne."

"You got that right!" I declared. "I drove all the way here to meet her plane and she starts a fight? Thank you, but no thank you very much. The same thing happened just before she left. She's become a raving bitch!"

Lucy held up her hands. "Roger, stop! Please. I'll listen to anything that bothers you but please, don't put Anne down. It takes two to tangle. So if there's a problem, you have some part in it, too. Am I wrong?"

I started to argue the point, but then I remembered some things and sighed. When I looked at it objectively, I had contributed to every argument Anne and I had ever had. Maybe to the one at the airport, too. "No, you're not wrong, Lucy. What's strange is getting marriage counseling from my lover."

"Anne's your lover, too, Roger. You've never seen me pissed and I prefer you don't, ever. I can be hell on wheels when I'm bent out of shape or stoned. Ask any of the people who knew me before recovery."

"I hope I never do, too. That's one of the things I like about us, you and me. We don't waste time fighting."

"We don't live together, either, lover. We're still minding our manners and trying to please."

"Speaking of trying to please, let's get out of here and find ourselves a room."

Lucy shook her head. "Not tonight, Roger. Tonight belongs to Anne. You need to make love to your wife. She needs it, too, and you need to remember you love her."

"That's odd advice coming from my mistress."

"I'm not your mistress, Roger. I'm one of your lovers, and not the most important one, either."

I looked at Lucy as if I was seeing her for the first time. This was a side of her I'd never suspected. "You know, Lucy, you're either completely sane or crazy as hell."

She smiled. "Well, not to argue, but I'm somewhere in between. None of us are playing with a full deck, lover, not one of us. The best we can hope for is being sane most of the time." She reached out for my hand. "Now get me home before I change my mind and boff you in the parking lot!"

♣

Lucy turned out to be absolutely right. When I got home that evening I found Anne on the couch, weeping. When she saw me come in, she threw herself into my arms. "I'm so sorry, Roger. I've been such a bitch."

"I'm sure there's every reason, my love," I said softly, lifting her chin and kissing her gently on the lips. I tried to be as open as I could but my memory of her acerbic tongue was still tender.

"That's not enough," she said. Taking my face in her hands, Anne kissed me again, this time with passion. "I missed you," she said, clinging to me tightly. After a few moments, I felt the tension go out of her body as she molded it to me, pressing tight against me with her mons veneris. It was as if all the passion she felt, all the anger and anguish and fear, along with every hope and dream, seemed to converge there, as fiery and focused as a cutting torch. I'm sure she felt me grow firm against her.

Suddenly we were on the floor, our clothes scattered around us where they were flung. Nor did we bother with foreplay. We tore at each other wildly, desperately kissing and clutching and crying out. We pounded our hot, crazed bodies together until they were forged into one flesh. We became a beast with two backs that roared as it shuddered again and again and again. Then we lay silent, totally spent in one another's arms.

♣

An hour later Anne and I were seated at our breakfast counter in the kitchen. This is where we took most of our meals and I had marinated a pork loin, one of Anne's favorites, before I left for the airport. I'd also made dinner rolls from scratch and prepared her favorite medley of mixed vegetables. For desert there was pie from the local bakery and a rich decaffeinated coffee Lucy had recommended.

"That was wonderful," Anne told me with a sly smile. "So was the food and I love the flowers." This, too, was something Lucy had suggested and I wondered how she would like the ones I'd ordered delivered to her place the next morning.

Shutting all thought of Lucy from my mind, I asked Anne about the near miss and the week that followed. "It really shook me up," she told me. "I don't really want to talk about it right this minute. I'm grateful to be alive and I want to stay in this moment. I'm also grateful I have such a sweet husband." She leaned across the counter and touched my cheek, smiling before she continued.

"The conference was great and I came back with almost a hundred orders for my new book. I was also offered a couple of commercial jobs working with one of the best architects around. That's going to mean a lot of traveling, I'm afraid. Do you mind?"

"Not really," I said. "I'm thinking about doing a book—not my novel—and I could use the free time for research."

"Oh, what about?" Anne asked.

"Nothing's really come together," I answered. "I'm still kicking different ideas around. You know my process. I think of a dozen ideas and then something else pops up out of the blue. I may even try to write a different novel."

"What about the other project?" Anne asked.

I frowned. "I'm not sure what you're talking about, sweetheart." This was not completely a lie. I always had a number of projects going, some of which I would complete. The dating project might be a sensitive subject, one that could lead to another fight. I didn't want that.

"The bet about the ad."

"Oh," I chuckled. "I expect to win the bet. There's not been a single response."

"It's only been a week or so. What did you expect?"

"Actually, I expected nothing. I believe you and the others are the ones who expected something to happen. You only win the bet if someone replies and we actually hook up."

Suddenly Anne was very afraid. "Why don't we just forget the stupid bet?"

I shook my head. "Our friends would never let me live it down. Besides, it's already running. I thought you knew. I placed the ad a couple of days before you left."

"We weren't communicating much," Anne observed. "I'm not arguing and I'm not pointing a finger except at both of us. It's not worth a fight, but we weren't on the same wavelength. Do you have a copy I could see?"

I got up and fetched the morning's paper, folding it to the right page. "It's the Sweet Gent ad."

Anne read the ad and smiled. "That's sweet. Did you notice they misspelled 'discreet'?"

"Yes, but not until after the ad was running. It would have cost too much to change. It didn't seem that important."

Anne nodded. "I think I might answer it, Roger."

"That doesn't count," I told her. Then I smiled. "Come to think of it, you already did."

Anne smiled. "No, I guess it wouldn't count. I see you wrote 'a broad life experience.' Why didn't you say broad minded?"

"I didn't want Lesbians answering the add," I replied with a wry smile.

"Ugh! You're bad," she told me.

"Yeah, but ain't you glad?" I shot back and Anne rewarded me with another smile.

"You could have said open-minded," Anne told me.

"I guess but I was close to the space limit," I told her. "Besides, who else would answer such an ad?"

Anne nodded. Then she started to say something but stopped. "What?" I asked.

"Oh, it's something that crossed my mind a while back. It's not important."

"Now you've got me curious," I told her. "Go ahead. I won't get upset. Cross my heart."

"Well, things are different these days and we don't have any children to worry about. We consider ourselves to be broad minded, but we've never done anything that outrageous."

"I don't understand where you're going."

"Well, I'm not suggesting we do anything but have you ever considered something like mild swinging?"

I shook my head. "That's too dangerous, Anne. STD's are not like they were when we grew up. There's AIDS and herpes all kinds of nasty stuff."

Anne nodded. "I know, but how about in principle? Would it make you jealous?"

"Wouldn't it make you?"

"Probably, but it might be all right with me if it was just sex. You know, no romance. Could you handle that?" Anne looked frightened even asking the question.

"I don't know," I said. "I'd have to think about it. Why are you asking? Do you want to have a fling?"

"No, that's not what I was asking. I just read something and it made me curious."

I nodded and shrugged, even though I knew Anne was lying. Her nose always flared in an odd way when she lied, though I'd never mentioned this to her. Nor did I think Anne would even ask the question unless she was already involved. I wondered who it was, then decided not to push the issue.

"Are you curious yellow?" I was referring to a movie that was quite controversial when it was released in 1967. We'd ordered a copy and watched it. Neither of us could understand why it seemed so outrageous.

"No, I'm curious Anne." She knew I was trying to get the conversation to safer ground. "Curious George is my cousin."

"You mean there's only two degrees of separation between me and the President? How about that!"

♣

The next few weeks were very busy for me. Classes resumed

the day after Anne got home, which meant I found it hard to find time to be with Lucy. We settled for early morning runs together. These sometimes ended with lovemaking, but mostly not. We also took lunch together every time we could at Lucy's. I had the more flexible schedule, so I'd bring sandwiches or soup. We always made love before we ate.

I asked Lucy about this one day while we were eating. We had been uncommonly in synch that day. It was like we'd been together for years. It started with Lucy in the shower when I arrived. There had been a chemical spill at work. This required her to get into the emergency shower immediately, clothes and all. She had come home to change. Even with the first shower, she could still smell the ugly odor of chemical and she wanted to be fresh for me. So she stripped off her wet clothes, dumping them in the mud sink to soak in hot soapy water. Then she bathed in the hottest water she could stand.

Lucy told me that as she showered, she remembered the first time I came to her place. Then she recalled our very first time together and began to tell me every detail: my hot, sweaty smell as we talked on the path; the feel of my wet skin when I got in the shower; the beauty of my long, thick love-maker with its pink tip; the smell and taste of the small smear of fluid around the opening; how it felt as she took me into her mouth; the resistance of my tight rosebud at first; the feel of probing me when I relaxed; the way I trembled and jerked and cried out when I came; and the wonderful, tangy taste of my semen.

Lucy told me that as she recalled these things, she became more and more aroused. When she heard my voice telling her I was there, she shivered with pleasure. As she went to the door to greet me, wet and dripping inside and out, it was all she could do to hold back. Then she kissed me and there was nothing she could do. As I slipped my tongue into her mouth, she felt herself falling over the edge as shudders of pure delight washed over her like surf.

Then something strange and beautiful happened. She said that as she went over the edge, she found herself growing faint. As if from a great distance, she heard me call out her name. When I did, she said my voice sounded like beautiful hand-bells and that she was surrounded by a wonderful silver light. It was then she wondered if she was dying, but the thought didn't disturb her. She knew there was nothing to fear and she would be content to remain here forever.

Even so, Lucy could feel my arms lifting her from the floor and laying her gently on the couch. The feel of me drying her off was so wonderful she said she could scarcely bear it and she found herself becoming aroused again. Opening her eyes, she saw me looking at her with great concern but she couldn't speak. All she could do was to attack the buttons of my shirt, almost ripping them out of the hole in her haste. Then she grabbed my belt, releasing it, and lowered my zipper. She said the sound was incredibly sensual, as if she could feel it as well as hear it. It was at that point she grabbed my still flaccid member in both hands, and began to stroke it rapidly. Then she shoved me inside her wet inferno once she felt me grow hard. "Fuck me, Roger!" she moaned. "Fuck me! Fuck me! Fuck me!"

Realizing Lucy was not in danger, I withdrew for a moment to free myself of my pants and shoes. When I did, Lucy began to keen until I plunged back into her, driving so hard and furiously I began to release my seed right away. Feeling me discharge my burden within her, Lucy flipped us off the couch. Wailing like a banshee she rode me until we both collapsed, exhausted.

As I drifted off I identified the strong odor I'd smelled. It was solvent. I'd smelled it before at the newspaper when they were cleaning machines. Then I smiled. I wondered how I'd ever explain smelling like I'd thoroughly fucked a printing press.

♣

When we ate lunch I was ravenous. "I'm not complaining, but I was wondering why we make love first." I said. "I think I just learned the answer."

"Yes," Lucy laughed. "Now you know, silly man. They teach us to take first things first in NA. Besides, I don't like to rush. If we run short on time, I can always take my lunch to the office."

"I take it there's not a safe place we could go where you work," I said. I didn't know why, but the thought of having sex at the newspaper excited me. "Don't you like an occasional quickie in the closet?"

"We're a long way from quickies, superman. Maybe after five or ten years but then I'll be running the place and have a private office. I can jump you across my desk."

I smiled. "Only if you must. I was thinking about doing it on one of the presses."

Lucy looked at me like I was crazy. "It would take a week to scrub the ink off."

"Just a thought. Actually, I like the place along the running path much better."

Lucy frowned. "You know, Roger, you're the only one I've ever taken there. I hope you will honor my secret."

"Of course I will. I promise."

"Even after we go our separate ways?"

"Lucy, I don't ever intend for that to happen. I love you and I want you in my life as long as you want to be."

To my surprise, I saw tears come to Lucy's eyes. I opened my arms and she came into them, weeping quietly. "Shit!" she said. "I promised myself this wasn't going to happen."

"What wasn't going to happen?" I was at a loss.

"I wasn't going to fall in love with you," Lucy told me. "We were just going to be friends and sex buddies. Now it's too late. I liked you too much. Now I'm in love."

I sighed. "I know, Lucy, I know. I thought that was happening. It was happening to me, too. But I can't do anything about it but what we're doing. Do you think we need to end it? Or do you want to learn to live with it?"

"What do you want, Roger?"

"I would rather learn to live with it but that's not fair to you, love, and maybe not to anyone else. What you want has to come first." Lucy told me my eyes were grave as I said this. That's when she realized that I really meant what I'd said. The decision was up to her.

"I can't have what I want," Lucy told me. She reached out and hugged me gently. "I guess we'll have to settle for what we can have. I don't want to lose you, Roger. Not ever."

"Neither do I, Lucy."

Later, when I thought about it, the way I said this didn't make much sense. When we speak from the heart it sometimes doesn't. Yet, Lucy understood exactly what I meant.

# CHAPTER EIGHT

# First Reply

The school year was coming to an end before the bet came up again. I'd signed up to teach a summer class and Anne had taken a professional commission that required her to be out of town for weeks at a time. She'd flown to New York the month before for two weeks to help plan the project. This delighted me, though I didn't dare show it. It meant Lucy and I could spend more time together.

Anne was excited about the project, more so than I'd ever seen her. She told me the chief architect she would be working with was someone famous and the site would be in Jamaica. She said that having her name alongside his as the architects would do wonders for her career. Yet, the way she talked about it told me the famous guru was probably her lover. *Sex, sand, and the sea*, I thought, trying not to be caustic. *What more could a married woman want?*

The custom among our friends was to gather to celebrate the end of the school year. That year Anne and I were the hosts, and the menu was pork loin. Dead pig was how I described it on the invitations. Everyone else brought side dishes and there was lots of beer in a large ice chest on the patio. We also set out wine and iced tea for anyone who preferred those.

As one might expect, it was Al who brought up the subject. "So you won your bet, Roger. Congratulations. I suppose you collected big time."

"I never kiss and tell, Al," I declared, hugging Anne and earning a laugh from the group. "Besides, the ad was expensive. So you could say I lost. Unless, of course, you're interested in helping out. I won't say no."

"It wasn't my bet," Al replied, holding up his hands, and three of the women booed.

"So you didn't get a single inquiry?" Shirley asked.

"Not from the local ad and not off the Internet, either. What I did get was lots of junk mail offering everything from phone sex to penile enhancement." The group laughed and I added, "I forwarded those to you, Al."

"Well, I can tell you Roger doesn't need enhancement!" Anne quipped. She had been visiting the beer cooler quite a bit and there was an embarrassed silence from the group.

"I think this pig is about done," I told the group, trying to shift their attention. I didn't know why Anne drank so much at times. We had it made, or so I thought. "Grab your plates. Two minutes and I'll start carving."

Over the meal the conversation drifted from the new book of short stories I was writing to Anne's news about the project in Jamaica. Then it turned to campus gossip and the discussion was lively. One of the deans was facing a sexual harassment suit and opinions of how this should be handled differed sharply.

"I say suspend the bastard without pay," Al declared.

"He's innocent until proven guilty, Al," one of the men reminded him. "You want him suing the university if he isn't convicted?"

"Where there's smoke, there's fire!" Al insisted testily. "When they start digging they'll find a can of worms!"

"What's that coming out from around your collar, Al?" Shirley asked sweetly. "Steam or smoke? You better be careful about throwing stones."

"What's that supposed to mean?" Al demanded.

"Don't play dumb with me, Al," Shirley fired back. "I've seen the way you look...."

I intervened, holding my hands up in the sign for a time-out. "Hold it, guys. We're all friends here. Let's stay that way. OK?"

"Good old Roger," Anne said. Her words were slurred. "Always refuses to fight." Seeing the hurt on my face, she tried to apologize but the damage had been done. Still, it had deflected the conflict between Al and my hecklers.

"All right!" I said, trying to ignore the hurt from Anne's dig and failing miserably. "We have black and white tonight, double chocolate cake and vanilla ice cream. The line forms at the rear and I'll need some help bringing it out." Nor was I surprised when Helen and Shirley followed me into the kitchen. They were usually the ones who helped out.

"That was the beer talking, Roger," Helen said. "I hope you know that."

"There's been a lot of booze under our bridge lately," I replied, noncommittal. "Not just beer. I've been thinking of finding a support group."

"We're your support group," Helen assured me. "All you have to do is call." Shirley nodded her agreement. It was no secret that Helen was a long time member of Al-anon, or that her husband, Roy, was an unrepentant drunk. This was why he was not there that evening. He'd been drunk by mid afternoon and Helen had refused to bring him along.

"Well, the most immediate support I need is getting dessert from here to there," I said, trying to make it clear I didn't want to discuss it. "Aprons are in the closet if you want one and the ice cream is in the freezer. Forks and spoons are in the drawer." I picked up the cake and left the kitchen.

From the reflection in our patio door I saw Shirley and Helen look at one another. I saw Shirley shrug and open the freezer. As the patio door closed I heard her say, "That went well, didn't it? I'll get the ice cream."

♣

I was grading essays a week later when I got a call at my university office. "Dr. Jahnsen?" asked a distorted voice from the other end of the line. It sounded vaguely familiar but the connection was poor.

"Yes, this is Roger Jahnsen. If you're calling for Dr. Samuel Johnson I'm afraid he won't be available for some time." Sam was one of my closest friends on the faculty. He took a lot of kidding about his famous name. He was currently on sabbatical and his namesake had been dead three hundred years.

The lady at the other end of the line was apparently having a hard time hearing, too. "Are you the one who placed the Sweet Gent ad?"

I finally guessed who the mystery caller was. "Lucy, is that you? Why don't you call me back? We've got a poor connection."

A moment later the phone rang and I recognized Lucy's voice. "Actually, we have a pretty good connection," she said and I laughed. "I wish we were connected right this minute."

"Your wish is my command," I told her. "Just say the word."

"I can't. Audrey's here." Audrey was a part time administrator who came in from time to time. Whenever she heard someone use earthy language she always said, "Don't talk trash!" She also fined anyone did this a quarter per vulgar word. No one knew what she did with the money she collected. Nor did anyone dare ask. Audrey was a force of nature.

"She's just jealous," I laughed. I looked at my watch and saw it was running. "Am I late for lunch?"

"No, but I'll have to watch the time." She was quiet for a moment and I wondered why. "The reason I called is that you have a response."

"Well, I should hope so. It's not much fun if you just lie there eating an apple."

Lucy laughed. "I don't think that's likely. You have a response to your ad. Do you want to come in and pick it up or should I put it in the mail?" She was speaking casually but there was something in her voice that concerned me. I decided to wait until we were together to ask. Lucy could not speak freely with the Dragon Lady present.

"Why don't you bring it when you go home for lunch?"

"Certainly," she said. "It's on my way."

♣

I was early getting to Lucy's place and I let myself in so I could start the coffee. Then I put our subs into the fridge and set out cups. Normally I felt very relaxed at Lucy's but that day I found it hard to sit still. There was something odd about getting an answer this long after the ad expired, but there could be a reasonable explanation.

With that thought in mind, I sat down and began going through a centering exercise. I wanted to be calm when Lucy arrived. So I imagined myself as a large rock on the Oregon coast, withstanding the surf and every storm. I was almost successful.

*Yeah, right!* Jolly Roger responded as the picture came together in my mind. *A real rock, like Rock Hudson! A rock star, too, no doubt. The only stones here are between your legs.*

I had to laugh. *All right, I'm taking myself too seriously. I am worried about this response, though.*

*Why? Play it like it lies.* I could almost see Jolly shrug.

*That's just it. There are too many lies,* I responded.

Jolly laughed. *What's one more? Your whole life's shot through with lies. It's the human condition.*

That last sentence hit me where I lived. "The human condition" was a phrase I often used in my lectures, and never without irony.

Having that irony pointed inward on myself hurt. It lay too near the truth. My whole career was based on distortion, now called spin. There was no escaping that harsh fact. I even gave a lecture every year to my lower level students called Original Spin that began, "In the beginning was the spin; and the spin was spun spinning apples."

*Yo, Roger! Lighten up. You're about to get laid by a beautiful lady.* It was Jolly Roger again. *First things first, man! Nooky rules!*

At that moment the door opened and Lucy came in. When she saw the troubled look on my face, she ran to me, her arms open. "It's going to be all right," she whispered, holding me close. I nodded and we stood there a long time.

"Wow, I haven't done that in a long time," I said, pulling back and kissing Lucy lightly on the lips. "I wanted to be strong for you and I thought myself into a funk. Would it be all right if we just had lunch and talked today?"

"Of course," she replied and then smiled. "As a matter of fact, the original meaning of 'intercourse' was communication. Or did you know that?"

I chuckled. "Yes, I did, but thanks for reminding me. I take myself way too seriously sometimes."

"That goes with the turf, doesn't it, being a high muckey-muck professor? It takes lots of gravitas." The way she said this sounded like "grab-it-ayuss."

"I just love it when you do Texan," I said, giving her a kiss that shivered my timbers.

"I'll talk Texas any time for one of those," Lucy replied when we were done. "Only we need to talk."

"The four scariest words in the English language," I said, letting her go. "I gather it's about the reply."

"It is." She opened her purse and pulling out a cheap white envelope. She handed it to me.

I looked at the envelope before taking it, handling it very carefully, as I would a poison snake. I walked to the kitchen table, sat down, and laid the envelope down. I made no move to open it.

"We could just ignore it," I suggested. "The ad's been closed for what, a month?"

"More like two," Lucy answered. "I looked it up."

"So what do you think?" I asked.

"I don't know what I think," Lucy answered. "But I know how I feel. I feel like a jealous fish-wife. I'd like to claw the bitch's eyes out!" She sat down opposite me. "I don't like the way I'm taking this, Roger. It was the ad that brought us together and I should be grateful for that."

I nodded and smiled. "When I say I should do something it usually means I have no intention of doing it."

Lucy smiled back. "Let me rephrase that. I need to be grateful for the bet. When I need to do something, I do it. Eventually."

I nodded and grinned. "You mean like taking a dump?"

Lucy snorted. "You are so delicate, Roger! I was thinking of something more basic, like breathing."

"You do that so nicely," I replied, taking several slow, deep breaths before starting to pant and moan.

"You better watch out, buster. You're going to get it!"

"God, I hope so," I said, then held up my hands in surrender. "Sorry. I get distracted when you're around."

Lucy smiled and looked at the envelope. I nodded and slit the top with a penknife. I didn't take out the single sheet of folded paper I saw inside. "It's not too late," I said. "I can still burn it."

"You can burn it after we read it," Lucy answered. "I want to see what the bitch has to say for herself." Then she shook her head. "Listen to me! I never get jealous!"

I didn't know how to respond so I picked up the envelope and took out the folded sheet. It was expensive off-white bond paper and carried a watermark. Someone had also taken time to mark it with scent, too. "That smells familiar but I can't tell what it is. Violets, I think."

I handed the sheet to Lucy without reading it and she sniffed it cautiously. "I don't know, either," she said. "It's something my mother used to wear. The scent is violets." She handed it back. "You going to read it?"

I didn't answer right away. I knew someone who wore that scent but I couldn't remember who. Nor did I think it wise to share this with Lucy. "I can't think of any reason to read it," I and started to crumple the sheet.

"God, Roger!" Lucy exclaimed, snatching the note out of my hands and reading it. It only took her a few seconds. When she was done she said, "No big deal. She wants to meet. She says where she'll be and when, and it's a very public place. All you have to do is show up."

"Why bother? I have every thing I want."

Lucy frowned, ignoring me. "It's funny she wants to meet in person so soon. People usually start with email and instant messaging. Do you think she knows who you are?"

"I don't see how but the bet's no secret. The whole thing's become a campus joke." Then I laughed. "I know who she is! She's Dragon Lady."

"Audrey?" Lucy laughed so hard she almost fell on the floor. Audrey was anything but attractive. I'd once described her as the face that stopped a thousand ships.

"Thanks," Lucy gasped, wiping her eyes. "I needed that. I forgot Rule 62."

"Rule 62? What's that?"

"It's from AA. It says don't take yourself too seriously."

I nodded vaguely. "There's something I need to say. To put it simply, you're number one with me, love."

"You mean I'm a real pisser?" Lucy snorted. "Sorry, Roger, I'm having trouble being serious right now."

I nodded, smiling. "I know. I do serious too well. Yet, I meant what I said. You're at the top of my list."

"Not Anne?"

I shook my head sadly. "I wish I could say she was. A month ago I could. We're going through a really rough time. I think she's having an affair." I told Lucy about Anne's question about an open marriage and the way she talked about Jamaica. "That doesn't mean I'm not committed, because I am. I don't know why. I just am."

"It's history," Lucy told me. "You've been together for more than half your life, but it's more than that. It's who you are as a man, Roger. It's why I love you."

"I don't want to end up hating each other."

"Then you need to make sure it doesn't happen," Lucy told me. Seeing the look on my face she said, "I assume you were talking about you and Anne."

"I was actually talking about you and me."

Lucy reached out and touched my face and I kissed her hand. "Are you tied up this afternoon?" she asked and I shook my head. "Wonderful! I'm going to call in and give myself a mental health day. First, we're going to finish talking and then we're going to eat. After that I'm going to fuck your ears off!"

♣

"Wow!" Lucy said. The clock read almost four and the afternoon was growing old. I needed to leave for home soon. She hated to see me go. She was lying next to me on the couch with one leg draped over mine. She held my flaccid staff in her hand and stroked him gently. Yet, I was too spent to respond.

"I know we're good together, lover, but that was awesome!"

"Twat's that?" I asked, cupping a hand over my ear. "Did you say something, Lucy? I cunt hair."

Lucy chuckled and snuggled closer. I knew she was recalling every detail of our tryst. It started over lunch when she picked up a large sweet pickle, holding it up before slowly inserting it into her mouth. She moved it back and fourth slowly, and I was surprised at how erotic this was. Then she dipped it in mayonnaise, holding it up and closely examining it before licking it like a cone. I saw a shiver of pleasure ripple up her back and I knew she was getting quite aroused.

I watched this closely, my sub half raised to my mouth, forgotten in my hand. "Ummm," I murmured, seeing her shiver. When I caught her eye, I opened my sub and began to run my tongue from the bottom to the top. There a small piece of meat stuck out by itself. Kissing it, I began to run my tongue around and around it. Then I backed off to lash it with the tip of my tongue. Lucy moaned, barely able to restrain herself from leaping across the table and attacking me.

Suddenly I growled, burying my face in the open sub and shaking it back and forth forcefully. Lucy gasped, shuddering as I did this. Then she laughed when the sandwich disintegrated. I was left with a handful of slippery lettuce and lunch meat.

This was more than Lucy could stand. Jumping up she drug my chair back from the table. She attacked my belt and fly. Then she stripped down my pants and underwear, leaving them in a heap around my ankles. Tearing off her panties, Lucy mounted me in my chair. Skewering herself on my slippery schlong, she rode me like a bronc buster. She dug her heels into the rungs of my chair as my fingers locked onto her ass like a vice. Then we cried out together in rapture. She exploded time after time, like lightning and rolling thunder. And like the rain, I began to fill her to overflowing.

Our timing was immaculate. With her last shudder, I felt the chair give way. We crashed to the floor but I kept lunging into her. She matched me stroke for stroke until I yelped as the final salvo shot up my rigid length. Then I slumped and for an awful moment, Lucy thought I had stopped breathing completely.

I gasped and took several deep breaths before I started to laugh. "Talk about bringing down the house," I said and Lucy giggled. "My, miss Lucy, we're something else. First the table, and then the chair." Then I reached up and kissed her gently on the lips. "I love you," I whispered. "Don't ever think I don't."

"Thank you," she said. "I'm going to make a pot of coffee. We can drink it in the loft. Or are you too tired to move?"

I groaned and sat up, looking at my hands, still covered with sandwich dressing. "I think I'll grab a quick shower first. This stuff is starting to get tacky."

"Go ahead. I'll join you if you want company."

"Your company, always," I told her. I blew her a kiss and padded into the bathroom.

When Lucy joined me in the shower my head was covered with shampoo. She picked up the sisal mitt and began to wash my back, working her way down each leg and then doing each arm. The odd thing, she said, is that she found this very sensuous and tender. Yet, somehow it was not erotic. I apparently felt the same. My little big man remained asleep, even when she carefully washed it.

Then it was my turn. When we were having coffee the next day, Lucy told me she was surprised how gentle I was as I scrubbed her from head to toe. It was oddly touching, she added, and she wondered at her lack of arousal. Yet, when I dried her off and lightly slapped her tush it was like a delayed switch turned on and she felt a delightful surge of passion. As she dried me off, she avoided my sleeping monk until she was almost done. Then she carefully pushed his hood back and took him into her mouth.

There was only a feeble response from my little soldier. "I think you wore me out," I laughed. "At least for today. It feels wonderful but...." I shrugged.

Lucy stood and smiled. "You better get going. You need to be home soon."

♣

*Lucy.* I watched Roger get dressed and then kissed him goodbye. He seemed reluctant to leave but it was getting late. When he was gone, I sat at my kitchen table a long time, sipping a cup of decaf as I recalled the afternoon.

As I remembered our time together, I felt tears gather in my eyes. I went to my purse and opened my billfold. I took out the only picture of Roger I had and looked at it a long time. He was not aware I had it. I took it at our special place by the river as he looked up from tying his shoe. There was a strange expression on his face. He looked so very sad, even though we'd just made love. I wondered what he'd been thinking.

*Never mind Roger*, I told myself. *What am I thinking? This was not supposed to happen. So what am I supposed to do about it?* It was then I remembered something one of my alcoholic friends once told me. When all else fails, it's time to pray.

# CHAPTER NINE

# The Cat's Palace

*Roger.* Although I was late, I arrived home before Anne. I had supper going by the time she arrived. "I didn't know it was your turn," she said.

I shrugged. "I don't know if it is or not. I felt inspired. I hope you didn't have something special planned."

"Actually, I'm relieved," she told me. "I was wondering what I was going to fix." She gave me a knowing look. "You must be hoping to get lucky."

"Not at all," I replied, smiling at her. "This is simply because I love you."

Anne looked at me closely. "Is something wrong, Roger?"

I shook my head. "No, there was something on the news and it really got to me. I shouldn't have turned on the tube. I wanted to hear the weather."

"What was it?"

"Please, Anne, let it be. I'm trying to get away from it. It wasn't that big a deal but it got to me. Somebody else's tragedy. Let's drop it. It's not worth fussing about."

"Nothing's worth fighting about with you," Anne said bitterly. "I'm your wife. We're supposed to share things."

"I said fussing, not fighting. We're supposed to respect each other's need for space."

"Well, you can have all the space you want, Roger. Do you want me to move out?"

"Geez," I said, truly surprised. "I come home and get a little depressed about starving people. I try to do something I think will please you. Two minutes after you get here our marriage is on the line. That doesn't make a bit of sense to me, Anne. What's going on? I'm here. I'm committed. Why do I get the idea you're not?"

Suddenly Anne burst into tears and fled. I followed her down the hall to our bedroom but Anne slammed the door in my face.

I heard the lock click. I stood there for a minute, then knocked on the door. "We can talk about it later, Anne. I'm going for a long walk. I may be late. Supper's in the fridge."

I ate quickly and put away the food. Changing into running shoes, I opened the front door. It had started to rain. Normally, I don't mind running in the rain. That night I was in no mood to get soaked. So I decided to drive to the mall. I don't particularly like walking inside but it was a weeknight. I expected the mall would be deserted at that hour.

I was half way there before I remembered the reply to my ad. Pulling over, I dug the sheet out of my pocket. I read it again and saw I was right. The woman signed the note as Gypsy Girl. She said that she would be at the mall that night from seven until eight if I wanted to meet. She added that she would be the only woman sitting alone and reading a copy of *Don Quixote* in the original Spanish.

What I found odd was her choice of Gypsy Girl for a *nombre de amor*. Coupled with *Don Quixote* it stirred a vague memory. Yet, I couldn't connect the dots. Now I was curious. Since I was headed there anyway, I decided it wouldn't hurt to meet this once. I was almost an hour early. That would give me plenty of time to walk and I could keep an eye on the food court with each lap. Since I was still anonymous, I could always look things over. I would simply walk on by if I picked up bad vibes or didn't like what I saw.

That resolved, I began to walk at a fast pace. I let my mind drift back to the afternoon with Lucy. How did this ever happen? I didn't regret that it had. My life would have been much poorer without Lucy in it, though I'd never have known what I'd missed. Or even that there was something to miss.

*So where do we go from here?* The thought was barely formed before there was an answer.

*Who says we have to go anywhere?* Jolly Roger asked me. *Live today to the fullest and grab life by the balls! You think too much, dude. All you have is right this moment.*

"Carpe diem!" I whispered. Seize the day.

*You got it, baby,* Jolly declared.

Then I laughed, remembering something Al once said at one of their parties. "Crappy diem is more likely!"

To which Anne answered, "You've got a shitty outlook,

Albert." She knew he hated to be called by his proper name.

"Yes," Helen chipped in. "He was dropped when he was a baby and his anal nerve fused with his optic nerve. People in AA call it ocular rectitis. It gives you a shitty outlook." Everyone thought this was funny but Al.

"So what are you laughing about, bubba?" said a familiar voice.

I glanced to my left, startled. *Oh shit! It's Shirley!* That meant there was no chance of a rendezvous. I was just as glad. She was wearing a tee over shorts and running shoes. I thought she must be here to walk, too. It surprised me that she was able to match my pace without effort.

"Hi, Shirley. You startled me," I told her. "I was thinking about that time Al stepped on himself talking about *carpe diem*. Helen got on his case for having such a shitty outlook."

Shirley laughed. "I remember. Anne helped her nail his hide to the barn, too. What brings you here tonight?"

"The rain. I didn't feel like getting soaked and I can get in two or three miles. Not much of a crowd tonight. How about you?"

"The same, but I had an errand at the bookstore, too. Odd us running into each other like this." She gave me a knowing look.

Suddenly, I remembered something from a literature class years before. Cervantes was famous for *Don Quixote*. But one of his shorter works was called *La Gitanilla, The Gypsy Girl*. I remembered Shirley talking about it at one of our parties. "Let me buy you a cup of coffee," I suggested.

Shirley smiled. "That's the best offer I've had all night."

We made our way to the coffee shop. We took a table away from where others were sitting. "Just so you know," Shirley said, opening her backpack and taking out a copy of *Don Quixote*. She handed it to me and I opened it at random. It was printed in Spanish. This was no surprise.

I closed the book and laid it on the table between us. I looked at my companion directly. "*La Gitanilla*. Does this mean you want to have sex with me, Shirley?"

"That's a rather harsh way of saying it, Roger. I prefer to call it lovemaking."

"There are lots of crude terms I could have used if I wanted to be harsh. You didn't answer my question."

"All right, I will. Yes, I'd like to make love with you. I've wanted to for a long time. This was a safe way to bring it up."

"I trust you're not making a crude pun," I answered. "Anne is your friend, Shirley."

"I'm not trying to take you away from her," Shirley told me. Then she smiled. "I just want to borrow you from time to time."

I nodded. There was no question Shirley was an attractive woman and she obviously kept herself in shape. Not many could keep up with my pace when I walked. "Have you talked with her about this?" My tone was gentler.

"God, no!" Shirley said. "She'd scratch my eyes out."

I chuckled. "She probably would. What about when she finds out?"

"There's no reason for her to find out. Don't you find me attractive, Roger?"

I chuckled. "You know I do, Shirley, or you wouldn't be here. That's not the point."

"What is the point?" Shirley asked.

"The point is that secrets always come out, sooner or later. I've been told they poison relationships, too. People who carry secrets act differently." I wondered if anyone had seen a difference in me over the last three months.

"Like Anne is acting lately?" Shirley suggested. There was an odd edge to her tone.

"That's dangerous territory, Shirley," I warned. "Are you telling me she's having an affair?"

Shirley shook her head. "No, I'm telling you she's showing all the signs. Ask Helen. She's noticed, too."

I thought about this. Having suspicions on my own was one thing and I could easily be wrong. Having them confirmed by women who were her close friends was something else. "Shit!" I said. "That's all we need."

"Did I tell you something you didn't know?" Shirley asked. "I didn't think I was."

I shook my head. "No, but I was hoping I was wrong. I'm committed to my marriage, Shirley. I wanted us to get past this and move on." Even as I spoke, I realized that I'd used past tense. "Shit!" It was all I could do not to weep.

I closed my eyes and took a deep breath, then another and still another. When I had my feelings more or less in control I looked at Shirley. "How are you and Ed doing?"

"Ed and I are doing fine, Roger. The age gap has caught up with us and he can't use any of those magic pills they advertise. The Parkinson's is getting worse. The doctors tell us he's stable but I can tell. It's not going to be long before he has to go into a nursing home."

Shirley sighed. "Thanks for showing up, Roger," she said sadly. "I didn't think it would work out. I'm sorry if I offended you."

I reached out for Shirley's hand. When she took my mine, it was like a spark of static popping. She jumped but didn't let go. Then she laughed. "That's the most fun I've had with a man in a long time."

"I'm not saying I won't do this," I told her, not believing I was saying what was coming out of my mouth. "You surprised me and I need some thing to think it through. It's not like we've fallen in love."

"Don't play games with me, Roger," Shirley told me. She looked so vulnerable I reached out with my other hand. After a moment she took it.

"I won't," I assured her. "I'm your friend first, and foremost. So if we do this, we'll screw our brains out and stay friends. I don't want to lose your friendship."

Shirley laughed, the deep belly laugh I had heard so many times before. "Fair enough," she said. "Would you like to see the trysting place I had picked out?"

"Here in the mall?" I asked, looking around.

Shirley nodded and I said, "Sure, why not? Or do you want to finish your coffee, first?" Her smile was eloquent but I made a point of finishing my coffee.

♣

Shirley led me down a back hallway lined with service doors. I couldn't help noticing the marvelous sway of her hips as I followed. "We have to be quiet," she said. She stopped at a door and slipped a key into the lock. "I need to lead so you don't trip. This is a home decorating store that's gone out of business. I think some of the furniture's still here. We can see out in places, but with the lights off, nobody can see in."

"I'm impressed," I told her. "You did a lot of planning."

Shirley shrugged. "No, it fell into my lap. I know the people who owned the shop. I used to help out and they gave me a key.

Then they went bankrupt and I forgot to give it back. Now be really quiet."

Reaching back for my hand, Shirley grabbed my package. "Oh!" she whispered. "I'm so sorry, Roger. I was reaching for your hand."

I shook my head and smiled. "I know you were, Shirley," I whispered back. "But it felt good."

Shirley leaned toward me and whispered in my ear. When she did, her breast brushed my arm and I could feel the hard nipple under the cotton fabric. I was surprised she was not wearing a bra. "This is how we have to talk now. And, yes, it did feel good. Now let me lock the door."

As Shirley reached around me, the space was so narrow that she had to press against my chest to get by. I felt her full breasts like large oranges ripe for harvest, the nipples hard against my own, and I felt myself getting aroused. I also knew she could feel me growing hard against her, and I could see her smiling in the dim light. I leaned close to whisper in her hear. "There's no question I find you very attractive, is there?"

Shirley snickered and leaned toward me to whisper back, "None at all, Sweet Gent." Her tongue darted into my ear, startling me though I liked it. I could feel her breathing deepen, knew she was getting aroused, too.

Shirley pushed by me again. She paused a moment to wiggle her full breasts back and forth against my chest. When she did, her mons pressed directly against my package and she rolled her hips, bringing them into contact. Through the thin fabric of her shorts I could feel the generous lips of her sweet spot and I took one of her taut buns in each hand and pulled her as close as I could. "You're so hot!" I murmured, slipping my hands under the fabric of her shorts. I was not surprised to find that she was not wearing panties.

I started pulling Shirley's shorts down but she stopped me. "There's a better place," she whispered in my ear. Again her tongue flicked out, this time lingering before she withdrew it. I was amazed how much this turned me on.

Giving me a gentle squeeze, Shirley took my hand and led me deeper inside. It was very dark. The papered display windows in front let in just enough light to see large shapes. Twice I almost stumbled over something that made the footing unsure. Yet,

Shirley steadied me and I didn't fall.

When Shirley finally stopped she let go of my hand and I bumped into her. Reaching around and slipping my hands under her tee, I filled my hands with her smooth breasts. I teased the nipples between my thumb and forefinger. Shirley moaned, arching her back against me. She reached around to grasp me firmly. Running my hands down her belly, I cupped her mound in my hand. Then I ran my middle finger down the cleft between her full nether lips. As I moved my finger back up, I slipped the tip of it between her warm, moist labia. I curled it up to tease her. She gasped as I did and thrust her pelvis upward, catching my finger inside her. I could feel her vaginal walls contracting. As she went over the edge, Shirley moaned, pumping hard against my hand.

"Oh, shit, that's good!" she whispered, breaking free from my hand and turning toward me. I could see her stripping off her top and slid my hands under the band of her shorts, slipping them all the way down and freeing her feet. Leaning forward, I kissed her love spot. She gasped again, grabbing my head and pulling it tight against her. I teased her with the tip of my tongue. I heard her moan, as if she were stifling a scream. She suddenly jerked once more as spasms racked her full body.

When she pushed my head away, I stood and held Shirley close as she began to sob. "It's been so long," she told me. "Ed lost his potency three years ago, just when I was hitting my peak. It's been hell." She pulled back and looked at me in the darkness. "You're a good man, Roger, and a better friend. Thank you."

"It's my pleasure," I chuckled giving her a hug. I was still hard as a nail. I wondered if that was all Shirley wanted.

My question was answered as soon as it crossed my mind. I felt Shirley's hands pull my shirt up, tossing it aside before reaching for my belt buckle and zipper. Following my example, she slipped my pants and shorts down to my ankles and took off my shoes. As I raised each foot she slipped off a sock and this felt wonderfully intimate. Then she took me in hand, kissing the tip of my length and running her tongue up and down it.

"My goodness," she murmured as she stroked me. "Anne said you were big but I had no idea. I don't know if I can take that much, Roger."

I could barely speak. Despite the fact I had come several

times that afternoon, I felt myself getting very aroused. "Let's lie down," I suggested.

"Getting weak in the knees, are we?" Shirley giggled softly. "Step to your left and you'll feel the edge of the mattress. It's only a foot or so."

Leaning over, I felt a plush silky surface and began to crawl onto it. As I did, Shirley goosed me playfully and I jumped. "You better watch out!" I warned her. "Or I'll get you back."

"Oh! Is that a promise?" She tried to goose me again but I was too quick for her. Grabbing her by the arm, I pulled her down beside me and tried to pin down her hands. This turned into a wrestling match until I finally pushed both her hands down over her head and was holding her body down with my own. "I like this," she said, opening her legs wide. "Are you going to have your way with me now?"

I answered by lifting up, drawing myself slowly down Shirley's belly until the very tip of my manhood reached her clitoris. Moving back in forth I massaged the little girl in the boat until Shirley whispered fiercely. "For heaven's sake, Roger! Fuck me! And fuck me hard!"

"I don't want to hurt you," I said, taking one of her nipples between my teeth and pressing down until she moaned.

"Yes!" Shirley begged. "Hurt me, Roger, hurt me!"

Moving my hips back a bit more, I found the doorway to Shirley's tunnel of love. She was so wet by now I had no trouble pushing in, though it was very tight. I stopped at half my length and began to slowly move my hips back and forth.

"All of it, Roger!" Shirley moaned. "I want it all!" So I pushed farther in until I felt myself hit bottom and began to move back and forth again. "All of it, damn you! All of it!"

So I pushed deeper and deeper until my pubic hair was mashed flat against her mound, her vagina stretched tight over my shaft. "Yes!" Shirley moaned. "Now fuck me, Roger, fast and hard. Don't hold back!"

So I pulled back slowly, then quickly rammed myself in to the hilt. Shirley gasped, almost a scream, but she didn't tell me to stop so I did this again. Picking up speed, I began to pound Shirley's mound with my own. She was moaning so loudly I was afraid we'd be heard. Suddenly I was at the peak and there was no turning back. I pumped like fury until I felt myself explode.

It was so violent it felt like I was being turned inside out. As I did, I felt Shirley jerk with violent spasms as she came with the mother of all orgasms.

Then it was over and I fell over onto the mattress beside Shirley. "Are you all right?" I asked anxiously.

Shirley replied with a throaty chuckle. "I'm more than all right. I'm great! Though it may be a while before I can do that again."

"Did I hurt you?"

"You hurt me just right, sweetie," she answered, giving me a sweet kiss. "You did exactly what I asked, which Ed never would. Of course, he isn't as well packaged." She giggled at her play on words.

"I see why he wouldn't," I said. "It was scary. I've never come like that before. It was like I was shooting my whole self out through my penis. I thought I was dying but couldn't stop."

Shirley laughed quietly. "So it was good for you, too." Suddenly she tensed, then rolled us off the bed and onto the floor. "Be very still," she whispered in my ear.

A bright beam of light blazed out above us. I ducked even lower against Shirley. As I did, my hand fell on her taut derrière. Remembering how she had goosed me twice, I ran my hand up and down the cleavage between her nether cheeks, stroking the crack with my middle finger. As I did, Shirley tried to move away but there was nowhere to go. She couldn't get up without being caught naked. When she stopped struggling, I dipped my finger into her rosebud and began to massage it.

"I would have sworn I heard somebody in here," a deep voice said as the light beam crossed above them.

"Couldn't prove it by me," another deep voice answered.

I started to remove my hand when I realized that Shirley wasn't tense any more. She had relaxed the gluteus maximus in both cheeks and was pushing back against my finger as I massaged her anus. It was then I decided to do something I never had. Pushing my hand lower, I ran my finger into Shirley's love tunnel which was incredibly slippery. Then I withdrew it and gently pushed at the center of her rosebud. As I did, she pushed back and I was suddenly deep inside her and began to feel around with my finger, probing as deeply as I could.

Shirley responded by beginning to swivel her hips and push

higher and faster. I matched her pace, running my digit in as far as I could and then out to the very tip. Then, just as the bright beam was sweeping over us again, I felt her jerk as love spasms seized her body again.

"Nobody here now," the second voice spoke. "It could have been the cat."

"What cat?" the first voice asked.

"The cat they put in here to keep the mice down. There's its box right over there."

"Well, shit! Why didn't you tell me?"

"You didn't ask and I thought you knew."

"Let's get the hell out of here," the first voice said. "This place gives me the creeps."

"It's the ghosts of dead mice," the second voice laughed.

Shirley and I heard the door close and the lock engage. Yet, we waited ten minutes before we moved. "You can take your finger out any time," Shirley said. "Just don't touch me with that hand."

♣

"So what do you think?" Shirley asked. She and I were sitting in the food court again, sipping a cup of coffee. For the first time in years I found myself craving a cigarette.

"I think you're a wonderful woman," I answered with a smile that hopefully said much more. Then I added, "You are also a brilliant scholar, at least you were until we screwed our brains out. I'm still trying to find mine."

"Are you being obtuse or are you avoiding my question?" she asked, her eyes seeking me.

I blinked. "I'm sorry, Shirley. I wasn't kidding. I'm still out there somewhere beyond the moon. Could you ask it again?"

She laughed. "You really aren't kidding, are you? You look a little … disoriented. Do you need me to drive you home?"

I chuckled. "I'd say you already did that." Then I added, "Were you asking if this is a one time thing?"

Shirley nodded. The look in her eyes told me this was a very important question to her, one I needed to answer well. "First of all, the only thing that's changed is that my admiration of you is much greater," I told her.

Shirley blinked. This was not an answer she had expected. "I am really in awe of you," I continued. "And that's not the little man talking. To answer your question, I would be honored if we could get together like this from time to time. How about you?"

Shirley smiled. "I want to jump you in the parking lot when we leave, Charley Brown," she said. "You're a good man."

"I'd rather be Schroeder," I said. "I always wanted to play a piano. The only problem I see is working out times and places. I don't think a local motel is a good idea. I hate to push our luck here, too."

"You're not going to tell me that almost getting caught didn't excite you, are you?" she replied. "You were hard as a rock when you were 'massaging' me." She giggled. "I'm trying to be discreet, Roger but just thinking about it stirs my kettle."

"So are you asking me to pull your taffy?" I asked and Shirley laughed quietly. "I think it would be easier to do if we set up a schedule," I added. "It probably needs to be a bit random, too. So when do you think would work for next time?"

"Why don't you meet me in my study carrel in the library next Friday?" Shirley suggested. "My last class is at one and nobody will be around."

"Great. Maybe we can find my brains there somewhere."

# CHAPTER TEN

# Love Play

Anne was still locked in the master bedroom when I got home. I knocked on our bedroom door and asked to come in, but she told me she wanted to be alone. "All right," said. "I'll be in the guest room if you change your mind. I will need to get into there to dress tomorrow morning." There was no response.

I turned to walk down the hall, then stopped and came back. "I love you, Anne," I said. "I don't know what's going on but nothing else really matters. We'll find a way through it. Good night, sweetheart."

I stood there for a moment, hoping for an answer, but there was only silence. This worried me but I was also relieved. Our arguments almost always led to lovemaking. I was feeling so tired it was all I could do to undress and get into bed. It had been an exhausting day. All I wanted was sleep.

We had two guest rooms in our home, both about the same size. The difference was that one had twin beds and looked out over the street. The other was more private, looking out over our back yard. It was furnished with a queen-sized bed and, like the master bedroom, it had its own bath. This was small, not even as big as a walk-in closet. Yet, it was equipped with a shower and toilet, and a small sink. A medicine chest built into the wall held everything a guest might need, from aspirin to antacids to tooth paste and deodorant.

That night I took a long, hot shower. Drying off, I slid between the cool sheets naked. They felt good against my bare skin. I closed my eyes, intending to think about the day. Yet, I fell asleep quickly. As I did, something fluttered across the back of my mind. I couldn't quite see what it was and this troubled me. Still, there was no help for it and I fell into a deep, dreamless sleep.

Something awakened me in the early hours of the morning, a soft sound. I lay there for a moment, listening. Looking at the clock, I saw it was just past four—too early to get up for good.

Then I checked the intruder alarm. I'd forgotten to arm it, but all the zone lights were green. So I went into the bathroom to relieve myself and returned to bed.

As I slid under the sheets, I was surprised to find a soft, naked body next to me. "Georgia?" I whispered, feeling around. "Is that you?"

Anne giggled. It was one of the games we sometimes played. "Be quiet," I said. "We don't want to wake Anne."

Familiar hands felts my face. "Roger? Oh, my God. I thought you were Wilbur or maybe Hank."

I ran my hands over Anne's breasts. Her nipples were hard and crinkled. "You don't feel like Georgia," I said.

Anne reached down and took my rigid wand in her hand. "Yep, you're Roger, all right." She began to move her hand slowly down and up, pausing to play with my foreskin. She knew it drove me crazy. "Come to think, you could be Orval, too."

"The plumber?" I asked, aghast. "Why in the world would you make it with the plumber?"

"He lays pipe pretty well," Anne laughed. "I needed plumbing at the moment." My hand had moved down to her belly and she moaned softly. "Um, that feels nice. I think I need some plumbing right now." She gasped when I cupped her nether lips in my hand and slipped my middle two fingers between her nether lips. Her hips began to undulate, following the rhythm of my fingers as they fluttered inside. She moaned again, louder this time.

"Something feels wet," Ann murmured. "Maybe I should take a look...." It was my turn to gasp as she slipped out of my arms and bent down under the covers. She fastened onto me with her warm, wet lips, giving me a thorough tongue lashing. I felt the sensation spread from my pelvic area down to my ankles and all the way up again. I began to tremble with anticipation as I approached the edge.

"Lie flat on your back," Anne told me and I did. Then she swung a leg over me, neatly impaling herself without touching my wet shaft with her hands. Then she lay forward on top of me, rocking back and forth. I could feel her wonderful breasts pressed against my own. Then she raised up a little and I felt her nipples rake my chest. She knew this drove me wild, too.

A moment later Anne began to raise herself up and down,

taking in more and more of me as she rocked back and forth. Then I was completely inside and she could feel my tight scrotum pushing against her. She sat upright and began to swivel her pelvis around and around, grinding as she slowly moved up and down. She knew that this, too, was something that I liked. She wound her body up my shaft slowly before plunging down again quickly. Then she wound it up again.

By this time I was squirming madly beneath her, groaning fiercely. I was clutching her legs so hard I knew she'd have bruises the next day. Yet, I knew she didn't care. She loved the way I filled her, even stretching her a bit after all these years. She loved riding me like this, too. She knew how to hold me right at the edge and she knew exactly when to push me over. She once told me she liked the sense of power this gave.

Nor was the knowledge one-sided. I knew her like a familiar book, what pleased her and what did not. I also knew how she liked to be touched and where. I was very sensitive to her moods, too. More than once I'd brought her to almost instant release by simply laying my hand on her neck in my special way when she was working.

♣

*Anne. Why am I fooling around?* I had asked myself self this when Roger left the house earlier. The thought returned again as we were making love. Michael and Ben were both wonderful lovers, but nothing like Roger.

Thinking about Michael reminded me of what Roger taught me about riding a man like this. It was something we both found incredibly stimulating. So I began to clench the tight muscles where my legs meet as I rose up Roger's length. It was like trying to pull him totally inside me through my birth canal. The sensation was as incredible as ever. No, it was even better. I cried out with him as he began to erupt within me, shooting out spurt after steaming spurt of seminal lava. It set my body ablaze with fiery passion.

The sensation was so intense I swooned, falling to one side. Roger, thinking this was some new game, rolled me over on my back. He grabbed my ankles and held them high as he ran his still spurting spout into me and began pushing like a madman. I came to and cried out over and over as I clutched his driving buttocks. Digging my nails into his powerful buns, I began to come again and again until there was nothing but darkness.

*Fucked to death!* This last thought made me want to laugh. *Who would have ever thought?* Then the warm, welcome darkness overcame me as I slipped away into the gentle night.

♣

*Roger.* The doctor looked grave as he walked out of the exam room and approached the waiting area where Shirley and I were sitting. "Mr. Smythe?" he asked, looking at me.

"It's Dr. Jahnsen," I answered automatically. "I'm Anne's husband."

"A medical doctor?" the physician asked.

I shook my head. "Academic."

"Ah," the doctor nodded. "I only ask so I know how to talk to you. We're not sure exactly what happened. We think your wife experienced a TIA. That's a transient ischemic attack, which is also called a mini-stroke. The symptoms had resolved by the time she arrived, so we can't be sure until the lab work gets back. Your wife is out of immediate danger but we want to keep her overnight for observation. May I ask what she was doing when this happened?"

I felt my face flushing. "We were, um, making love."

The doctor nodded but didn't smile. "You'd be surprised how often we hear that. People don't realize how stressful it can be. Is there any history of TIA or stroke with your wife or her family?"

"Her mother died of a stroke. Anne was very young and her mother was in her early fifties. Anne told me it came as a complete surprise to everyone. Her mother had never had any trouble with high blood pressure or anything like that."

"That's good to know. That means we definitely need to keep Anne overnight for observation. Her blood pressure is not dangerously high. Does she exercise?"

I nodded. "She swims several times a week—at least a half mile. She also takes a small aspirin every day, but nothing else."

"No other medications?"

I started to shake my head but stopped. "Yes, there is something. She was having problems with stress at work so she started taking…boo something."

"Bupropion?" the doctor asked and I nodded. "When did she start that?"

"I don't know," I said. "Not that long ago. Maybe a month or two. Not over three months."

"Well, she needs to stay off it until we know more," the doctor said. "Just to be safe. I'll be sure to mention it to her. It could be that this was a side effect of the new medication, but I don't think so. We'll know more when we get the labs back. You can see her now, if you wish."

❦

Shirley was quiet as we drove home. I pulled into the double garage and lowered the door, then sat there for a while. I looked over at Shirley. "It's a hell of a thing, isn't it?"

Shirley nodded. "I feel like such a shit," she said. Seeing the surprise on my face she said, "Anne's one of my best friends, Roger. And here I am schtupping her husband the very night she gets sick."

"The two things aren't related, Shirley," I replied. "I'm the one who was making love with her but this is not my fault, either. There's no fault here at all except genetics. Anne takes care of herself and does all the right things and it happens, anyway."

Shirley looked dubious and I reminded her, "Don't you remember that marathon runner they found dead on the running path several years ago? He was in top shape. The next thing we knew, he's having a heart attack and was gone."

Shirley looked at me, unconvinced. "I don't know," she said. "I feel somehow responsible. That doesn't make any sense, either, does it?"

"Not a bit," I said, reaching out and taking her in my arms. "Thank you for coming over and helping me dress her. I didn't want the EMT's to see her naked."

Shirley nodded. "I think Anne would agree. So would I if it was me. It would have been rather embarrassing if they had. Who else would you have called?" She pulled away and kissed me lightly on the lips. "You're a good man, Roger. I won't hold you to our date on Friday."

"Let's see how we both feel by then," I suggested. "Do you want to come in?"

Shirley shook her head. "I better get home. Ed will worry." She reached out and touched my cheek gently. "Call if you need me. Please."

❦

"So Roger's becoming a pussy hound," Lucy said the next

morning, nodding. "I guess I can't bitch. I pushed you to make the meeting." We were standing at the turn-around on the river trail, taking a short break before running back to her place. "Are you jealous?" I asked.

Lucy nodded. "I am and I don't like it at all. It feels yucky." She looked at me intently. "As much as I've tried not to be, I'm jealous of Anne, too. She gets to sleep with you every night. Now there's another competitor on the field."

"Shirley's a friend, not a competitor," I said. "I've known her for years and it's not the same. I told you about her husband and their situation."

Lucy sighed. "Yeah, you're being honest, Roger. Do you mean it when you say you love me?"

"Yes, I do, Lucy. I love you the same way I love Anne. Were I not married I'd stay with you every night you'd let me."

Lucy grinned. "You wouldn't get much rest if you did. I'd drive you crazy." She looked up and down the path. No one was in sight. "I'd like a kiss," she said, moving close.

I smiled back. "I think that's about all I could give you. I am totally worn out."

Our kiss was gentle and very tender. "Um," murmured Lucy. "I like that kind best." She released me and stepped back. "Now we better head for the special place or back to the house. That kiss gave me ideas." There was no mistaking the look in her eye.

I laughed. "I'm not sure if I could even get it up. Like I said, yesterday really wore me out."

"I can see how it might," Lucy laughed, too. "First it was us and then your friend, and when you got home, you were attacked again. Your cojones must be shriveled up like prunes."

"It took me a while to find them when I showered," I agreed. "I thought I'd grown a pair of warts overnight."

"Well, I want to know everything," she told me. Seeing my distressed look, she said, "Roger, I'm not being a voyeur. Well, a little bit, maybe. I want to know everything about you I can. Women love the details. I want to know what pleases the man who made me fall in love with him."

"You please me, Lucy. Just be who you are. That's who I love."

"Among others," she murmured. "I'm sorry. I really didn't want to say that. I just...." Lucy shook her head and took off up the path, running fast. Nor was there any question of my catching up. It was all I could do to keep her in sight.

♣

When I arrived at the hospital the next morning, Anne was sitting up in an arm chair in her hospital robe, waiting for the clothes she'd asked me to bring. "The doctor was in earlier," she told me, slipping on the bathrobe I brought. "He says I can go home if the last test results are good. They took blood just before breakfast, so they should be available soon."

"So what did he tell you?" I asked, taking a seat on the bed. There was no other place to sit. The bed and service tray took up most of the space.

"Nothing more than he told me last night," she answered. "He thinks I had a mini-stroke but the blood work was inconclusive. That's why they took more blood this morning." She smiled. "I think they don't want to admit there was nothing wrong. It was so good I simply fainted." She smiled. "The old fashioned word for that is 'swoon'."

I shook my head, unconvinced. "Sweetie, you were unconscious for over an hour. Do you remember Shirley coming over or the EMT people?"

Anne frowned. "No, I don't. Why did Shirley come over? Couldn't you get me dressed by yourself?"

I shook my head again. "I needed someone to wait at the door until the EMT got there. I had to get some clothes on you and I didn't want to leave you alone."

"Thank you," Anne said quietly. *Oh, shit!* she thought. *I told the doctor nothing like this had never happened to me before. But this isn't true. It happened twice in Phoenix. Once was with Ben. Then it happened again with Michael. Dear God! I thought it was only a swoon! It's just like my mother!*

I saw something change in Anne's face. She blanched and I thought she was having another stroke. Then I realized she was terrified. I didn't know what it was but I knew something must have happened in Phoenix. Nor did I think she would tell me. I was the one person she had always turned to for strength. So I knew it was bad and I suspected it had to do with an affair. She was afraid she would lose me.

There was an awkward pause. It was clear that Anne was embarrassed by the incident. She didn't want to hear the details. Talking about it would make her more uncomfortable. Yet, there was nothing else we could talk about. Assuming I was right, neither of us wanted the other to know what was going on in our lives. Nor was small talk something we did when alone. When we talked, we had real conversations. These might be about current affairs or the people we knew. Or it might be our work. We discussed what we thought and what we felt freely. We'd never been a couple who simply lived our separate lives without sharing.

Now we had to take care what we said. Neither of us dared speak freely. Even the small things that made up each day were risky. It would be too easy to slip up and reveal a secret. So we sat quietly listening to the random sounds of a busy hospital wing. Each of us was lost in our own thoughts, alone with our own fears. To feel free we would have to speak the painful truth. Now was not the time for that.

I was the one who broke the silence. "You don't suppose it could be some as simple as hormones, do you?"

When Anne looked at me it was hard to read the expression on her face. She looked both guarded and frightened.

"You mean menopause?" she asked and I nodded. "I guess it might be that," Anne told me. "It could explain why I've felt so moody lately." She seemed to relax a little when she said this and I wondered why.

"It's certainly something to ask the doctor," I said.

Anne was quiet for a moment, then frowned. "I hope it's that simple. I need to get back to Jamaica next week. I'm supposed to supervise part of the construction."

"Can't what's-his-name do that? You know, the architect you work for?"

"That's not his job," Anne replied. "Besides, he may not even be there."

Once again I could see Anne was lying. *Is this who it is?* I wondered. *What's the fucker's name, Littlejohn?* Then I had another thought. *Do I even want to know?*

Jolly was quick to answer. *What if it's more than one, asshole? What if she brought home a present from the islands? Just like Columbus did with French Gout, the big syph?*

"So what are you thinking?" Anne asked. She knew whatever it was distressed me. I always rub my jaw a particular way whenever I'm really disturbed. I'm aware of this but that doesn't mean I want to stop it. It can be useful.

I looked at Anne. When I did, it was as if she was not really there. I sounded like I was talking to myself. Maybe I was. "I think I need to go for a walk and sort some things out." I glanced at my watch. It was almost eleven. "I'll be back about two. You think the doctor will be here before then?"

Anne shook her head. "No, I told him it would be at least three before you got here. So take your time. I'm not going anywhere. I need to sort some things out, too."

*I bet you do, sweetie.* It was Jolly speaking. I forced myself to be present and kissed Anne on the cheek before I left. "Don't worry, Anne," I heard myself saying. "No matter what the doctor has to say, we'll be all right." Even as I said this, I was not sure I really believed it.

♣

I was surprised how Lucy responded when she heard what I was thinking. "I'm pretty sure she's sleeping with someone else." I said this, explaining why I thought this. "I'm not sure who it is. But I think it was someone she met in Phoenix. She seemed different after that. At first, I thought the difference was me." I smiled and touched Lucy's cheek. "I met this wonderful lady who turned my world upside down."

"There is that," she said, showing nothing in her face.

"The only thing that really tells me I'm right is that thing she does when she lies. I used to think it was cute. Now I almost wish I didn't know."

Lucy nodded sympathetically and I went on. "I assume it's only one guy. It could be more or the guy could have more than one partner. Anne is pretty wise in picking her friends, but who knows? Whoever it is may have put her at risk."

"And, therefore, have put you and me and your friend from the mall at risk, too," Lucy pointed out. "I can't remember her name and I don't think I want to remember. God, I hate being jealous, Roger."

"I can break that off, Lucy. She's Anne's best friend and I think she's feeling guilty."

Lucy got up and poured herself another cup of coffee. Rather than sitting down again, she leaned against the counter as she sipped it. I thought she was feeling agitated but nothing of this showed in her features. "I guess the question is if you want to break it off," she replied. Her voice was almost too quiet. "I'm not asking you to do that. It can't be up to me."

"I really would like to," I said. "Things were complicated enough when it was just you and me."

"You and me and Anne," Lucy pointed out. Again, there was nothing in her voice that told me how she felt. She sounded oddly detached, not like her usual self.

"You seem to be taking all this very well," I observed. "Maybe a bit too well."

Lucy smiled sadly. "You're looking in from the outside," she answered. "You don't know how close I am to a wall-eyed hissy." Seeing my surprise, she explained. "I want to scream and cuss and throw things, Roger, but I don't dare. It's something they teach us in recovery. Screaming and yelling and tearing my hair wouldn't do much good. It's the same as getting drunk or wasted, maybe worse. When I'm done, the issue will still be there. I'd also have the emotional hangover to deal with. It's easier to stay away from going crazy."

"What can I do to help?" I asked.

"Just hold me for a while," Lucy answered and I could see she was trembling. "Hold me and tell me you love me. Tell me you'll always be there for me no matter what happens."

"Of course, I will," I said, opening my arms. Lucy came into them and began to weep like a child, crying out as great sobs wrenched her frame. As I held her, I tried to shut away my own feelings, to remain strong for her sake. Yet, before long I found myself weeping, too. This was something new. It had been years since I'd shed tears.

☘

For a long time after the storm passed, Lucy and I sat holding each other quietly. She was the first to speak. "You want to hear something weird, Roger?" she asked, smiling as she wiped her cheek. I nodded and she went on. "I've never felt closer to you than I do right now. Isn't that strange?"

I shook my head. "I don't understand it, either, Lucy. I feel the same way. What's weird to me is that it feels so right." I looked at her, not trying to hide how I felt.

"I've never done that with anyone before, Roger. I've never let anyone get that close."

"Neither have I, Lucy. Not even Anne, and that really bothers me. As close as I thought we were, I've always held back. That wasn't fair to her, was it?"

"Maybe or maybe not. What's different now?"

I was perplexed. "I seem to feel completely safe with you, Lucy. I can be who I am with no bullshit."

Lucy held me close and nodded. "I'm glad you didn't know me back when I was so crazy. You wouldn't have liked me much back then. The bullshit was deep and stinky."

I pulled back and smiled. "I don't care about back then, Lucy. Back then brought you to me the way you are now. I love you for being the kind of person you are now."

"I hope so, Roger" Lucy said sadly. "I really hope so. It would just about kill me if you ended up hating me. The way things are now, that could happen."

"Only if we let it, love, only if we let it. I guess the only thing that's changed is that we know we need to be careful now."

"Or you need to be careful at home. I don't want you at risk, Roger."

"That would rip the scab off, wouldn't it? 'Sorry, Anne. I know you're boffing somebody else and I don't want to catch anything.' I can't imagine what unmitigated hell that would unleash."

Lucy opened her mouth to say something, and then stopped. "You might as well say it," I told her.

Lucy shook her head. "I'm in no position to comment," she told me. "I only know what you tell me and I may be wrong."

"Maybe I want to know what you think, anyway," I told her.

Lucy shrugged. "Well, I can talk about it but you may not like what I have to say."

"Please. I need to know."

"Well, for what it's worth, you make your relationship with Anne sound like a war zone. I'm not saying that's what it is, but that's what it sounds like from the way you talk. Or the way you've done with me."

I thought about that a moment. Then I gave Lucy a wry smile and nodded. "We don't complain about the good stuff, do we? I think you're right. That's the way I must sound. Maybe that tells me it's the way I think about it, too. We do fight a lot, Anne and I. We always have. We even fought on the way to get our marriage license. I almost walked out then."

"What kept you from it?"

I sighed. "I couldn't have told you back then. Now I'd say it was fear. I was afraid of winding up alone. We also enjoyed being together when we weren't fighting."

"So you were thinking about yourself, about what you could get out of the relationship."

I didn't understand what she was saying. "Yeah, I guess so. But that's how people talk about it, isn't it? We put something in and we expect to get something out."

"What if the other person has nothing to give? Does that mean you don't love them any more?"

I thought about this. "Wow, you get right down to the nut cuttin', don't you? Do not pass Go or collect your hundred bucks. What are you driving at, Lucy?"

She shrugged. "I'm not driving at anything, Roger. I just think you're wrong. You do things for people because you love them. And when I say 'you' I mean Roger. I think love comes first with you. I don't think you're someone who asks what he can get out of it before he jumps in. You'd be on Wall Street if you were."

I looked at Lucy intently, then smiled. "You could be right, Miss Lucy. But it takes one to know one, you know. One of the things I like about you most is that you will receive what I have to give. It doesn't have to be on your terms, either. That makes you easy for me to love."

"So it wasn't my tits and ass? Pa-shaw, Mr. Jolly."

"Speaking of aforesaid tits and ass...."

"Yeah, I know. Me, too. All this serious talk is getting me as randy as a humpy-bird."

"Well, in that case, how about an Aussie kiss?"

"An Aussie kiss? What's that, like a kangaroo?"

"No, it's like a French kiss. Only the Aussies kiss the girls down under."

"I can't believe I actually fell for that," Lucy laughed. "You're going to pay for that, Jolly Roger."

"Promises, promises...."

# CHAPTER ELEVEN

# Complications

It was after two when I arrived back at the hospital. It was only a mile-and-a-half from where Lucy lived and since the weather was pleasant I had chosen to walk. I didn't want to give up my parking space near the back door of the hospital. This entrance was used mostly by the medical staff and it was close to the cafeteria and the elevators to the patient floors.

Even though the hour was later than I told Anne, I was in no hurry. As I walked, I thought about my visit to Lucy. Normally our lovemaking was quite passionate and intense. That afternoon it had been gentle and unusually tender. It was so loving I found myself sad when it came to an end. "I hoped we'd never stop," I told her. I kissed her face and neck gently before seeking her lips. "I wanted it to go on forever. To die in each other's arms."

Lucy nodded, tears running down her cheeks. "I love you too much, Roger," she told me simply. "I hate it when you're not here or can't spend the night. Then, when you're around, it's all I can do to keep my hands off you. It scares me."

"Why does it scare you, sweetheart?" This was her favorite term of endearment.

"I'm a pretty level-headed person," she told me. "Yet, when I'm around you, I don't seem to have a bit of sense. Sometimes just hearing your voice is almost more than I can stand. And when you touch me...." Lucy shivered, pulling me close.

"Why is that so scary?" I wanted to know.

"Because there is going to come a time when I lose you. Even if we stay together the rest of our lives, one of us is going to die and if I'm the one who survives...." She shook her head and began to cry softly.

"Don't you guys have a saying about this?" I asked.

"What guys?"

"You and your friends in recovery. Don't you say something about living life a day at a time?"

Lucy snorted. Then she smiled. "I guess I was taking myself a little to seriously, wasn't I?"

"That's not what I was saying," I protested.

"No, but you were reminding me that today is all we have. I had myself wedged pretty tight on the pity pot, didn't I?" She reached out and touched my face. "You're something special, Jolly Roger. *Carpe diem.*" Then she gasped as I touched her in a tender place.

"I love it when you do that." I laughed, kissing her lightly and heading for the shower. "I've got to get back to the hospital and you need to get back to work. I'll call you later."

Now, as I entered the hospital, I set all this firmly aside. As I waited for the elevator, I reminded myself that my first duty was to Anne. Then I realized what I'd just told myself. *Is this how I think about Anne?* I wondered. *As a duty to be done? Whatever happened to us?*

*Maybe you should ask what never happened between you,* Jolly answered.

*What do you mean?* I demanded, but Jolly was silent. I had the sense that the answer lay in how I was with Lucy. *It's not Anne's fault!* I declared. Still, it was not clear to me just what I meant. Any question of fault seemed irrelevant.

When I walked into the door of Anne's room it was half past two and I was surprised to find the room empty. I assumed she'd been taken somewhere for further tests. Someone had moved a narrow recliner into the room while I was gone, cramping the space even more. So I sat down to wait. There was nothing there I wanted to read and I decided to take a short nap. Leaning back in the recliner I stretched out and quickly fell asleep.

When I awoke the clock in the wall told me it was half past three and I was surprised to find Anne still gone. Walking down to the nurse's station I asked the clerk where Dr. Smyth might be. The young woman was someone I had not met and she gave me an odd look. "Which Dr. Smith do you want?" she asked.

"Dr. Anne Smyth," I answered. "The patient in 407."

"Are you family?" the clerk asked and I found myself becoming impatient.

"I'm Dr. Jahnsen," I told her, exasperated. "I'm Dr. Smyth's husband."

"No need to get snippy, Doctor," the clerk told me. "Doctor

was moved to Intensive Care."

"For God's sake, why?" I asked.

"I think I better let the nurse explain," the clerk replied. "I'm not supposed to give out medical information. Please be patient."

Fortunately, the floor supervisor was close by and it was someone who knew me. "Oh, Dr. Jahnsen, I'm glad you're here. We've been trying to reach you for over an hour. Your wife had another seizure and the doctor ordered her moved to the ICU."

"I've been waiting in her room," I said. "How bad was it?"

"I really don't know," the nurse told me. "I just came on at three and your wife's chart is there with her."

I nodded. "So where is the ICU?"

The clerk handed me a hospital map. "It's kind of hard to get there from here," she said, taking a yellow high-lighter and tracing a route on the map.

"Never mind," the floor nurse interjected. "There's the chaplain. I'll ask her to take you direct."

The hospital chaplain was a mature woman who looked familiar and I wondered where I'd seen her. "I took a course from you about three years ago," she told me when I asked. We were walking down a corridor to the medical elevators used to transfer patients and the staff. We crowded into a large cage with two orderlies and an elderly patient in a wheel chair.

"What are you in for?" the patient asked me. The old man had a faded military tattoo on his forearm. I thought it was Marine Corps.

"Armed robbery," I answered. "How about you?"

"Gun running," the old Marine replied, chuckling. "You look pretty healthy to me."

"It's my wife," I answered. "She had a stroke."

"Aw, geeze, that's the shits!" Then the older man looked at the cross around the chaplain's neck. "Begging your pardon, Sister."

Just then the doors opened and the orderly told them he and the patient in the wheel chair were going to a higher floor. The chaplain led the way but I turned back to the old man. "Good luck with the judge!" I said and I could hear him laughing as the doors closed.

"That was good of you, Dr. Jahnsen," the chaplain remarked. "It brightened up his day." She pointed to a set of doors. "Go through those and turn right. The ICU desk is right there."

I looked where the chaplain was pointing. When I turned to thank her, she was gone. Just then I heard someone call my name. I turned to see Anne's doctor waving for me to join the group he was with. "I'm glad to see you," the physician said. "We were just discussing your wife's condition. She had another seizure just after two this afternoon, a rather bad one, I'm afraid. That's why we moved her up here."

"How bad?" I asked and the doctor led me to a wall panel with a large piece of film clipped on it. A grid of what looked like small X-ray images filled the large film.

The doctor pointed to a spot on one of the images. "This is from a CT scan we did thirty minutes ago. What you see are horizontal slices about half a centimeter apart. What I'm pointing at is a blood clot that wasn't there when we did this last night." He pointed to a second sheet of film. "This is the same area we scanned then and, as you can see, there's nothing there."

"So what does this mean?"

"The area where it's located is not good. There could be full paralysis of one side as well as impaired cognitive processes. There could also be aphasia or total loss of speech. Or your wife could die, Dr. Jahnsen. Since her own mother died of a stroke at about the same age, that is a real possibility."

Suddenly, I felt very weak. The doctor reached out and grabbed my arm, supporting me and a passing orderly took the other. Together they moved me to a chair and sat me down gently. "Sorry," I said. "I've never had that happen before."

"You had a pretty severe shock," the doctor assured me. He frowned. "I need to ask you something else. Were you aware that your wife was pregnant?"

"What?" I was stunned. "No. They told her we couldn't have children. There was something wrong with her system."

"Did she ever take birth control pills?"

I nodded. "She did the first five years we were married. Then she stopped when we decided to have children. When she didn't get pregnant, she never started again."

The doctor nodded, sadly I thought. "Birth control pills and pregnancy are both risk factors," he said. "Especially at her age with a family history of strokes. I was planning to talk to you about this when we met this afternoon, before your wife had a stroke. We didn't know she was pregnant then. You indicated she was not when we admitted her last night."

"Are you sure she is?" I asked. I was having trouble accepting this.

The doctor nodded. "I had the lab run a second sample. It was positive, just like the first. Then I asked one of our gynecologists to examine your wife and she confirmed the diagnosis."

"Do you need to abort the fetus to save Anne?" I asked.

The doctor shook his head. "I don't recommend that at all at this point. There's not enough evidence to warrant it and we might end up doing more harm than good. Later on we can visit the issue again, if need be."

"I don't understand what you're telling me," I said.

"I'm telling you that there is a difference between a potential risk factor and solid scientific data that shows that pregnancy contributes to a woman having a stroke. To induce abortion at this point I would have to know that there is evidence it might improve your wife's chances. I don't have that evidence."

I nodded numbly. "When can I see Anne?" I asked.

"Right now, very briefly. Then once every four hours for five minutes. The hours are posted in the waiting room."

I was shocked when a nurse took me to see Anne. Part of it was seeing all the tubes and wires hooked up to her body. The worst was how old she looked. Her beautiful skin was an unhealthy pallor and the unforgiving light of the ICU showed every blemish and wrinkle. There seemed to be more white than blonde in her fine Nordic hair, now pulled back behind her head. Her warm, vibrant lips were a pale, ghastly pink.

I nodded numbly when the nurse told me it was time to go and followed her to the waiting room. There were about a dozen people there and they all looked up when I entered. I took a chair in a corner as far away from the other people as I could get. I sat there trying to get my mind around what had happened. Suddenly I jumped up and ran to the wastebasket on the wall opposite me and began to wretch violently. When I was done, I stumbled down the hall to the restroom and washed my face. The cool water seemed to help.

When I came out, someone was standing near the restroom door but I didn't pay any attention. Then a familiar voice asked, "Is there someone I can call to be here with you?"

Thinking of Lucy, I started to shake my head. I knew she would come if she was called, but how would we explain it? Then I had another thought. Looking up I saw it was the chaplain who had asked. "Yes," I said, taking out my cell phone.

"You can't use that here," the chaplain told me. "It interferes with the machines."

"Would it hurt to show you a number?" I asked and the chaplain shook her head. Scrolling through my address list, I stopped at Shirley's number. "Shirley is Anne's best friend," I told her. Then I added, "One of my best friends, too."

The chaplain wrote down the phone number and was about to leave when I stopped her. "Where do I have to go to use my cell phone? Outside?"

"The lobby or the cafeteria is all right," she told me.

"I've got to call work," I explained, thinking that Shirley would probably do that for me. "Some of our other friends need to know, too. Come to think of it, I need some air. I'll make the calls myself. Thanks, anyway."

The chaplain looked doubtful but nodded. "I'll check back with you later," she said. When she walked away, I couldn't help noticing her elegant stature or her full womanly derrière. *You ain't doing too bad if you're checking out the ladies,* Jolly Roger observed. *I bet you could talk her into it, too.*

*She's the chaplain, for God's sake!* I retorted, heading for the elevator. *Have some respect, damn you!*

*Feeling well enough to fight, too!* Jolly answered. *Don't you know that sex and prayer are kissing cousins?*

The chaplain stopped when I called and waited for me to catch up with her. "What's the best way to get to the cafeteria?" I asked. "This place is a little confusing."

"The easiest way is to show you," she replied. I noticed she had beautiful eyes, too. "This renovation has everyone going in circles. We'll take the staff elevator so I'll have to go with you. It's not far."

The chaplain led me through a couple of double doors marked "STAFF ONLY" to an elevator marked the same. The cage was crowded when it arrived but she got in and waved for me to stand in front of her. Reaching for the control panel, she pushed the button for the cafeteria level.

As she did this, I felt her pressed against me. "Sorry," she murmured and started to move back but the cage shifted and she was pressed even harder against my back. Not only could I feel the tips of her breasts stiffen against my shoulder blade and arm. I could also feel her mound pressed against my leg. It felt warm and I heard Jolly chuckle.

As the elevator descended, it swayed slightly, moving the chaplain back and forth from side to side against me and I felt my body begin to respond. "I beg your pardon," I said, as I looked back at her and tried to turn away. This only made things worse and I saw a nurse who was watching us smile. She could tell exactly what was happening.

The elevator was slow and stopped at almost every floor. No one was getting off and there was no room for anyone to get on. "Would you rather get off and take the stairs from here?" I asked.

The chaplain shook her head and then realized that I couldn't see her. "No," she said. "It's just one more floor. As slow as this is, it's still faster to take the elevator."

The doors closed but the elevator didn't move. "Excuse me," the chaplain said, leaning around me and pushing the down button again. When she did, I could feel the heat coming from her loins. "Whoo," she said. "It's close in here."

Suddenly the elevator lurched and started going up instead of down. A groan went up from the whole group. "Shit!" someone in the back said. "Not again."

"Well, I just hope we make it to the next floor," someone else added.

"Anyone have a can opener?" a jovial voice asked. Everyone laughed nervously. "Folks, I think we need to wait to see if there's any reason to worry," the voice added calmly. I had the speaker pegged for an administrator.

A moment later the elevator jolted to a stop at the next floor up and the doors opened. I stepped out and the rest of the group followed. When I looked at the chaplain her face was flushed. "I must be having a hot flash," she said, fanning her face with a hand.

*Hot flash, hell!* Jolly Roger declared. *What she means is a red-hot twat!*

*Cool it, damn you!* I scolded. *Have some respect. She's a woman of the cloth!*

*Yeah, right. The only cloth she'd like to feel right now is a silk sheet against her back.*

"Sorry," I said. "I'm sort of out of it." I was feeling a bit light-headed for some reason.

"I can imagine," the chaplain responded, concerned. "Would you like to lie down for a moment? My office is just down the hall and there's a comfortable couch."

*Holy cow, Red Rider!* Jolly quipped. *There you have it!*

*Shut up, asshole!* I snarled. "Thank you," I replied. "It might be good to sit down for a moment. When the elevator acted up it bothered me." Looking at the chaplain I could see concern in her face. Yet, there was something else, too. *Told you so, big guy!* Jolly laughed.

The chaplain chuckled. "To tell you the truth, it did me, too. The office is down this way." I followed, thinking about what Jolly was saying. *You're reading way too much into this,* I told him. His only answer was a knowing chuckle.

The chaplain led me to a door about halfway down the corridor. Slipping a key out of her pocket she unlocked it and turned on the lights. "Have a seat," she invited, pointing to a long wide couch. "It's comfortable. That's where I sleep whenever I'm on call."

I sat down and watched as the chaplain went to her desk and picked up a sign. She hung it outside the door. It read, "IN SESSION. PLEASE TRY LATER."

"That will keep anyone from disturbing you if you want a nap." The chaplain took a seat in a chair at the corner of the couch. "My name is Martha, by the way. I'm one of the volunteers. We don't have a paid chaplain."

"I'm Roger," I said, automatically extending my hand. This surprised Martha. She hesitated for a moment before taking it. When she did, her hand felt warm and a little moist.

*Just like a hot, moist....*

*Shut up!* I interrupted, silencing Jolly. I felt the chaplain wince and realized I had grasped her hand too firmly. "Did I hurt you?" I asked, worried. "I'm sorry. I didn't mean to squeeze so hard."

Martha laughed. "No, you just startled me." She was still holding my hand in hers and reached to pat it with the other.

I found this very sensuous. "That feels good," I said. As Martha began to massage my hand. I leaned my head back and closed my eyes. "You have a very nice touch." The office was quiet and I could hear her breathing deeply.

"So do you, Roger. You have a very sweet aura."

I opened my eyes and looked at Martha, amused. "I didn't think you guys talked about auras," I said, smiling. "Do they teach that in seminary."

"I wouldn't know," Martha answered. "I'm just a lay person. I usually do filing and stuff. The regular chaplain is off today."

Jolly began to hum an old Bob Dylan song, "Lay, lady, lay," and I smiled. "Sorry," I said, seeing the question in Martha's features. "I just remembered something funny."

"I'm glad you did. That's the first time I've seen you smile." She started to add something but didn't. She was still holding my hand, stroking it as if petting a cat. I noticed that she was not wearing a wedding ring.

Martha saw my glance and said, "No, I'm not married. I'm a widow. That's why I volunteer here, for something to do." She smiled. "Would you like to talk?"

I shook my head. "No, I think maybe I'd like to stretch out." I slipped off my shoes and Martha hung my jacket on a coat rack by the door. "Would you mind sitting with me for a while?" I asked. "Just being quiet? I don't want to be around people right now, especially our friends. But I don't want to be alone, either."

"Of course," Martha said. I expected her to pull the chair around so she could see me but she sat down on the floor beside the couch, instead. When she did, her blouse gaped and I caught sight of lovely breasts nestled in a surprisingly sexy bra.

"You remind me of my Sam," Martha said. "We used to sit like this for hours." She took my hand in both of hers and her eyes clouded. "He's been gone eight years now. So I know what you're going through."

"How long were you married?"

"Twenty-six years. We married right out of college." Seeing me trying to calculate, she chuckled. "Friends tell me I don't look like I'm fifty-eight," she said. "I don't feel like it, either, not in the last six months. Before that, I didn't want to live. I don't know what kept me going. My friends, I guess."

"I would have guessed early forties," I told her. "At first I thought you were a kid in her thirties."

"What gave me away?" Martha asked.

"Certainly not how you look," I said. "I don't know how to describe it." Then I remembered. "It was your aura."

"Now you're teasing me," she replied but she didn't seem to be offended.

"Actually, I'm not," I told her. "It takes lots of life experience for someone to have the beautiful feel you have."

"You're a very kind man, Roger," Martha whispered. "Your wife is a very lucky woman."

"I need a time-out, Martha," I said. "Things have been pretty intense at home for a good while. I need to keep my mind off them. All this is a little overwhelming."

"How clumsy of me," Martha said, reaching out and touching my cheek. I something was different between us but I didn't know what had changed or how. Yet, there was no mistaking what I saw in Martha's eyes. It was desire.

Taking the hand that had touched my cheek, I kissed it. When I did, Martha shivered. I saw the dark pupils of her eyes grow wide. She opened her mouth to speak but I stopped her, touching her lips gently. Smiling, she kissed my hand. "It's been a long time," she said simply, slowly unbuttoning my shirt. "I'm trying very hard not to think about this."

"Let me help you, then," I answered, raising my head and kissing her on the lips. For several moments our lips kneaded each other but then Martha's mouth opened and I caressed her with my tongue. As I did, I raised my hand to one of her full breasts and squeezed gently, causing her to moan with pleasure. Then I began unbuttoning her blouse. I could feel her hand rubbing my leg, then grasping my hardness firmly.

"Goodness," Martha said. "Is that all you?"

"Yes, all me. Just the way it naturally grew."

"Good," Martha whispered. "Sam was a big man, too, down there. You'd have never guessed, looking at him." She had unzipped my fly and undone my belt, pulling my shorts aside to grasp me firmly. Then she smiled and said. "You know, Sam wasn't circumcised, either. I like it that way."

I slipped Martha's blouse off her shoulders and reached for the clasp to her halter. A moment later her ripe breasts were swinging free. I took a few moments to graze. When I did, Martha gasped and trembled. "God, it's been so long," she said. I wondered if she was talking to herself or to the deity.

Martha pushed my trousers and shorts down, freeing my legs. Then she pushed my shirt off and began to kiss my chest, slowly moving down until she was nibbling my belly. "You taste so good," she said. She took me into her mouth, circling the tip with her tongue.

I found myself growing incredibly excited and headed for the edge. Reaching down, I took Martha's head in my hands. "I'm about to explode," I told her. "You better stop." She shook her head and began to draw me in, deeper and deeper. She began moving her lips up and down, using her tongue like a flail.

I gasped and within seconds I began to twitch. I felt my semen forcing itself out of my loins. With one almost unbearable spasm after another I came until I was drained. Then I slumped back against the cushions of the couch, almost comatose.

I was amazed to find myself still hard as a rock. I watched as Martha took off her blouse, followed by skirt and panties, folding them carefully and laying them aside. Then she moved me over toward the edge of the couch. When she mounted me, she easily took my full length within her. "Oh, yes," she whispered as she began to ride. "Oh, God, yes!" She picked up speed as if she were galloping a thoroughbred and began to swivel her hips.

Drained as I was, I found myself responding. The sensation was unbelievable. Never had I felt anything as soft and smooth as Martha's blind alley. Then it began to contract rapidly, pulling me even deeper. I felt her jerk as she reached her peak, whimpering and moaning. As she tried to pull me completely within her, I felt myself building up to another eruption. It overtook me, like a mighty wave thundering down the beach. It lifted me to the heavens and dashed me to the sand, and as it flowed back to the sea it took all thought and emotion with it. All that was left was a wonderful sense of emptiness in the warm darkness.

# CHAPTER TWELVE

# More Surprises

When I awoke, Martha was dressed and sitting in the chair next to the couch. She looked very troubled and I got up and went to her naked, kissing her softly and gently on the lips. "Thank you, Martha," I told her. "That was wonderful."

"Yes, it was," she answered. "It was also very wrong."

"It depends on how you look at it. I look at it as an act of compassion. I was in need and you reached out to me. How could anything that beautiful and that...healing for both of us be considered wrong?"

A ghost of a smile played around the corners of Martha's lips though she remained grave. "I can agree with the compassion, at least on your part. With me it was mostly passion." She frowned and shook her head. "I don't like being that out of control, Roger. I do apologize."

"I would accept it but there's nothing to forgive," I told her. "We're both consenting adults and we were both in need. Maybe it was a divine gift to us both."

"Oh, it was divine, all right," Martha smiled. "I can't say I'm sorry it happened, either. It's just that you're the husband of a patient and I'm a staff member. They frown on stuff like this."

"Well, what they don't know won't piss them off. They're not going to hear it from me. Are you going to bare your soul and get cut to pieces for something that really doesn't matter in the larger scheme of things?"

"Are you a lawyer?" Martha asked gravely. There was a wary look on her face.

I chuckled. "No, but I used to be in advertising. A spin master, as a matter of fact. But what I just said isn't spin. I really mean it, every bit."

"But what about your wife? Didn't you just cheat on her?"

"Not really," I told her. "She wants an open marriage and I

guess I just agreed. What we've done doesn't make me love her any less. It's brought me comfort when I needed it, and I made, I hope, a good friend." I held out my arms and she came into them. "So I owe you one, Martha."

Martha looked at me seriously. "You really are a spin master, aren't you? You're very good with words."

"I'm not spinning. I'm telling the truth as I see it now."

Martha gave me a wry smile. "Well, I may call your bluff Mr. Spinner. I may call in that marker some time. Now you better get dressed before someone wants in and we all get embarrassed."

"I thought we already were," I chuckled as I dressed. Seeing Martha's puzzled look I added, "Em-bare-assed."

"Dear God," she said, shaking her head. "A spin master and a punster, too."

♣

When I got to the ICU waiting area that evening, Shirley was there with Helen. The rules of the ICU only allowed two visitors every four hours and after I left the hospital I had gone home to shower. Then I called Shirley, asking her to spread the word. After that I paid a visit to Lucy's to let her know what was going on with Anne. Yet, I didn't tell her about the spontaneous combustion with Martha.

"Oh, God, Roger," Lucy said, hugging me close. "I wish I could come to the hospital and be with you, but that wouldn't be wise, would it?"

I shook my head. "Not really. As far as I know, no one else knows about us. I'd just as soon keep it that way. People can be pretty vicious, especially academic people."

"So will you be coming back here tonight?" she asked.

"I'd like to, Lucy, but I don't think that's wise. I don't think it would be smart for you to come to the house, either."

"God, no! That would be asking for it," she replied. "I just don't want this to come between us."

"There's only one thing that's going to come between us," I smiled. "I believe he's making his presence known."

"I didn't think that was a pistol you were packing," Lucy laughed. "You feel like letting him loose?"

I shook my head. "Not right now. I will this evening after we run. But I may have to take a rain check."

"Either way will be fine," she said. "I want to be there for you any way I can, Roger. I mean that."

"You are," I told her. "I carry you around with me just about everywhere I go, right here and here." I touched my breast and my temple. "I love you, Lucy. That's the long and short of it."

Lucy chuckled. "I really like the long of it, Roger. I don't think I've seen the short yet."

I answered by tapping the tip of my tongue with a finger and Lucy laughed. "I stand corrected," she said.

I left for the hospital soon after. I was glad to see Shirley and Helen in the waiting area. I would have been taken aback if they hadn't been. The three women were like sisters in many ways, though they were very different, too. Somehow the chemistry worked. Even when they argued their differences passionately, this only seemed to bring them closer.

*That might be it*, I thought as I walked up to them. *They're all passionate women.*

*Anne and Shirley, for sure*, Jolly agreed. *You can't say for sure about Helen. Not yet.*

There was no time to argue. Seeing me, Shirley jumped up and threw her arms around my neck, pressing herself tight against me. "Oh, Roger, we were so worried about you."

"It's only been an hour or so since I talked to you," I said. "I had a couple of errands to run and a bag to pack."

"Are you going to stay here overnight?" Helen asked. "You won't get much rest."

I shook my head. "No, I'm going to sleep at home tonight after my run. The bag is for Anne."

"You want company running?" Shirley asked but I shook my head. "I need time to sort through things," I answered. "I also need to let the people on her project know what's going on." I handed Shirley Anne's cell phone. "Would you mind doing that?" I asked. "There's a number under Jamaica. I don't know who to ask for, maybe someone named Littlejohn."

Shirley understood immediately. I did't want to risk talking with whomever might be sharing Anne's bed. "Of course," she said. "How much do you want me to say?"

"Tell them it's life threatening and that she's in intensive care. So no flowers, and no visitors are allowed except family. Tell them that the prognosis is not hopeful." There was a raw edge to my voice when I said this and the two women exchanged a significant look.

I saw the look and said, "I'm sorry. I'm upset about the whole thing. That's why I want someone else to call."

"Who shall I tell them I am?" Shirley wanted to know.

"Tell them you're her lover!" I declared and Helen snorted. Shirley simply looked sad. "No, don't tell them that," I added. "Tell them that you're a family friend. That's the truth. Tell them someone will call when we know more."

Shirley opened Anne's phone to dial but I stopped her. "You have to go outside or down to the cafeteria to use a cell phone," I told her.

"Excuse me," someone else in the waiting area said. "You can go up two floors and use the waiting room at either end of the hall. It's easier to get there and reception is very good."

♣

*Adams.* Shirley thanked the lady who had spoken. She headed for the elevator, leaving Roger in Helen's capable hands. When she got to the right floor she found it was mostly office space but there was a lounge at the end of the hall with a couch and a couple of chairs. It looked like it was rarely used and Shirley sat in the chair and dialed the number in Anne's phone.

A mellow male voice answered on the third ring. "Hi, there, Hot Pants," it said. "How did you know I was just thinking about you?"

*Oh, shit!* Shirley thought. *It's true.* "I beg your pardon," she said pleasantly. "I must have the wrong number. I was calling on behalf of Dr. Anne Smyth."

There was a brief silence. "No, you have the right number. I was teasing her about sitting on a hot metal bench without touching it first."

*Right,* Shirley thought. *You're one smooth, lying bastard, too.* "To whom am I speaking?" she asked.

"This is Dr. Littlejohn, Michael Littlejohn. Who are you?"

"I'm Dr. Shirley," she answered, avoiding giving her last name. "I'm a close friend of Anne's. Are you the chief architect in the project she's on in Jamaica?"

Littlejohn admitted he was and Shirley continued. "Anne has suffered a stroke, two of them, actually. They are not sure she will survive." *Take that, you asshole!* She was surprised at the anger she felt though she was careful to keep it out of her voice. Many years in the academic world had taught her how. Acerbic sarcasm was acceptable, as was passive aggression. Honest anger and outrage were not. *You hypocritical bitch!* Shirley scolded herself. *You're riding the rail with her husband.*

There was a long silence from the other end and Shirley let the man swing in the wind. "Sorry," he said after a moment. His mild British accent was much stronger. "This took me completely by surprise. Can you tell me more?"

There was real concern in the man's voice and Shirley relented. "I'm sorry. That's all the medical people are telling us now. Anne suffered a milder incident last night and we got her to the hospital right away. They were hoping to discharge her this afternoon but she apparently had a major stroke. Luckily she was in the hospital when she did. She might not have made it at home."

"How is her family doing?" Michael asked. Shirley was surprised by this. Surely Littlejohn knew that Anne had no children. So he must be asking about Roger. Shirley wondered why. *Probably guilt,* she thought.

"We're all doing as best we can," she temporized. "It came as quite a shock. Listen, I need to go. Someone will call when we know more. It may be a few days so please be patient."

After she hung up, Shirley spent a few minutes thinking about the conversation and the man on the other end of the line. Even with the limited conversation she'd had with him, she understood why Anne found him attractive. Assuming he looked as good as he sounded, it was no wonder she found herself in his bed. She also wondered if Anne was planning to leave Roger.

Shirley shook her head. There were too many unknowns, too many issues. So she mentally set the conversation aside and found her way back to the waiting room.

When Shirley got back to the waiting room, Roger was talking to Helen. Then he turned and saw her and smiled. When he did, a delicious shiver ran up her spine. She was glad he couldn't see Helen who was trying to hide a smile. Helen knew her almost too well and understood that it was all Shirley could do to keep her hands off the man.

*God, he's gorgeous,* she thought. Then she realized she was falling in love a little. Though a part of her was glad they had not made love since the mall, most of her wanted to ravish Roger right there on the waiting room floor. *Down, girl, damn it! Down!* she admonished herself sternly.

"Listen," Roger said when Shirley sat down. He wondered why she had chosen to sit by Helen instead of by him. *Maybe she's being discreet,* he thought. To which Jolly answered, *The hell you say, dumb-ass! She's trying to keep from raping you right here in front of God and everybody. Can't you tell?*

"I've been thinking," Roger continued, ignoring Jolly. "They will only allow two members of the immediate family in at a time. Then for only five minutes. Why don't I tell them that you're Anne's sisters?"

"Better hers than yours," Shirley said under her breath but Helen heard her and chuckled.

Roger heard it, too, and Helen's smile told him she knew what had happened between Shirley and him. He chose to ignore it for the moment and went on. "So one of you can come in to see Anne with me first and the other can go in next. Why don't you two decide?"

"Why don't you go first, Shirley," Helen suggested. "After all, you're the eldest."

"You want to compare our driver's licenses, sis?" Shirley smiled sweetly. Helen was, in fact, a week older than she.

"No," Helen relented. "You were here last night so you go on in first. Then you can go home to Ed and I'll stay here with Roger until he needs to leave. I'll go in when you're done or the next time they allow it."

♣

It was four hours later and Roger was saddened to see that there was no apparent change with Anne. She looked worse, if anything, and he wondered if she would ever make it back to normal. Even if she survived the stroke he knew there would be weeks, if not months of rehabilitation. He also knew this would be almost as hard on him as it was on her. Nor was he sure if she would be released home or sent to a rehab center or nursing home. It all depended on how she responded.

"I love you, Anne," Roger told her, taking her hand. It was cold and felt lifeless, and there was no response. "Shirley is here with me and Helen will be coming in soon. I explained to the people here that they're your sisters." This was something he knew Anne would like if she could hear him and understand what he was saying. She loved putting one over on the system, especially if it was harmless. Roger nodded to Shirley to speak.

"Hi, sweetie," Shirley said. Her voice was far more cheerful than she felt. "You really gave us a scare last night but you'll be up and kicking ass before you know it." She went on in this vein until the nurse said it was time to leave.

"Can I bring her other sister in?" Roger asked. "She's been waiting, too."

"Just for a moment," the nurse said and he left to escort Helen.

Helen gasped when she saw Anne and slumped against Roger, who put an arm around her waist to steady her. When he did, he was struck by what he could feel below her light skirt and full blouse. Then Helen straightened up, giving him a sweet smile as she thanked him, and went to Anne's side. Yet, when they were done, she leaned heavily on Roger's arm as they left the unit. There were tears in her eyes when they got to the waiting room.

Leaving Roger, Helen threw her arms around Shirley's neck and they held each other, weeping. Watching them, Roger felt his eyes grow moist and he had to fight back the tears. Even as he did so, he wondered why. While he didn't think it unmanly to weep, there were strangers present in the waiting room. He felt reluctant to display how he felt in front of them. Score another victory for Mad Ave, he thought bitterly. Never show anyone how you really feel. It's a weakness.

♣

*Roger.* When I got home from Lucy's late that evening, I was surprised to see a car I didn't recognize parked in the driveway. I was even more surprised when I let myself into the house and found Helen waiting for me in the living room. "Shirley was here but I sent her home," she told me, giving me a gentle hug. I was surprised how good it felt, but then Helen was a surprising woman.

Seeing a question in my eyes, she said, "Roy's passed out on the pool table and I left him there." With a wry smile, she added, "I did turn him on his side so he wouldn't aspirate his puke, but I sometimes wonder why I bother. He's obviously trying to drink himself to death."

"Why do you stay?" I inquired. It was something I'd wondered about many times but had never asked.

"You tell me and we'll both know," Helen answered, holding up her hands. "I didn't come here to bitch about Roy. Al-anon's plenty good for that. I came here to be with you." She looked at me gravely, then effortlessly slipped into my arms, tucking her head against my chest. "When things are bad, it's good to have someone hold you," she said.

I was amazed how good Helen felt in my arms. Her body seemed to flow easily against mine, as if she was hugging me with every square inch and I could feel taut muscles below the soft surface of her body. She was almost as tall as I am and I could also feel the soft heat of her loins pressed directly against my own.

While I knew I should break the embrace, I felt so completely at home in Helen's arms that I could not. It was as if she had flowed around me with her whole being, encompassing me completely and holding me close. Nor was there any question of the tension I could feel from her lady below.

"I've wanted to do this for a long time," she told me, looking directly into my eyes. Then her lips were against mine, leisurely exploring whatever they might find. This stoked the furnace within my groin. I found myself becoming unbelievably firm and there was no doubt that Helen felt it, too. Shifting very slightly and doing something with her legs, Helen settled against me and I could feel her nether lips pushing against my staff.

Helen kissed me again, then moaned as she began to move herself up and down my length. "Helen!" I said. It was almost a cry of desperation, but I couldn't stop. I began pushing myself against her.

"We don't have to do anything," Helen whispered, pulling back. "Just lie down with me and let me hold you close." Then taking my hand, she led me into the guest bedroom. There she gently undressed me, and then herself, and lay down next to me on the large, soft bed. "This is so nice," she said, cuddling close and laying an arm across my stomach. Her hand fell across my rampant knight and she sighed. "So nice," she said, moving her hand down my full length without grasping me and then cupping my seed. "Just let me hold you. It feels so good."

I turned and looked at Helen. Her gray eyes met mine and she smiled. "You're a wonderful man, Roger," she whispered as she reached around my waist and pulled me close. "Kiss me and make me feel loved."

This was more than I could stand. Raising up, I kissed Helen full on the lips, teasing her lips with my tongue until she opened her mouth to me. I spent a long time there, pouring the whole of my attention into my lips and tongue until I heard Helen moan. I began kissing my way down her neck, between her breasts and then to the very tips, which were crinkled and hard.

Raising myself up, I moved Helen to the middle of the bed and gently opened her legs with a hand. When I did, I could smell her fragrance and I moved until we were face to face with my firmness lightly touching her soft, moist center. Then I bent down and kissed her belly button, working it with my tongue before I began to move lower, lightly licking her stomach until I felt the cleft and the tiny hard button within it.

Helen lifted her legs and grasped my head. She pulled me to her as I began to explore her valley of joy with my nose. Flickering out my tongue and teasing her lips, I moved down them. Then I slipped my tongue into the gate. She cried out with a loud voice and raised up, rigid as one jolting tremor after another surged through her. Then she collapsed, mewling softly as the aftershocks rolled in, making her twitch gently in my arms. When she was done she looked at me and smiled. "Wow!" she said. "That was something!"

I smiled and started to pull away but Helen grasped me tight. "Now I want you inside me," she insisted. Reaching down, she gently claimed my length and pushed it inside herself. It was a very tight fit and I started to pull back, but Helen insisted. "No!" she said, rocking her hips and forcing me inside. "I want it all! All I can stand."

Tight, Helen might be, but she was incredibly wet and I gently pushed myself deeper and deeper. I expected her to stop me when I reached bottom, but Helen pushed harder until my full length was inside. "Now fuck me, Roger," she whispered in my ear. "Fuck me like I've never been fucked before."

To emphasize her point, Helen began to undulate slowly and I quickly fell into her rhythm. "Harder!" she demanded, beginning to thrust against me quickly. "Fuck me harder!"

I was surprised at Helen's choice of words. She was such an elegant soul and I had never heard her use the F-bomb. It was hard for me to believe I was hearing this. Yet, I did as she demanded and Helen began to keen, softly at first, but then louder and louder. I found myself wondering if the neighbors could hear, but didn't care. Her tight, wet channel felt incredibly good and I felt myself building toward an explosion. As I did, I pushed harder and Helen lifted her legs as high as she could, grabbing her knees and pulling them to her breast, crying out with inarticulate pleasure as she began to crest. As I exploded for the fifth time that day, she dug her heels into my butt. Locking me to herself so tight I could barely move, she wailed, "Fuck me, Roger! Fuck me! Fuck me! Fuck me!"

# CHAPTER THIRTEEN

# Sisters-in-law

"Surprised?" Helen asked. We were lying quietly, cuddled close together in the early morning light. The clock on the bureau told us that it was half past five.

"You're full of surprises," I told her. "I'm really surprised you spent the night."

"It's been a long time since I've slept with anyone, Roger. I don't mean sex. I mean being together in the same bed all night. Ed has his own room. It was his preference but I'm just as glad. He always smells like cheap booze." There was a bitter edge to her voice.

"I'm wondering something," I began, hoping to move the subject to something besides Ed.

"You're wondering why I'm still with him?" Helen said, frowning. When she did, it was the closest I had ever seen her to being ugly.

"Well, yes, I've wondered that, but I really meant something else." Helen looked at me, surprised, and I smiled. "I mean if what we did last night was 'not doing anything,' as you put it, how could I ever hope to survive making love with you?"

Helen laughed. It was a wonderful sound, a deep belly laugh not unlike Shirley's. Any other response she might have made was cut short by the phone.

I answered on the second ring, expecting it to be the hospital. It was Lucy. "Roger, are you all right?" she asked, clearly worried.

"Yeah, I'm all right. I'm just a little groggy. Are we meeting to run this morning?"

"You sound funny," Lucy told me. "Are you sure you're all right? I'm sorry to call but I woke up worried about you. I had a bad feeling."

"All right," I answered vaguely, aware Helen was listening to everything I was saying. "I'll meet you there in an hour."

"Is someone there?" Lucy asked. "And you can't talk."

"No, I don't mind," I replied. "I'll see you then." I hung up the phone. "Someone I run with from time to time," I told Helen. "I almost forgot we were running this morning. Excuse me." I got up and headed for the bathroom.

Helen was dressed by the time I returned. "I better go," she said, clearly ill at ease. "I hope my staying over didn't make problems for you, Roger."

"Hey, Helen," I said, reaching out with both arms. After a moment she came to me. "Your staying over was exactly what I needed. Thank you for knowing that."

Helen looked like she was about to cry. "I'm so scared about Anne," she said. "She looked so bad." Then she looked at me, eye to eye. "Was that really someone you run with?"

"Yes, it was, and I really did have an early appointment to run this morning."

Helen nodded. "I guess I was wrong. I had the sense it was…. Never mind what I thought. I guess I'm a little groggy, too. I guess I better go."

"Not without a kiss," I told her. "We'll talk about all this later this morning, if you like."

"I'm not going to be a problem, Roger," Helen assured me. "Just be careful, will you? I care about you as much as I do about Anne. So does Shirley." She kissed me lightly on the lips. "I best move my car before the neighbors wonder."

"No problem," I said lightly. "If anyone asks, I'll tell them it was my sister-in-law."

♣

"So Roger is becoming a cocks-man," Lucy murmured softly. Her normally animated voice was flat, neutral and I knew she was fighting back tears. "But I guess I can't bitch, can I? I pushed you to make that first meeting."

"I don't understand it, Lucy," I told her. "That's not what I wanted to happen. It just did and I don't know how or why. I probably should have said 'no' to Shirley but I think that would have been wrong. She's a close friend and I really didn't want to hurt her that way. I told her I'd have to give it some serious thought and then it just happened. It didn't occur to me that Shirley would tell Helen, or that Helen would approach me."

"You're leaving somebody out, aren't you?" Lucy asked. "How about the chaplain? What was her name, Martha?"

"That was the strangest thing," I said. "We were just sitting there talking about things and then something changed. I don't have any idea what it was, but it did. The next thing I knew it was over. What is it, Lucy? Do I have a tattoo on my forehead that says, 'Fuck me?'"

Lucy shook her head sadly. "No, it actually says, 'Big Dick Needs Cave.' You really don't understand, do you?"

"No, I don't. Up until a few months ago I was a married man who loved my wife and wasn't interested in anyone else. Then we made that damned bet and things changed. I wish we never had."

"Then you wouldn't have met me," Lucy replied.

"I like to think I would have, sooner or later. Maybe we could have been close friends."

Lucy gave me a dubious look. "Do you really believe that, Roger?"

"No, not really. I was interested in going to bed the moment I first saw you and that hasn't changed, Lucy. What has changed is that Anne started having an affair with someone she met at the conference over spring break."

"How is she so different from you?" Lucy wanted to know. "We are having an affair, too, if you didn't notice."

"I didn't start out to have an affair," I replied.

"Do you honestly think Anne went to the conference looking for a lover?"

"No, she was invited to present and it was a good career choice. It pissed me off that she shit-canned our vacation before she talked to me. But I encouraged her to go, anyway. I was right, too. It paid off." I sighed. "The irony is that I had decided to ditch the bet before she left but she was such a bitch that I decided to go ahead with it."

"Don't make her the bad guy, Roger. She doesn't deserve it. None of us do. Sometimes things just happen." Her face twisted just like she'd tasted something foul. "Like fucking the chaplain."

I nodded. "That was weird, Lucy. I don't know why I let that happen. I could have stopped it but I didn't." I frowned. "I can't blame anyone else for that one."

Lucy reached out and took my hand. It was the first time we had touched since I explained my early morning visitor. "Stop it, Roger!" she insisted. "Think about it. You had just been told your lifelong partner had suffered a stroke and might not live.

You once told me that you shut down in emergencies and then go to pieces later. I think you held together as long as you need to and then you fell apart. Coming close to death does that. It doesn't matter if it's us or someone we love. And you love Anne. You wouldn't get so pissed if you didn't."

"Oh, shit!" I said. I told Lucy about Anne's near miss in Phoenix. "I bet that's what it was. She told me they came so close she could see the other pilot screaming."

"Are you up to a little anthropology?" Lucy asked and I looked at her like she was crazy. "Seriously, do you know anything about old time country funerals in Ireland?" I shook my head and she went on. "After the funeral and the meal afterwards, couples used to go out into the fields and fuck themselves silly. It was their way of telling death to fuck off."

I nodded. "I heard something like that once. I thought it was pure myth."

Lucy shrugged. "It may never have happened but it's still true. I think that's what you were doing diddling the chaplain. What I don't understand is why she let it happen."

"She's not clergy. She's a lay volunteer."

"So that's what that means, lay people," Lucy laughed. When she did I was relieved. We were past the crisis.

"She's a widow, too. She told me she's only now coming alive. I think she said it's been five or six years."

"So you were both vulnerable and it happened." Lucy nodded and was quiet for a moment. "Well, at least it's very unlikely you were exposed to HIV. Now give me a hug, Roger. I need to feel your arms around me."

Lucy and I held one another for a long while. There was a great deal of tenderness in our embrace and neither of us thought it odd that there was so little passion. Even when I lifted her chin and kissed her softly.

"I love you, Lucy," I told her simply. "I don't want to lose you. Not ever."

"I know, you big lug," she smiled back. "That's why I didn't bash you with a chair."

"You mean there's one we left unbroken?" I kissed her again. "So where do we go from here?"

"For a run," Lucy said. "I have the afternoon off and I think we need to visit our hideaway." Nor was it lost on me that she said "our" rather than "my."

I was relieved to find a different chaplain on duty late that afternoon during ICU visiting hours. There had been no change in Anne's condition and what the doctor had to say was indefinite. "We really don't know that much about the healing process of the brain," he told me. "We know more than we did ten years ago and a lot more than we did fifty years back. Compared to what there is to know, however, it's very little. We are still not completely clear how physiology and consciousness are related."

The doctor paused. "With your wife, there does not appear to be that much damage. Yet, there is no way we can tell when, or if, she will come out of the coma. I wish I could tell you something more definite, but I can't. We're doing everything we can to help her body heal itself." He cleared his throat. "I understand that you two don't have children, correct?"

I told the doctor he was right. "That's too bad since one's family can help the healing process. Children seem to be the best medicine, but at least her sisters are here. Spiritual resources help a great deal, too."

"We're not church folk," I told him. "I did have a good conversation with the chaplain yesterday. Martha, I believe her name was. She has a very calming influence."

"Yes, she does. The nurse told me she came in last night and prayed for your wife. She's a widow, you know."

"Yes, she told me that. We all need all the help we can get."

"Well, if you are a praying man, I would suggest you do so. Your wife is a long way from being out of the woods."

I wondered why the doctor always called Anne "your wife" rather than using her given name. When I mentioned it to Lucy later on she said, "It's simple. He needs to stay detached to be most effective. Naming his patients would make them real people to him, not symptoms or cases. I think that's a mistake but I'd bet that's why he does it."

Shirley and Helen arrived together just before visiting hours started and both of them hugged me. "Thank you for letting Helen stay over," Shirley whispered in my ear. "She needed it." Then she chuckled and added, "Me, too."

Despite what the doctor had told me, Anne looked worse to my eyes. Both Shirley and Helen thought the same. "It's like nobody is there," Shirley said. "It's Anne's body but no one's at home."

"Maybe she's just gone for a while," Helen suggested. There were tears in her eyes.

I nodded. "I surely hope so. The doctor isn't encouraging. The longer a person stays in a coma, the less hope there is for any recovery. Even if Anne survives physically, she may not be able to function normally."

"I called a friend over at the nursing school," Helen said. "She's had a lot of experience with stroke victims and people in a coma. The big thing right now is making sure Anne doesn't catch pneumonia or develop some other kind of infection." She started to say something else, but stopped.

"Come on, toots, don't hold back," Shirley told her.

Helen looked at me. I was watching her intently. "Well, my friend told me one of the big factors is will to survive. People sometimes come back when there's little hope and that's one of the big factors."

"Anne has that in spades," I replied.

Shirley and Helen looked at one another and it was Helen who spoke. "We think Anne has a drinking problem, Roger. That could make things worse. Drunks don't have much hope."

I nodded. "I wondered about that, too. I looked it up. She has a lot of the symptoms. Were you aware she's pregnant?"

"No!" The two women said in unison. I had no doubt they were telling the truth. "Will she lose the baby?" Shirley asked.

"They don't think so, at least not at the moment. But she could. The doctor tells me there's not much danger in her being pregnant now, but I don't really understand. He also said that being pregnant was a risk factor for having a stroke in the first place."

"I've heard that it is," Helen replied. "I don't understand it, either. It doesn't make much sense to me." Shirley nodded her agreement. "Her drinking definitely raises the risk," Helen added. "That's pretty well recognized."

"There was something in the news about that," Shirley told us. "Are you headed for home now? You're welcome to stop by for supper." She looked at Helen. "How about you, dear?"

"I don't want to intrude..." Helen began, hesitant.

Shirley cut her off. "Do you really want to go home to Roy?"

she asked. "Besides, Ed would like the company. He needs to see someone besides me."

Helen looked at me. "Sure," I said. "That would be good. I can pick up some take-out and we can have a picnic. Hospitals give me the willies." I was also thinking there was safety in numbers. With Helen and Shirley both there, I wouldn't have to say no to either.

⚜

I was at the Chinese restaurant waiting for their order and lost in thought when I heard a familiar voice saying something to me. Turning to see who it was, I found Martha, the volunteer chaplain, looking at me with concern. "Are you all right, Roger?" she said, repeating herself. "Did something happen to Anne?"

"No," I told her, trying to smile. "There's been no change since yesterday. The doctor doesn't sound very hopeful." *Shit, I thought. What next? A man can't even think without someone barging in.*

*You need a "Do Not Disturb" sign,* Jolly told me. *Or maybe one that says "In Session."*

"Oh," Martha said. "You looked… I don't know, lost, maybe, and I wondered." She smiled, hesitant. "I stopped by to see Anne last night. I hope you don't mind. I prayed with her and read from the Psalms."

"Thank you," I said automatically. "I appreciate that. Anne's not much of a religious person. Neither am I. At least, she hasn't been," I added, wondering why I said this.

*She sure calls on God a lot,* Jolly reminded me. *Maybe she's still in the closet—a secret holy roller.*

There was an awkward silence and it was clear to me that Martha was nervous. "Look," I said. "Don't worry about it. I'm not going to complain. I appreciate your going by to see her and you were very…helpful to me yesterday."

"Our, um, conversation was very helpful to me, too," she told me, smiling. "I'm here if you'd like to talk some more." There was no mistaking the invitation in her eyes.

The clerk came with our order and I paid for it. Then I turned to my companion and said, "Thank you, Martha. At the moment I'm a little overwhelmed. Perhaps when things calm down a bit."

"At least you're eating well," she said, looking at the sack I was carrying.

"Oh, this is for a sick friend and his family," I told her and headed for the door. Even though it was true, it sounded like an excuse, and a lame one at that. So I paused at the doorway and looked back. "Thanks, Martha," I said. "I do appreciate it. I'm a little out-of-it right now."

♣

When I knocked at Shirley and Ed's door, it was Helen who answered. "Shirley's giving Ed his bath," she said, taking the food and setting it on the kitchen counter. Then she turned back to me, giving me a hug and a tender kiss on the lips. Then she looked my in the eyes and smiled. "To hell with that!" she said and gave me a kiss that brought me to full alert.

I was saved from any reply by sounds from the hallway. Ed walked in a moment later, leaning on Shirley's arm as he shuffled along. Holding out a hand I greeted him warmly. "Damned shame about Anne," he growled. "Damned shame."

As Shirley helped Ed shuffle to the kitchen table he spotted the distinctive white take-out boxes. "Chinese, is it?" He observed. "We haven't had that in a while, have we, Spunk?" Turning to me, he said, "Of course, I don't do well with chopsticks these days. Takes a big shovel and a good operator, eh, Spunk?"

"You do very well, Eddie," Shirley answered. Yet, I noted she put a plastic apron over Ed's pajamas and a large teaspoon by his plate.

As supper progressed, I found myself forgetting about Ed's illness. One thing the disease had not dampened was his quick sense of humor. He unleashed it toward our state governor who had done something particularly stupid the week before. "I guess it serves us right," Ed observed between bites. "If we elect a clown we really can't expect anything else."

"At least he can speak in complete sentences," Helen said. "Not like Curious George."

"The chump looks like a chimp, doesn't he?" Ed laughed. "Have you seen the photos of him side by side with a chimp? Put a shirt and tie on the chimp and it's hard to tell the difference."

The conversation turned in other directions and I was surprised how fast the time flew by. However, I could see it took a toll on Ed. By the time my host said good night, he could barely keep his eyes open. Yet, when Helen took one of his arms to help Shirley take Ed to his room, he looked at me and grinned. "I can't be doing too bad, can I, Roger? I've got two beautiful ladies taking me to bed!"

While Helen and Shirley were gone, I cleaned up the kitchen and put away the food. That didn't take long and I was seated at the table sipping a cup of decaf then they returned. Shirley was trying hard to hold back tears and Helen had her arm around our friend. "Let's go to the den," Helen suggested. "We can talk freely in there."

I had never been to the den, which turned out to be on the other end of the house. It was clearly a man's room and I liked it immediately. Most of the seats were canvas director's chairs. Yet, there was also a large overstuffed sofa with a wide flat section along one wall. The middle of the floor was dominated by what looked like a wrestling mat and along the walls was a full set of lightweight dumbbells. An exercise bike in one corner faced a large screen television and there was a small refrigerator to one side. There were also lots of comfortable pillows scattered across the central mat.

"Welcome to Ed's man cave," Helen said to me. "I've never been able to tell if it was a study or a gym." She pointed to a wall full of books and a built-in sound system.

"Kick off your shoes, if you don't mind," Shirley told us, taking her seat on the huge couch. "Ed doesn't like street shoes on his exercise mat."

I did so, taking off my socks, too. The textured surface of the mat felt good against my feet. "Oh, my," I sighed, taking a seat next to Helen. "I need a room like this at our place."

"Move over here," Shirley told me, patting the sofa beside her. "I need to be surrounded by friends right now."

I did as she asked and Shirley put her arms around us both. She hugged us close for several minutes, quietly sobbing, then pushed us away. "Thank you," she said. "Sometimes it's just too much."

"You don't have to do it alone, sweetie," Helen said, giving her a hug and rubbing her back. When Shirley looked up at her, Helen nodded, and Shirley turned to me. "I need a big favor, Roger," she told me. I could see excitement in her eyes and wondered what she meant.

"Of course, Shirley, whatever I can do."

"I would like to see you kiss Helen."

I hesitated, then looked at Helen, who was smiling. I leaned across Shirley and kissed Helen lightly on the lips. She seemed surprised when I broke off.

Shirley ran her hand up my neck and turned my head toward her. "Kiss her like you mean it," she said. "Like this." She pulled me toward her and locked her lips to me. This time I did not hesitate. I kissed Shirley as thoroughly as I knew how and as I did, I felt Helen take my free hand and press it against one of her breasts. I also felt Shirley grasp me and run her hand up and down my length.

"You guys have been plotting," I said when Shirley released me. Helen nodded shyly and I leaned across and kissed her like Shirley had kissed me. As I did, I ran my hand up her inner thigh and when Helen opened her legs, I grasped her firmly where they met. She moaned.

Freeing my hand, I started unbuttoning Helen's blouse but Shirley stopped me. "Stand up, Roger," she said. "I want to watch you do it."

Getting to my feet, I helped Helen to hers. Then I kissed her, and backing away a bit, circled around and began kissing her neck and shoulders as I continued slowly unbuttoning her blouse. Helen arched her back, bringing her derrière up against me, rubbing up and down. I could feel her tremble as I freed each button and she moaned when I dropped her blouse to the mat. Then I slowly unfettered her breasts, gently releasing the clasp and keeping each of them covered as I kissed my way around her to the tips. When I dropped her bra, she sighed, and as I unbuttoned her slacks and dropped them, she caught her breath. Then, gently slipping her panties down her long, lovely legs, I began kissing my way down her belly until I arrived at her cleft.

Looking up, I smiled and deftly skipped my tongue between Helen's nether lips, flicking her little girl with the tip. I felt Helen fill her fists with my hair and pull me toward her and I lashed her sweetness with my tongue without mercy. She cried out suddenly and began to twitch wildly, opening her legs wider and driving her mound into my face. When I slid my tongue completely into her, she groaned as spasms of rapture shook her elegant frame.

Then she pushed me away and slid to the mat. "Stop!" she whispered urgently when I started to follow. "It's too much! It almost hurts!"

Suddenly I was tackled from behind. "My turn!" Shirley declared, throwing her clothes aside with abandon as she pulled me to the floor and stripped me. Then she mounted me. Impaling herself completely on my full length, she began to rotate her hips as she ran herself up and own my length.

Then I felt something touch my head and when I opened my eyes, I could see Helen and Shirley kissing as they caressed each other's breasts. Reaching back and grasping Helen by her hips, I drew her down to me and began teasing her again with my lips and tongue. The sensation was like nothing I had ever felt before and it seemed to last forever.

Then it happened. Just as I felt myself begin to explode within Shirley, I felt their spasms as both women reached the peak. When I felt this I began to thrust wildly with my hips and my tongue and I heard my companions moan loudly, almost in unison, as they found release. Then, as suddenly as it had happened, they collapsed across me intertwined in an array of arms and legs and breasts. I had to push them off my chest so I could breathe. Then I lay back to rest a moment and floated away into a deep sleep.

# CHAPTER FOURTEEN

# No Change Blues

When I awoke the next morning, I was in Lucy's big bed and she was asleep cuddled next to me. I lay there for a few moments trying to remember how I got there. After supper there had been a visit to the hospital and a brief visit with Anne. There was no change in her condition but when I first saw her, I thought her complexion had more color. Then I realized that it was probably just the light. The sky was still bright from a marvelous sunset and the skylights over each bed were deep orange, warming the hard, cold brilliance of the fluorescent tubes overhead.

Helen asked if I wanted her to spend the night again as we left the hospital. I thanked her and said I needed solitude and rest. Yet, when I got home, I found the silence oppressive. Unable to fall asleep, I got up and dressed again, then headed for Lucy's, hoping she was still up.

Lucy was in her bathrobe when she answered the door. Seeing the look in my eyes, she pulled me inside and gathered me into her arms. She held me for a long time. Then, without a word, she led me upstairs to the loft. There she undressed me and tucked me in. "Do you need anything?" she asked.

"Just you," I whispered. She dropped her robe and joined me under the covers. When she put her arms around me there was no ardor in her embrace, only tenderness. I quickly fell into a deep sleep.

Looking at the clock, I saw it was almost nine and I started to wake Lucy. Then I realized it was Saturday. She didn't have to work. So I got up and headed for the bathroom, brushing my teeth when I was done. Not wanting to dress, I draped my robe over my arm and returned to the loft. When I got there I saw she had turned over and was watching me. "Who's this naked man in my bedroom?" she asked softly. "He looks familiar."

"I'm the milkman," I said, smiling as I laid aside my robe and slid under the covers. "I brought you some special cream."

"Ha!" Lucy said, throwing the covers back and getting to her feet. "Then I better visit the biffy before he makes delivery." She was down the steps in a flash.

Lucy wasted no time in the bathroom but I pretended like I'd fallen asleep when she came back. Then she saw movement under the covers and jumped on top of me, pinning me under the covers. "Faker!" she laughed as she gave the bulge she'd seen a gentle squeeze. "Mr. Jolly doesn't lie."

I managed to free an arm and pulled her down so we were face to face. "Good morning, sweetheart," I said, grinning as I gave her an ardent kiss. "It's good to see you."

"It's even better to be seen," she told me, returning my passion with interest." Then she threw off the covers and straddled me, setting my little big man free. "It's even better to be held."

"It is, indeed," I admitted. I could feel the heat of her loins rubbing against me. Then she closed her legs, capturing her prize in between them. "Gottcha!" she murmured.

"Yes you do," I answered, moving my shanks and opening my legs. When I did, Lucy dropped down between them, changing the angle of our conjunction. "Oh, that feels good," I told her.

"I'll be the man," she whispered, beginning to move her hips gently back and forth. "Just lie back and enjoy."

"Like you do?" I murmured and Lucy chuckled. "Or can I be a lively wench?" Then I gasped as she began to rotate her pelvis as she moved up and down my length.

"This is called screwing," she told me. "Lie back and enjoy."

"I would never have guessed," I moaned and did as I was told. At least, I did as long as I could stand it. The sensation was intense and Lucy quickly brought me to the edge. She knew me well enough now to hold me there. With a mischievous grin she kept me from passing the point of no return. By then I was squirming and groaning beneath her, clawing at the bed covers. It was only when she felt her own pleasure grow so intense she could no longer hold back did she relent. She rode me wildly until we both exploded in wave after wave of carnal delight. Then she fell to one side and lay motionless on the bed.

"Lucy!" I cried out in alarm as I sat up and began shaking her.

"What?" Lucy snarled, glaring at me until she saw the alarm in my eyes. "What is it, Roger?" she asked, concerned, as I buried my face into my hands and began to sob. Yet, all I could do was shake my head and Lucy held me close until the tears were done.

"God, you scared me," I said when I caught my breath. "The way you fell over I thought...." I clouded up and could not finish the thought.

Suddenly Lucy understood what I was trying to tell her. "You thought I was having a stroke?" she asked gently. I nodded. "Was that what happened to Anne?" I nodded again, trying to fight back tears. "So you thought you were losing me, too." The tears streaming down my face told her she was right.

"I'm not going to die on you, Roger," she told me, holding me close, stroking my head like she would a child. "Not if I can help it. I promise."

I pulled back and looked at Lucy. "I'm sorry," I told her. "I thought I had a handle on things. Apparently I don't." I didn't like how much this admission troubled me.

"Roger, you're allowed!" Lucy told me. "You've been the one who's been carrying everyone else. It just caught up with you, that's all. You've been there for everyone but yourself. It's like stretching a rubber band too far too often."

"I hate being needy," I told her. I knew Lucy could see the shame in my eyes.

"I do, too, but welcome to the human fucking condition. You don't have to be Iron Man for me," she added. "I kind of like it when you're human. Now get your butt out of this bed and go fix us some coffee. I need it! God, I want a cigarette!"

I looked pointedly at the juncture of her legs. "Gee, I didn't know you smoked after sex."

♣

When I got to the hospital just before noon, I found Shirley and Helen sitting in the waiting room. "I overslept this morning," I told them, giving each of them a hug before sitting down. When I did, both of them were a bit reserved. "Is something wrong?" I asked.

The two women looked at each other. It was Shirley who spoke. "We drove by your house but the car wasn't in the drive."

"No, it wasn't," I told them. "Did you check the garage?"

Helen shook her head. "No, but we were worried about you so we let ourselves in. You weren't there."

"What time was this?" I asked.

"Almost nine," Helen told me.

I nodded. "I was having breakfast with a friend and I walked here from there."

"The one you run with?" Shirley asked.

"As a matter of fact, yes," I said. "Why the third degree?" I asked, frowning. "Did I do something wrong?"

"I don't know," Shirley said. "Did you?"

I responded with an intensity that startled the two women. "Who the hell do you two think you are taking that tone with me?" I demanded. "Who the hell are you to judge? I thought we were friends."

Shirley flinched at the hostility behind my words and Helen burst into tears. Just then the doctor came through the double doors of the unit. Having no idea what was going on, the doctor ignored the situation and spoke directly to me. "Good morning, Dr. Jahnsen. We moved your wife from intensive care to critical care this morning. That's one floor down."

"So she's better?" I asked. Helen told me later there was no mistaking the relief in my voice.

"No, there's been no change, really. However, she is breathing on her own and her vital signs are good, so there was no reason not to move her. We needed the intensive care bed. We had three people come in from a car crash, all critical. The good news is that you can visit her during normal visiting hours."

"The good news will be her waking up," I reminded him gently. "What room is she in now?"

After the doctor left I looked at Shirley and Helen. "I don't know what's going on with you two but I can't deal with this right now. I need to go see Anne." My voice was calm, as it normally was.

"Do you mind if we tag along?" Helen asked.

"Of course, not," I answered. "We're friends. I'm sorry I popped off. I don't know why I did."

"You're as stressed out as we are, Roger," Shirley told me. "May I have a hug?"

"Of course," I told her holding out my arms. "You, too, Helen," I added. "We need to hang together. We are friends."

Shirley giggled. "Lovers, too."

The visit to Anne's room was disappointing. The room was much more inviting than the ICU but it was still a hospital room. Anne was attached to an IV drip and to a machine with several leads. There was also an oxygen line fitted to her nose. What looked like an electronic alarm was clipped to her gown.

Even with the blinds on the large window partially closed, Anne looked better than she had under the harsh lights of the ICU. Someone had shampooed her hair and combed it back in a style Anne would not be caught dead wearing. I smiled at the thought, then sobered. I realized this was exactly what might happen. The truth was that Anne still looked terrible. I also realized that the doctor had not softened the blow. Anne was still in danger and things could go south in a heartbeat.

I moved to the side of the bead and reached for Anne's hand. Her beautiful skin was still sickly green and felt cold and lifeless. When I touched her forehead it felt the same. Except for her slow breathing, she was motionless and completely still. Only the display attached to the leads told me she was still alive. I had no idea how to interpret what I saw on the display, but Anne's heartbeat seemed strong and steady.

"Good morning, love," I said, stroking the back of the hand I held. "It's a beautiful day out. We're glad you have a private room now. Shirley and Helen are here." I moved to make room for the two women. They stood at the other side of the bed. "You gave us quite a scare the other night," I added, not knowing what to say. Then I laughed. "You wouldn't believe what they've done with your hair."

"Don't worry about that," Helen told Anne, giving me a sharp look. "Shirley and I will have you spruced up in no time."

"Yeah, what does a silly man know about hair?" Shirley asked. "Us girls have to hang together."

*Yeah, right!* Jolly Roger snorted. *They're balling your husband's brains out but what's a little fucking among friends?*

The two of them talked to Anne for a while longer before they each said goodbye and moved into the hallway. "I think you're going to need some help," Shirley told me. "Someone needs to be with Anne during the day and you'll need some time away, too, Roger. Why don't we set up some shifts? Why don't you stay the rest of the morning and I'll come back about two and stay until dinner."

"I don't mind coming in for the evening," Helen interjected. "I usually watch TV by myself and I could do that here."

"I can't ask you to do that," I said. "I don't know how long it's going to be."

"You're not asking," Shirley replied. "We're volunteering and I don't have any classes until September. Let us help out, Roger. Please. It's what we want to do." Helen nodded.

"All right," I said. "We'll do it your way for the next two weeks. Then, if there's no change, we can talk about where we go from there."

"Thank you," Shirley said, giving me a hug. Then she gave me a wry smile. "For that and a lot of other things, too."

"Me, too," Helen added, hugging us both.

♣

My next visit to Anne's room was unsettling. Even though the nurse told me there had been no change, it was discouraging to see this with my own eyes. Shirley or Helen had combed Anne's hair and her private room was quieter than Intensive Care. Yet, I thought she looked even more pale than the night before and her skin felt as cold and lifeless as it had that morning. It was all I could do to keep this out of my voice when I talked to her.

Shirley and Helen showed up a bit later and I was glad that they were there. They jumped in whenever I faltered and kept the conversation upbeat, but I could see it was an effort for them, too. As far as I could tell, we were talking to an empty body whose resident was no longer there.

However, the nurses in ICU had stressed that it was very likely Anne could hear us. They said that it was important to talk to her. They said our talking would help her find her way back, but it seemed hopeless. Yet, what other choice did we have? I was not ready to give up hope and neither were Helen or Shirley. Watching them gave me heart and I was grateful for their presence.

At one point the chaplain on duty stopped by and asked if they wanted prayer. I looked at my companions and shrugged. "It can't hurt," I said. "Who knows? It might even help."

The chaplain smiled at this and laid her hand on Anne's arm, reaching out to me with the other. Helen and Shirley did the same and we stood in a circle as the chaplain delivered a simple but eloquent prayer, one that I suspected she had used many times before. Yet, I found myself with a lump in my throat. Then the chaplain began the Lords Prayer. I was surprised to find myself mumbling the words as tears ran down my cheeks. I wondered what Jolly thought of all this, why he was silent.

*There are some things you don't joke about,* the familiar voice told me. *I'm not a devil, you know. I'm not even a fallen angel.*

*So you think there's something to this?* I asked but the inner voice didn't answer. Then I realized the answer was implicit in Jolly's silence. This surprised me even more.

Suddenly I realized the prayer was done and I opened my eyes. The chaplain and the two women were looking at me oddly and I found I was still holding their hands. "Sorry," I said, letting go. The chaplain nodded and smiled. Then Helen handed me a tissue and I realized my face was wet.

The chaplain stayed a bit longer, waiting to see if there was need. When it became obvious that I had no desire to talk about whatever was going on with me, she took her leave. "You can have the nurse page me if you want," she told me. "Someone will be on duty all night."

I thanked her. When she was gone, I asked Helen and Shirley to have supper with me in the cafeteria. Shirley said she needed to get home. "Ed told me to stay as long as I needed to be here, but I need to fix his supper. It's one of the few things I can do for him." She looked very sad.

"I'll come with you," Helen told her. "Roy's probably so drunk by now he won't eat, anyway."

"Maybe we can use the conference room," I said. "I need to talk to both of you privately for a few minutes."

The hospital was fairly new and every floor had a room doctors used to talk to families of their patients. The room on Anne's floor was not in use and I got right to the point. "There is something you need to know," I told them. "There was someone who knew about the ad before it ran. They responded to it before it was in the paper." I shrugged.

"Why didn't you say anything?" Shirley demanded.

"How could I?" I answered calmly. "How do you think Anne would have responded? Then she hinted around about having an open marriage. Telling her seemed moot at that point."

"Who is it?" Shirley demanded, clearly angry.

I shook my head. "I don't kiss and tell," I said. When I did I heard Jolly Roger laugh. *No, turkey, you don't fuck and tell. Except to Lucy.*

"Is this the person you run with?" Helen asked.

I nodded. "Yes, as a matter of fact, it is."

"So if we see you out running with some woman we'll know who it is?" Shirley asked. She was still angry.

"Why do you think it's a woman?" I answered and Jolly laughed again. *Brilliant, Sachmo!*

Shirley and Helen were too stunned to speak. "I run with lots of people," I added. "So keep that in mind."

Shirley looked stunned. "You sleep with them all?"

"Of course, not. Only one of them."

Shirley gave me an intent look. "You sure don't seem gay, Roger. This isn't something to joke about." She seemed calmer.

Helen spoke up. "I think the term is bi, dear."

I decided truth was the best way to go. "No, I'm not gay, Shirley, or bisexual, either. There is a woman I'm involved with."

"I bet she's younger," Shirley declared. It was clear that she was not pleased by the news.

"Forgive me for pointing it out, but you're older than I am," I answered. "Age doesn't have anything to do with this."

"Roger's telling us he's an equal opportunity fucker, dear," Helen explained. Once gain, the word sounded strange coming from her.

"Jesus!" Shirley said. "It makes me wonder what you've passed along to us."

"Nothing that Anne didn't pass along to me," I shot back and Shirley glared at me.

"Come on, dears," Helen broke in. "We need to remember that we are friends."

"Just for the record, I don't think there's anything to worry about," I said. "The lady and I are both clean and I assume you both are, too. If there's any doubt in your mind, you can always be tested."

"I wish it was you rather than Anne in that bed!" Shirley said sharply.

I looked at her sadly. "Don't you think I do, too, Shirley? Despite what you may think, I love Anne. I love her more than anyone else in this world." There were tears in my eyes.

It was Helen who reached out and touched me. "Of course, you do, Roger," she assured me. "We know that." She gave her companion a stern look. "Don't we, Shirley?"

I had never seen Helen so forceful. Yet, she did it without

raising her voice and I was surprised to see Shirley back down. She sighed and her shoulders slumped. "Yeah, we know that, you dumb shit. You laid a lot on us, Roger, but I'm glad you told us. At least, I think I am." She shook her head and walked away.

"She'll be all right," Helen told me, reaching up for a hug. "I better go with her. You'll be all right, won't you?" I nodded and she hurried to catch up with Shirley.

As much as I appreciated their help, I was glad to see the two women leave. I headed to the cafeteria, which was still open. When I was done eating I returned to Anne's room. I stood at her bedside a long while, holding her hand in one of mine and stroking her hair with the other. It was something Anne liked me to do. "It's just you and me, babe," I told her. "I sure wish you'd come home." As I said this, I was unaware of the tears running down my cheeks. Yet, in the waning light I didn't see the tears that formed in the corners of her eyes. The nurses told me about them the next day.

♣

"So they know about us now," I said. I was seated at Lucy's kitchen table, sipping a cup of coffee. For some reason she didn't have to go in to work until late that morning and we slept in, cuddled together like spoons in a drawer.

"Will they make trouble for you?" Lucy asked.

"I doubt it," I told her. "They don't want everything known, either. Helen may not have much to lose but Shirley does. We live in a liberal community and she has tenure, but if it were known she had another woman for a lover...." I shrugged. "A lot of people we work with would be scandalized. They wouldn't admit it, of course, but they would."

"You're not going to rat them out, are you?"

"Of course, not." I frowned. "I'm surprised you had to ask, Lucy."

"I didn't think so," she said. "It was just the way you said it. I may be wrong but I think you may have some resentment there."

I thought about this and then nodded. "I do. I don't want to have it but there it is. The truth of the matter is that Shirley is a bit pushy. Sometimes more than just a bit. Still, she's a long time friend. I like her most of the time."

Lucy smiled. "You know, Roger, you may eventually see a side of me that you don't like. I can almost guarantee it."

"What? Are you going to start picking your nose and flipping boogers or something?"

"You're gross!"

"Guilty as charged."

"Well, I hope you'll tell me before it gets to be a resentment." She regarded me seriously. I saw her reach a decision. "There is something I need to tell you."

"You're not running off with a drummer in a country band, are you?" While I was miming shock, she saw there was also real concern behind my words. She told me later she didn't like to admit how much this pleased her.

Lucy laughed. "Been there, done that, Lee Roy. Got the tattoo and the t-shirt, too."

"I haven't spotted the tattoo. Yet."

"It only shows up under black light," she assured me. Then her face grew grave. "I need to be serious for a moment, dear man. I'm a couple of weeks late."

It took I a moment to understand what Lucy was saying. "Oh," I said. "Are you sure?"

"I haven't been to the doctor yet, but my body's doing some funny things." Seeing my knowing smile, she said. "No, don't say something funny, please. I'm scared."

I reached out and took her in my arms. "I think the first thing is to see the doctor. Lots of things can make you late, or so I've read. And if you're...with child it's not the end of the world. I'll do the right thing."

"'With child?' 'The right thing.' Let's call it what it is. You may have knocked me up, Roger. I may be pregnant. And what's this 'right thing' stuff?'"

"No," I said, shaking my head. "We may have knocked us up. I'm part of this thing, too." Then I frowned. "Or are you telling me it's someone else?"

"Would it matter?"

"Only for medical reasons, inherited stuff. You know, like hemophilia or diabetes."

"You're taking this rather calmly."

"I've had time to think about it," I replied. "There's a good chance Anne's child is not mine. But as far as I'm concerned, her child is mine to raise. I'm his dad. Or hers." I reached over and patted her flat stomach. "So is this one if she's there."

"He. My family runs to boys." Lucy gave me a searching look. "Are you sure, Roger? It's a lifetime commitment. I could have it taken care of."

"No!" I almost yelled. "Don't you dare! I know it's your body but it's my child, too." Seeing the tears in Lucy's eyes, I added. "I'm sorry for yelling. I feel very strongly about this."

To my surprise, Lucy threw herself into my arms and began to weep. "Lucy, I really am sorry. I didn't mean to hurt your feelings...."

"No, you idiot," she said, pulling back and smiling through her tears. "That's not why I'm crying. I'm crying because you're the best man I've ever known and I love you."

"I'll try not to yell again," I replied.

"You'll fail miserably, too," she assured me. "I don't mind you yelling because you care." She began to unbutton my shirt.

"What are you doing?" I asked, confused.

"I'm getting ready to rape you. Hold still."

"Not that I mind, but do I have any choice?"

Lucy smiled. "Not a bit. That's why I said 'rape.'"

# CHAPTER FIFTEEN

# New Dimensions

The young doctor was smiling when he came into the office where Lucy and I were waiting. "Well, Mr. Parker, it looks like you're going to be a father."

"I'm Parker," Lucy told me. "This is Dr. Jahnsen."

The doctor nodded as if he clearly understood, though it was clear he did not. "Well, Ms Parker," he continued, "the tests were positive and your pelvic confirmed it. You're about five or six weeks along and you're going to be a mother." He started to smile but stopped. "I gather this is not good news."

"No," Lucy told me. "It's wonderful news but it's not a good time. It was not something we anticipated." She looked at me. She later said I was beaming like an idiot. Then she smiled and added, "You can see he's as pleased with himself as he can be."

The doctor nodded. "Well, things seem to work themselves out. The main thing is to keep a positive attitude and take care of yourself. It's a big plus that you're not a smoker and don't drink. You might want to cut back on salt and caffeine, too."

"You mean no coffee?" Lucy asked.

"No, but I would suggest decaffeinated coffee and green tea. There is very little caffeine in that."

"What are you smirking about?" Lucy asked me.

"Lucy's a coffee junkie," I told the doctor. "Decaf is heresy."

The doctor smiled. "Yes, well, withdrawal is not too bad. I was a coffee junkie, too. These days it's tea for me. Do you have any questions?" Lucy and I shook our heads. "Well, then, I'll want to see you again in four to six weeks. You can set up an appointment at the desk when you go out." He started to say something else but shook his head and showed us out of his office.

"So what do you think?" I asked as we drove home.

"I think I'm scared," Lucy told me, reaching out for my hand. "I'm a bit old to be having a first child."

I pulled over to the curb and took Lucy in my arms. "You are also in very good shape," I reminded her. "Mentally as well as physically."

"It doesn't feel like that right now," she murmured. "I feel like I want to cry. I'm sorry."

"What in the world are you apologizing about?" I asked. "You never have to apologize for how you feel, Lucy."

"But you're so happy about this," she said. "I don't want to ruin that."

"I'll tell you what. I'll smile and you cry. That way we'll have all the bases covered." Lucy snorted when I said this. "I'm scared, too, Lucy, but I'm too happy to be there right now. I'm going to be with you every step of the way, too."

"Even for Lamaze? It might raise a few eyebrows if you show up there with me."

I nodded. "It might, but I don't care. That's still a bit down the road, isn't it? Or do you start right away?"

"I don't know," Lucy told me. "I don't know shit about being a mother."

"What about your own mother?"

"My mother was lost in her own little world. She never let anything unpleasant in, either. She put the big 'D' on denial."

"You seem to have gotten along with your dad pretty well. You have a good role model there, don't you?"

Lucy looked up at me and smiled. "Yes, he raised us pretty well. He also protected us from my mother's insanity." She shivered at the memory. "It got pretty bad sometimes. She could get real scary when she missed her medication. I don't want to be like her. Never, ever."

I smiled. "You're not on any medication, sweetheart. There's nothing for you to miss."

"What do mean?" Lucy asked, indignant. "The doctor's taking me off coffee!"

♣

When I arrived at Anne's room that afternoon, Helen and Shirley were there. I'd not seen them since I told them I was seeing someone and there was a distinct reserve in the way they greeted me. They were friendly enough but when they hugged me it seemed perfunctory, almost impersonal. They kept up their part of the conversation. Yet, they also seemed to communicate with looks and smiles and subtle facial expressions I couldn't understand. It was as if they were using an unspoken language known only to themselves. And I sensed they were enjoying my confusion.

*They're probably miffed about Lucy and me. They'll just have to get over it.* I thought. *Fuck them!* Then I smiled when Jolly Roger reminded me. *You already have, dude. Quite thoroughly.*

Setting this aside for later, I turned all my attention to my wife. Though the nurse told me there was no change, Anne seemed different. She lay quite still, her only movement the rising and falling of her chest as she breathed. She still felt cold to my touch, too. Taking her hand in my own, I turned to her two friends. "Is it just me or does Anne seem different today?" Even to my own ears my voice sounded strange and I realized I was close to tears. I desperately wished that Lucy was there.

It was Helen who answered. She moved around to my side of the bed and patted my cheek gently. "There's no change, Roger," she said softly, looking me in the eye. "Someone gave her a bath and washed her hair. That's what you're seeing. She's not home, dear. Not yet."

I nodded, turning back to Anne with tears streaming down my face. Helen moved closer and put an arm around my shoulders. "I'm so sorry, Roger," she murmured and the way she said it told me her words were about far more than the situation with Anne. "I wish there was more we could do."

I let go of Anne's hand and turned to Helen. When I hugged her, she hugged me back and there was nothing perfunctory about it. Then I looked up and saw the look on Shirley's face. It was almost a grimace, a mixture of anger and resentment, and something else, too. Then it was gone and Shirley nodded, trying hard to smile.

There was nothing else to say. After a while the two took their leave. I stood there a long while, saying nothing as I held Anne's hand. Then a question crossed my mind and I pulled the covers down far enough that I could feel Anne's tummy.

A nurse I had never seen before walked in just at that moment. "What are you doing?" she demanded harshly.

"I was wondering if she showed yet, " I answered, turning to glance at the nurse before turning back to Anne. "I'm her husband, you know."

"No, I don't know," the nurse declared. "You need to stop that. Now!"

I shrugged and answered calmly. "Call security if you want to embarrass yourself, nurse. Or ask the desk clerk."

"He is her husband," said a familiar voice from the door. It was the chaplain, Martha, and she deftly moved around the nurse and put a hand on my back. "How are you doing, Roger?" she asked.

"Not worth a damn, to tell you the truth," I said, trying to smile. "How do you that?" I asked. "You always seem to show up just when I need help most."

Martha smiled. "I don't know. Call it intuition. I oftentimes find myself going somewhere without knowing why. More often than not it's right where I need to be."

"Well, I need to get vital signs," the nurse said crossly. "Why don't you and Mr. Smythe step outside, chaplain?"

"It's Dr. Jahnsen," Martha answered sweetly. "They have different names."

This clearly took the nurse off guard. "Oh, I didn't know, doctor. I still need to get vital signs," she announced.

I nodded. "Let me buy you a cup of coffee, chaplain."

As we walked down the hallway to the elevator I turned to the chaplain. "Thanks," I said. "I think you saved me from decking the bitch."

"Glad to be of service," she replied without thinking. Then she flushed, realizing how that could be taken.

"You're terrible," I teased gently. "I thought you guys didn't think about anything but angels."

"I was actually thinking of Moses," she replied. Seeing my confusion, she smiled. "You know, like Charlton Heston, parting the Red Sea with his staff." Then she shook her head. "We shouldn't be talking like this."

"Why not?" I asked. "It does get my mind off...." I stopped and shook my head sadly. "I'm sorry. It's really getting to me today. Could we go to your office and talk?"

"I'm not sure that's a good idea, Roger," she replied.

"I'll be good," I promised.

"No, as a matter of fact, you would be far beyond good," she told me. "I would really like it, too, but it's too risky. We could go to the chapel." Seeing the surprise in my eyes, she laughed. "To talk, Roger, to talk. Maybe to pray if you want to do so."

"Will you hold my hand?" I asked.

Martha told me later she found the vulnerability in my eyes almost heart breaking. "Of course, I will," she said. "In the chapel."

❦

"I was really surprised," I told Lucy that afternoon. We were sitting at her kitchen table drinking decaffeinated coffee. "I don't know what happened. But I felt a lot better after we prayed together. It wasn't so soul crushing after that."

Lucy nodded. "Yes, it does work. It does for me and a lot of very spiritual people tell me it works for them, too. What wasn't so soul crushing?"

"My whole life," I said simply. "Everything's so up in the air right now. The only solid ground in my life is right here with you."

"And we're facing some pretty scary things here, too," Lucy answered. She looked at me, urgency in her eyes. "Roger, I can't be your higher power. I'm not wise enough or strong enough. I can barely manage my own insanity. No, that's not right. Only the one whom I choose to call God can manage my insanity. No human power can keep me clean. I can help you. I can stand by you. But I can't save you. Only God can. Your God, not mine."

"I don't have one," I said simply. "I never thought I needed it. Where do I find one?"

"It sounds like you made a pretty good start today," Lucy told me. "Did you feel anything? See anything?"

"No, but I had a strong sense that someone or something was present while we prayed. It seemed like a very friendly presence. It seemed to surround us on every side. To hold us like a baby."

"You sound surprised. Why wouldn't it be friendly?"

"That's not the image I got growing up. The God the preachers talked about kicked ass and took names."

"Maybe that says more about the preachers than about God," she suggested. "Why do you think they were right?"

"I guess because that's what I was told as a child," I said. "Everyone seemed to think the preachers knew what they were talking about. I knew I could never measure up to their standards of perfection, So I quit going to church as soon as I graduated high school. Later I discovered how hypocritical they were.

A couple of years after I left home one of the preachers at my mother's church ran off with twenty thousand dollars of church money. He took the organist along with him, too." I shrugged. "Religion made even less sense then."

"So tell me about this friendly presence you felt today. Have you ever felt it before?"

"No, not in the same way. The first time I saw the Grand Canyon I sensed something like it. It was strange, like the Architect was letting me know he or she was glad I liked it. I've had a similar feeling seeing some of Anne's work for the first time. It wasn't as strong, but similar. I never thought of it in religious terms before."

"No, Roger, not in religious terms, in spiritual terms. What you are telling me has little to do with religion. I know because I've studied every major religion there is and some of the others, too. Prayer is where it's at, not dogma or doctrine. Religion is heavy on those." She paused. "Haven't we had this conversation before? Or am I not remembering right?"

"Yes, we have, but I was distracted by your presence."

"And here I thought it was my aura." Lucy gave me a look I knew well. "I don't know about you but all this spiritual talk is getting me all stirred up."

"I thought so. Your aura is getting bright red."

"That's my vulva," she told me moving close. "Be careful you don't get scorched."

"How you talk, Miss Lucy," I said, putting my hand over my heart. "I'm torched."

⚜

The afternoon was growing old when I arrived at the university. There was a book I needed to pick up from my office and I decided to stop by there on my way to Shirley and Ed's. Shirley had left her billfold on the bedside table in Anne's room that afternoon and never came back to get it. So I decided to return it in person.

On an impulse I decided to see if Shirley was in her office but her graduate assistant was locking up when I got there. He told me that Shirley had been in but had left for the library a few minutes earlier. "She's probably in her carrel," the young man told me. "She's reviewing a paper for publication and there's something she needed to verify."

I started to leave the billfold in Shirley's office but had second thoughts. Too many people had master keys to the building, so after I retrieved the book I needed from my office, I headed for the library. Nor was I surprised to find the place almost deserted when I got there. It was a three-day weekend and I saw only a few graduate students still hard at work.

The clerk at the main desk gave me the number of Shirley's carrel and told me how to get there. It was on the forth floor and when I got off the elevator there was no one else around. When I got to the right aisle and looked in the direction the clerk had told me, I saw Shirley's number above the door. I could also see light shining through a sheet of paper taped over the eye level window.

I was just about to knock when I heard a voice coming from inside the carrel. The voice sounded familiar though it was too soft for me to make out what was being said. Another, stronger voice answered it. I recognized that as Shirley's voice and raised my hand to knock. Yet, I didn't. I moved close enough to peek through a crack between the window frame and the paper.

What I saw through the crack surprised me, but not much. Shirley and Helen were locked in a passionate embrace. Helen's blouse was open and Shirley was kissing her breasts. At the same time, her right hand was also out of sight beneath Helen's skirt and the movement of the fabric told me she was massaging the area between Helen's widely spread legs. As I watched, I saw Helen grow rigid and heard her moan loudly, and I found myself becoming aroused.

"Hey! What are you doing?" I turned and saw a security guard approaching me.

"I was looking to see if Shirley was in," I said back in a loud voice. I could hear the two women scrambling behind the door. "I stopped by to return her wallet." I held it up.

"Oh, it's you, Dr. Jahnsen," the guard said. He was a senior in my department. "Why didn't you knock?"

"I thought I heard someone talking and didn't want to interrupt," I answered easily. I turned and knocked on the door.

"Who is it?" Shirley's voice demanded from inside the carrel.

"It's Roger. You left your billfold at the hospital."

Shirley opened the door and glared at me. "I don't like to be interrupted," she said in no uncertain terms. "That's why I come to the library."

"My apologies," I said, handing her the wallet. "I understand completely. Good luck with your research."

Shirley grabbed the billfold and slammed the door. I looked at the guard and shrugged. The young man grinned. As we walked down the aisle the guard chuckled. "I guess it's true. No good deed shall go unpunished."

"Yeah," I said. "But I know how she feels. I don't like to be interrupted like that, either."

"Do you think there was someone else in there with her?"

"No, I don't," I said, chuckling. "It's an occupational hazard. Hang around a university long enough and we all start talking to ourselves." I hoped Helen and Shirley made it out of the library before the guard spotted them. What I'd seen explained the look Shirley had given me when Helen came to my side. It was jealousy, pure and simple. I wondered why the two had decided to come to the library rather than go to Shirley's place.

*Are you kidding?* Jolly answered. *Shirley is a risk junkie. She likes the thrill of it, almost getting caught. Why do you think she took you to that shop in the mall?*

For once I had no riposte. Jolly was right.

♣

A number of things changed in my life over the following weeks as summer wound itself down and the days grew shorter. One was that Lucy began to show. Her hips began to grow broader and her breasts, larger. She was also ravenous. She was still able to run, which kept her weight in check.

I was worried and begged her to switch to speed walking until our child was born. "I don't want to lose our baby," I told her bluntly. "You can burn all the calories you need walking fast and it's easier on your body."

"You just want to see my ass roll that funny way it does when they speed walk," she replied, smiling. "I will when it's time." Then she got a mischievous look. "How about sex? I suppose you want to cut back on that, too."

I nodded. "There will come a time when we need to do that, too. I don't want to harm the baby."

Lucy snorted. "The time to do that is when we're on the way to the hospital," she told me. "I expect you to break my water, bucko." Then, seeing the look of horror on my face, she laughed.

"I'm teasing you, Roger. We'll know when it's time and there are lots of other ways to make love."

"I guess I could let my fingers do the walking," I said, walking two digits up her leg. When I did, Lucy shivered with pleasure. "Or I could smother your breasts with kisses." I grinned, seeing the effect I was having and dodged the couch pillow she threw. Then I moved close, kneeling on the floor and gently lifting her skirt and pushing her knees apart. I leaned forward, running my hands over her tummy and gently fondling her breasts. She was breathing deeply when I kissed her.

Lucy slid forward on the couch and locked her heels behind my hips, pulling me tight against her. She felt me stiffen against her and began to move her pelvis up and down. "Are we going to do it dry?" she asked. "We seem to have a lot of clothes in the way."

I reached down and dropped my trousers. Then I straightened myself so my full length pressed against her through my shorts. "We never have, have we?" I asked. "What do you think?" I pushed back, matching her pace.

"I think I want you inside me," she murmured. "But this feels so nice I don't want to stop."

"Me, neither," I whispered, groaning softly as I felt myself slide across her softness. Only two layers of light fabric separated us and I could feel her moist against me. The sensation was unlike anything I had ever felt. Then Lucy began to move faster and faster, and all thought was lost as the two of us became one in the dance of love.

Over these same weeks change was taking place with Anne, too, though the difference from day to day was gradual and not easy to see. Though she remained unconscious and unresponsive, her heartbeat was strong and regular, and with the constant care of the nursing staff, her lungs remained clear and functional. Nor did she develop bedsores or secondary infections. Other than being unresponsive, she was in good health. The only thing that never changed was that her pregnancy became more evident each passing week. As her tummy continued to swell, she began to look more healthy. This was due to change in her hormones.

After three weeks in the hospital, the doctor recommended moving Anne to a skilled nursing facility that specialized in stroke treatment. I agreed since there didn't seem to be any real alternative other than moving her to a nursing home. However, the facility the doctor recommended was fifty miles away. This meant that I could not visit as often. Nor could Shirley and Helen, though Helen often rode along with me when I drove over to spend an afternoon.

Whenever Helen rode with me, the time passed quickly and I began to look forward to these trips. There was an easy intimacy with her that felt much like my time spent with Lucy. I found myself asking her a great many questions about her life with Roy and his alcoholism. Yet, after a while I also found myself talking a lot about Lucy on these trips.

Helen was curious about Lucy and didn't seem to resent her presence in my life the way Shirley did. When I asked about this, Helen smiled. "It wouldn't do much good, would it?" she asked, then laughed. "One of the wonderful things Al-anon has taught me is not to judge," she added. "Life became so much simpler and more pleasant when I found I don't have be critical. All that does is push people away."

I turned and looked at her. "Forgive me for bringing it up, but it felt like that was what you and Shirley were doing that day at the hospital. Don't you remember?"

"Yes, I do and I've been meaning to apologize for that. Being in recovery doesn't mean we don't fall back into old behaviors from time to time. What it means is that when we do, we apologize and try to make things right."

"I wish some of that would rub off on Shirley," I replied. "She's almost cold to me these days."

Helen sighed. "I know, Roger, but we're lovers." She gave me a wry smile. "As you well know. I saw you peeking in at the library. The point is that I'm not comfortable with the two of us talking about her. It's...." She shook her head.

"I understand that but how do I make things right with her?"

Helen held up her hands. "I really think you need to ask her that, Roger. I'm really uncomfortable with this."

I nodded. "Sorry. I didn't mean to push but she was such a close friend. You're right. I'll ask her myself."

We drove in silence for a few miles before I glanced her way and saw Helen smiling. "A penny for your thoughts," I said and was surprised when she blushed. "I beg your pardon," I added.

"I can't seem to help intruding today."

"Oh, you're not. I was just thinking about that lovely night we spent together."

"Doing nothing," I replied, chuckling. "So you still think about that?"

"Quite often, as a matter of fact," Helen told me. Seeing my surprise, she went on. "Roger, just because I have a woman for a lover doesn't mean I've lost my pleasure in being with a man." She looked down and I could see she was embarrassed. "I was just remembering how big you are and how wonderful it felt to have you explode inside me."

I glanced her way, then pulled over and stopped the car. I reached out and touched Helen's cheek. She looked at me gravely, then leaned across and kissed me on the mouth. When she did, I kissed her back with passion, then reached over and squeezed her thigh.

Helen pulled back and looked deep into my eyes. "Don't toy with me, Roger. Please."

"I'm not," I said. My voice was husky. "I wouldn't hurt you for all the world. I was remembering how wonderful it was, too." I caressed her breast. "I'd show you right here and now, but I don't think this is a very good place."

"No, it's not," she replied, reaching over and taking me in her hand. "I'm not sure it's a very good idea, either."

"You may be right," I replied, nuzzling her neck. Then I sat up and shook myself. "I better get us out of here before we're run over by a truck."

Helen nodded and I started the car and pulled onto the road. Still, she didn't release me for a moment or two. When she did, she gave me a gentle squeeze. "And that's a promise," she murmured, smiling sweetly. Then she leaned down and kissed me, nibbling me through the fabric with her lips. It was all I could do to stay on the road.

The visit with Anne that evening was very disjointed. I was acutely aware of Helen's presence and I knew she was just as aware of mine. Every time she moved close or touched me I wanted to take her in my arms. By the time we left, an hour earlier than usual, it was all I could do to keep my hands off her. Walking down the hallway she bumped me with her hip, smiling sweetly at my response, and when we were outside the door, she took my arm, pressing it against her breast. When she did, I ran my hand run up her thigh. I felt her shiver.

It seemed to take us forever to get across the parking lot, which was poorly lighted. It had been late afternoon when we arrived and the main lot had been crowded, so I'd been forced to park at the back of an overflow area a block away. When we returned that evening we discovered the overflow lot was not well lighted. It was so dark we had trouble finding the car even though it was the only one there.

When I unlocked the door and started to open it for Helen, she pushed it shut and turned and embraced me. Nor did the way she kissed me leave any doubt where she wanted this to end. Then she moved to the front of the car, leading me by the hand. Leaning back over the fender Helen pulled me close and began to open my fly. When she did I lifted her skirt, pushing aside her briefs. Once I was free I pushed deep inside her. She was warm and slippery and I began to thrust.

After hours of foreplay, release came within seconds for both of us as we exploded in unison. The sensation was so intense I almost fainted and I had to lean against Helen to keep my balance. When I did she held me tight against herself and gently moved her hips back and forth, delighting in my presence within her. We stayed there for several long, lovely minutes tightly joined and clinging to one another.

There was sweet sadness when we slowly disengaged and Helen kissed me tenderly. "I'm sorry we can't spend the night together," she whispered.

"I'm not sure I could survive, but who cares?" I chuckled and Helen laughed.

"I do," she told me. "I want to do it again. And again and again. I envy Lucy being able to sleep with you. I'd love to be your girlfriend."

"Really? What about Shirley?"

Helen looked at me seriously. "Roger, she's the consolation prize but don't you dare tell her I said that. I'll deny it if you do!"

"Well, I'm pretty committed to Lucy," I replied lightly. "Did I tell you we're going to have a child?"

"No!" said Helen. "How wonderful! I wish it was me. Even if we aren't married."

"Well, it's a good thing you're past menopause. I seem to be quite virile these days."

"Well, we're a match. The doctor's tell me I'm quite fertile. Of course, with Roy there was never much exposure." Then she looked around uneasily. "We better go. I'd hate to get arrested."

No sooner had I started the car and started to pull out of the parking lot than a security patrol drove by, checking us out as it passed. The guard recognized the car and simply waved as she drove by. "Great timing!" I said and we laughed.

We drove for a long while in silence, holding hands and lost in our own thoughts. After a while I looked at Helen and she turned and smiled back. "I need a little clarification," I told her.

"Oh, dear, that sounds serious. What is it?"

"You said that the doctors tell you you're quite fertile. Present tense. Haven't you gone through menopause, yet?"

"Oh, no, not at all. It tends to run quite late in my family."

"So we just...exposed you?"

Helen laughed. "That sounds so delightfully vulgar. Yes, Roger, we exposed me rather thoroughly. I really get wound up about the time I ovulate, too. So your little guys may be courting my egg even as we speak."

"Doesn't that bother you?"

"Of course, not! Having your child? Never, and don't worry. I'm not about to raise a ruckus."

"How would you explain it?"

"Easy as pie. After all, I am married. I'll tell Roy he did the sweet deed in one of his blackouts."

"You're dangerous."

"I know. Ain't it fun?"

# CHAPTER SIXTEEN

# Phone Calls

It was about a month after Anne's stroke that I got a call one afternoon when I was home sorting through Anne's papers. I was looking for her credit card file. The company had called and left a message, asking Anne to call them back right away and I needed to be informed when I talked to them.

When the phone rang I had no idea who it might be and identified myself as Dr. Jahnsen. A melodious man's voice on the other end told me I was speaking to Dr. Michael Littlejohn. "Sorry to bother you, Dr. Jahnsen. I'm calling about Dr. Anne Smyth. Is this her home?"

I allowed that it was and the voice continued. "I'm calling to find out how she is. I'm the architect she's working with on a project in Jamaica and someone called some time ago and told me she had suffered a stroke. I haven't had word since."

I took a deep breath and let it out slowly. "This is her husband, Dr. Littlejohn. Anne is in a coma and is unresponsive. Things don't look very good. She's in stable condition but that can head south at any moment."

There was a moment of silence from the other end. "I'm very sorry to hear that," Littlejohn said. "Anne is an esteemed colleague and I consider her a personal friend."

*I bet you do!* Jolly Roger piped up but I remained silent and Littlejohn continued. "I need to talk with you about some practicalities. Do you mind my asking the prognosis, assuming she survives?"

"It's very poor," I answered. "The doctor is surprised she's still alive. He hasn't said that in so many words but he's told us not to get our hopes up. Even if Anne comes out of the coma she has a long recovery ahead of her. Months, if not years."

"I was afraid of that, especially after this long." There was a long silence and I waited for the other man to continue. When he did there was something in Littlejohn's voice that told me he really cared for Anne. "Sorry, I'm afraid this is all rather unsettling. I can't imagine how it must be for you. Anne is so brilliant, so full of life. I can't imagine her...." He broke off.

'Yes, she was," I agreed. "Hopefully, she will be like that again but the odds are against her."

"Yes, they must be. Well, I wish you both the best. I'm sorry to intrude but there are some practical things that need attention. We owe Anne some consulting fees and I need to know how you wish this handled. I believe I have your correct home address." He read it off to me.

I told me this was correct. "You can make the check out directly to Anne and I'll see it's deposited to her account." I paused. "Listen, I really appreciate your honesty, Dr. Littlejohn. I really do. There are those who wouldn't have made this call. They would have simply pocketed the consulting fees."

"Please, call me Michael. I believe we're beyond formality."

"Yes, I suppose we are. You can call me Roger. Please feel free to call whenever you wish. Right now I need to go. Why don't you put your email address in with the check and I'll try to make sure you know what's going on."

"Of course. I must say, this is all very decent of you, Roger."

"That's us, Michael," I answered. "We belong to the same club. The Society of Decent Blokes."

♣

"I couldn't helping liking the guy," I said. Lucy and I were seated at her kitchen table savoring a cup of green tea. This was her answer to the caffeine interdict. "I guess I must be getting mellow in my old age."

"Pa-shaw, Dr. Jahnsen," Lucy replied. "Are you trying to get me to show you how young you are?" She took a sip of tea. "Of course, you liked him. Anne has excellent taste in men. Who did you think she'd have a fling with, some scum bag?"

"To tell you the truth, I never gave it much thought. I had no idea she might have an affair." I paused. "You know, I almost started to tell him she's pregnant but I didn't."

"No reason you should. It's really none of his business." She smiled. "Unless you're going after him for child support."

I chuckled. "Not likely. I'm making sure my name goes on the birth certificate as his father, her father. I don't want there to be any question of paternity. Anne and I are married and she and I will be having a child. I thought about having a DNA test done, but I'm not sure about that." I laughed. "Later on when our child hits the teens I may change my mind, but I don't think so." I looked at Lucy intently. "I want my name on the birth certificate of the child you and I are having, too. I'm unanimous about that, sweetheart."

"I am, too," she told me. "You know, you might want to get a sample of Littlejohn's DNA. Just to have if you need it later."

"How am I supposed to do that? 'Hey, mon, can you spare a guy a cuppa cum?' I'm damned if I'll offer him a blow job."

Lucy laughed. "I don't know. Maybe he chews gum and you can get it from that. I'm just the idea person, not the doer of deeds."

Just as she said this, Lucy's stomach growled. "Hey, Dude," she said. "Your kid wants to know when you're going to feed us."

"Funny you should ask. I got some lean pork and a bag of stir-fry mix. I thought I'd whip us up a batch of that and maybe a bit of rice to go with it."

"Stir-fry? Where is it? I didn't see you bring it in."

"You were in the can and I put it in the fridge. I brought some sweet and sour sauce, too, but it's probably laced with MSG and all kinds of other unhealthy crap."

"We could use lemon juice if I had some."

I chuckled and reached into a sack on the counter, pulling out four fresh lemons. "I thought you might say that." Lucy used fresh lemon for a number of things.

"Wow! I just thought you were good before. If I wasn't so hungry I'd jump your bones!"

I smiled. "Speaking of which, I thought I might spend the night." To my surprise Lucy burst into tears. When I started to go to her, she waved me away.

"Don't touch me now or I'll totally lose it. These are happy tears, sweet man. It's all these hormones."

"Hormones?" I grinned. "That's when you doesn't pay them, ain't it?" Despite her tears, Lucy snorted and threw her arms around my neck. "God, I love you! Puns and all."

"Punzinal? Wasn't he that strange fellow in the fairy tale?"

"Yes, the one who liked shagging pregnant women."

♣

The dog days of August were in full swing when I got a

call from Anne's doctor. He was brief and to the point. "There are some care issues we need to discuss, Dr. Jahnsen," he said. "There's not been any new development but some things are coming up down the road. Could you meet with me either today or tomorrow?"

When I arrived at the hospital that afternoon I was pleasantly surprised when the doctor didn't keep me waiting. He showed me into a family conference room and got right to the point. "I was talking with my colleague at the care center. We both agree that she probably conceived in mid March or early April. This is based on the stage of development of the fetus. We also agree it might be a good idea for you to consider amniocentesis. Are you familiar with what that is?"

I nodded. "That's the test to tell if the baby has birth defects, isn't it? You take a sample of amniotic fluid."

"Yes, it's useful for that and some other things, too. In this case we are concerned about the possibility of what you refer to as birth defects. Our concern stems both from your wife's age and her current status. It's enough of a challenge to raise a disabled child for a normal family. To have one with your wife in a coma would put a rather heavy burden on you. At her age the risk of the procedure is significantly higher than if she was twenty."

"So if the test shows that there is a birth defect, you would recommend aborting?"

"Yes. We would recommend terminating the pregnancy. On the other hand, the situation may resolve itself. It is very unusual for a woman in a coma to carry a child to full term."

I nodded. "I understand your concern. Assuming Anne does make it full term, what would you do, a Caesarian?"

"No, actually. My colleague and I talked about this. We think that it's safer for your wife to do a vaginal delivery, if possible. The big concern is the effect that anesthesia might have on her general condition."

"It could kill her?"

"Yes, that would be the primary issue. The other is the effect of the anesthesia on the child."

"How soon does a decision need to be made?"

"Today would be preferable," the doctor said. "Do you need some time to think it over?"

I shook my head. "Not really. Assuming we have a healthy

baby, the child's health has to come first. I've given it some thought and I'm pretty clear on that. What are the risks?"

"The primary risk is damage to the fetus. The procedure could also set of a spontaneous miscarriage and the fetus is not far enough developed to survive outside the uterus."

"What are the risks to Anne?"

"Well, as with any surgical procedure there is the possibility she might die." I was surprised the doctor was blunt. "While this is a very remote possibility, it's one I have to mention. There is the usual risk of infection and anaphylactic shock, too. Normally these are acceptable risks but your wife being in a coma complicates things. All in all, I'd say the risk is fairly low. It's probably safer than driving home from here."

"What if this were your wife? What would you do?"

The doctor shrugged. "I would order the procedure. However, I'm not in your shoes, Dr. Jahnsen."

I nodded. "Let's do it. Is there something I need to sign?"

The doctor smiled for the first time that day. "Always, in this day and age." The form was on a clipboard and he checked where I needed to sign.

"Assuming you're right, it could be a Christmas baby, right?"

"Yes, but it could be earlier or later, too. It happens when it happens unless we induce and that would not be indicated here. Again, any procedure is risky."

I nodded. "Is there anything else?" The doctor shook his head. "Well, thank you, doctor. I appreciate everything you and the staff are doing. Could you page the chaplain for me?"

"Certainly," the doctor replied, dialing a number from memory and speaking to someone on the other end. A moment later I heard the page. "She'll be here in a few minutes," the doctor said and I thanked him.

The chaplain arrived right away and I was pleased to see it was Martha. "We've got to stop meeting this way," I said as I gave her a gentle hug and she laughed. Then I added, "We need to pray. At least, I do and I'd like some company."

"Of course," Martha replied. "Is there something special we need to pray about?"

I explained the situation and Martha nodded, holding out her hand. When I took it there was an almost electric connection and a very sensuous one. Martha started to pull back but I held tight.

"Please," I asked. "I just want to be held."

Martha looked at me for a long moment, then nodded and opened her arms. When I came into them she trembled as the connection encircled us both and, as she put it later, set her whole being ablaze. "Dear God," she said and fell silent. I didn't know if it was an exclamation or a prayer, nor did I care. Once again I felt the strong presence I'd felt before. All I wanted was to be held close in this wonderful embrace.

It was not long after this that Helen rode along when I went to see Anne. She'd made the trip a couple of other times since our tryst in the parking lot but Shirley had come, too. When she did so it had done a lot to heal the breach between Shirley and I, but things were still not as easy as once they were. Nor did I have a chance to speak with Helen privately.

Now the leaves were beginning to turn and there had been no change in Anne's status over the summer. The amniocentesis had gone well and showed that the child Anne was carrying was a normal male. Yet, the doctor warned me once more that Anne might not be able to carry to full term. "As I told you before, this would be most unusual for a woman in a deep coma. We really don't know what may happen. All we can do is wait and see."

One thing that surprised the doctor was that I had asked for a full DNA analysis, one that could be used to establish paternity. "May I ask why you want this?" the physician had asked.

I shrugged. "It's information we may need to know. We may need it for medical reasons, possible genetic disorders."

The doctor was clearly disturbed and I asked, "Do I really need to explain, doctor? I will legally be this child's father regardless of the results of the results. That is the law and it's there for my protection as well as the protection of my child. On the other hand, if the child is by another man and there's a medical problem in his family tree, I need to know, as will my son or daughter when they're grown."

The doctor had little choice but to agree. The results showed the child as a male of mixed ancestry. It revealed that one of his parents was of African ancestry and this confirmed what I suspected. Yet, I said nothing of this to the doctor. "We're all mongrels," I told the man. "There is no such thing as pure genetic ancestry, as I'm sure you know. Some of my ancestors were slave owners in the South and I've often wondered if one of my other ancestors might not have been a slave. There's no shame in this. Look at the offspring of Thomas Jefferson. I'm in good company if it's true."

The doctor was not convinced but accepted this with good grace, as I had suspected he might. Nor did he suggest DNA testing for me to make sure. Lucy, on the other hand, was delighted. "Wow! I guess what they say about you guys is right," she teased, holding her hands a foot apart. "I get to sleep with the catfish aristocracy."

Helen responded in much the same way. "Well!" she declared, arching an eyebrow and giving me a wry smile. "That explains a lot, doesn't it?"

Shirley thought it was downright hilarious. "Wow! What do we call you now, Massa Roger or Dr. Boy? But don't worry, we won't tell the chancellor. You won't have to be his poster child for affirmative action."

"Oh, I don't know. He could dress me up like Kingfish," I said. "I used to watch old episodes of 'Amos and Andy.' That was back in the good old days when we could be Politically Incorrect."

"Yes," Shirley quipped. "The good old days of Affirmative Inaction."

Remembering this, I smiled. I looked across the seat at Helen who was smiling, too. We'd driven twenty miles in comfortable silence, taking in the bright fall colors and enjoying our quiet intimacy. Since we were alone, we were holding hands.

Nor was there any question Helen was delighted with this. There had been an odd, mischievous glint in her eye ever since I had picked her up. There was no question she was amused about something. I had no idea what it was until she laughed. "I can't stand it any longer," she said, turning toward me. "I have something funny to tell you."

"I wondered," I replied, looking her way. For some reason Helen looked even more beautiful than ever.

"Well, the irony is killing me." She paused, smiled demurely. "I'm going to have a baby."

"What!" I almost drove off the road. Releasing Helen's hand, I managed to pull off onto a field ramp and stopped the car just short of a fence. "Don't tease me, Helen," I said. "That's not funny. Not at all."

"No? I find it rather amusing. Guess who the father is?"

"This is for real?" I asked. I was half smiling though she later said it looked like I was about to cry.

"Yes, dear," she laughed. "My doctor confirmed it. Mr. Roger strikes again. You should have seen Roy's face!"

I was speechless. "I don't understand," I stammered.

"Oh, dear. Do I have to explain what happens when the bee puts his little thing in the bird? Or is it the other way around?" When I still didn't respond, Helen said, "Poor Roger. He's got three pregnant women on his hands." She reached out and gently touched my cheek to take any sting out of the words.

"Have you told Shirley?" I asked.

Helen grimaced. "Yes, but I'm afraid I told a lie. After the night we put me in a delicate condition I told Shirley that Roy had jumped me. So when I missed a period, she wasn't surprised. The hardest part has been keeping her from punching Roy out. I pointed out that he is my husband and he does have certain conjugal rights. I also said it had not been unpleasant. As you can imagine, she liked that even less."

Helen paused and looked at me gravely. "None of that really matters to me, Roger. What matters is how you feel about this. Shirley wants me to have an abortion, not that I ever would. I love you and I want to have your child. I don't expect you to love me the same way but...." She trailed off miserably.

I reached out and took her in my arms. Nor was I surprised when she began to cry. "Oh, shit!" she murmured. "I told myself I wasn't going to do this."

"I do love you, Helen," I murmured. "Don't ever think I don't. I don't know what I can do about it except promise to always be your friend. I'll do whatever I can for our child, too. Will you be all right having it? Physically?"

"Of course, I will, dear. That's what I'm built for. Age isn't a factor, either. I've had a child before, you know."

"No, I didn't but that's good."

"Yes, it's supposed to make later ones easier. I was very young and foolish and gave it up for adoption. I've regretted that ever since." She smiled. "Now I have another chance, and with such a lovely man." She touched my cheek tenderly.

I nodded and smiled. "I'm very honored, Helen. I'm also a

little overwhelmed."

"Yes, I can imagine. I was too when the doctor confirmed it. Even when I knew there was a good possibility. Somehow it's different when it's real." She leaned forward and kissed me. "You don't suppose...." she whispered.

"I don't suppose what?" I asked, puzzled.

Helen shook her head. "No, it's probably not a good idea. I'm sure you're busy, anyway."

Then I understood and smiled. "You're asking if we can make love again."

"No, dear. I'm asking if I can spend the night."

♣

I was still a bit overwhelmed as I ran the next morning. Since I was by myself, I took a different route, one that I had used rather often before I met Lucy. She was gone for the weekend, visiting her sister in St. Paul, and would not be back until late Sunday evening. So I ran alone, pushing myself harder than usual, trying to get my mind around Helen's news. Helen and I had made love that morning before I left, and I had asked her to be there when I got back.

"I need to check on Roy and run a couple of errands," she told me. "But I can come back this afternoon. Do you mind if I bring a toothbrush and change of clothes?"

"That would be wonderful," I said. "Let yourself in if I'm not here. I need to stop by the office."

As I was finishing my run, lost in thought, I passed someone walking the same route. I looked back when I heard a cheerful greeting. It was Martha, the chaplain. She was dressed in running clothes and I could see she had been working hard. Her tee was so wet with sweat I could see the running bra beneath it. Her face was flushed bright red.

"Are you all right?" I asked, turning and trotting back.

"Just a little winded," she replied, breathing heavily as she looked at her watch. "I just walked five miles in one hour and twenty-eight minutes. That's a mile every seventeen-and-a-half minutes."

"Maybe you should sit down," I suggested, pointing to the curb. "You look over-heated."

"My home is just up the block." She pointed to a small two-story house with a wrought iron fence in front.

"I'll walk you to the door," I said. "Let's take it easy."

Martha smiled. "Thank you, Roger. That would be nice. We can have a cup of tea on my patio. I usually take a swim once I've cooled down."

I hesitated, then heard myself agreeing. *I better, just in case she keels over,* I thought. *Right,* Jolly Roger laughed. *Just in case she lands on her back with her legs spread.* I didn't bother to respond.

The chaplain's home was tidy. It reminded me of a yacht. There a specific place for everything and everything not in use as put away. Martha saw me looking and smiled. "Sam was diabetic. The last two years of his life he was blind, so everything had to be in exactly the same spot and things had to be kept picked up." Her eyes clouded. "Sorry, Roger. Even after all these years it still creeps up on me." She wiped her eyes with a tissue. "Would you like something to drink? I have bottled water and stuff to replace your electrolytes. I have iced tea, too."

"Bottled water would be fine," I said. "Why don't you have a seat and let me get it? You're really flushed."

"I've got too many layers on," she said, stripping off her soaked tee-shirt. The black running bra she was wearing accentuated her figure. Seeing my look she said, "Oh, I'm sorry. Did I offend you? I didn't think."

I chuckled. "How could you offend me, Martha? We've pretty much seen it all, haven't we?"

Martha laughed. "I guess we have. I know I'm all sweaty but could I ask a favor? I really need a hug." The look in her eyes was heartbreaking and I nodded. "I'll be good," she said, moving into my arms.

"You'll be delightful," I answered. "You always are." When I felt Martha's hands running up my back under my tee, I felt myself becoming aroused. "Just a second," I said, stepping back and pulling off my sweat sodden tee. Then I hugged Martha again. It was much better but the outer surface of the jogging bra felt like fine sandpaper.

"I want to feel your chest against mine," she told me and shed the bra. Her breasts were every bit as magnificent as I remembered them and when our sweaty skin touched it felt very erotic. I heard Martha sigh, felt her pull me close, her hands sliding down beneath the elastic band of my shorts to grip my buttocks. When she raised her head, I kissed her passionately and my own hands found their way to her smooth derrière. Then I began to strip her of her shorts, kissing my way down until I came to her sweetness. There I paused, teasing with my tongue, and I felt Martha's hands grasp my hair, pulling me closer.

Suddenly we were on the floor and Martha turned to the side to take me inside her mouth. When she did, I turned the other way to busy myself with my tongue while she worked wonders with hers. The intensity of the sensation of this always surprises me. It seemed to go on and on, as if time had been drawn out and each moment extended. After what seemed like hours I felt myself moving to a peak and redoubled my efforts. Martha responded in kind and the feeling grew ever more intense until I thought I couldn't take it any more. The explosion took me by surprise and I felt Martha jerking and twitching beneath my lips until we collapsed where we lay. As I drifted into darkness a thought swam lazily across my mind. *Not in my wildest dreams....*

# CHAPTER SEVENTEEN

# Complications

When I awoke I could hear the sound of a shower. I picked up my wet running clothes and followed the sound to the bathroom. Knocking on the door, I said, "Leave it running for me, all right?" "Come on in," Martha called and I found the door unlocked. When I walked in I could see her through the glass wall of the shower stall and slipped inside. "Do you mind?" I asked and she shook her head.

"Do my back," Martha ordered. I had a strange sense of *dèjá vu* as I picked up a sisal glove identical to the one at Lucy's and soaped it with a blue bar of glycerin soap. Then I gently worked my way down Martha's back and hips, pausing to carefully wash her sweetness before moving farther down. When I reached her ankles, Martha turned around and I worked my way back up, removing the glove before I washed her breasts and under her arms. It was very sensual and my hand moving across her skin felt like I was stroking the finest silk. Then it was her turn and by the time she was done, I was surprised to find myself fully aroused again.

"You know, Roger," Martha said as she carefully dried me with a soft towel, her lips lingering and causing me to moan. "You left me a bit unfulfilled."

"I did?" I asked, surprised. "I thought you enjoyed it."

"Oh, I did. It was wonderful but I'm greedy. I want to feel you deep inside me the way you were before."

I chuckled. "Well, it looks like I'm up to it. I'd rather do it on a bed if you don't mind."

Martha smiled and led me upstairs to a large bedroom. As we climbed the stairs the roll of Martha's beautiful bottom inspired me to bend forward and nip her lightly on the cheek. She squealed when I did and shook a finger at me, laughing. "That was naughty, Roger."

"Just call me nautical," I laughed and Martha held her nose.

The large bedroom had a king sized bed and Martha moved

to the middle and lay on her back. "I want you on top this time," she told me and opened her thighs. "Use a little love jelly if you don't mind." She pointed to a bedside table.

I took a tube from a drawer and squeezed a bit of jelly on myself, spreading it with my fingers. When I did so, I was startled to find myself becoming warm. "It's got pepper stuff in it," Martha told me. "It drives me wild. Or it used to when Sam was alive. Maybe it still does."

I applied a little more jelly then moved until I was on my knees, poised over Martha. As I did, she raised her legs, rolling her hips up until there was nothing between her softness and my rampant little man. Slipping myself inside I was surprised once more how smooth the walls of her love canal were and the pepper in the gel seemed to intensify the sensation.

Slowly I began to work back and forth, pushing myself to the depths and withdrawing so far I almost fell out. As I did, Martha began to push back and I found myself unusually aroused. "So sweet," I murmured. "So soft and sweet."

I heard Martha moan softly. "Harder, Roger, harder."

I began to thrust more forcefully and as I did, I could feel Martha squeezing down against me again and again. This aroused me even more and I plunged even harder. Then I passed the point of no return and as I felt the pleasure grow ever greater, I began to plunge rapidly. Yet, just as I released my seed, something hard and furry bounced on the bed and struck me full in the middle of my back, knocking me over and spraying Martha's belly with my semen.

"Pumpkin!" Martha cried out, rolling out from under me. "No!" I felt a hot, rough tongue licking my nose and saw a furry brown terrier eye to eye with me. I wondered where in the world it had come from.

"Oh shit!" Martha said. "Stay here! There are clothes in that dresser." She grabbed a robe and headed out the door. With a glance at me, the terrier followed.

"Janice," I heard Martha call down the stairway. "Call Pumpkin, will you." Another woman's voice said something I couldn't understand. "Of course, I'm all right. You just came at a bad time."

The other voice asked something and Martha laughed. "No, I'm not sick. I have company."

"Company?" I could hear Janice's question clearly. She sounded much like Martha. "What kind of company?"

"Man company, silly. What did you expect, another woman?"

"Well, aren't you going to introduce me?"

Martha laughed even harder. "Not in my present state, sweetie. I'm a little bare at the moment."

"A bear! What's it doing here?"

"Not a bear! Bare as in naked."

"What were you doing naked?"

"What do you think? Do I have to spell it out for you? I have a guest. We were fucking."

"MOTHER!"

By this time I was laughing, too. I had been exploring the dresser Martha pointed out and had dug out fresh underwear, a worn pair of jeans and a black Grateful Dead tee-shirt. These fit perfectly and I pulled on a dry pair of socks. Then I joined Martha at the top of the stairs. "Hi!" I said, waving to a young woman at the bottom of the stairs. "I'm Roger. I'm one of your mother's neighbors. I'm a dressed bear now."

"What are you doing in those clothes?" Janice demanded. "That was my dad's favorite tee-shirt!"

"Your mother told me to put them on. I'm just borrowing them until I get home."

"Well take them off!"

"Oh. All right," I answered, raising the tee and beginning to strip off the jeans.

"No, stop!" Janice told me and I heard Martha laughing in the bedroom.

"Janice!" I said in what Anne called my command voice. "Take a deep breath."

I was surprised when she complied. "Now take another." Again she minded me.

"Now, let's start over. I'm Roger Jahnsen. I live two blocks up the street. Why don't you have a seat and your mother and I will be down in just a moment." I turned around and almost bumped into Martha. She was dressed much the same as I.

"How did you do that?" she asked, clearly impressed. "I haven't been able to manage that since she was fourteen."

"They teach you how in Bear College," I answered, grinning. "I hope I didn't mess things up for you."

"Are you kidding? I haven't had this much fun in years."

❧

I was still chuckling about this when I got to my office. On the way I stopped by Martha's to drop off the clothes I'd borrowed and reluctantly agreed to have a cup of tea with the two women. Pumpkin adopted me the minute I arrived, jumping into my lap and flopping down, licking my hand as I petted him. Janice tried to order Pumpkin to get down but the terrier ignored her, nudging my arm when I stopped petting.

"Pumpkin rules," Martha laughed. "I'm surprised he's taken to you so quickly. He usually doesn't with men."

"I guess I'm a doggy soul," I replied lightly. "Us guys have to stick together. Maybe he thinks he's a bear, too."

Martha laughed and Janice glared at me. She looked like she'd just bitten into a very sour pickle. Martha simply ignored her. "So what brings you our way, Jan?" she asked.

"I had to get out of the house," Jan replied bitterly. "Jerry's off playing golf and when he comes home he'll be drunk as a skunk."

Martha shrugged. "Maybe so, but I've never seen him drunk. He usually has one or two drinks and then stops. He seems to know how to handle it."

The conversation was making me uncomfortable. "This sounds like a family discussion," I broke in. "Perhaps I need to be on my way."

Janice nodded her head but Martha shook hers. "No, don't feel you have to go, Roger. Jan and I can talk about this later. It's not like it's the first time we've discussed it." Janice glared at her. "At least have some lunch with us. I make a very good omelet. That's what I was planning to have, anyway."

I reluctantly agreed to stay and followed Martha into the kitchen. So did Pumpkin, stationing himself to catch anything she might drop. When a small flake of cheese fell to the tile, he was on it like a tiger. After a few moments Janice joined us and the two of them talked about cooking. I was surprised to learn that Martha had been to chef school and hoped one day to be certified as cordon blieu. "The thing is," she told me, "the French are so chauvinistic. They don't think women can really cook, not at their level."

"That's no surprise," I said. "It's where we get the word.

Nicolas Chauvin was one of Napoleon's soldiers and a real martinet."

"And Jean Martinet was were we got that term," Jan added, surprising me by being civil enough to join in.

"Really?" Martha asked.

"Yes, he was the original drill master from hell."

"I learn something every day," I replied. "That sure smells good, Martha."

"Grab your plates. It's almost done."

Over lunch Janice relaxed even more. I learned she had taken one of my introductory courses years before and earned an A. "You must have really busted your butt," I told her. "I didn't give as many of those back then. Not that I give that many now."

"I did," she told me. "I almost majored in business because of that course, but I stayed with English."

"Then you must know Shirley Fields," I said.

"Better than I ever wanted to. She was my advisor. Talk about a real chauvinist." Seeing the look on my face she added, "I hope she isn't a friend of yours."

"A very good one," I told her. "But that doesn't matter. It's much different being someone's student. I hear that she's a real taskmaster, much worse than I am. I'm not talking behind her back, either. I think she enjoys having that reputation."

The conversation moved on from there and I was surprised when the clock in the living room chimed two o'clock. "I really must go," I said. "I promised to be somewhere later this afternoon and I need to stop by my office."

"I'll see you out," Martha said. When they got to the door she looked back to make sure we were alone. "Thanks for staying for lunch," she murmured. "The third degree won't be so bad."

"My pleasure," I murmured in response, then gave her a hug. "That's a bare bear hug," I whispered in her ear. "Consider yourself soul-kissed."

Martha laughed. "Right back at you!" she declared, reaching up and giving a peck on the lips. "Now that you know where I live, don't be a stranger."

"You know," I said, "I don't even know your last name."

Martha smiled sweetly. "Believe it or not, it's Mitchell." Seeing my response, she nodded, "That's right. Just like the Mouth of the South."

"Oh," I said. "I would have guessed Deep Throat." She was still laughing when she shut the door behind me.

✣

Lucy and I had our first real fight Sunday evening when she got home from St. Paul. As might be expected it was over the way I'd spent the weekend and it took place as we were lying on Lucy's bed, resting from a rather joyful reunion. It began with a simple question. "So how was your weekend?" Lucy asked and something in my eyes told her she wouldn't like my answer.

"I went down to see Anne," I said. "Helen went along and told me she's pregnant."

Lucy looked like she had been kicked in the gut. "I see. And I suppose you're the father." I nodded. "When is she due?"

"Some time in March," I said.

"So you fucked her some time in July." Lucy declared. "Why didn't you tell me about this?"

"I didn't want to upset you," I said. "You knew we had been together before and I thought it was an isolated event."

"An isolated event?" Lucy's voice was growing heated. "You mean like the isolated event we just did."

"What we did was part of our life together. I don't have a life together with Helen."

"No, you just have random fucks! Who else did you fuck this weekend?"

"Well, I ran into Martha when I was out running. She looked like she was about to collapse, so I walked her home."

"And fucked her eyes out!" Lucy was almost screaming.

"Actually, we were interrupted by her daughter."

"So you fucked her, too!"

"Actually, I didn't. We had lunch. Could you keep your voice down? I can hear you quite clearly."

"IT'S MY FUCKING HOUSE AND I'LL FUCKING YELL IF I WANT TO!"

I held up my hand. "Stop it, Lucy! I know you're angry and maybe you have every cause to be...."

"YOU'RE FUCKING RIGHT, I AM!" she interrupted. When she screamed this, I got up and headed for the stairs. "WHERE IN THE BLUE FUCK DO YOU THING YOU'RE GOING?"

I turned back and answered calmly, though it cost me a real effort. "Lucy, I'll talk to you and I'll answer your questions but I won't listen to you scream at me."

"**YOU ASSHOLE!**" she screeched and grabbed a coffee cup and threw it at me. I dodged and it shattered against the wall. Yet, a shard bounced back and cut a gash in my leg deep enough to start bleeding. Looking at the gash, I grabbed my clothes and stalked down the stair, dripping blood. Barricading myself in the bathroom, I bandaged the cut and dressed. When I came out, Lucy was standing in the kitchen in a robe, fuming. Without a word I turned and went out the front door.

"Roger, please!" I was about a dozen yards away when I heard her voice. I turned back and Lucy was at the door. Her robe was open and she was weeping. "Please come back inside," she pleaded. "I won't yell any more."

As angry as I was, the sight of Lucy standing there with her belly bulging and weeping almost broke my heart. Turning, I went back and took her in my arms. "I love you, Lucy," I said gently. "I am sorry I hurt you." Then I closed her robe and led her back inside where I held her for a long time.

"Please don't hate me," she asked when her tears had dried. "I try to keep that side of me in the past."

"I can't hate you, Lucy," I told her. "But I can't stand your screaming. I grew up with that at home and it makes me shrivel up inside."

"I need to be able to trust you, Roger." She rubbed her swelled midriff. "Especially now. I need to know I can count on your being there when I need you."

"You can," I answered. "It's not like I'm going around behind your back. I told you the truth and I didn't lie about it. Would you prefer me to have lied by my silence?"

Lucy shook her head. "I would rather you kept your pecker in your pants!"

I nodded. "I know and I do. These aren't new conquests, Lucy. I don't do conquests. These are good friends. For what it's worth, I'm not seeing Shirley any more."

"Yet," She replied. Though her voice was quiet, there was heat in it, and steel.

"Ever. You need to meet Helen. Martha, too. These aren't bimbos. They're friends."

Lucy shook her head. "That's even worse. Bimbos wouldn't upset me so much. Friends are something else. You could fall in love with a friend."

I shook my head. "It's not going to happen. I'm in love with you. You're the mother of my child. I'm not going to leave you, Lucy. Not ever."

"You just did, Roger. You just walked out."

"Only to protect myself. I also came back."

"Didn't you believe me when I told you I was monogamous? I told you that when we first started seeing each other."

I nodded. "Yes, I remember. You also knew I was married and told me that you prefer married men. I didn't think you meant me to be monogamous the way you are. You must have known I'd be sleeping with Anne."

"Yes, but Anne's your wife."

"Who is having another man's baby," I replied. There was a bitter edge in my voice I wished wasn't there. I hate being jealous.

"What does that have to do with anything?"

I nodded. "Nothing, to do with us. The point is that you knew about Helen and Martha, both. This is nothing new."

"Yes, but I don't want to have to take a number."

"You don't. You've already got one. You're already number one, even before Anne."

"What's to keep the same thing from happening to me, Roger? What's to keep you from changing your mind?"

I nodded. "I understand your concern. It's going to take me years and years of being together to show you it's true. I love you more than anyone else, Lucy, but that's what it's going to take to prove it." I paused. "I knew you wouldn't like what happened, Lucy, but I didn't know it would hurt you like this. I thought you were all right with these things. It won't happen again."

"What about Anne?"

"I am not going to abandon Anne or our child. I couldn't live with myself if I did, and you couldn't trust me, either. Am I wrong?" Lucy shook her head and I continued. "So I guess we're going to have to take it a day at a time."

For the first time since the argument began Lucy showed the hint of a smile. "What a concept," she said. "You ought to copyright that. Tomorrow. Right now I need you to hold me." Then she patted her tummy. "Or should I say 'us?'"

§

Things were different for Lucy and me after that. During the week following the fight I sought out both Martha and Helen, and I did so with Lucy's knowledge and approval. Helen understood the situation completely. "Thank you for being so honest with me, Roger," she said. "I pretty much figured that the weekend was our last tango in Paris. I wish it wasn't but we all have our commitments." She smiled. "I don't put much hope in it but Roy was really affected by the news that I'm pregnant. He's still drinking but he actually showed up at AA this week. He's done that before, but maybe it will stick this time."

Martha was surprised to hear about Lucy and but not about Helen. "I didn't think she was your sister-in-law. The way she looked at you didn't fit, though it happens in some families. I would like to meet Lucy sometime. I take it she knows about us." I nodded. Martha smiled. "I don't suppose she'd lend you out from time to time, would she?"

I laughed. "I don't know. You'd have to talk to her about that. Would you do so in her place?"

"Heavens, no!" Martha laughed. "On the other hand, I might. It depends on who the woman was, her circumstances. I know how it is for widows."

Martha paused, then asked. "May I ask a personal question?"

"Of course, you can," I answered. "We have a pretty personal relationship."

"What about Anne? Are you going to divorce her?"

"No. I'm not even considering it. I signed up for better or for worse. If she was healthy, it might be different, but she isn't and I am not about to abandon her. Even if she comes out of the coma, she may not be functional."

"That's got to be a real burden. I hope you have good health insurance."

"Health care and disability both," I told her. "If need be, I can sell the house."

"Well, don't forget Social Security, too. After all these months Anne would certainly qualify." Then she held up her hands. "I'm sorry. None of this is my business but I admire you, Roger. Anne and Lucy are very lucky women, as am I. Or maybe I should say 'blessed.'"

"I'm very lucky to have them in my life. I'm very lucky to know you, too, Martha. You've been a real Godsend. Literally."

Martha smiled again and gave me a look I knew well. "Well,

you better get out of here while the getting's good. Hang around for another two minutes and I'm going to jump your bones."

I even saw Shirley that week, though I didn't seek her out. She came to find me and caught me at my office. Closing the door behind her, she took a seat by my desk. "That's quite a story Helen's been telling me," she said. "I came by to apologize for being such a bitch. I don't know why I got so jealous."

I smiled. "I do and in your place I'd have gotten jealous, too. Helen and I have a wonderful rapport. As do you and I, if you recall. I seem to remember a wonderful evening at the mall. You and I have been friends for too long to let stuff like this get in the way."

"You're being very noble," Shirley said. While her voice was neutral, I knew it wasn't a compliment.

"Horseshit," I replied and she grinned. "I can be as selfish and tacky as anybody and you know it."

"I know but what's a little tacky among friends? I just wanted to clear the air."

"We're good," I said. Then I shook my head. "No, I'd have to say we're great."

"I still have the key."

"I'd tell you to get thee behind me," I laughed. "But then you'd goose me."

Even so, the biggest surprise came a couple of weeks later when I came home for lunch. Lucy was off that day and I was running late. I was surprised to hear two women's voices talking when I let myself in Lucy's door. When I looked down the short entry hall I saw Lucy and Martha sitting at the kitchen table smiling.

"Speak of the devil," Lucy said, giving me a hug and a kiss. "We've been talking about you."

"I wondered," I said, giving Martha a hug and taking a seat between the two women. "My ears were burning."

"Yes," Lucy told me. "She's been trying to talk me into hiring your out."

"What did she offer, two goats or a ram?"

Martha chuckled, too. "I actually went as high as a yearling bullock." She looked at Lucy, who nodded. "What we were really talking about was you. In pretty direct terms."

"Martha was telling me about how you handled the situation

with Janice," Lucy informed me. "She didn't know Jan and I were drinking buddies back in the days she was here in school. Why didn't you tell me about that?"

"I don't kiss and tell," I said.

"Well, us girls don't have that burden," Lucy replied. "I didn't realize Martha the chaplain was actually someone I knew. I think she still lives in the same house as back then."

Martha nodded. "I don't know what Jan will say when she finds out my...visitor was your...?" She held up her hands in question.

"My soul mate," Lucy filled in. "Well, I'm not going to tell her. Are you?"

"No," said Martha. "But I don't want to lie about it."

"No reason you should," Lucy said. "If she's nosy enough to ask, then tell her."

"Oh, Jan's nosy enough. But I imagine you know that."

"Oh, yeah! I could tell you some stories about it."

As the two women continued their conversation, I got up and went to the kitchen. There I washed my hands and looked in the refrigerator, taking out a large bowl of salad. There was also a pot of soup on the stove and I got out three bowls and spoons and took all these to the table. The women moved out of my way a bit but paid about as much attention to me as they would to a waiter. When the table was set, I sat down and put out my hands. The women stopped talking and I asked Martha if she would like to return thanks. I was touched by the elegant, simple prayer she used.

The women resumed their conversation, pausing only to eat and I sat listening. When they were done I cleared the table and out away the food. Then I washed the dishes and put those away, too. Coming back to the table, I interrupted their conversation by kissing Lucy and giving her a hug. "I've got to get back to work," I said. "I have a committee meeting at two."

Walking around the table I gave Martha a hug and kissed her, too. "Thanks for stopping by," I told her. "Try offering her a puppy. She's crazy about mutts." Then I waved and walked to the door. Looking back, I saw both women looking at me oddly and smiled at them. Waving again, I closed the door behind me. I had the strangest feeling I'd just emerged from the twilight zone.

That evening when I returned home, Lucy was waiting for me

with supper on the stove. We ate in comfortable silence, letting our eyes and smiles speak what was in our hearts. When we were done, Lucy brought out vanilla ice cream and chocolate syrup. I laughed. "I know a bribe when I see one. What is it you're after?"

"Nothing," Lucy replied, innocently. Then she smiled and I knew she was about to ask. She surprised me. "Martha is a wonderful woman, Roger," she observed. "I told her you are welcome to visit her any time you wish."

"Lucy," I began, clearly worried.

"No, sweet man, I mean it. Just to be clear, that means taking her to bed if the two of you wish. Just let me know when you do. I don't want any more surprises. It doesn't include anyone else."

"You really mean this, don't you?" I asked and she nodded. "Well, I just have one question."

"What's that?"

"What are we going to name the dog?"

Lucy was puzzled at first. Then she began to laugh.

# CHAPTER EIGHTEEN

# Test Results

My doctor greeted me at the door offered me a seat on the other side of his desk, then sat down and picked up a file. "As I told you on the phone, we have the results of your tests. Not many men ask for these and I ordered the additional analysis you asked. The good news is that your DNA file does not show any known propensity for hereditary disease. So you chose your grandparents well." I smiled at the joke.

"Your ethnic profile is interesting. There are European markers from the British Isles, including those associated with Celts, and there are American Indian markers the testers identified as being Choctaw."

The doctor paused and cleared his throat. "This brings us to the other question you asked. There are no African markers and you are not genetically related to the male charted in the profile you brought us to compare. This raises some medical questions I need to ask." The doctor took off his glasses and looked at me gravely. "I am your doctor, so anything you tell me is totally confidential. The answers to these questions will not even be noted in your file since it has no direct bearing on your physical health."

I nodded and the doctor continued. "It would help me to know why you asked for the second comparison."

I sighed. "The second profile belongs to the child my wife is carrying."

"I was afraid of something like that. Are you going to use this as the basis for divorce?"

I shook my head. "No. My wife is in a coma and has been since May. I know she may not carry the child to full term, but if she does, I intend to raise the child as my own. That's why I needed the information about the second profile. When the child is born I'll have him tested for hereditary disease."

The doctor thought a moment. "I take it the results came from an amniocentesis?" I nodded. "Well, I admire your choice but you need to realize it's a lifetime commitment. What caused your wife's coma?"

I explained Anne's family history and what had happened after the first TIA. "Thinking back, I believe there were smaller events before but we had no idea what they were."

The doctor nodded. "Well, for what cold comfort it may be, knowing may or may not have helped that much. There are the obvious things we can do to help prevent these things but it sounds like Anne was living a healthy lifestyle. You need to understand that you are in no way to blame, Roger."

"I realize that but there's still a small wedge of doubt that says that surely there was something we could have done knowing her family history."

"I understand, but that's wrong. No matter what we do there is always the question of what else we might have done. It can drive us crazy. Your driving yourself crazy will not help your wife or her child."

"My son," I corrected gently. "The amniocentesis did show healthy boy. I just hope Anne can deliver him."

"I know you do but the odds are really against it. On the other hand, I see the odds beaten all the time. No one knows how this happens but spirituality is often correlated."

"A good friend tells me prayers are always answered, one way or another. It may be the answer we want or it may not. What she says is that either way, it helps us if we pray."

"Your friend sounds like a very wise woman," the doctor replied. "It's good to have someone like that in your corner. So do you have any other questions?"

I shook my head and the doctor closed the file and walked me to the door. I offered my hand and he shook it. "Thank you, doctor. I really appreciate all you've done."

The doctor smiled. "That's what we're here for. Don't hesitate to call me if you think of something later."

As September drifted into October, Anne's pregnancy began to become more and more pronounced. Her vital signs remained good and I began to hope that she might carry her child to full term. Even her doctor became more hopeful as did his colleague at the nursing center. Yet, they were both quite cautious in how they expressed this. "Every day she carries is a small victory," her doctor said. "But we may still lose the war."

Lucy, too, was hopeful and the irony of the situation not lost on me. Lucy would be helping raise two children if Anne did give birth. I wondered if she might not have second thoughts over the long haul. I had no doubt that if she had to choose between me and her child, she would choose her child.

Nor did I see this as betrayal. I might have to make the same awful choice myself. I knew it would tear my heart out if it came to that. Even so, I knew I would choose in favor of my son.

It was about a month after Martha had come to visit Lucy that I ran into her in the grocery. "Hello, stranger," she greeted me warmly. "How is Lucy?"

"She is as awesome as always," I said. "She also thinks she is getting fat and ugly. It's all I can do to convince her she's wrong. Other than that, she's the same wonderful woman."

Martha nodded. "She is that, all right." Then she frowned and gave me a stern look. "Why have you been such a stranger?"

"It's not intentional," I assured her. "Between teaching and visiting Anne and Lucy's La Maze classes, the hours seem to evaporate."

"Instant hours," Martha said. "Too bad you can't bottle that. I wondered. Didn't Lucy tell you we had her imprimatur?"

"*Nihil obstat*," I replied, smiling. "She told me that the evening after you came to lunch. I'm afraid I've simply let the time get away from me."

"Well, then, what are you doing right now?"

I smiled. "I'm buying groceries but I think maybe that can wait. There seems to be a widow lady I need to visit."

"There is, indeed. You can leave your car here and ride with me. I'll drop you off when I'm done ravishing you, stud muffin."

"How you talk, Miss Martha."

"It's not just talk, buster, as you well know."

"Well, just so we bolt the door. We were sort of interrupted the last time."

Martha laughed. "Jan's still talking about that. No, she's still scolding me about that."

"Better Jan than a neighbor borrowing a cup of sugar," I suggested.

"Now, wouldn't that be something?"

When we arrived at Martha's house, she used a remote to open the door and drove directly into the garage. She immediately closed the door behind us and turned to me. "I want a kiss," she said putting her arms around my neck. The kiss she gave me was very tender, like those exchanged by lovers after they have made love. "You are so gentle," she said, looking into my eyes. "Why don't we go inside?"

No sooner had we opened the door into the house than the phone started ringing. Martha ignored it, looking at the caller ID. "Wouldn't you know," she said, shaking her head. "It's Jan. Her timing is incredible. I better take it or she'll be calling here all afternoon."

"Hello, Jan," Martha said. "No, I just walked in the door. I haven't had time to check my messages. What do you need?" She listened a moment then said, "Look, I've got a full afternoon." She smiled at me when she said this. "Yes, I've got things I need to do right now. I'll call this evening…. Well, then, I'll call tomorrow…. Yes, I had a hard day at the hospital and it feels like a headache coming on…. No, I just need to take a shower and stretch out." Again she smiled at me and this time she winked. "No, I definitely do NOT want you to drive up. There are some things I want to do if I get to feeling better…. No, just some personal things…. Well, if you must know, I thought I might jump the neighbor again." Anticipating the loud squawk from the other end, Martha held the receiver away from her ear. When the squawk abated she said, "Come on, Jan. Where's your sense of humor? Pumpkin thought it was great fun."

Martha rolled her eyes and listened for a few minutes more. "You know, this isn't doing my headache a bit of good. I'm going to hang up and head for the shower. No! I will talk to you tomorrow…. Well, if it's that much of an emergency, call 911." She hung up the phone and held up a finger. A moment later the phone rang again and Martha turned off the ringer. Then she made herself a note and posted it on the oddly bare refrigerator door. "If I don't make myself a note, I'll forget to turn the ringer back on."

Smiling, Martha put her arms around me and kissed me. Once again there was more tenderness than passion in it and she sighed. "It feels so good to have you hold me," she told me. "Do you mind if we go slowly this afternoon? I mostly just want to be held close."

"Not at all," I answered. "This is very nice."

"Well, it would be nicer if we were both naked, but I need a shower. You're welcome to join me, or not." Then she laughed. "I don't know why I said that, what I did on the phone. It just eggs Jan on."

I shrugged and Martha added, "I wasn't telling a fib, either. Some awful things happened at the hospital today, not to me but in the Emergency Room. I need to talk about them but not now. Right now I do need to wash them out of my mind. I like to imagine them swirling down the drain."

I followed Martha up the stairs and when we got to the bedroom, I followed her lead and shed my clothes. "Oh, my," she said. "I forgot how lovely you are. I'm feeling a twinge of urgency, after all."

"Let's shower first," I said. "Then let's see how you feel. You may just want to rest."

"Not very likely," she laughed. "Not after all that work stalking you at the grocery store."

When we got in the shower, I took a washcloth and the blue soap and began to wash Martha's back. Then I washed her arms and legs, washing the delicate places but not dwelling there. "You're so gentle," she said, taking the washcloth and soap from me and working her way down. As she did, she carefully avoided my now firm erection. Yet, she did wash my sack, very gently. Only when she was done with my legs did she return. Laying aside the cloth, she soaped her hands and then began to carefully wash my length, gently pushing back my foreskin to wash there. Though she was more tender than passionate, the sensation was intense and by the time Martha was done, I felt like I was about to burst. Then she took me in her mouth and I could not hold back any longer. I cried out when I came.

"There," she said, smiling and giving me a kiss. "That will take the edge off." Then she took a towel and began to pat me dry.

After Martha dried herself she led the way into the bedroom. When she lay down on the bed, I asked her to lie on her stomach. "I really don't like the Greek way," she said.

"Neither do I. I want to give you a rubdown. It will help you relax. You may even fall asleep."

Martha turned and gave me a wry grin. "Not likely," she said.

Then she settled back and closed her eyes as I began to knead her neck and shoulders. "Mmm," she said, almost as if she was purring. "That feels so good."

As I rubbed Martha's back, I was struck by how smooth her skin was. I wondered how she managed this. "You want me to rub in some lotion?" I asked.

"No," she told me. "I rarely use the stuff." Then she chuckled. "That doesn't keep Jan from buying me some every year on my birthday, but that's all right. I give it to my friends who need it."

I was done with Martha's shoulders and moved down to the middle of her back, working up and down the muscles on either side of her spine and the areas around her shoulder blades. "You have a wonderful touch," she murmured. "You have no idea what a gift this is to me." She sighed as my hands reached her waist and when I began to massage her buttocks, I heard her breathing change. I remained there, gently working the powerful muscles that formed her derrière until I felt them relax as the tension melted away.

"Now for the legs," I said, starting with her calves and moving up to the strong muscles of her thighs. As I did, I worked with a hand on either side of her leg, massaging my way up until I felt my hand lightly brush the ends of the dark tuft of hair concealing her sweetness.

When I touched her tuft, Martha gasped quietly and began to move her hips up and down. Spreading her legs wide, I rubbed higher up her thighs. She moaned as the soft skin of her labia brushed the back of my hand. Yet, I avoided touching her directly with my fingers. When I was done I placed a hand on the side of each of hip and lifted her gently.

Martha knew immediately what I wanted and raised her derrière until she was balanced on her shoulders and knees. Only then did I begin to explore the mystery between her thighs. When I parted her lips I found her hot and moist. Then I ran my hand up the cleft until my fingers found what I was seeking. I began to massage the spot lightly. When I did, Martha gasped once more and moaned. "Roger!" she whispered urgently. "I'm almost there."

"Go ahead," I encouraged her. "Don't wait for me."

"I want you inside me!" she insisted and I raised myself on my knees behind her and pushed myself deep within her.

Martha cried out as I did this and I felt the spasms of her canal as she began to reach the peak. Then she cried out even louder and began to push back hard against me. She reached back to grab my shanks, twitching and jerking as a tsunami of rapture crashed over her and bore her away. As it did I plunged wildly against her, releasing my seed deep within.

Afterwards, as we lay quietly in each other's arms, Martha kissed me lightly on the cheek. "This is as good as it gets," she told me. "You know, when I felt you coming inside me, I wished I was still fertile enough to conceive."

I looked down and smiled. "Thank you." Then I kissed her on the lips.

"Wouldn't that be a hoot?" she asked. "Jan having a brother or sister young enough to be her child."

"That would be something," I said. "Exactly what, I'm not sure. You know, I have a question. It's none of my business but I have wondered. Why haven't you tried to find someone else? Have you ever thought of one of those dating services?"

Martha nodded. "I thought about it and I even tried it for a while." She smiled. "I didn't like it and now I don't have to. I have a part-time boyfriend courtesy of my full time girlfriend."

I smiled back. "No, I'm serious. A man would be very... blessed to have you in my life. I am."

"Have you seen what's out there?" she asked.

"Not really."

"It's pretty dismal. You wouldn't believe what crawls out of the rocks."

We were quiet for a while after that, each lost in our thoughts. Then I looked down at her again. "What happened at the hospital today?"

Martha shook her head. "Not now, please. Just hold me close, like we've been married a long time."

I did as she asked. After a few minutes, she began to talk, telling me about the child who had died of cancer and the young man who came in with his skull smashed from a motorcycle crash. She'd been the chaplain on call. She was the one who had to be there for the mother when the angry father stalked out of the emergency room, cursing God for allowing this to happen to his eldest. She was the one who had sat with another grieving family as a young man in his teens barely clung to life. He might live but it was doubtful h'd ever be the same again.

By the time she was done, Martha was weeping, barely able to talk through her sobs. When she stopped, I bent down to kiss her on the forehead. But she turned and kissed me passionately, taking me in her hand and bringing me to full arousal. A few moments later she was riding me like a crazy woman, tears running down her cheeks as she made love furiously. It was as if she was trying to burn the memory out of her mind by thrusting herself at me relentlessly.

Then all thought was gone as she shuddered and cried out. When she slumped to the bed, I wrapped my arms wrap around her as if I were holding a child. "I love you, Roger," I heard her say. She told me later she thought she said this to herself as she fell asleep. She said she could have sworn she heard me answer in kind.

I assured her I had. "I don't understand how it's possible for me to love so many people so deeply."

"Oh, it's really quite simple," she told me. "Love is not like money in the bank or even personal power. It's a paradox. The more you give it away, the more you have."

♣

"Well, look who the cat drug in," Lucy said from the kitchen when I finally got home to her place.

"Sorry I'm late." I set the sacks of groceries on the counter and gave her a gentle kiss. There was affection in it, but little passion. "I was shopping and ran into Martha. I'm beat."

Lucy chuckled. "I bet you are. Is this the first time since I told you it was all right?" I nodded and she added, "I wondered why you hadn't said anything before."

"I wouldn't have stayed so long but she needed to talk. There was some terrible stuff that happened at the hospital today and it really got to her. She needed someone to listen."

Lucy nodded. "I bet she needed some of Dr. Roger's sex therapy, too."

There was a slight edge of jealousy in Lucy's voice but I decided to ignore it. I looked at her gravely. "You know, if I'm not around at the moment sometime and you need someone in an emergency…."

"I'll call Martha," Lucy interrupted. "She and I talked about that the day she came to visit."

I smiled. "I should have known."

"I told her it worked the other way, too, to call either of us. I hope you don't mind my volunteering you. She lives alone and doesn't have any family in town. She's not comfortable calling her friends. She doesn't seem to have anyone else she can trust."

I nodded. "You know how vicious small town gossip can be. We're outside that loop, so I think we're safe." I shrugged. "I may be wrong."

Lucy smiled. "That's what she told me. Not in so many words, but that's what she meant."

I chuckled. "Not in so many words or in so few?"

Lucy smiled. "You know us girls. We have to be sure we're heard. So we say it three times."

"Not like us hairy types with two snorts and a grunt."

♣

A week later Lucy and I were out walking along the river trail. It was a glorious day. The maple trees were reaching their peak in a hundred shades of red. This was accented by the yellows and browns from other trees. The sky was bright blue, the air was crisp, and the two of us were ambling along arm in arm, soaking up the mellow October sun.

I was lost in thought, as I often am when we walk or run. So I was surprised when Lucy let go of my arm. I glanced at her and then looked in the direction of her gaze. Someone was seated at the bench at the turn-around holding the leash of a small dog.

"Are we still being discreet?" I asked.

Lucy looked at me oddly. The look on my face must have belied the innocence of my question. "I thought so," she said. She looked at the dog again. "I hope whoever it is picks up the piles. I hate to step in the stuff." She looked at me and smiled. "You're up to something, aren't you."

"What?" I asked. "Me?"

"Never!" She laughed and took my arm again. "It looks like Martha," she said. "I've never seen her here before. I didn't know she had a dog, either."

"It looks like Pumpkin," I answered. "I think I told you about Jan's dog."

"The one that knocked you out of the saddle?" Lucy laughed. "That's who it must be. Look at its tail wag! He recognizes you. He wants to do it again."

When we drew close the little dog was jumping up and down and jumped into Lucy's arms when she stooped to pet it. "Hello, Martha..." she began but the pup was licking at her nose and scored a direct hit on a nostril. Lucy laughed and pulled back. "No more kisses," she said and handed the dog to Martha.

There was room on the bench for us all and Lucy sat in the middle. When she did, the pup kept trying to get at her, lapping with a surprisingly long, pink tongue. "Why don't you hold him?" Martha asked and Lucy took the dog, laughing as it struggled to score another kiss.

"I didn't know Pumpkin was a puppy," she said to Martha.

"He's not," Martha replied. "That's not Pumpkin. He just looks like him."

"Then who are you?" Lucy asked the dog. Having been unsuccessful getting a kiss, the pup was chewing at a button on Lucy's coat.

"That's up to you," Martha said and Lucy turned to me.

"You turkey! I knew you were up to something!"

"Do you like him?" I asked and Lucy nodded. "Martha and I picked him out at the humane society yesterday. He was the best of the litter but you don't have to keep him. This is just a home visit. We can take him back if he doesn't work out."

"What do you think, little guy?" Lucy asked. The pup let go of the button and tried for her nose again, catching Lucy's chin as she leaned back. "Will Roger be in charge of picking up all your messes?"

"Of course," I said. "Unless I'm away on a trip. You can take care of the other end—food and water. Our girl needs a pup to grow up with."

"So it's a girl?" Martha asked.

"The doctor thinks so." She looked at me and grinned. "If it was a boy, I'd think it would be rather obvious if he takes after his father."

Martha blushed and Lucy reached out and touched her arm. When she did, the pup made a bid for freedom but I grabbed him and held him secure. "I'm sorry, Martha. Is that something we can't talk about?"

"No," Martha said. "I'm still not used to our situation. I'll get there. Did Roger tell you my Sam was a big man, too? Big in the right place."

Lucy laughed. "Really? No, he didn't. He doesn't kiss and tell, so I guess it's up to us girls. Do you mind?"

Martha shrugged. "No, not really. Maybe we can compare notes."

"Ladies, please!" I said and the two women looked at me. I was holding my hands over the dog's ears. "Not in front of the puppy!"

# CHAPTER NINETEEN

# Deliverance

I was visiting Anne one day in mid November when her doctor asked to speak with me. As it happened, Shirley and Helen were both with me. The state legislature had declared a three-day weekend in honor of Veteran's Day and the university had cancelled classes. So we were able to drive over during the day for a longer visit. While there was no indication that Anne was aware of our presence, the doctor had told us that there were observable changes in her brain activity after a visit.

"You know she's probably able to hear you?" The doctor had told me this early in her stay at the facility and I nodded.

The doctor continued. "The point is that she may not be able to comprehend what you say. But she can probably recognize familiar voices, especially of those she loves."

The doctor paused a moment. "It's somewhat like the response of a pet, especially a dog. They may not know what the words mean but they do pick up on the feelings behind them. So it's very important that you remain positive and relaxed whenever you're in her room."

"I understand," I said, but the doctor pressed on.

"Pardon me for bringing up what may be a sore subject, but I sense some conflict between you and one of her sisters. It is vital that the two of you come to some resolution of this so it doesn't carry over into Anne's presence. Pretending will only make things worse."

I nodded. "Actually, doctor, they're intimate long time friends of hers, not relatives."

"Oh," the doctor said, opening Anne's chart. "I guess someone made a mistake in the chart."

"No, to be honest, that's what we told the hospital so they could visit her in the ICU. Anne is the only member of her family left. They're the closest thing she has to sisters."

"I see," the doctor said. "That makes me wonder what else

you are not telling me, Dr. Jahnsen."

"I can see how it might. That's the only direct lie I've told. There were some other things going on in her life that were stressful but I don't think any of them are germane."

"I wish you would let me be the judge of that."

"Well, for one thing, her professional career took off last spring and she was in the middle of a major architectural project when she had her first mini-stroke. She was doing a lot of traveling and just had a book published. It was well received and she found herself much in demand. That's all positive stress, but it's still stressful."

The doctor nodded. "That's true. What else?"

I sighed. "How much of what I tell you is totally confidential?" I asked. "There are other people who could be badly hurt."

"I can't be party to anything illegal, but other than that I can remain silent under patient-physician confidentiality."

"Well, her two friend-sisters think Anne is an alcoholic. Helen is married to one and I think Shirley has personal experience with the disease, too. I do know Anne's drinking was causing stress in our marriage."

"I wondered," said the doctor. "Anne does show symptoms of early alcoholism, but it could be other things. How about you? Are you a heavy drinker, too?"

"No. I went through that with my dad. He drank himself to death. At least, that's what his doctor told my mother. She died six months after that." I paused. "Sorry. I'm giving you more information than you asked."

"Not at all," the doctor replied. "It's a disease that runs in families. Is there anything else?"

I thought for a moment. "This is hearsay, all right?" The physician nodded. "Shirley and Helen have told me they think that Anne was having an affair. It could be true, but I don't have any evidence that convinces me it is. Except for the DNA. Nor am I looking for it. It doesn't matter either way. I'm committed to my wife and my marriage."

"That must be very difficult. You're still a young man and I imagine you must still have the desire for sex and companionship."

I nodded. "I do but I have close friends for companions and emotional intimacy. Shirley and Helen are two, but there are others. No one takes priority ahead of my marriage."

"I may seem to be very nosey," the doctor said. "My concern is for Anne's care. What is the issue between you and the older friend—Shirley?"

I chuckled. "I don't mind telling you but it must go no further, no matter what. Agreed?"

After a long moment, the doctor nodded. I said, "I need to hear the words, doctor."

A flash of annoyance crossed the physician's face but he said, "Yes, I agree, so long as it doesn't put Anne in danger."

"It's not my secret but Shirley and Helen are lovers, even though both are married. Yet, Helen has a crush on me and Shirley picked up on that." I shrugged. "That's about all I'm going to say."

The doctor nodded. "You have a very complicated life, Dr. Jahnsen. I hope it doesn't come back to bite you."

I nodded. "Yes, I do. It's going to become even more complicated if Anne has a live delivery. I have a lot of support and our son will have lots of unofficial aunts and uncles." I paused. "As to our visits, I'll make sure that Shirley and I don't both visit at the same time.  Helen and I are all right together."

"I couldn't help noticing she seems to be pregnant, too. Is she…?" The doctor stopped.

"Her husband is a full-blown alcoholic, doctor. That's a fact. Helen says he does become amorous from time to time when he's in a blackout." I shrugged. "Your guess is as good as mine. I know she is one of the most dependable friends Anne and I have, and she is someone I really admire. Is there anything else?"

The doctor was far from satisfied but he shook his head. "I do appreciate your candor, Dr. Jahnsen. I'll call if I have any other questions. In the meantime, I need some things signed." He handed me a lengthy piece of paper. "This authorizes us to do the delivery and to induce labor. That makes it easier to get your wife into position to deliver. I think I told you earlier that we want to steer clear of general anesthesia but a spinal block will be necessary to relax your wife's legs so she can deliver."

I nodded, signing the form. "When are you planning to do so? I need to be here."

The doctor glanced at his watch. "Oh, we're still four to six weeks out. I'll let you know ahead of time."

"There is one thing," I told him. "I want it noted in the chart that there will be no circumcision."

The doctor frowned. "May I ask why?"

I gave him a wry smile. "We're not Jewish. Besides, I consider it a barbaric custom."

"I see. I don't think of it that way. There is some medical evidence that it is useful—hygiene and that sort of thing."

"It's also unnecessary surgery. I don't want my son to be given any anesthesia."

The physician shook his head. "I assure you, it's a routine procedure. It really doesn't hurt them that much, you know."

"You can't know that, doctor. Any surgery is risky and it won't be your pride and joy under the knife." The doctor nodded but didn't seem convinced. So I added, "Not to be unpleasant, but you do need to understand this very clearly. If my son is circumcised, I will file a criminal complaint for assault on a minor and a malpractice suit, too. That's how seriously I take it."

♣

"I really didn't lie to him," I told Lucy that evening when I got back. "I didn't think you and I are any of his business. He did bring up a good point about Robin."

"Robin?" Lucy asked. "Is that what you're going to name him, Robin?"

"Yes. Anne really liked the name. She has always been a big fan of Robin Williams—all the way back to Mork and Mindy. I'm a fan of Robin Hood."

Lucy laughed. "Why am I not surprised? You're a downright socialist at heart, Roger."

"No, I'm just a refugee from Mad Avenue. I'm more of a pirate, I think. I like to swash my buckle."

"Ooh! You're getting me all hot and bothered, Jolly Roger."

"I'll hot your bother!" I declared, giving her a resounding kiss on the lips. "Man the sails. Raise anchor! There's booty at hand!" When I said this, I clutched her derrière.

"I'll raise your anchor!" Lucy laughed, pushing against me. "Ooh! It's already up! We're ready to sail."

♣

A while later she asked, "What was the other point you were going to bring up? You said the doctor brought something up about Robin."

I chuckled sleepily. "I have no idea."

"Maybe we need to jog your memory," Lucy purred, stroking me gently.

"You already did," I said. "That's the problem. You jogged it right out of my head."

"New dimensions in jogging," she replied. "I've heard of being jiggered but never joggered." I was drifting off when she said this and the only answer she got was a snore.

§

The doctor decided it was time to deliver about a month later. The morning it was scheduled I was back at the facility with Helen. Shirley had classes and meetings that day that she couldn't cancel or assign to a graduate assistant.

As we drove to the facility Helen turned to me. "I'm glad it's just us, Roger." She reached out and touched my arm. "We haven't had much time to be alone in a good while."

I glanced at her and smiled. Helen was about four months along and I could see the difference. Her breasts were fuller and her normally lean abdomen was beginning to swell enough to be noticed. Helen had also begun to wear looser clothes and that day she was wearing a loose frock. "You look radiant," I told her and she smiled, suddenly self-conscious.

"I look fat," Helen corrected me. "I don't mind bigger boobs but my butt looks like a sack of potatoes."

"It looks great to me," I told her, smiling. "It always has."

"Lecherous beast!" Helen declared, smiling and moving her hand to my lap and squeezing gently. My response was immediate. "I don't suppose?"

I chuckled. "That's a hard offer to turn down but I don't think it's a good idea."

Helen nodded but didn't take away her hand. "It's probably not but I can't see any harm in it. It's not like you're going to knock me up."

I laughed. "No, we seem to have done that already. Right now I'm concerned about Anne."

"There is that," Helen sighed, taking away her hand. "Don't worry. I'll be good."

"You'd be wonderful," I told her. "You always are, in bed or on the floor. And, especially, over the fender."

"That's reassuring," she said, laughing. "A girl wonders when she starts to get fat."

Anne was in labor by the time Helen and I arrived. This was a surprise. "We decided to start a little earlier," the doctor told me. "This is her first delivery there's no way of predicting how long she'll be. I'd suggest you go have breakfast if you haven't already. This could be a long day."

Helen took my arm as we made our way to the cafeteria. "We could always get a room at a hot-sheet motel," she murmured as they were passing a group of candy-stripers.

One of the aides overheard her and looked around sharply. "It's all right, sweetie," Helen assured her. "We're married." Then seeing the odd look I gave her, Helen laughed. "Well, we are, silly man," she told me.

"That's true," I agreed. "To other people."

♣

As things turned out, it was good that the doctor started early. Anne was in labor fourteen hours, giving birth to a healthy boy of seven pounds six ounces at half past nine that evening. When the doctor came out to tell us, he had other news, as well. "Your wife woke up late in her labor," he said. "She opened her eyes and began to track people around the room. But she didn't speak or respond to our questions. She doesn't seem able to move her arms or legs, either. I'd suggest you both go into to see her now. Maybe she'll recognize one of you and respond."

When Helen and I entered her room, Anne was in bed with her head raised and her eyes open. She watched us as we came near, turning her eyes but not her head. Yet, she didn't respond when we greeted her. Nor did she seem to recognize us, either.

"We have a healthy baby boy, sweetheart," I told her but Anne didn't even blink at the news. "You're awake now, too. You've been asleep a long time." I took her hand and squeezed it gently but again there was no response.

"Hi, sweetie," Helen said but Anne didn't even look her way even though Helen kept talking. Anne kept her eyes on me but they held no sign of she understood anything we said. Her flat expression never changed.

A nurse came into the room a bit later, carrying our newborn. "Hi, Dr. Smyth," she said. "You have a beautiful baby boy." When the nurse said this, Anne didn't shift her eyes from my face. When Anne failed to respond, the nurse brought the child to me. "Would you like to hold your son, Dr. Jahnsen?"

"Of course," I said, opening my arms. Looking down into the dark eyes of the child I smiled and said, "Hi, Robin. I'm your dad. Welcome to planet Earth."

Looking over my shoulder Helen caught her breath and murmured, "Oh, Roger. He's so beautiful." She reached out and touched his silky black hair. Yet, the most striking features of the child were his obsidian eyes and dark complexion.

Helen looked at me and I returned her gaze and nodded. She could see that there was no doubt in my mind that I had not sired this child. Even so, I looked at young Robin with a smile and said, "We're in for some real adventures, son. I can't wait." I looked at the nurse. "Can he nurse his mother?"

"We may have to use a breast pump," she replied. "She can't hold him up to herself."

"Let's give it a try," I said, lifting one of Anne's arms to make a cradle and lifting her gown to reveal a breast. I laid Robbie down and lifted Anne's nipple to his lips. Robbie opened his mouth and began to nurse. "Yeah, little guy," I said. "You know what's good, don't you?"

"Now that's something you don't see every day," Helen said. There were tears in her eyes and she ran a hand across my back. "You're a good man, Roger Jahnsen."

⚜

"So are you going to tell him?" Lucy asked, looking at pictures Helen had taken of Robin. We were at her place, sitting in our usual places at the kitchen table, drinking coffee. I felt tired, almost haggard, and Lucy had told me I looked it as well. Between the drive to the nursing center and back, and the long wait for Anne's delivery, I'd been up most of the day before. I was too wired to sleep that night and had ended up dozing fitfully in the recliner at home.

"I don't know," I answered. I poured myself another cup of coffee. "Right now I'm more concerned about finding a good nanny and bringing Robbie home. I'm not sure what else I'll need."

"I know but you can pick it up as you go," Lucy assured me. "The basics are pretty simple." She smiled, thinking of all the things she already bought for the birth of our child two months hence. "Of course, that's the voice of inexperience speaking."

I smiled back. "Inexperience? One would think that in six hundred years you'd have picked up quite a bit of information."

Lucy smiled but looked at me gravely. "Roger, you need to remember you don't have to do this alone. We're in this together and we have a lot of experience we can call on if we need. Martha, comes to mind but there are others, too."

"Are you sure you want to raise someone else's child?" I asked.

Lucy gave me a stern look. "Are you trying to piss me off? Or are you having doubts about raising someone else's child yourself? It's understandable if you are. It's a life-long commitment."

I shook my head. "Robbie is my child born into my marriage. The law is pretty clear about that. I checked."

"I'm not talking about the law, Roger. I'm asking about your heart, how you feel about it."

"I wish you could have been there when he was born," I told her with a smile. "When I first saw him, something happened. I really don't care whose genes he carries. He's beautiful and he is my son."

Lucy smiled and nodded. "That's what I thought, Roger, but I needed to hear it."

"That's just the point. Robbie is my son but he's not yours. I can't expect you to raise Anne's child."

"I know, but I will if you let me. And if I raise him, he'll be my child, too." She smiled and looked at the floor where the pup lay chewing a rawhide bone. "Just like Bowser. We don't share genes but he's mine."

Hearing his name, the pup looked up and wagged his tail. Deciding he'd not been called he returned to worrying his prize.

"Doesn't take much to please him, does it?" I said, smiling. Then I looked back at Lucy and reached out for her hand. "I'm sorry, love. Things are pretty complicated and it all got to me at once."

Lucy gave me a smile I knew well. "Well, maybe Roger needs a bone, too."

I laughed. "To tell you the truth, I'd be satisfied with a hot shower and a long nap."

Lucy nodded. "That can be arranged. I'll even scrub your back and dry you off, and I promise to be good."

I laughed again. "You're never good, Lucy. You're always great."

"Whoo!" she responded, fanning her face with a hand. "Talk like that and you might get jumped, but I promise to control myself." She got to her feet and pulled my hand. "Come on, dear man. Let's get you rested up. I'll have my way with you later."

Lucy led me into the bathroom where we had first made love. When I started to unbutton my shirt she pushed my hand aside. "No, let me do that. All you need to do is to keep standing until you fall into bed."

"That sounds like a winner," I replied, trying to kiss her but Lucy ducked and kept undoing my buttons. Then she pushed the shirt down off my shoulders, tossing it out the door, and started to unbuckle my belt.

When I felt my pants and shorts being pulled down I felt myself growing firm. "None of that!" Lucy laughed, giving my love-maker a playful slap and taking off my shoes. Getting to her feet, Lucy turned on the water, adjusting it to the right temperature, and held the door open. As I entered the stall she gave me a playful slap on the rump. "God, you have a nice ass," she declared.

While I stood under the hot water, Lucy shed her clothes and grabbed the sisal mitt. Lathering it with soap she began to scrub my back vigorously and then worked on my arms and legs. Then she washed my torso and the front of my legs, carefully avoiding my erection until she was almost done. When she took me in her soapy hand, I moaned and grew even more aroused. "Lucy," I murmured.

Lucy didn't linger over her last task. She rinsed me quickly and turned off the water. She wrapped me in a large towel and gently patted me down until I was dry. Then she draped a dry towel over my shoulders and led me upstairs to our bed. There she gently pushed me down and covered me with a warm blanket, laughing when she saw the tent it made above my erection.

"I guess we need to do something about that," she observed. She ducked under the blanket and took me in her mouth. When I started to move my hips, she said, "Lie still and take your medicine like a man."

I chuckled and forced myself to be lie quietly. Then I gasped as Lucy's tongue touched a very tender spot. Within seconds I was on the edge, exploding a moment later, and was wracked by tremors. Then darkness descended as I fell into a deep and dreamless sleep.

♣

When I woke, the loft was filled with morning light and I was snuggled next to Lucy. I lay there for a moment before glancing at the clock. It told me the hour was half past ten and I sat up suddenly, waking Lucy. "I've got to go," I said. "I'm supposed to meet with the doctor this morning."

"There's no hurry," she told me. "I called the doctor and he said you were exhausted. He told me to let you sleep."

"He did?" I asked. "I've only been asleep for a couple of hours." Then another thought struck me. "What day is this?"

"It's Friday. You slept all the way through Thursday. I got worried about you but the doctor said it was all right. He said you needed the rest."

"How did you know who to call?" I asked.

"I used your phone and talked to Helen. She's the one who suggested I call the doctor. His number was in your phone, too." She paused. "I hope you don't mind my using it." Then she gave me an odd look. "I think she's in love with you, too."

"She's married," I said, realizing as I uttered the words just how lame this was.

Lucy shrugged. "So are you and here we are."

"Lucy, love," I said, taking her hands. "I will never forsake you for anyone. Not Anne, and certainly not Helen. We're very close friends and I think the world of her, but not like I do you. I need you to believe me when I say that."

Lucy looked at me uncertainly. "I want to, Roger, but it's very hard for me. I'm really scared."

"What do I need to do to help you not be afraid?"

"Nothing. It's my fear and it's up to me to deal with it. I just need you to be faithful."

"I'd marry you this moment if I could," I told her. "I consider you my wife."

"What about Anne?"

"The Anne I knew is gone," I said simply. "It's like she's dead. I will never abandon her but she's no longer my wife—not in my heart. She's the mother of my child and I have an obligation to her as long as she is disabled. But my heart belongs to you. Stick around and you'll see."

Lucy nodded and came into my arms, weeping quietly. When she was done she looked at me and said, "I need you to make love to me, Roger. I need you to make love to me right now."

# CHAPTER TWENTY

# Good Old Dad

I was late getting back from meeting with Anne's doctor. When I arrived home, Lucy held up my cell phone. "I think you forgot this," she said. There was an odd look on her face.

I took her in my arms and kissed her. "You seem upset," I observed.

"Not upset, worried," she answered. "You got a call. The number was on the screen. I didn't answer but I looked up the area code. It was from Washington, DC."

I took the phone and punched some keys. The number on my missed calls list was not one I recognized. Then I took out my planner and looked in the address book in the back. "Speak of the devil," I said, looking at her. "It's Michael Littlejohn. You know, the architect Anne was working with on her last project."

"I know who he is," Lucy said, watching me put my cell phone down. "Aren't you going to call him back?"

"I don't know," I told her. "I told him I'd call and let him know how Anne's doing, but he doesn't know she was pregnant. I'm not sure I want him to know."

"Why not? What harm could it do?"

"He might want to see Robin. If he does, he'll know he's his biological father. He might try to get custody."

Lucy looked at me for a long moment. "Roger, I've stayed out of your family business so far. At least, I've tried. Now it affects me and I think you're making a big mistake. You're reacting out of fear, not love."

"What do you mean?"

Lucy looked troubled. "I don't know quite how to say this, so bear with me, all right?" I nodded and she continued. "Your son is not something you own, like you might a dog or cat. He's a challenge the universe... No, let's call it like it is. His presence in your life is a gift from Whomever is in charge of things, given to you for a reason. But Robbie belongs to this Higher Power, not to you. At least, that's how I see it. Maybe Michael is part of what the One I call God has in mind for Robbie's life. So maybe you need to let Michael know, but not all at once."

"All right, but I am scared. I want the best for my son."

Lucy sighed. "All right, here I go off the ten-meter board. To put it in a nutshell, Anne doesn't choose losers. She chose you and I happen to think you're a keeper."

"I'm glad to hear that. So you think Littlejohn may be...?" I couldn't find the right words.

"I think he may be a winner, too, but I don't know the man. I have never talked to him, but you have. Taking Anne out of the equation for a minute, how do you think you would feel about him if you met him professionally?"

I nodded. "That's an interesting thought. I'd have to say, based on one phone call, that he might be interesting to know."

Lucy shrugged. "There you are. Tell him you have a new son and that, as a result, Anne is awake now, but not responsive. It's the truth, but my point is that you didn't get this far not knowing how to handle difficult situations." She smiled. "I think that knocking two women up in the same year constitutes a difficult situation."

"Two women?" I asked.

"Yes, dear man, two women. Isn't Helen's child yours, too?" When I started to answer immediately, she raised her hands and stopped me. "Please, Roger, don't lie to me. I can see it in your eyes. I don't buy Helen's story about her husband being the father. That may be the truth but I'd have to see a DNA test to believe it."

I nodded. "You're right, but Shirley doesn't know. That's why she made up the story about Roy getting amorous. Shirley is jealous enough of me as it is."

"Has there been anyone else?" Lucy asked. She looked terribly vulnerable.

"Aside from Martha, no," I said. "Do you want to know how it happened?"

Lucy shook her head. "The usual way, I'd imagine," she replied dryly. "It happened since your ménage à trois, didn't it?" I nodded my head and held out my arms but Lucy held up her hands, stopping me. "No, I just want to hold myself right now. I'll get over it, Roger, but I need a little time. I need to talk to my sponsor."

"We haven't done it since," I told her. "That probably doesn't help much, but I did stop it after that."

Lucy nodded. "Thank you. Just be patient with me. I just need a little time. I think you need to go now."

I got up from my chair. "You have my heartfelt apology, Lucy. It won't happen again." She nodded and I walked to the door. As I was about to close the door behind me, I heard Lucy call and looked back. "I'm not breaking us up," she told me. "I want you to understand that very clearly. I just need time to get my soul around this. I *will* call."

Two days later I was sitting in my office at the university. I picked up my cell phone from where it lay on my desk and started to make a call to a colleague. When I began to dial, the phone was unresponsive. Checking further, I discovered I had forgotten to turn it back on after my last lecture two days prior and when I corrected this, I could see I had missed several calls.

Afraid that Lucy might have called while my phone was off, I dialed the number of her office at the paper. It was Lucy who answered and when I heard her voice, I choked. "Hello?" she said. "Hello? Anyone there?" Then, before I could respond, she hung up.

I quickly hit the redial button and when Lucy answered, I said, "It's me, sweetheart. My phone's been off and I was afraid you'd called."

"Was that just you who called a moment ago?" she asked.

"Yes," I told her. "I choked up when I heard your voice."

"Goodness, Dr. Jahnsen, you know how to get a girl all hot and bothered. It was on my list to call you today but you weren't at home and I didn't want to leave a message there. I miss you."

"I miss you, too," I said and felt tears running down my face. "God, I've missed you!"

"I'm glad to hear it," she told me. Her voice was as husky as mine. "We need to do something about that, don't we? Are you coming over for supper."

"Are you kidding? I wouldn't miss it for the world. I'll be bringing Robbie, if you don't mind."

"Oh, he's home now?" There was no mistaking the excitement in Lucy's voice. "Of course, I don't mind, silly! I want to hold him and he needs to meet Bowser. He can try out our new crib."

"You want us to stay over?" I asked.

"Of course, I do! We can put the crib in the loft with us. Is there a problem with that?"

"No, not at all. I just didn't want to presume," I answered.

After I had hung up, I checked to see what other calls I had missed. There was nothing critical but I did notice that Michael Littlejohn had called again. Deciding it was time to bite the bullet, I dialed the man's number.

Michael answered on the fourth ring. "Littlejohn here," he said with a distinct British accent.

"This is Roger Jahnsen, Anne's husband."

"Oh, yes, thank you for ringing back. I was wondering if there had been any change with Anne."

"Actually, there has been. Anne was pregnant when she had the stroke and she delivered a healthy baby last week. When she did, she woke up but she's still unresponsive. She can track movement with her eyes but she can't speak or use her arms or legs. Even so, it's better than the way she was. She could have had a stroke during delivery but she didn't."

"Congratulations," Michael responded. "Was it a boy or a girl?"

"He's a beautiful boy."

"Wonderful. Is he...." Littlejohn apparently realized that what he was about to ask was not apropos but he couldn't think of anything else to say.

I understood exactly what Michael wanted to know but I decided to be obtuse. "Is he what?"

"Is he normal? No birth defects?"

"No, none," I answered. "We lucked out there, being older. He's a beautiful baby boy who has his mother's smile and is built like his father." I was referring to the fact that at Robin was born with a longer penis than most newborns. "I'm a runner," I added, clouding the issue. "I was also surprised how strong he is."

"Well, he's a very lucky child to have you for his father. Please keep me posted on Anne's progress. Several of our colleagues have asked about her."

♣

Lucy laughed when I reported the conversation verbatim. "You're terrible!" she told me. "What got into you?"

I reached out and patted her swollen belly. "I'd rather talk about what got into you," I answered.

Lucy leaned forward and kissed me, reaching out to grasp me firmly. "Goodness," she murmured. "I think it's the same thing that's about to get into me again."

At that moment Robbie awoke, hungry and needing a change, and not a bit hesitant to let the world know. "Be right back," I said, scooping my son out of his child seat and grabbing the diaper bag. "Oops, I guess I'll need this first," I added, setting down the diaper bag and picking up a folding changing table.

"You're pretty good at that," Lucy observed as I quickly replaced Robbie's soiled nappie. Then she laughed as a stream of bright yellow urine arced up just as I was about to fasten the tabs. Most of it ended up on my shirt. "Good thing you're not wearing a tie," she told me.

"I wear a bib at home," I answered, securing the diaper and holding Robbie out to Lucy. "Would you mind feeding him while I change?"

"I'd be happy to," she answered, taking Robbie in her arms and putting the nipple of the bottle in his mouth. "Goodness, what a hungry little man," she said as he sucked noisily. When I got back to the table, she said, "You know, I'm going to wear you out. This is an incredible turn-on."

"That might have something to do with the fact it's been several days since we were together," I pointed out dryly. From the bulge in my trousers it was clear that I was wound up, too.

Lucy grinned "I guess it's true," she said. "Abstinence does make the frond grow harder."

"That was awful," I said with a grimace. Then I looked toward the kitchen. "Something smells delicious." I got up and walked in to see what was on the stove.

"Mama Lucy's chicken stew," she informed me. "It's done any time you want to eat. It's simmering in case you want to eat later. I thought we might be distracted at first."

"Definitely," I answered. "First things first. Isn't that what they say in your program?"

Lucy laughed. "Yes, but I don't think that's exactly what they had in mind."

I came back to where she sat. Bending over from behind, I kissed Lucy on the neck and nibbled her ear. Lucy closed her eyes and shuddered. "Don't make me drop Robbie," she said.

"You're not about to drop him," I told her, kissing her neck again. "I'm just fooling around."

"Why don't you fool around with his crib and take it upstairs? I couldn't figure out how it goes together. The screwdriver is in the second drawer from the bottom in the kitchen."

"One of them is there," I replied. "I'll show you the other one later."

"Well, if you can use it to put together the crib...."

"No, I wouldn't want to screw it up," I laughed. "Or the crib, either."

I was finishing up with the crib when Lucy clumped heavily up the stairs. "It feels like I weigh a ton!" she told me. "I've only gained thirty pounds but it feels like a hundred."

"You're carrying another ten pounds of healthy kid, too," I reminded her. "That's what? An additional third of your normal weight? It's not surprising it feels so heavy. That would be like me carrying, what, two-fifty? Two-sixty?""

"How can you love me?" she asked. "I'm so fat and ugly."

"I think you're beautiful," I told her, taking Robbie and laying him on his back in the crib. My son stirred a bit when I did, but didn't wake.

I went to Lucy, who was sitting on the side of the bed. "I think you're beautiful," I repeated. "Even more than when we met and I love you more than ever. You're my soul mate, Lucy, and I feel very blessed to have you in my life."

"That's a word I've never heard you use," she said. "Are you sure you don't mean lucky?"

"Lucky is something that just happens when the odds line up," I told her. "Blessed is when the universe gives us a great gift, one like you."

"Pa-shaw, Dr. Jahnsen! You're getting me all stirred up."

"And I didn't even have to use a swizzle stick," I grinned.

Lucy grinned back and began unbuckling my belt. "Let's see what happens when you do." She pulled down my pants and I sprang out. "My goodness! Would you look at that," she added, gently taking me in her lips and grasping my hips, pulling me even closer.

"Lucy!" I cried. "I'm about to...." I never got to finish the the thought. A sudden wave of passion took me over the edge and

I twitched again and again as Lucy extracted every drop. Then, when there was no more I could give, I collapsed on the bed and fell into a deep sleep.

When I woke it was dark in the loft and Lucy was lying next me, naked. Feeling me stir, she kissed me lightly on the lips and said, "Hi, there, stranger. Going my way?"

I smiled and kissed her back. "What time is it?" I asked. "I need to feed Robbie."

"It's just after nine," Lucy answered. "He woke up about seven and told me he needed to be changed and fed. So I did. What a beautiful little man he is. He and his sister are going to be a handful—two in diapers at once."

"Do you know something I don't?" I asked.

"Well, I did have a doctor's appointment while you were gone. She did the ultrasound and there was something we didn't see in the picture. The doctor said we wouldn't know for sure until she's born but she's pretty certain it's a girl."

"Wonderful!" I said. "So your family doesn't always run to boys, then. They'll be like twins."

"Yes, I imagine they will. Except they'll be totally unrelated, of course—genetically."

I started to respond and Lucy held up a hand, stopping me. "We can talk about this later. Right now the mother of your daughter needs some personal attention—if you're up to it."

"I think that can be arranged," I answered, rolling her over on her back and giving her a kiss that left her almost in a swoon. Then I began to kiss her neck and breasts, leisurely working my way down over her distended belly.

When I reached my prize, Lucy stopped me, pulling me up by my ears. "I want you inside me," she said. "I want to feel you as deep inside me as we can go."

"I don't want to hurt the baby," I murmured.

"You won't," Lucy told me. "She's up above where you'll be."

"You're tight," I told her a moment later as I gently pushed myself inside.

"Are you complaining?" She moaned and a moment later began to push back, twisting her hips the way she knew drove me wild. "Oh, God," she said and as I responded she felt me grow even harder. "That feels so good."

My answer was a distracted utterance somewhere between

a groan and a yelp of pleasure as I picked up the pace, gently pushing in and out. Then Lucy felt herself approaching the edge and pushed back even more urgently. A moment later she flew over the crest and cried out loudly, "Oh, God, Roger! Oh, God!" She began moaning, almost keening, as I rode her over the peak and down the other side. Then, when I found release within her, she came again and we slumped side by side.

♣

An hour later Lucy and I were seated at the kitchen table again, this time eating her chicken stew. Robbie was watching us from his carrier, his dark eyes moving from one of us to the other. The pup had abandoned his chew for the chance of something to eat from the table and he sat intently watching each bite I lifted to my mouth. As I watched, he licked his chops.

"I can't stand it," I said, breaking off a piece of bread and dipping it into the stew. "This won't hurt him, will it?"

"You're as bad as I am," Lucy replied. "I didn't put much seasoning in—just a little salt—so it ought to be all right if you don't give him too much. Just remember to hold it flat in your palm or he'll nip your fingers. He's been doing that lately."

I did as she suggested and Bowser wasted no time gobbling up the bread and licking the juice off my palm. "Wow, that went down without chewing," I said. "He didn't even taste it, did he?"

Bowser made an odd sound, somewhere between a growl and a whine. "He's talking to me," I said, picking up another piece of bread and rewarding the pup. Again Bowser made the strange noise, and again I rewarded him.

"You're creating a monster, you know," Lucy told me. "You're teaching him something he won't forget."

This time Bowser barked and Lucy said sternly, "No, Bowser! When she did the pup looked so contrite that I laughed. He made the strange sound again, this time looking at Lucy, and she laughed and fed him a piece of bread. "All gone!" she said and the pup looked at me.

"All gone!" I said, using the same tone as Lucy. The pup's ears drooped and he looked sad. Then he remembered his chew and after a minute flopped down to worry that some more. Even so, he didn't take his eyes off us.

"He's easy to please," I observed.

"Yeah, not like us complicated types," Lucy said. "Have you

seen Martha lately, Roger?"

"No," I told her. "Under the circumstances it wouldn't have been appropriate."

Lucy shook her head. "That's not what I meant, but I appreciate your restraint."

"I didn't even think about it," I told her. "Who I was thinking about was you."

"Keep talking like that and I'm going to have my way with you, buster," Lucy replied. "No, seriously, I haven't heard from her and she hasn't returned my calls. I'm worried. Would you mind going by and seeing if she's there?"

"Sure," I told her. "I'll take Robbie by. She hasn't seen him Yet, and I want her to see him."

"No, leave him with me," Lucy suggested. "There's something going around and I don't want him to catch it if she's sick." She looked at me and added, "Or to cramp your style." There was no mistaking what she meant.

I reached out and touched Lucy's cheek. She turned her head and kissed my hand. "You're going to be a wonderful mother," I told her. "You're already concerned about our little man."

"All both of them," she murmured, kissing my hand again.

♣

I parked the car at my house and walked the three blocks to Martha's. When I arrived, the house felt deserted. Two neighbors were out in the yard and I greeted them. "Have you seen Martha?" I asked.

The woman looked at her husband and went into the house without saying a word. Her husband gave me an odd look. He looked uncomfortable. "Well, I guess you didn't hear," he said.

"I didn't hear what?"

"About her daughter, the one down in the Cities. She lost her husband, you know."

"No, I didn't know. We have a new baby at our house."

"No kidding? I thought your wife was … sick."

"She's still in pretty bad shape but she had a healthy baby boy. What happened to Martha's son-in-law?"

"Car accident," the old man said. "The paper said it was a drunk driver."

"I guess I missed it," I told me. "When did it happen?"

"I guess it was about a week ago. Where I saw the story

was in the *Pioneer-Post*. Wasn't a word in our paper." His face reflected his disapproval but I couldn't tell if it was due to the drunk driver, the late husband for getting himself killed, or the lack of local news coverage. Given the deep frown wrinkles that lined the man's countenance, I decided it was probably all three.

"I don't suppose you have the daughter's phone number, do you?" I asked, but the man shook his head and without another word, went into the house.

I wanted to leave a note but had neither paper nor a pencil with me. Trotting back to my place, I wrote a brief note, sealed it in an envelope with Martha's name on the outside, and trotted back to her house. I'd just pushed the note though the mail slot when I heard the sound of the garage door opening. Looking around, I saw Martha turn in from the street.

Seeing me, Martha waved and held up a finger asking me to wait. I saw the garage door close behind her car and a couple of minutes later, the front door opened. "Come in, Roger," Martha said, holding the door open. "I'm so glad to see you," she added, closing the door behind me. Then she threw herself into my arms and began to weep.

Not knowing what else to do, I simply held her until the grief had passed for the moment. Then she looked up. "Thank you for being here," she murmured, kissing me passionately before pulling back. "I need you to hold me." Seeing my confusion, she added, "Upstairs."

Locking the front door, Martha took my hand and led me upstairs to her bedroom. Once there, she wasted no time taking off my shirt and pants and shedding her dress and undergarments. Then she led me to the bed and lay down. "I want you inside me," she told me and I lay down gently between her open legs. Reaching down and grasping me firmly, Martha placed me within herself and I was surprised to find her moist and ready.

"I've been thinking about this all the way home," she said as she began to push against me. "I was so glad to see you standing at the door." Then she began to push harder as tears streamed down her face and she reached her peak. Crying out incoherently, she shuddered again and again, and then collapsed, beginning to weep as hard as she had before. When she did, I rolled off to one side and held her in her arms.

Once the tears had passed, Martha blew her nose and turned

to me. "Thank you so much for being here," she said. "I dreaded coming home to an empty house. Even after all these years it was just like when my Sam died, maybe worse. I was so numb at first back then."

We lay quietly for a long while. Then Martha stirred. "We need to get dressed. Janice is coming up to stay for a few days. She'll be here before too long."

I dressed quickly and was seated at Martha's kitchen table when I heard a key turn and the front door open. "Hi, Mom! It's me," Janice called out.

"She's in the shower," I called back. "I'm here in the kitchen."

A moment later Jan walked into the kitchen and looked at me suspiciously. "What are you doing her?" she demanded.

"I stopped by to see if Martha was all right," I told her. "She asked me to fix some coffee. I hadn't heard of your loss."

Jan's eyes clouded when I said this and I could see she was fighting back tears. "Maybe you better go," she said.

I shook my head. "With all due respect, Jan, your mother asked me to stay. She's expecting me to be here so I better stay, at least until she comes out." I started to get up. "I'll let her know you're here."

"Never mind!" Jan snapped, bolting toward the stairs. "I'll let her know myself! Please go."

I rose but made no move to leave. "I need to tell her goodbye," I answered. "It would be rude if I didn't."

"Jan, is that you?' Martha called out from the top of the stairs.

"Yes, mom. Your neighbor's here. He won't leave."

"That's because I asked him to stay," Martha answered, coming down the stairs, drying her hair with a towel. "I didn't want to be alone. Let's all have a cup of coffee. He has a new baby boy."

"Where is he?" Jan demanded.

"He's with his mother," I answered calmly. "We didn't know if your mother was sick and she didn't want him to catch anything."

"I thought his mother was in the nursing home," Jan declared.

"His surrogate mother, then," I said. "Anne isn't able to take care of herself, much less him."

"I haven't seen him," Martha told her. "He was due home from the hospital but the accident happened before I got by.

How's Lucy?" she asked me.

"She's more beautiful every day," I told her, my eyes softening.

"I imagine she is," Martha nodded, smiling. "It won't be long now, will it?"

"We still have six weeks to go," I answered, smiling.

"Well, I expect you to let me know," Martha said. "I hope you'll let me keep Robbie while Lucy's in the hospital."

"This is just too weird," Janice said, getting up from the table and leaving the room.

Martha started to say something to her but I shook my head. "I think I need to go," I told her. "Jan needs her mom."

"Yes, but her mom needs to see Robbie. We'll come by very soon, all right?"

"Don't push her, Martha. She's been through a big loss. You, of all people, know how that is."

"Yes," Martha answered, "I do. I also know that she and her husband were about to separate."

"I'm sorry to hear that," I replied. "I think that might make it even worse."

"It does," Jan said. She was in the dining area looking into the kitchen. Neither of us had seen her come back. "I apologize for being such a bitch, Roger."

"No need to, but thank you," I replied. "It must have been a shock seeing me here." I got up. "I really do need to get going. If and when you feel like it, why don't you and your mother come by for supper? You can see Robbie. Bowser, too."

"Bowser?" Janice asked. "Is that what she named the puppy?"

"Sir Bowser the Chewer," I said, taking out my wallet. "He's the one on the right." I handed them a picture of the pup and Lucy I'd taken weeks before. She was holding Boswer in her lap and he was going for her nose with his long tongue.

As if on cue, they heard a small dog barking. "Oh!" Jan gasped. "I forgot all about Pumpkin," she said as she rushed out of the kitchen. "Coming, Pumpkin!" she called and Martha and I heard the front door close.

"Thanks," I said, taking the opportunity to give Martha a thorough kiss. She returned it just as thoroughly.

"No, thank you," she murmured, tears gathering in her eyes. "It was exactly what I needed. I wish you could spend the night."

"I do, too," I said giving her a gentle hug. I kissed her again, lightly. "I promise to stay in touch."

"That would be nice," Martha murmured, giving me a saucy wink. "Especially if you mean that literally."

# CHAPTER TWENTY-ONE

# A Child Is Born

When the call came, I had my hands full. I was helping Martha and Janice move furniture into the garage and felt my phone vibrate. I was on one side of the door between the house and garage and Jan, on the other. "Could you get that, Martha?" I asked. She was standing behind me. "It's in my left pocket."

"Let's just set this down," Jan suggested, lowering her end of a heavy tall dresser.

"It's more fun this way," Martha laughed as she reached into my pocket and gave me a playful squeeze. It was all I could do to not drop the dresser. "It's Lucy," Martha told me, excited. "She says it's time to go to the hospital."

"Tell her I'll be right there," I said. Turning to Jan, I said, "Let's get this monster into the garage." Together we wrestled the rest of the dresser through the door, setting it down on the garage floor. "I'm sorry I have to leave," I told Martha.

"We're almost done," she replied. "Jan and I can get the rest later. I'll follow you there."

"Thanks," I said. "I'd like that. I'm a little nervous."

When I arrived at Lucy's, she was waiting at the door with the suitcase she'd packed two weeks before. "My water broke just before I called you," she said once we were on the way. "The contractions began to get stronger after you left this morning. I didn't want to call you until I was sure."

This was not surprising. Lucy had experienced several incidents of false labor and she was ten days past her due date. We had made the run to the hospital twice before, only to be sent home by the staff. Her doctor had wanted to induce labor then but Lucy was firmly against it. "I want to give her the best start I can," Lucy told her. "Every ounce she gains inside gives her a better chance outside."

"That's one way of looking at it," the doctor agreed. She was a gynecologist in her fifties. "We may be wrong about gender. The size of the baby seems a little large for a girl, judging by you, and ultrasound doesn't always show everything."

"Big mamas don't run in my family, either," I added. "The women tend to be small and tough as nails. Smart, too, like my sweetheart."

"See why I like the big lug?" Lucy asked. "That's how he got me this way. Sweet talk."

The doctor smiled. Roger's looks and charm were not lost on her, not at all. "All right, then. But if the baby holds off much longer, we'll need to talk about this again."

Once they got to the hospital Lucy was whisked off to the delivery area while I donned scrubs. When I was done an aide led me to where Lucy was waiting. Her doctor was there, too, and she looked up when I arrived. "It looks like this is it," she said. "Lucy is dilating nicely and the baby is in the right place."

*Where else would the baby be?* Jolly snorted. As if she had read my thought, the doctor clarified. "I mean the right position. I don't think we'll have to turn the child at all."

*Turn her what?* Jolly asked. He was on a roll. *Into a pumpkin? Or maybe a toadstool?*

The gynecologist looked at me oddly. "Are you all right?"

I nodded my head and smiled. "I'm fine. This is all a little overwhelming."

"It is for me, too, Kemo Sabe," Lucy. Then she gasped and gave my hand a hard squeeze. "Whoo! That was a big one," she told me. "I think it's time to start counting."

I glanced at my watch. A while later another contraction began. I looked at the watch again as I began calling out the seconds while Lucy sucked in air and puffed. "Hey, they're right," she told me when it was past. "That really helps."

"Glad to be of service, m'am," I replied and Lucy laughed. Then she gasped as the next contraction began, and I looked at my watch once more. Again I counted off the seconds in units of five. This contraction was unusually long and one of the nurses came over and examined Lucy.

After she was done the nurse went to the phone on the wall and asked the operator to page Lucy's doctor. It didn't take the physician long to call back and I heard the nurse tell her that Lucy was dilating very quickly. Lucy was in the middle of a hard contraction just then and when it was done, I passed along the news. "You're opening up fast," I told her.

"Good!" she declared and then almost crushed my hand when another spasm overwhelmed her. By then she was not taking deep breaths but started panting as she rubbed her belly with her free hand.

"See what you did to me?" Lucy growled at me when the contraction had passed.

"You're doing fine," I told her. "It will be worth it. I promise. Just focus on your breathing and think of Robbie. We'll get through this together."

"I want to call her Martha," Lucy told me. "Martha Anne."

I knew Lucy could see I was touched but I didn't have time to reply. Another contraction began right after she stopped speaking and this was another long one. She was panting by the time it was over and my hand felt like it had been run through a wringer. When it had passed, I changed hands.

"What's the matter, tough guy?" Lucy laughed then gasped as another cramp began. This time I managed to cup my hand to take the compression and my voice was much more relaxed as I called out the intervals.

As we moved through the hours, I lost all track of time. I was surprised when the doctor came in and said it was time to go to the delivery room. Once we were there, Lucy delivered very quickly and the gynecologist chuckled as she received the baby and a strong cry rang out. "Well, we were wrong," she said. "Congratulations, Lucy, you have a beautiful baby boy." She handed the baby to a nurse who showed him to Lucy, who held him for a moment. Then she handed him to me.

"We did well, love," I told her, kissing her on the forehead. "I guess we better think up a boy's name."

♣

Martha was the first person I saw when I came out of the delivery room and she smiled at the grin on my face. "It's a boy!" I told her, hugging her close. "Nine pounds, nine ounces and ten fingers and toes!" Then I whispered into her ear. "He's going to be built like his dad, too!"

Martha laughed. "How is Lucy?" she asked.

"Lucy is wonderful," I told her. "Just like she always is. She came through it fine." Then I saw Janice standing behind Martha. "Hi, Jan. I guess you heard our good news."

Janice smiled. "I'm glad to hear Lucy's all right. So many things can go wrong." Then the corners of her mouth turned down. Her mother frowned and shook her head. "What?" Jan asked.

"Nothing," Martha said, giving me another hug. "When can we see Lucy and the baby?"

"Any time," a nurse told her. She had just come out of the delivery room. "She's in the recovery area. We're going to take her to her room in about an hour. It's 2114."

"I know the way," Martha said. Turning to me, she said, "I imagine you must be starved. Why don't you let me treat you to lunch after we see Lucy? We haven't eaten, either."

"I need to check on Robbie first," I told her.

"I'm sure Helen's doing fine," Martha replied, taking out her cell phone and dialing a number. "He was being fed when I called an hour ago." When the number at the other end began to ring, she handed the instrument to me.

"Two boys the same age," Helen chuckled when I told her the news. "You're going to have an interesting time raising them, Roger. Tell Lucy she's a very lucky woman to have the three of you in her life. Robbie is a real charmer. What are you going to name his brother?"

"I don't know. The men in the family are Roger and Robin. Maybe we'll call him Reuben. I really don't care for Ralph or Raymond."

"Well, I'm sure Lucy will have some ideas, too," Helen said.

Lunch with Martha and her daughter was an odd experience. Even though Jan didn't contribute much to the conversation, her presence inhibited the easy intimacy I normally felt with Martha. Jan's dour mood also cast its shadow over everything that we discussed. Finally, Martha had enough.

"For heaven's sake, Jan," she exclaimed. "I know you're sad. I've been there, too. As you well know, I was shattered after your father died. It took a long time to do even the simplest things. That doesn't mean we have to nurse it and rain on everyone else's parade. Think of someone else besides yourself."

Jan gave her mother a stricken look and fled the cafeteria. Martha sighed. "I'll pay for that," she predicted. "Oh, well, seize the moment."

"You can always sleep over at my house," I suggested with a

wry grin.

"Don't tempt me," she told me, shaking her head. "You don't know how much I'd like to sleep with you, Roger."

"You could always stay at my house and Robbie and I can stay at Lucy's if you'd rather."

Martha's eyebrow went up and she gave me an odd look. "I hope you're teasing, Roger. If I spend a night at your house I want to spend it next to you in your bed, whether we have sex or not." Then she sighed. "As much a pain in the tush as Jan can be, I don't want to leave her alone."

"Pumpkin is there with her," I suggested, reaching out and taking Martha's hand. "I'm sure Lucy would be all right with it. Caregivers need respite, too. How long has she been here, two months, three?"

"Almost three," Martha replied. When she did, she looked so weary it was all I could do not to take her in my arms.

"It might do you good," I said. "Let's see what Lucy says."

When we got to Lucy's room, she was nursing the baby. "I hope you don't mind," she said to Martha. "The little guy was hungry and telling the world about it."

"Not at all," Martha said. "It reminds me of a very good part of my life—when my Sam was still alive and Jan was just born. That was our happiest time, when it was just the three of us." With a visible effort she shook off the sadness that had crept into her voice. "Enough of me! This day is about you and the baby. The big guy, too," she added, nodding toward me.

"What?" I asked. I had not heard a word. The sight of Lucy nursing our son had transfixed me. "That's the most beautiful sight I've ever seen," I said reverently.

"It's a good thing I have two of these," Lucy laughed. "Can't you just see me, a babe at each boob. Too bad I don't have three," she added, looking at me and Martha flushed. "How is Robbie?"

"Helen says she wants to keep him," I told her. "She can't wait until her baby arrives."

Lucy nodded, looking at Martha. "I don't suppose you could stay over with Roger tonight, could you? He's been deprived so long his eyes are starting to cross." Then she stopped. "Oh, damn, never mind. I forgot all about Janice."

"Jan is a big girl now," Martha replied. "She has Pumpkin for company." When she said this, I gave her an odd look.

"So you will?" Lucy asked and Martha nodded, her eyes were filled and she looked like she was about to cry.

Lucy reached out and took Martha's hand. "Care givers have to take care of themselves, too," she said.

"That's what your hus...Roger told me," Martha answered.

"It's all right to call him that," Lucy told her. "I think of him as my husband, too. My husband, the bigamist," she added and the two of them laughed.

"Whose special friend sleeps over when my wife's in the hospital having their baby," I quipped, shaking my head. "It's confusing!"

"Then don't think so much," Lucy answered. "Follow your heart and not your head, husband." She pointedly looked down at my fly. "Particularly not that head!"

Seeing Martha's blush, Lucy was immediately contrite. "Oh, Martha, I'm sorry. Did I embarrass you?"

Martha shook her head. "No, I embarrassed myself. I'm afraid my silly mind went.... Oh, never mind."

"It's been a while for all of us," Lucy said, patting her hand. "I really want you to stay over tonight. Please?"

Martha nodded, her eyes turned down. I looked at her but for the first time in our friendship, she avoided my eyes.

♣

"That wasn't so bad, was it?" I asked. Martha and I were sitting in my kitchen sharing breakfast the next morning.

Martha laughed. "No, it was wonderful. I don't know why I feel so uncomfortable about it. "Maybe because I liked it too much. You'd think by now I wouldn't feel that way."

"To tell you the truth, I felt a little strange, too," I said. "We've always done it at your house."

"Except for the first time," she laughed. "That still blows my mind whenever I think about it. We could have been caught so easily."

"Maybe that's what God wanted to happen," I suggested.

"You know, I've wondered that, too. You've been such a.... I can't think of a better word than 'blessing.' I can't see how something so beautiful can be bad. It's made so much difference to me. I was beginning to sink into old age, Roger."

"It's hard to see myself that way, Martha, as a blessing. On the other hand, there's no doubt in my mind what a spiritual gift you are. It seems like a wild thought, but I think what we do when we make love is a form of prayer."

Martha got a mischievous gleam in her eye. "Well, maybe we need to have another prayer meeting before we leave," she said.

I laughed. "I don't think my back could take it!"

However, as I recalled our night together I found myself becoming aroused again. It had started in the car on our way to pick up Robbie. Martha had asked Jan to drive her car home and rode with me to pick up Robbie. On the way there she had reached over and stroked my leg, getting an immediate response. "Are you going to be able to get out of the car?" she teased, giving me a gentle squeeze.

"Not if you keep that up," I replied, laughing. I was wearing baggy jeans and there was no question I was aroused.

Martha laughed and sang a childhood doggerel, "Roger's got a hard on." To which I sang back, "And Martha wants it in her!" It became a game, one spontaneous verse leading to another, and by the time we arrived at Helen's door, we were laughing so hard we could barely stand.

When Helen answered the door, she took one look and said, "If I didn't know better, I'd think you two were drunk!"

"We are," I told her. "We're drunk on life. It's been a marvelous day. How's the little guy?"

"I finally got him down to sleep," Helen said. "We got him so wound up playing buzz lips he had a hard time settling down. I hate to wake him."

"We?" I asked. "Roy, too?"

"Yes," Helen nodded. "He really hit it off with Roy. You know, Roy's been sober for a week now." Tears gathered in her eyes. "It's been like it used to be, so good. I'm afraid to hope it will last." She cleared her throat. "It's late and you need some rest. Why don't you leave Robbie with us over night? I'll give you a call in the morning when he wakes up."

"Are you sure?" I asked.

"Oh, yes. He's a delight and it's late. Go get some rest. I'm sure he'll be up bright and early, ready to play."

"How is Roy?"

Helen shrugged. "Well, he went to bed sober. He says he doesn't have any desire to drink. I'd like to believe him but it's happened before. I don't know what makes this time different."

I looked at Martha. "Robbie will be in with me," Helen assured me. She patted her swollen abdomen. "This is the most beautiful gift I've ever had. Playing with Robbie made me realize that even more." When she said this she was looking at me and Martha suddenly understood.

"What happened was a miracle," Martha told Helen. "At least, that's how I see it."

"Thank you," I told Helen. "I'll be over the first thing in the morning to get him."

Martha was quiet on their way to Lucy's place. When we got there she turned and looked at me. "Helen is carrying your child, isn't she?" I nodded. "Does Lucy know?" she asked.

"Yes, she does," I replied. "She tells me she's all right with it. I think she is." I shrugged. "How about you?"

Martha smiled sadly. "I wish it was me, Roger. I wish I could have your child. Helen and Lucy are so lucky—no, I take that back. Luck had nothing to do with it. They've been given a gift, a real blessing." She sighed. "I think I just hit the wall. It's been a long, stressful day. Would you mind if we just go to sleep and make love in the morning?"

"Of course not," I told her. "I'm pretty tired, too."

Yet, when we got undressed and crawled into bed, I found myself erect. "Sorry," I told Martha. "It's just a reflex. It happens in your nude presence."

"A gallant one," she smiled, snuggling close and taking me in hand. "Do you mind if I just hold him for a while?"

"Of course not," I said, turning and giving her a kiss. "Good night, sweet lady."

"Good night," she answered, kissing me back gently. "Wake me if you get any wild ideas." I'm afraid her answer was a snore.

The next thing I knew I was completely awake and in the middle of a full-blown orgasm. When I could look around, the covers were pulled back and I was still lying on my back. "Sorry," Martha said, looking up. "I just couldn't help myself. I wanted to kiss him and I got carried away."

I somehow managed to smile and nod. I glanced at the clock. It was half past three and it took me several moments before I could organize my thoughts. Before I did, Martha went back to work and any thought of anything but what was happening below fled my mind.

Feeling myself approaching the threshold again, I stopped Martha and pulled her up to me. Kissing her deeply, I rolled us over until I was on top. When her legs opened to receive me, I slipped inside and slowly began to slide my full length in and out gently. As I did, Martha tried to move faster but I kept my deliberate pace and after a moment she relaxed and followed my lead. When she did, she began to moan, almost as if she was humming or singing to herself, and to roll her hips. The sensation was unbelievable and sensing she was growing close to the edge I began to pick up the pace. We finished together at a wild gallop. As she reached the peak, Martha cried out, calling to God time after time before we kissed gently and fell apart.

After a while Martha heard me chuckle. "What?" she asked, her voice heavy with sleep. When I told her, she laughed. "Yes," she agreed. "That was some a prayer meeting, wasn't it?" A minute later, she was sound asleep and I soon followed.

⚜

As tired as I had been, I was awake early, feeling rested and full of energy. Slipping out of bed and into the shower, I washed myself quickly and walked up to the bedroom drying myself with a large towel. When I did, Martha rolled out of bed and stumbled into the bathroom, closing the door after her. Still needing to shave, I got back into bed and pulled the covers back over me. After a bit I heard the shower and dozed off as I waited for Martha to be done.

I woke again when Martha crawled back into bed and cuddled close. As she did, she gently took me in hand. "I'm not trying to start something," she murmured as she felt me growing hard. "I just like to hold him. I'm still a little sore from last night."

I kissed her tenderly and laid back, enjoying the sensation as she stroked me gently. Yet, after a while I found myself becoming aroused and began to move my hips slowly, matching the rhythm of Martha's hand. A moan of pleasure escaped my lips.

"I didn't mean to start something," she murmured. "I guess I better see it through." Ducking under the covers she sought me with her lips and quickly brought me release.

"I just can't get enough of you," she whispered, snuggling close when she was done. Yet, I couldn't answer her just then. I was lost in a pleasant, haunting dream I could not quite recall when I thought of it later. All I could remember, with a sense of sadness, is how wonderful it had been.

When I mentioned this to Martha, she nodded and smiled, and tears formed in her eyes. "I have dreams like that, too, Roger. I think what we're dreaming about is place I call Home. I think my Sam is there, waiting for me."

# CHAPTER TWENTY-TWO

# Calls in the Night

As the days melded into weeks and months, Lucy and I fell into a pleasant domestic life together raising our two sons. At first this took some getting used to, particularly before Paul began sleeping through the night. Every time he awoke, crying out to be fed or changed, it woke Robbie, who demanded equal attention. So both of us had to get up, and normally Lucy fed one of them while I changed the other. "It's a shitty job," I often groused, laughing about it. "Sometimes more than others, but I can't complain too much. The fringe benefits are wonderful."

What I was referring to was the fact that getting up together to tend our boys in the wee hours also often led to what Lucy called "close encounters of the best kind."

The two of us had settled on naming our second son after Lucy's father. When I pointed out that both I and Robbie were given names in the R's, or "arse," as I put it, Lucy had suggested Ringo for our firstborn. "Why Ringo?" I asked when she first suggested it. "That sounds like something out of an old western."

"Well, we could always call him Kid," she laughed. "You know, like the Ringo Kid." I rolled my eyes when she said this.

"I bet you can't name his side-kick," Lucy said.

"I'm not sure I'd want to, but I'll bite. What was it?"

"Dull Knife," she laughed. "His horse was called Arab. It was one of Marvel Comic's first creations."

"Wasn't there a movie character named Ringo?" I asked.

"Yes, John Wayne played the part in Stagecoach in 1939, but that's not who I was thinking about. I was thinking about Ringo Starr—the drummer for the Beatles."

"Ah," I nodded. "That does seem apropos for Lucy in the Sky, doesn't it? So does Paul, John, or George. Or if we wanted to stick with arse, he could be Robert or Randall."

"My parents were randy enough for one family," she laughed. Her eyes grew moist. "Would you mind Paul, after my dad?"

"Of course, not," I told her. Then I grinned. "I'm just glad your dad's name wasn't Harley or Roscoe, or Rasputin. Or even Richard, for that matter. There are enough dicks in this family." It was Lucy's turn to roll her eyes.

So we named him Paul. Yet, unlike his brother, he was not a little man, as the name implied. Where Robbie was long and slender, some wild Viking gene had managed to sneak through with Paul. He quickly surpassed Robbie in length and weight, just as he had at birth. Nor was this a bad thing for Robbie. As a result, he had to learn other, more subtle skills to deal with his more powerful brother. Yet, there was no question who the leader was.

Nevertheless, Robbie learned to be careful not to push Paul too far. When he did, retaliation was swift and painful, though Paul never seemed to hold a grudge. Lucy was the first to mention this one morning when the two of us were enjoying our first cup of coffee and watching our sons play. "Have you noticed what a little sneak Robbie is?" she asked me one day when they were in the park with the boys.

"Oh, yeah," I remarked. "He's a real little spin artist like his dad. Those little eyes don't miss much and you can almost see his mind spinning, figuring out how to use what he sees. He doesn't forget much, either."

Lucy nodded. "Well, Paul is no dummy," she pointed out. "It didn't take him long to learn he needs to watch his brother like a hawk. Robbie has taught him all kinds of tricks."

"Not all of which are good," I agreed. "God help us when the two of them hit their teens."

Lucy gave me an odd look. "Funny you should mention the Boss," she said. "I was thinking the other day that we need to do something about their spiritual development."

"You know a lot more about that than I do," I said, trying to nuzzle her neck.

"No, I'm serious," she said with a smile, reluctantly pulling away.

"I am, too," I told her. "I'm seriously in love. Let's do something about it."

"We will but we need to talk about this," she insisted.

"All right," I agreed, running my hand up her thigh. Then I sighed and released her. "What do you want to do, find a church we both like?"

Lucy shook her head. "No, I don't want the bible thumpers to get at them. It's too important."

"Well, they're going to have to deal with the thumpers sooner or later," I observed.

"That makes it all the more important for us to give them a solid base of spirituality. It's up to us. I don't think it's something we can delegate. I want to teach them a healthy way of looking at religion and spirituality."

I nodded. "You do realize that whatever we teach them, they are going to rebel against it, don't you?"

"Of course, but we can teach them some good habits before then."

I frowned. "I'm not sure what you have in mind."

"Well, I'm thinking of the simple things, like beginning their days with gratitude. We need to teach them that there's nothing shameful about their bodies, too. Especially when it comes to sex and affection."

I nodded. "All right, but it needs to come from someone besides us, too. It needs to be someone they respect."

"Someone like Aunt Martha?" Lucy asked and I laughed.

"You're reading my mind." I shook my head. "I guess that means I'm going to have to learn something about it, too. You can't teach what you don't know." Seeing the look in Lucy's eyes, I gave her a lecherous grin. "Are we done talking about this?" I asked, running my hand up her leg to her hip.

"For the moment," she told me. "I think it's time for our boys to take a nap."

⚜

We were awakened in the early hours one morning not long after that. I was the one who answered the phone. Nor could Lucy tell who was calling from my end of the short conversation. "That was Helen," I told her, getting up and reaching for my clothes. "She needs a ride to the hospital. Roy is drunk and Shirley has the flu." I shrugged. "I hope it doesn't piss you off, but I think I need to be there."

"Go!" Lucy told me. "Let me know when you can. Wait!" She added, getting up and giving me a hug. "It's all right. You need to do this." Then she smiled. "I hope you haven't forgotten what you learned in LaMaze."

"No, not at all. I hope they let me help."

Lucy gave me a wry grin. "Tell them you're the father of the child. Now get out of here, you big lug."

✤

It was late that afternoon when I called. "It was an easy delivery and Helen's all right," I told Lucy. "She had a healthy baby girl—seven pounds, six ounces." Then I laughed. "You should have seen their faces when Helen insisted on having me with her. She told them I was the father."

I told Lucy that I needed to stay for a while, that I'd be home in an hour or so. "I'm beat," I added. Lucy told me she could hear the weariness in my voice.

"You're a good man, Jolly Roger," she told me. "You can tell me all about it when you get home."

What I didn't tell Lucy was what Helen had whispered in my ear on their way to the delivery room. "I'm glad it's you here, not Shirley. But don't tell her I said so."

"My lips are sealed," I replied.

"God, I hope not!" Helen replied, giving me a bawdy wink that made the nurses smile. Then her face softened and her eyes grew moist. "I hope you don't mind, Roger," she said. "I want to name her Anne."

"I don't mind," I told her. "I think Anne would be honored if she could understand. I know I am."

Then Helen grinned. "Although I guess I could name her after her dad—Rogella. Shirley would never forgive me."

"Neither would your daughter," I laughed. "How about Rogene? Or Rogina!"

"No, Dana Dana Roganna!" Helen quipped and the nurse left, shaking her head.

✤

The second call in the night came two weeks later, long after midnight. When I answered my cell phone I wondered who would be calling so late. A ringing phone in the wee hours of the morning is almost always bad news. It means someone is in trouble or something bad has happened. My personal phone was unlisted and it was rare to get wrong numbers or calls from drunks. So my first thought when I heard it ring was that it was bad news about Anne.

The call turned out to be from someone well on the way to being drunk. I was about to hang up when I recognized the gentle Caribbean accent. "Who is this?" I asked, irritated at being awakened by a drunken fool.

"Oh, sorry, old man," the caller replied. "I must have got you up. I'm terribly sorry. I'm in Ankara in the middle of bloody Turkey. Must have got the time zones wrong. Terribly sorry."

"Why are you calling?" I asked, still not completely sure who was on the other end of the line.

"Oh, that. Well, I'm going to be in Minneapolis in about three weeks. Wondered if I might drive up and visit Anne. I hope you don't mind."

"Is this Michael Littlejohn?" I tried to keep the irritation out of my voice.

"Oh, yes, sorry. Should have told you right off. What time is it there? It's almost nine in the morning here."

"About one in the morning, if it matters." I wondered why Littlejohn was drunk so early in the day. Then I realized the man might be just then getting to bed.

"Oh, dear. No wonder you're out of sorts. I do apologize. I had it at half past nine there. Perhaps I should call later."

"Don't worry about it. When are you going to be here?"

"It looks like the twenty-seventh, if that's convenient. I thought I'd rent a car in Minneapolis between meetings."

"You better plan on spending the night. It's a four-hour drive up here from the Cities—from Minneapolis."

"I didn't realize it was that far. I assume it's a large enough place to have a decent hotel."

"Yes," I said dryly. "We got indoor pluming last year and all the rooms are electrified."

There was dead silence, then a bust of laughter from the other end. "Sorry. I deserved that. You wouldn't believe what I've seen in the way of hotels in the last ten days here. It's unbelievable."

"I can imagine," I told him. "What time I can expect you? I've got classes that morning."

"How about having a late lunch together?" Littlejohn asked. "I plan to get an early start and that will give me plenty of time to drive up there."

"Just be sure to bring a shotgun," I told him.

"What in the world for? Do you have bears?"

"Yes, but you won't need it for bears. It's the mosquitoes. Up here they're as big as buzzards."

When I hung up Lucy was looking at me oddly. "So Michael Littlejohn is coming to town. I assume it's to visit Anne. Are you going to let him see Robbie?"

I shook my head. "I don't think so. That might confuse things even more. I don't want to risk it. I know how I'd respond in his place."

"Care to share that?" Lucy asked.

"It's the same old thing. Robbie is my son, legally and morally. I don't want to put that at risk."

"Robbie's going to want to meet his biological father some day," she answered. "I'd think the sooner that is, the better."

"I'm not even positive that Littlejohn is his father."

"You aren't? Do you seriously think it might be someone else?"

"No, but I could be wrong."

The third call waking us in the night came at just after four in the morning six weeks after Helen gave birth to her daughter. This time there was no urgency, though I still had to get dressed and respond. The call was from the doctor at the stroke care center, Anne's doctor, letting me know that Anne had suffered a third and fatal stroke.

"I know this is hard news," the doctor said. "On the other hand, it may turn out for the best. In my mind it was never a matter of if this would happen, but when."

When I first got the news, I was stunned, unable to do more than respond to the doctor in monosyllables. Then, when Lucy asked who had called, I choked and fell apart when I tried to answer. As I grasped my head in my hands and buried it between my knees all the grief of the last year broke free, releasing deep sobs so wrenching I could barely breathe.

"It's Anne," I managed to say when I caught my breath. Then I choked and began to weep again.

"Something happened to Anne?" Lucy asked, distracted by the wailing of Robbie and Paul who had been frightened by my cries. Getting out of bed she picked up both boys and comforted them as best she could.

"She's dead," I managed to gasp. "She had another stroke." I reached for Paul and Lucy handed him over. Once he was in my arms, he stopped crying and Robbie did, too.

"Wow," I said softly a few minutes later. My voice was flat, even to my ears, and it sounded like it was coming from a great distance. "I really lost it, didn't I? I'm sorry."

"You never have to apologize for how you feel," Lucy told me. She put her free arm around my shoulder. "I'm not surprised."

"You're not?" I asked. I felt drained of emotion. I got up and carried Paul to the changing table. "Paul messed his pants," I told Lucy as I began to unbutton the bottom of Paul's sleeper.

"Robbie did, too," she replied. "You know, I've been expecting this, Roger. You've been the strong one carrying all the rest of us. I've been worried about you. Something had to give."

I handed her Paul and reached for Robbie. "No," Lucy said. "Let me change him. You sit down. You look as white as a ghost."

I nodded dumbly. "I feel like I've run a full marathon," I said. "I'm beat."

"Grief is hard work, love," Lucy replied. "Do you want to talk about it?"

I sat down on the bed and began pulling on my socks. "No, not right now. I need to get over to the care center."

"You're not in any shape to drive," Lucy pointed out. "I'll take you. Let me call Martha."

I started to protest but Lucy was adamant. "No, Roger, I mean it. If you don't want me taking you, at least let Martha."

I nodded dumbly. "Yeah, it might be a little awkward if you did. They know Martha. She's been there and somebody needs to stay with the boys."

Martha was there within twenty minutes. "Oh, Roger," she said as she came in the door. She took me into her arms like a small child. "I'm so sorry."

I nodded dumbly, tears running down my cheeks. "I thought I was ready for this. Apparently not."

"Nobody is," Martha assured me. Turning to Lucy she said, "I don't know when we'll be back. I'll stay there with him until he's ready to come home."

"Take your time," Lucy replied. "I'm staying home from work today. I'll call the university and let them know, too."

♣

Later I had trouble remembering much about my visit to the care center, though Martha remembered it all. I insisted that she come with me when I talked to the doctor. "Martha is my pastor," I said. "I'm having a hard time with this."

"I know you must be," the doctor told me. Yet, I know he wondered, curious about the look on Martha's face when I said this. He must have sensed that there was far more to our relationship that this. "You've had a long, tough ordeal, Dr. Jahnsen, and it's not over yet."

Later, when the doctor asked what church Martha was with, she told him, "I'm a lay pastor. I was the chaplain on duty when Anne had her first stroke and Roger has come to me for spiritual support ever since." As she said this, Martha told me, she asked forgiveness, reminding the God of her understanding that it was none of the doctor's business, anyway. *After all, I'm the one who helped him learn how to pray,* she added. She said she could have sworn she heard a celestial chuckle.

When all the arrangements had been made and we were done at the nursing center, Martha got behind the wheel while I collapsed in the passenger seat. Leaning my seat back all the way, I was asleep before we were out of the parking lot and didn't awaken until Martha dropped me off at Lucy's. Together the two women got me undressed and into bed.

"He's beautiful, isn't he?" I heard Lucy observe as they draped the top sheet over me.

"Yes," Martha replied. "Thank you for sharing him with me. I don't know what I would have done without him."

Martha told me later about the conversation that followed. She said Lucy looked at her and smiled. "Why don't you stay with him? I need to take care of the boys and catch any phone calls." To be clear what she was saying, Lucy apparently held up a corner of the bed clothes.

"I'd like that," Martha replied. "Do you have a night gown that will fit me?"

Lucy snorted. "Is that what you wear when you're with him? I wear a smile." Seeing Martha's blush she reached out and touched her cheek. "I'll get you a night gown if that's what you want."

Martha laughed. "Never mind. What I need is a shower and a bath robe." Twenty minutes later she was asleep, nestled close to me, her arm across my bare stomach. Nor was she wearing a night gown. At least, she wasn't when I woke up.

♣

*Adams.* Martha awakened just after noon. When she turned to the warm body cuddled close to her, intending to give Roger a good morning kiss, she was surprised to find herself looking into the eyes of Lucy. "Good morning," Lucy whispered. She leaned forward and kissed Martha lightly on the lips.

"Where's Roger?" Martha asked, flushing. Everything she had ever been taught told her to pull back, but she found herself strangely reluctant. Lucy's body was soft and Martha found it quite sensuous. Nor did she turn away when Lucy kissed her once again. This time she felt the first tinglings of arousal.

"Roger is up and tending to the boys," Lucy answered, kissing Martha gently on the neck and throat. Then she lowered her head and kissed Martha's breast, lingering at the nipple, teasing it with her tongue. Martha gasped, pulling Lucy closer, then lifted Lucy's face and kissed her full on the lips. Then she surprised herself by inviting a response with her tongue.

Lucy rolled on top, deftly using her tongue to tease Martha's lips and neck. Without thinking, Martha opened her legs and felt Lucy's soft nest against hers. She began to gently push herself against Lucy. When she did, Lucy kissed her like she'd never been kissed before. She began to work herself down Martha's breast until she reached the softness below her belly. There she began to flail Martha with her tongue. Martha cried out as she came without warning, holding Lucy's head tight against her warmth and crying out to God.

When Martha released her, Lucy slid back up Martha's body and held her close. Martha stroked Lucy's cheek gently. "Thank you," she said. "I've never done that before."

"Neither have I," Lucy answered, kissing her full on the lips. "I just did what I like Roger to do to me."

Martha was surprised to taste herself on Lucy's lips. The taste was not what she might have expected. It was mellow and fruity, like apples or peaches allowed to ripen on the tree. "Is it my turn now?" Martha asked.

"Only if you want to," Lucy told her, smiling. "I get as much pleasure giving as receiving, but I need to shower first. I'm afraid I'm not very fresh."

Just then Roger's head appeared over the top step of the loft. "I don't want to interrupt," he said, smiling. "It sounded like the two of you were having a prayer meeting."

Martha blushed, pulling the sheet over herself. "I hope you don't mind," she told him. "It was wonderful."

"Then I'm glad it happened," he answered, climbing the rest of the stairs and slipping off his clothes. Getting under the covers, he added, "The boys are asleep. Are you two done for the moment or would you like to rumble some more?"

Martha and Lucy looked at each other and smiled. Without a word they grabbed Roger and pinned him to the bed. Then they went to work and when they were finished, he was out like a light. "Fuck you, death!" Lucy murmured.

"And the horse you rode in!" Martha added. "And thank you, God, for good sex!"

Later, when the two women compared notes, they would have sworn they heard Roger whisper, "Amen!"

# CHAPTER TWENTY-THREE

# Requiem

*Roger.* The toughest time I had in the week after Anne's death was at her funeral. To be discreet, Lucy sat with Martha in the seats behind me, along with Helen and Shirley. Since I had no family who could get away in time for the funeral, I sat with the pallbearers and two of Anne's distant cousins who happened to live in the Twin Cities. Neither of them had been close to Anne and neither had ever met me. However, they had read Anne's obit in the Minneapolis paper and had gotten up early to make the long drive north. Fortunately, it was not winter.

The most surprising arrival was Michael Littlejohn, who I asked to be one of the pallbearers. The call from Michael had come about six in the morning on the day before the funeral. He was calling to let me know he was on the way. I had forgotten all about him. Yet, there was no question of the man's grief when I informed him that Anne had died. "I left word with your office yesterday," I said. "I guess you didn't get it."

"I've been traveling," he replied. "I'm sure they'll let me know when I get back. They didn't know...." He paused and I could almost see him shake his head.

"They didn't know you were coming here," I said as gently as I could. "Don't worry about it, Michael. The important thing is that you can be here to say goodbye."

"That's terribly decent of you, Roger."

"What's done is done, Michael. I don't hold grudges and any friend of Anne is a friend of mine. As someone pointed out to me a while back, the lady had good taste in men." I paused, then decided to plunge on before I changed my mind. "Just so I don't forget it, there is someone I want you to meet while you're here."

"Who might that be?" he wanted to know.

"Just someone I think you'd like to know. It's a long story and I need to get going. There's a lot to be done. Would you like to say something about Anne's work at the wake?"

"Let me think about it, but thank you for asking," Michael

said and I took this as a decline. I was mistaken about that but it worked out well.

I also invited Michael and the two cousins to stay at the house I had shared with Anne. The cousins declined politely but Michael accepted, which surprised me. I also wanted Lucy there, too, along with the boys. "How do you want me to introduce you?" I asked when I brought the subject up.

Lucy smiled. "That's simple. Introduce me as Robby's nanny and Paul as my son. Any prurient soul that might titillate will be titillated by anything you say. I think most people will accept it at face value."

"You're so smart. Will you marry me?"

"Of course I will, but now is not the time to ask me. We'll have all the time we need later." Then she smiled. "I take it you've decided for Robbie to meet his biological dad."

"Yes, I think so. So does a very old and wise lady I know. She's teaching the spin doctor to live in the truth."

"I think the spin doctor already knew," Lucy replied. "All she does is point out the obvious."

"Well, if it's so obvious, why can't I see it?"

"Because you're in the thick of things. Like the fog of war."

I put my hands on Lucy's hips and pulled her close. "I'd like to be in the thick of your thing," I murmured.

"Well, I'd like to have your thick in my thing. We better do something about this."

Fortunately, the boys were sound asleep.

♣

The wake the evening before the funeral was tough for me. I was surprised at the depth of grief I felt hearing the kind words of our friends. What really got to me were the many anecdotes they told about Anne and me as a couple over the years. "I thought I'd said goodbye to Anne a long time ago," I told Lucy and Martha later that evening. "Why do I feel like I'm being torn to pieces and run through a hammer mill all over again?"

"That's because you are," Lucy said. "You're being pulverized, lover. You've been so focused on taking care everything else you haven't taken time to grieve. It's tough work." Martha nodded.

Seeing my lack of understanding, Martha spoke up. "Sex is a good way to short circuit grief, Roger. The only thing I know that's more effective is drugs. When I lost Sam, the worst thing my doctor did was to keep me sedated for months. That kept me from doing my grief work. Then the drugs ran out and there it was, still waiting for me. Then I decided to try sex, but that was worse. So I made myself face the loss and cried my eyes out. After that, it got a less and less painful and I cried less every day."

Martha's eyes were full of tears by the time she was done and Lucy put her arms around her. Turning to me Lucy said, "You're saying goodbye to a huge part of your life, Roger. The reason the wake tonight hit you so hard is that this is it. Anne is dead and the wake has put the seal on her death. It's over. Your best friend is dead and the funeral slams the door on it."

"What really got to me was survivor's guilt," Martha offered. "I kept having the same thought. 'Why Sam and not me?' I would have gladly died in his place."

"There was a time I felt that way about Anne," I replied. "I don't any more, but I feel that way about Lucy and the boys."

Lucy chuckled, but there was no humor in it. "Yeah, the little brats! There are times I'd like to...." She broke off, shaking her head. "Yet, I'd change place with either of them or with you, too, you big lug." She punched me in the arm. "You're not allowed to die, sailor. We all need you around."

"Lucy has a good point," Martha observed. "You may be feeling guilty for feeling the way you do.

I nodded, glancing at my watch. "We better get going, Martha." I said, giving her a hug. "Michael will be wondering what happened to us. Thanks for everything."

"Thanks for the ride home," she said.

"You know the hardest part?" I asked. "The hardest part was hearing Michael talk about Anne's work. He really made it come alive. The slides he showed us were incredible and he gave Anne all the credit."

"That's because he's not only an architect," Martha said. "He's also a good salesman. That's a large part of his success."

"Dead artists sell better," Lucy murmured. Seeing the shock in our eyes she was immediately contrite. "God, I'm sorry, Roger. I didn't mean to say that out loud. I don't really mean that. It was just my twisted alcoholic brain misfiring."

"Maybe so, but it was also the truth," I told her. "The really good ones do and there's no question Anne was an artist. So don't worry about it, sweetheart. As a wise lady once told me, all it shows is that you're human."

♣

The day of the funeral was one of the most beautiful fall days anyone could remember. A thunderstorm had passed through the night before and the air was crystal clear. Still, there was still enough moisture in the air that the bright light was a mellow pale yellow, and the flowers in front of All Saints' were in a full riot of color. Nor had the green soul who tended the garden there exercised much restraint planting bulbs or seed for the annuals. One entire section was dedicated to wild flowers of every kind and these were what I asked to be used for the funeral.

The gardener agreed with my choice. "As beautiful as the tulips and roses are, there's something about wildflowers that seems to touch some people in a very special way," she told me.

Then she smiled in a way that told me she was one of those souls. "Maybe there's something in some of us that can never be tamed," she murmured. When she looked at me there was something in her eyes. What popped into my mind was the image of her lying in a pristine meadow carpeted with wild clover and dressed in a smile. Nor was there any mistaking the passion behind the smile or the urgency of my response.

*What's the matter with me?* I wondered. *I'm burying my wife! I'm happy with Lucy, and Martha, too. Enough is enough!* Yet, the image made me smile and there was something in the lady's eyes that told me she shared the thought.

*Sez who?* Jolly Roger laughed, distracting me. *"Consider the lilies of the field." Why did God put all these wild flower children here if not for us to pollinate?*

*Two children is plenty!* I snapped back. *She's no child, either.*

*Two per mother, maybe,* Jolly snorted. *As many as we can for us men. Hogamus, higamus, man is polygamous!" Who says you have to knock her up? I bet she's on the pill.*

"You may be right," I replied. *You're welcome,* Jolly answered. *I was talking to her, asshole!*

"Thank you," I added. "I really appreciate the trouble you've taken." Without intending to do so, I found myself reaching out and patting the lady on the shoulder. When I did, there was no mistaking the look in her eyes. "You've put a lot of work into the garden here. When did you start it? It must be years ago."

"Oh, it was here when we moved to town several months back. I just took over recently. The lady who took care of it died last spring and no one else was willing to step forward."

She stepped closer and bent over to pull a weed. "It was a labor of love, one she did it for over thirty years." She stood up, close enough that I could smell the delicate scent she used. "She used to complain about having to do it alone but the other ladies tell me no one else could work with her for long. They said she was a real tyrant." As she shrugged, her gray eyes met mine. Her pupils were large despite the bright morning light. "So there wasn't a lot I had to do when I took over. Just keep things going."

"Well, you've done a wonderful job," I said. Her gaze held me captive. "I've never seen anything quite like the wildflower arrangement you made."

"Do you have to be somewhere?" the lady asked.

I glanced at my watch. "No, not for a couple of hours. Everything else is being taken care of by friends. I'd just get in their way."

"Then let me show you the greenhouse," she said softly. "Perhaps we can come up with something you like better." Taking my arm she led me around the corner of the chapel and I could feel the soft warmth of her breast pressing against my arm through the thin fabric. It was evident she was not wearing a bra and out of the corner of my eye I could see her nipples growing firm where her bosom touched the loose material of her blouse.

Before I could think of a polite way to beg off, we were inside the small hut that abutted the rear of the chapel. It was warm there, almost hot, and I watched dumbly as the lady hooked the latch on the door and turned to me. "The wildflowers are at the back," she said, slipping by and leading me to the rear of the greenhouse.

As she passed, she brushed against my chest and I felt myself responding. "This way," she murmured, taking my hand and pulling me along behind her. I was so distracted that when she stopped I bumped into her. Settling back against me she pressed her derriere against my firm presence. "Umm," she said softly. "That feels good." Then she turned and came into my arms, and when her lips touched mine she pulled me tight against her. I could feel the heat of her loins pressed against mine and when I reached down to pull her closer, I discovered she had nothing on below the long skirt she was wearing.

Reaching lower, I raised the lady's skirt until I was grasping her taut, bare derriere. When I did, the lady moaned and I felt her tongue flickering over my lips. Then she reached down and unzipped me, probing my trousers until she clasped my manhood. "Oh, my!" she whispered as she raised herself and guided me into her sweetness.

I gasped when she did this. Her love canal was hot and wet and very snug. I almost exploded as I entered her. Then I felt the walls of her love canal tighten and heard her groan deeply as she began to shudder against me. "Oh, God!" she whispered over and over, thrusting violently with her hips and dragging me with her as she went over the edge. "Oh, God! Oh, God!" Then, with a final shudder that shook her from head to toe, she collapsed against me, still clutching me tight. I felt myself explode, planting my seed deep within the warm welcoming earth of her body.

♣

"Goodness," the lady said a few moments later. We were still locked together, leaning against a sturdy potting bench. She rolled her pelvis up and down over my still rigid erection. "That feels so good...." Then she giggled. "I'm sorry. I don't remember your name."

"Roger," I murmured, barely able to speak. "My name is Roger Jahnsen."

"So I've been rogered," she chuckled. The sound came from deep in her throat, causing me to grow even harder. "Well, I'm Susan. Susan Gladstone. So you've been sued."

Hearing her name, I pulled back and looked at her closely. "Gladstone? Are you the vicar's sister?" Even as I asked, I knew what her response would be.

Susan shook her head. "No, I'm the good father's wife. I hope that doesn't shock you, but I guess it does, doesn't it?" She could feel me growing flaccid.

"I don't know what to say," I replied. "I'm so sorry."

"I'm not," she told me. "That was a wonderful rogering and I enjoyed it immensely." Then she chuckled again. "Maybe I should say I enjoyed your immense-ness. Or is it immensity?"

"What about your husband?" I asked.

"I'm afraid he doesn't know what to do with me," she told

me. "I'm window dressing."

"Window dressing?"

"Yes, to please the good church folk. He prefers men." Then she stopped, her face serious. "I would prefer you didn't mention that to anyone else, Roger. Not that anyone would believe you. He and I have a good understanding with each other about this and we put on a good act. I hope I can trust you."

"Of course," I told her, wondering what I was going to say to Lucy. Or if I was. "But I don't think this is something we ought to do again, Susan. Or do you go by Sue?"

"Either one. Why not, Roger? We seem to be compatible."

"I'm in a committed relationship," I told her.

"I thought you were burying your wife," she answered, pulling back and giving me an odd look.

"She was in a coma," I answered. "We were estranged when it happened but I couldn't abandon her. Even though I was involved with someone else. Divorce wasn't an option."

Susan nodded, her face serious. "Just like it isn't for us." Then she shook her head. "I'm sorry, Roger. I didn't know. I hope you don't think I took advantage of you. I don't do things like this, not ever before. I've had lovers when we lived other places but nothing like this. God, I've made a mess of things! Please forgive me. Can you?"

I reached out and touched her face gently. "There's nothing to forgive, Sue," I assured her. "Sometimes these things just happen. Why don't we just accept it as a gift? I don't really think we've done anything wrong. At least, we didn't set out to. I can't see that we've done anyone any harm."

Susan nodded gravely. "I hope not. You're good people, Roger."

"So are you, Sue."

She smiled, then looked thoughtful. "You don't suppose.... No, I guess we better not."

I chuckled. "That would be tempting fate, wouldn't it? As pleasant as it would be."

"Joyful was the word I had in mind. We better get out of here before we cause talk. Just a minute." She unlatched the door and handed me a flower arrangement. "Just in case anybody sees us."

"Well, just for the record, I'm glad we met."

"Yes, I am, too," Sue grinned. "That was some introduction."

♣

The burial service for Anne was solemn and majestic, beautiful in the effortless way that only high church Anglicans seem to achieve. Unlike normal Protestant rites, the service began with the congregation being asked to stand. Then a hymn was announced, one I had never heard before. It was a repetitive chant called Ubi Caritas and was beautiful. It was sung *acapella* and led by the university choir, who followed an ornate processional cross into the nave, borne by a big, muscular acolyte with a bushy red beard and plain leather sandals. Next came a reader in black and white robes, followed by the priest, in full white regalia. Last of all came the casket and pallbearers.

When I asked the vicar about this at the reception, the priest smiled. "In a church procession, the place of honor is at the very end," the good father replied. "The idea is the first shall be last. It's one of those things the Teacher told us to do."

"I really appreciate your doing this," I replied. "With us not being members of your church."

"Oh, Anne was a member," the vicar told me. "My given name is Felix, by the way. Didn't you tell me Anne grew up and was confirmed in the Episcopal Church?"

"Yes, but she hasn't been to church in years."

"It doesn't matter," Fr. Felix replied. "We're one of the few churches around that doesn't kick people out. We move them to the inactive list. We can excommunicate them if they're really notorious, but we do not kick them out. Even if people lose faith, the church does not."

"I also liked what you said in the sermon," I told me.

"Oh, dear," Felix said. "You'll have to remind me. I may not have been listening." The way he said this told me it wasn't true and that he knew I knew it. I found myself really liking the man and I could see how he and his wife could get away with the masquerade, assuming she had told me the truth. I would not have pegged him as gay.

"It was your description of birth and death as gateways into a much larger life."

"I wish I could claim it was original, but the concept is one you can find in the *Prayerbook*. It's one of the prayers in the Rite I burial service." Felix gave me a thoughtful look. "You know, if you're interested in learning more about our wee quaint ways of looking at things, there is an inquirer's class coming up pretty soon. I'm not pressing, but you're welcome." Then he glanced around and grinned. No one else was nearby. "Or you can come by the office and we can shoot the shit."

Someone came up just then and claimed the padre's presence and I wandered into the nave and looked at the stained glass windows while I thought about the funeral. Michael Littlejohn had been surprised when I asked him to be a pallbearer. There was no doubt in my mind that Michael had been in love with Anne and still was. There was no mistaking the grief he was carrying and when he had met Robbie, he had been deeply moved. "Thank you," he told me in a private moment. "You didn't have to do that but I am in your debt for doing it. I take it...." He paused, unable to finish the thought.

I nodded. "As I told you, he's built like his dad. One of these days he's going to want to meet you, man to man. I've decided it would be best for him if you were involved in his life before then. That is, if you wish to be. You may not."

"I would be most honored," Michael Littlejohn told me. "How would we do this?"

"I don't know your schedule, but you're welcome to stay a couple of days longer and get to know him. You won't even have to change a diaper."

Michael laughed. "Oh, I'm a master at that. I'm the oldest of seven children." He thought for a moment, then nodded. "I can stay an extra night but I'll have to leave by six tomorrow evening. I have an early flight the next day." Then he gave me a searching look. "Are you sure about this, Roger? It's awfully decent of you but I really don't want to impose."

"You won't be. I have some friends coming by this evening and Lucy and the boys will be there. She's their primary caretaker. It's nothing formal, just the kids and my closest friends. One of them will be bringing her baby daughter."

# CHAPTER TWENTY-FOUR

# Breaking Point

Helen volunteered to drive our visitor to the house after the reception. She knew Lucy and I needed a respite, however brief. She had also spent a lot of time talking to Michael at the reception. Seeing how they responded to each other, I thought Roy was lucky that Michael lived in Jamaica. Roy had not attended the funeral and would not be coming to the house because he was drunk. My sense of it was that his remaining days with Helen were numbered.

Even so, I didn't have much time to think about this. Lucy had been quiet since we left the church and I sensed that she was upset about something. I didn't think it was the service, or even the homily, so I asked. "Did something upset you, sweetheart?"

"I think that woman craves your body," she told me.

"What woman was that?" I asked.

"That tall woman in the blue dress, the one who was talking to the priest and arranging things."

"That's the vicar's wife," I replied, intending to sound shocked and failing miserably.

"So? You'd like to fuck her, wouldn't you?" Seeing the look on my face, she added. "You've already fucked her haven't you?"

I shrugged. "I can't always help what pops into my mind, Lucy. She is an attractive woman...."

"I don't care what pops into your mind. I think it's more than just in your mind. I don't want you popping into her."

"Lucy, please don't do this," I asked. "I'm not going to fight with you. Not today. Please?"

She gave me a look that would curdle milk. "Is this how it was with Anne?" she asked. "Were you fucking around on her, too?"

"No, I was not," I replied, with some heat. "Not until after that stupid bet and you were the first. This is not a good time to talk, Lucy. Can't we do it later?"

"I guess you didn't see the way that woman looked at you, did you?" Her voice was sharp with sarcasm but I said nothing.

"She would have fucked you on the chapel floor in front of God and everybody!" she declared.

I pulled the car over and turned to her. "Lucy, you are the love of my life. I want you to become my wife as soon as we can decently do so. Please don't do this."

"What if I don't want to?" she shot back.

"What does that mean?" I asked, fearing the answer.

"That means I need some time away to think things through," she told me. "I think I'm going to stay at my house tonight and you're going to stay at yours."

"What about the children?"

She shrugged. "Paul will come with me since we've told people he's my child and Robbie can stay with you."

"Paul is my child, too," I said. "And you're Robbie's mom,"

"No, I think I'm just the nanny his daddy's been fucking."

"Can we talk about this after Michael leaves tomorrow?" I asked. "He's got to take off about six."

"Maybe," she said. "I need to talk to my sponsor and it depends on what I decide."

"That's the way it has to be?"

"It is. You can drop me and Robbie off at my place."

♣

Fortunately, I had plenty to do when I got home and I didn't have time to brood. Lucy had put a brisket wrapped in foil in the grill before we left for the funeral and it was done to perfection. Without her there to tend both children, I was torn between being host and dad, and Robbie had become upset over the tension between Lucy and me.

It was Michael Littlejohn who came to my rescue. "Perhaps I can help," he said. "I have a lot of experience with squalling babies." I handed Robbie over to him without hesitation and in two minutes he was perfectly happy on Michael's lap. I felt a pang of jealousy when I saw this, particularly when Helen and baby Anne joined Michael on the sofa.

Martha and Jan got there not much later and pitched in with the kitchen. "Where's Lucy?" Martha asked and I told her she was indisposed.

"I hope it's not the flu," she said. "Especially with the boys."

"It's the green eyed monster," I told her quietly, thankful that Jan was not in earshot.

"Oh," Martha nodded. "Over the vicar's wife. I thought she was rather indiscreet, the way she was looking at you."

"Was I the only one who didn't notice that?" I asked.

Martha gave me a searching look. "Roger, I love you dearly but sometimes you have your head up your butt. Was there anything behind her looks?"

The answer must have been written across my face because Martha shook her head and sighed deeply. "No wonder Lucy is indisposed. I'm surprised she didn't wring your neck!"

"It just happened," I told her. "Like you and me at the hospital the day we met."

"I know, sweet man. I can't throw stones but I know how Lucy must feel. It comes with being human. I'm a little jealous of her, too, to tell you the truth. That's not the point."

"So what is the point?" I asked but Jan came back into the kitchen just then. "What?" she asked, looking at the two of us.

"Nothing," Martha told her. "Just something Roger and I need to talk about."

"I think everything's ready and on the table," I said. "Let's call tell the others it's time eat." It was clear Jan was not satisfied with this answer but there was little she could do about it. I suspected that she would give Martha the third degree when they got home.

Thankfully, it was still warm enough outside to eat on the patio and I was glad of it. I was in no mood for polite conversation around a dinner table. I did manage to pry Robbie away from Michael to put him to bed. Helen followed me into the nursery.

"How are you doing, Roger?" she asked as we were changing the babies. "You seem a little tense. Trouble at home?"

"You could say that, Helen," I replied. "Lucy's in a real snit."

"Which is why she isn't here," Helen nodded. "I don't suppose it has anything to do with the vicar's wife, does it?"

"You're the third person who mentioned that," I said.

"Well, it was rather hard not to notice," Helen replied dryly.

"So I'm told," I answered. "The only one who didn't must have been her husband."

"Oh, I'm sure he did," Helen told me. "He seemed to be rather amused by it. I'm sure talk is all over town, too."

"Well, he was friendly enough at the reception," I told her. "So maybe he wasn't aware of it. He didn't seem jealous."

"That was because he wasn't, silly man. Unless I'm mistaken, he's about as straight as a three-dollar bill."

I was tired of talking about this and changed the subject. "Well I wasn't the only one giving people something to talk about," I observed. "You and Michael Littlejohn seemed to hit it off pretty well."

"Yes, he's a wonderful man." She smiled and it was clear to me that she was infatuated. "He really cared about Anne."

"I'm sure he still does," I told her. "That's why I invited him to stay. I think he's Robbie's father."

"He is," Helen told me, nodding. "You can see it in Robbie's eyes and nose, and in the way Robbie moves."

I nodded. "We better get back to the others. Thank you for not chewing on my ear about the vicar's wife."

"Oh, I'm not one to throw stones, am I?" She smiled and gave me a hug. Pulling back, she looked me in the eyes. "After all, I know what the poor woman's going through."

The rest of the evening went well and I thought I was safely through it until Shirley caught me in the kitchen. "I'm surprised you invited him here this evening," she said.

I glanced where she was staring and saw Helen and Michael in lively conversation on the couch. The erotic energy surrounding them like a fog was almost palatable. "You mean Michael?" I asked and Shirley nodded.

"Well he's a house guest, Shirley. He's also a charming man. It's easy to see why Anne liked him."

"Anne was a fool, Roger. She should have never let you get away from her."

I sighed. "It's a lot more complicated than that, Shirley."

"It always is," she replied. She glanced at Michael and Helen. "Look at him! If he loved Anne so much, why is he putting the rush on Helen?"

"These things happen, Shirley. Look at you and me. We both love Anne but we both love each other, too. There's plenty of love to go around."

Shirley was staring so intently at Michael and Helen she didn't seem to hear a word I said. "Look at him!" she said, taking a gulp from her drink. It was pure vodka, diluted only by melting ice. I know because I mixed it and made it a triple.

I heard Shirley growl. It was not a pleasant sound. "I've half a mind to march over there and punch him out!" she declared, finishing her drink in a single gulp.

I interposed myself between Shirley and the patio. "I'm not going to let you do that, Shirley." I told her. "So please don't embarrass us both by trying. I'll hold you down if I have to."

Shirley glared at me. "He's not worth it," I continued. "He's leaving town tomorrow."

Shirley glared at me a moment longer before she relented. "So am I." Her words were slurred by the vodka. "I have an early flight out the next morning." She glanced around. "Where are Lucy and Paul?"

"She's pissed off at me at the moment," I answered.

"Over the way the Vicar's wife looked at you? I don't blame her. I would be, too, you dumb shit."

"I guess I didn't notice," I replied. This was the truth. I'd been so busy avoiding looking at Susan that I had barely noticed the color of her dress.

"Then you were the only one in the place who didn't. I thought the bitch was going to rip your clothes off and have you on the altar," she declared.

I tried to pass it off as a joke. "Then I guess I'm lucky she restrained herself."

"You know, Roger," Shirley said. "I do love you as a friend. But sometimes you can be as dumb as dog shit!"

I started to observe that we all can but decided to remain mute. There was a good chance that Shirley could take it personally and she was spoiling for a fight. So I offered her another double vodka hoping that she might either get too drunk to stand or pass out.

♣

During the weeks after Anne's funeral Indian summer turned into early winter. The first big snowstorm came on Columbus day, a good bit earlier than usual. It left almost a foot of heavy, wet snow that stayed for the winter.

My mood darkened with the shorter days. Lucy had not been back in touch, though she cashed the checks I mailed for child support. She even wrote "Thank You" above her endorsement and I was temped to call many times. Yet, I did not, thinking that the first move had to come from her. It was she who had left and I was not about to crowd her. So I wrote her more than a dozen love letters I never sent. For some reason I didn't discard them, either. I even thought making them into a journal under that title but I didn't dare dwell on our separation. The ache was too deep, too devastating. I needed to raise my son.

To make matters worse, a small university in New Hampshire sent me a letter asking if I would consider joining their faculty. It was tempting to follow this up and make a clean break. Yet, I told them I needed to stay where I was. I cited concerns for my family as the reason and this was true. I didn't want to leave Paul in the lurch. Even though it didn't look like Lucy would ever come home, I thought moving to New England would put the last nail in the coffin for us. I don't know why, but I still held some slim hope we might get back together.

To her credit, after a couple of weeks separation Lucy arranged for Martha to bring Paul to spend a weekend and I reciprocated with Robbie the weekend after. This became a pattern and by Thanksgiving the boys had pretty much adapted to being shunted back and forth by Martha. The boys and I spent the holidays with Martha and Jan while Lucy visited her sister in the Cities and Martha and I consoled one another in the way only the grieving can. I even thought about making the arrangement permanent, but I knew Martha would turn me down if I asked.

However, there were some bright spots in those days. One was Robbie, whose enthusiasm for spontaneous games was boundless. We spent hours at play, making up rules as we went along, and when brother Paul joined us, Robbie quickly recruited him as an ally when the three of us played. Yet, the two of them preferred to spend their time with each other and quite often I was relegated to the role of observer and umpire.

Another bright spot was Helen and our daughter, Annie, who seemed to quickly figure out how to play the boys off against one another when they were all together. When Helen came over, she often spent the night, but I often wondered if she would rather it be Michael Littlehohn in her bed. They had been in constant communication by email and instant messaging, and they even talked by phone from time to time. Yet, Helen let me know quite clearly that she would prefer to be with me, given the choice.

"You know, I'd move in with you in a New York minute," she told me one day when I asked what she thought about her fling with Michael. "I'd have more of your babies, too, and I wouldn't care if we got married or not. Say the word and I'll be here before the echo stops."

"It's tempting," I answered. "I love you very much but I need to be sure I'm over Lucy first."

"Sweet man, you will never be over Lucy. Just like I will never be over Roy, despite the fact I have our divorce papers waiting to be filed. You'll never be over Anne, either. But relationships die just like people do. I think you and I could build a very good life together. We certainly know each other well enough."

I was surprised to hear Martha agree with Helen when I sought her counsel. "It would never be the same as with Lucy but you and Helen are a good match."

"I thought about asking you but I figured you would turn me down," I confessed.

"Oh, God, don't tempt me! But you're right, Roger. I would. I love you too much to saddle you with this old woman."

"You're not that much older than I am," I pointed out.

She shook her head sadly. "No, but I'm your friend first, Roger. And your occasional paramour. I prefer things the way they are." Then she smiled. "I'd rather stay a merry widow. Or was that before your time, young man?"

I had no idea what she was talking about. Nor could I think of anything else to say. Martha looked at me, her eyes full of compassion. "Poor Roger. So many women, so little time, so much confusion. It's called the midlife crazy and most men go through it. Sam didn't but he didn't live long enough, and you seem to have a worse case than most."

"So you don't think Lucy will come back?" I asked.

"That's something you'll need to ask her," Martha told me. "I'd guess it could go either way. Do you want her back?"

"I thought so," I told her. "Now I'm not sure. Why hasn't she called me?"

"That's also something you need to ask her. I'd guess she's still feeling terribly hurt and probably betrayed. You did sleep with the vicar's wife, didn't you?"

I told her what had happened and she laughed. "I'm sorry for laughing but I couldn't help but see the parallels to what happened with you and me. Have you slept with her again?"

"I didn't think that would be such a good idea, even if her husband is gay." Then I stopped, horrified at what I'd said. "That has got to stay between you and me, Martha. She told me that in confidence. I'm sorry I let it slip."

Again, Martha laughed. "You're such an honorable soul, Roger. The secret is safe with me. I wondered about the good father. He comes across to me as just a shade too masculine. Are you sure he's not bisexual?"

"That's what I was told, that he's gay. It makes sense. On the other hand, all my information comes from Susan. I didn't think it would be a good thing to ask him directly."

Martha smiled. "Who knows? He might give you a very direct answer." A devilish look came into her eyes. "Maybe a kiss, too."

# CHAPTER TWENTY-FIVE

# Dinner for Three

Oddly enough, it was just a few days later that Felix Gladstone called and invited me to dinner at the vicarage. I tried to beg off but he insisted. "Don't worry about things being awkward," Felix said. "Susan and I are used to living with ambiguity. I rather liked her greenhouse story."

I reluctantly agreed but dreaded the occasion and almost called to cancel the day I was supposed to be there. Yet, when I got to the vicarage, Felix shook my hand warmly and Susan game me a wonderful hug. Then, after he had poured us a glass of sherry, the good father raised his glass. "Here's to joyful shagging!" he said and Susan replied with a grin. "Hear! Hear!"

"Now, we've got that particular ice broken," Felix said, "let's get to know one another."

Susan spoke up. "No, there's something more to be said. I really am sorry if my attention caused you any problems, Roger. Felix said that at the service I looked like I wanted to have my way with you right there at the chancel crossing. I did but I didn't realize I was being indiscreet."

I nodded. "Several of my friends told me about it. I was trying to play it cool and avoid catching your eye."

Susan laughed. "Well, I wish I'd followed your lead. If I need to make amends, please tell me. Not that I'd know how to go about it. I do hope I didn't cause you too much grief, though I can't say I'm sorry."

I answered by raising my glass. "That's water over the bridge. As your husband said, here's to joyful shagging!"

"Amen!" Felix declared and took a sip of his sherry.

I found the rest of the evening delightful. At one point toward the end of my visit the padre looked at me and said, "I can't say how I know. Roger, but I hear you're responsible for a bit of the local population boom. Three for three, I'm told."

"Actually, it was only two. Anne's child was by another man. I hope you keep this all confidential. I'm not ashamed of it but this is a small town and the gossip is vicious. Other people could be hurt if it got out."

"Actually, my friend, it is three," Felix assured me. He looked at his wife and smiled. "The greenhouse effect produced more fruit. That's one of the reasons we wanted you to come to dinner."

I glanced at Susan who was looking very demure as she studied her plate. "No," I said, shocked. "Surely not."

Felix laughed. "I'm afraid so but not to worry. You did us a favor, my friend."

"We've wanted children for some time," Susan explained. "We even tried artificial insemination but that didn't work. Our body chemistries don't match and neither do our libidos."

Seeing the questions in my eyes, Felix interjected, "I'd be wondering why Susan and I married if I were in your shoes." I nodded and he explained. "We've been best friends since nursery school. No one else ever measured up for either of us. Even without the conjugal shagging, we have an intimacy that few seem to find. Sadly enough. There's nothing we can't talk about."

I nodded, then turned to Susan. "Are you sure?"

"Yes, I went to the doctor right away and she confirmed it. You're the...donor. I don't mean to be rude about it but Felix will be the child's dad."

I was quiet for a long moment before I responded. "I'm having trouble getting my mind around all this," I told them. "Although I agree that Felix should be dad. I don't know quite how to look at all this."

"I can understand why," Felix said. "It is most irregular, but I refuse to call it bad. And I hope you're not feeling guilty about it. What you've done is to establish my masculinity with the community in a way I could not."

"Couldn't someone figure it out, anyway?" I asked.

"People are too lazy to think that much," Felix replied. "Those who are not simply wouldn't be believed. People go for the easiest explanations." His smile was wry and very sad. I realized Felix was speaking from his own experience.

"Enough of this," the padre said. "Let's talk about something more interesting. I was fascinated by the presentation by that architect at the wake. Anne must have been an incredibly creative individual."

I started to agree but choked. Neither of my hosts seemed embarrassed by my reaction and waited patiently for me to respond. After a moment I got myself together. "Sorry," I said. "I thought I was beyond that. It came out of nowhere."

"I hope I wasn't being insensitive," Felix said. "It will probably help to talk about it. Not now, but at some point fairly soon."

Much to my surprise, I found myself talking about the bet and the strange direction my life had taken ever since. I also talked about Lucy and Paul and about her leaving. When I was done, Susan reached out and touched me on the arm. "I am so sorry, Roger," she said. "I had no idea. I thought you were a widower. I didn't see the harm."

"There's no way you could know," I told her. "It's entirely my fault."

"I'm not sure finding fault is very useful here," Felix said softly. "I think the important thing is what you want. Anne is gone now and so is Lucy. Do you want Lucy back?"

I sighed. "I thought I did but I'm not sure. I'm very confused right now. Even if she came back, how could she ever trust me again? How could I trust myself? I seem to have developed a set of round heels." I grinned but Felix later told me my face was a mass of pain. That was how he put it.

"I may be wrong but I have to disagree," Felix replied. "You strike me as a very honorable fellow, Roger. Nor do you strike me as either wanton or promiscuous. I think the issue may be that you take more responsibility for things than is honestly yours."

I nodded. "I've been told that, but could we talk about something else? I'm a little overloaded."

"Of course," Felix said. "Sorry. It's easy to fall into professional habits. What would you like to talk about?"

I thought a moment. "I suppose people ask you all the time, but why did you choose to become a priest?"

"The standard answer I give is that while the pay ain't the greatest, the retirement benefits are out of this world." Felix smiled and went on. "The truth is that the Hound of Heaven wouldn't leave me alone. Do you know the poem?"

I nodded. "Lucy has a copy and I read it. I can't say that I understand it. I mean, the story is quite clear. What I don't understand is why heaven might want to run someone down. It's probably good that I'm not God, if there is one."

Felix laughed and nodded. "Quite so! The hound is a dramatic metaphor beloved of drama queens. I actually like the concept of the good shepherd better. It's stronger. Do you know much about sheep?"

"In what way, Father?" I quipped, raising an eyebrow. We all laughed.

"I walked right into that one, didn't I?" Felix said. "Well, I'm not a farm boy or a sheep herd. Yet, I understand that when a sheep gets lost from the herd and can't find its way home, it lies down. I'm told it will stay there until it dies unless the shepherd comes and finds it. Even then, it won't follow the shepherd back to the herd. The shepherd has to pick it up and carry it all the way home. It's a wonderful metaphor for grace."

"I hear a lot of people use that term," I told him. "I'm never sure exactly what they mean. I sometimes think that they don't, either. But you haven't answered my question. Why would the good shepherd want to find a wayward sheep?"

"Because he loves them just like you love Lucy and your children. Wouldn't you go after them if they were lost and in trouble?"

That really hit me where I live. "Yes. The kids, for sure. Lucy, well, maybe." Then I corrected myself. "No, not maybe. I'd go after her, regardless. Which just goes to show what a hypocrite I am, doesn't it."

Felix shook his head. "Not at all. Are you familiar with the parable of the waiting father?"

"No. Is that in the Bible somewhere?"

"It's in the New Testament. It's commonly known as the parable of the prodigal son, but the parable is about the father, not the two sons. The point is that the waiting father doesn't care what either son has done. He simply wants them safely home. You might want to read it. I think you may find it has some bearing on your situation." There was no mistaking the depth of compassion in the padre's face.

"You mean I'm the prodigal son?" I asked, surprised.

"Actually, I was thinking more of you as the waiting father who wants his family home."

❧

"That one rocked me," I told Martha. We were seated at her kitchen table the morning after my dinner with the vicar and his wife. I had told her the full story, from the moment I arrived at the vicarage up to when Felix cited the parable. At the time I wanted to disagree with what he said but I had trouble sleeping that night. Finally, I'd called Martha at six-thirty.

"Well, Roger, the man has a point," Martha said. "I think it fits. Have you read it?"

"What if I reach out and she says no?" I asked. "I'm not sure I could take that, Martha."

"I think you're selling yourself short," she told me. "She may not agree at first so you need to be prepared to persevere. You may also have to learn to fight with her, and fight clean. Do you love her enough to do that?"

"I don't know how to fight," I told her. "Not without going nuclear."

"I bet she'd teach you," Martha smiled. "Particularly if you asked her sweetly."

"What do I say?"

"How about 'I don't know how to fight clean. Will you please teach me?' I think that covers the bases."

"What if she lashes out?"

"Simple. Let her blow off steam and ask again. And again and again, if you have to."

"I'm scared, Martha."

"Good. Keep that in mind. Lucy is not your enemy. Fear is but it can get us off our butts, too."

♣

It was two days later. I had called Lucy at home, blurted out what Martha had told me to say. When I did there was a long silence. Then Lucy answered. "I don't want to do it in front of the kids. Let me call Martha to babysit. Can you be here tomorrow afternoon?"

I had classes but nothing my graduate assistants couldn't handle. "I'll be there," I answered. "What time?"

"Let's try for two o'clock. I'll take the afternoon off. I'll let you know if things work out."

"Thank you, Lucy. For what it's worth...."

She interrupted. "I know. That's why we're doing this. Roger. We love each other."

Now there we were, face to face. Neither of us knew where to start. "Who goes first?" I finally asked.

"Why don't you start?" she suggested.

"I want my family together again."

"So do I."

"I don't know how to do this," I told her. "I never learned at home." I paused but she waited. "I think it's something I need to learn so I can teach our boys. I need your help."

"Ground rules," Lucy replied. "No taking inventory and no slashing. We each talk only about our own side of the street."

"I'm not sure I understand."

"I'll give you an example. When I think you've betrayed my trust I'm deeply hurt."

"OK, let me try it. When I've hurt you unintentionally, I feel awful."

Lucy nodded. "I don't understand how hurting me that way could be considered unintentional."

"I didn't do it to hurt anyone. It just happened."

Lucy took a deep breath and let it out slowly. "I'm getting angry all over again. I don't understand how something just happens or doesn't just happen."

"Didn't you and I just happen?" Lucy started to answer and I held up my hand. "No, wait. Let me withdraw that question. It was not a good question. When I first saw you I hoped that would happen."

"I did, too."

"The afternoon it happened I was angry with Anne. That was my excuse but I already wanted it to happen, Lucy. The fight with her was just something to blame it on. That sounds sick but I'm glad it happened."

"I agree," Lucy nodded. "To both parts. Have you been seeing anyone else?"

"Martha," I told her. "Helen sometimes brings Annie over to play and sometimes she spends the night."

Lucy looked like I had kicked her, but she nodded. "I'm not surprised. Are the two of you serious?"

"She wants to leave Roy and move in but that's not what I want. I want to live with you and our children."

"Do you know what's held me back, Roger?"

"Yes, I think I do. What assurance can you have that this won't happen again."

"That's right. How can I trust you?"

"I don't know," I told her. "I don't trust me very much these days, either. I can't offer you any assurances. All I can offer is the hope that things will be different. It doesn't seem to be a realistic hope. On the other hand, the only time it's happened is when I was going through a crisis."

Lucy nodded. "Yes, but there's always going to be a crisis coming down the road. I wish I could simply accept this as the way things are, Roger. I can't. I've tried but what happens is I end up full of resentment. Sooner or later that will drive me to drink and we'll lose what we have, anyway. Why not quit while we're ahead?" The way Lucy looked when she said this broke my heart. It was clear to me it broke hers, too.

♣

"That's where we left it," I told Martha later that afternoon. "I hate it and I believe Lucy does, too. But I don't see any way out. We both want to go on but we can't get beyond that point."

Martha gave me an odd look. "I need to take a risk with you, Roger. Please forgive me if I'm pressing on where I'm not wanted. What I wonder is if the two of you have given this much prayer. Why don't you ask Lucy if she will pray with you about this?"

"Jesus, Martha!" I said. "No disrespect intended but neither of us are religious people."

"No, but you're both deeply spiritual people," she pointed out. "You've prayed with me several times. Why not pray with Lucy?"

I couldn't think of a good answer to that, so I called Lucy and told her what Martha had said. It was quiet for a long time on the other end of the line. Then Lucy snorted. "You may not believe this, Jolly Roger, but I just hung up from talking with my AA sponsor. She asked me that same thing."

"So where do we go from here?"

"Are you kidding? We go to our knees, you big lug. Don't you understand? We go to our knees, together."

"That's very scary," I told her.

"I know, but it's worth a try. What do we have to lose?"

"I don't know, control of our lives?"

Lucy laughed. Hearing it gave me hope. "Right. As if we had much control over anything, anyway. How soon can you get here?"

"Ten minutes," I told her. I made it in four.

# Down the Years

It's hard to believe that's been twelve years ago now, twelve years next week. Lucy and I observe that day every year as our anniversary and very few days pass that we do not spend some time together in what she calls Step Eleven. Two years after we came back together we decided it was time to marry, and we exchanged our vows on our second anniversary. Or maybe I should say we renewed our vows.

We celebrated our wedding with all our friends and Felix did the service. It was Lucy who suggested him. Oddly enough, she and Susan have become very close. After Lucy and I got back together I learned that Susan had come to Lucy during our estrangement and asked her forgiveness.

As it turned out, we also celebrated our wedding by giving ourselves the gift of a baby girl we named Martha Anne. This created some confusion when we were all together, but confusion seems come with living in a family of five. The boys were talking by then and called her Marta-ann, which became her family name

No, make that a family six including Bowser, who is doing well for a dog of his years. The day we brought Marta-ann home from the hospital Bowser settled himself by her crib. There he has made his bed ever since and he follows her all around the house. The few times she's been gone to slumber parties or to camp, the poor old fellow has been miserable. He follows us around like a shadow. Then, when she comes home, he gets so excited he almost wags himself inside out.

We sold my house, the one I shared with Anne. We bought one new to us both and big enough for our family. Yet, we also kept Lucy's place overlooking the river for our get-away. We often run together on the path to our special place by the spring. When we do, we almost always make love there. We do so even in the late fall, on a bed of fallen leaves.

Helen finally filed divorce papers on Roy. It was about a year after Anne's funeral and she found a place of her own. From time to time Michael Littlejohn shows up for a week or two and when he does, we have the two of them over for dinner with our close friends. We also keep Annie when Helen flies off to Jamaica or some other exotic place where Michael is working.

Shirley and I have become good friends again. She has a standing invitation to our get-togethers. She often comes to help celebrate whatever occasion, particularly when Michael Littlejohn will be there with Helen. Oddly enough, Shirley and Michael were on the same flight on the morning he flew out of Minneapolis. He somehow managed to charm her out of her anger. And from what Shirley said later, I gather they shared a room on an unplanned layover. The look in her eyes when she told me about it let me know they hadn't wasted the opportunity.

Shirley often comes to these gatherings with one of my former graduate assistants. The two of them have been together long enough they are considered a couple by our friends. They are pretty much accepted as that in the larger community, too. Sadly enough, about a year and a half after the funeral, Shirley had to put Ed in a nursing home. However, he seems to be delighted with her new companion, Brenda, who often visits him by herself when Shirley cannot get away. When I go to visit, he brags about the beautiful women in his life and I have often wondered if he understands the nature of their friendship. It's none of my business, of course, but I do wonder.

We have a new crowd now made up of the friends we have in common. Nor is Al is part of it and I wonder why we tolerated him as long as we did. Lucy and I have become frequent companions with the Gladstones and their daughter June is Annie's best friend. Marta-ann sometimes hangs out with the two of them but she's younger. She seems to prefer the company of the boys. There she reigns as tyrant queen and she's tough enough to make it stick. Despite being two years younger.

Martha has become even more of a part of our family. So has Jan, oddly enough. Somewhere along the line Jan turned a corner. Now she's the delightful woman Lucy knew a long while back. She's given up trying to convince her mother not to shag the neighbor. When Martha and I need private time, she often pays a visit to our new home to baby-sit.

Nor does it hurt that Martha and I accidentally interrupted

Jan at a delicate moment. She was with a newly found friend, a man a good bit younger than herself. She calls him BT, for boy-toy, and he doesn't seem to mind. I suspect that's because Jan is as passionate as her mother. I've seen her in an unguarded moment, giving him a look that could scorch the wallpaper.

♣

Every once in a while in the wee hours of the morning I think of the bet Anne and I made so long ago. I think of all that happened as a consequence. I always wonder how things might have gone had we not made the wager. Or let our friends shame us into honoring it. Yet, there is no way we could know, as Felix pointed out when I went to talk with him about it. Nor did I withhold anything from him.

When I was done with my story, Felix nodded and sat for a long while, puffing the dead pipe he chews when he cogitates. Then he made a couple of observations. "First of all, Roger, life just happens the way it does despite our best efforts to control it. Yet, if you look really closely at all that happened, I think you see a fine celestial hand behind the scenes. You will see it making things come out as they need to be. Sometimes this is through direct prior intervention. My experience is that most of the time what happens is a work of redemption."

I asked him for an example and he smiled. "Well, it's like playing nine-ball with the legendary Minnesota Fats. The Boss lets us take the first shots but once we miss, he runs the table."

"I see what you mean," I answered. "You know, when I first saw the movie, I actually thought Fats was a real person. Jackie Gleason made him seem so alive."

"Just so," Felix answered, nodding. "To finish my thought, I am personally convinced it's impossible for us to defeat grace. I see it written all over your sexual adventures."

"That's hard for me to get my mind around," I told him. "Sex and grace seem worlds apart, although the gift of children is a strong argument for it."

Felix nodded. "Yes, they are, aren't they? But the connection is closer than you think. I once listened to a recording by Scott Peck. You know, *The Road Less Traveled* guy. He pointed out that spirituality and sexuality are two sides of the same coin. He called them kissing cousins. He also pointed out that in the original Hebrew, the Song of Songs is a lot more earthy than the translators let on. He said this is the reason that it is so popular with monastics. He cited St. John of the Cross to bolster his argument. There is no question that 'One Dark Night' is erotic literature."

"I bet that made the fundamentalists happy," I observed.

"Yes, well, I doubt many of them ever heard that recording or even read Scott Peck." The padre nodded, then frowned. "There's one other thing I want to mention. Very few people are aware what lies behind their words, but then, you know that. You told me you were a Madison Avenue spin-master, didn't you?"

I nodded. "I was, though I turned away from that. Or, if I understand the word right, I repented."

"That's what it means, to turn from something. 'Turn or burn' is how some of my more unenlightened colleagues put it. They seem to prefer scaring the hell out of people, as if that was really possible. I prefer to love the devil out of them."

Felix shook his head. "One of the words the great unwashed use without understanding is 'righteousness.' I hear it all the time and it makes me shudder. I know they are well intentioned but one of their greatest sins against humanity is trying to reduce human life to a set of rules. Look at the original Hebrew and you will find that righteousness has nothing to do with rules or codes of conduct. It does have to do with the relationships in our lives and with fulfilling the needs that grow out of those. The fact of the matter is that an act might be righteous in one situation and as unrighteous in another."

I shrugged. "That sounds like situational ethics. I pretty much try to avoid that."

"All ethics are situational, Roger. What matters is what drives them. If they are governed by the love of others, there can be no unrighteousness. The more unconditional our love is, the more righteous the actions that flow out of it."

"Forgive me, padre, but this sounds like spin."

"Perhaps it does, but if we use Minnesota Fats as a metaphor for the One To Whom It All Concerns, grace becomes a matter of divine spin. It's like turning all the pieces of the puzzle at once until they fall into place perfectly."

I shook my head. "All this is very new to me, very confusing."

"Oh, it is to me, too, Roger. Even after all these years. Trying to figure it out can drive you crazy."

"So how do you live with it? You're a priest."

Felix smiled. "As if that makes any difference. Priests are just as confused as anyone else and some of us go crazy or become rigid. Which may be the same thing. What I did was to accept the fact there are mysteries we simply cannot figure out. So I stopped trying to figure them out. I simply tried to figure out what the Boss, as you call him, needed me to do next."

"That's it?" I asked.

"That's it," he answered with a smile. "I jump in head first and trust God to redeem any mistakes I make."

"So you just take off in the fog and fly blind?"

"That's right, Roger," Felix told me. "Sometimes there's a clear beacon to follow, but most often it's onward through the murk." He smiled and shrugged. "It's certainly not boring."

Then, unaware he was doing so, he confronted me with my own words. "There's not much we can do about it, my friend. It's simply the human condition."

Jolly Roger thought this was hilarious.

www.ingramcontent.com/pod-product-compliance
Lightning Source LLC
Chambersburg PA
CBHW070855250626
47159CB00003B/1078